THE FAIR
MISSISSIPPIAN

THE FAIR MISSISSIPPIAN

CHARLES EGBERT CRADDOCK

Originally published in 1908.
Published by Wildside Press LLC.
Visis us at wildsidepress.com

CHAPTER I

The simplest fact of this life of ours is subject to manifold and diverse interpretations. It was the faithful belief of Edward Desmond, and his inward protest, that he did not care for money. He had the true scholar's disdain of the froth and fret of fashion that can but scantily disguise the mental shallowness of society. He was not fond of luxury. He had an ardor for hard work and a passionate ambition for achievement. He desired but a modest competence and the opportunity for mental development along the lines which his expanding capacities gave promise of compassing. Nevertheless, at twenty-four years of age, his elaborate education at length complete, in the prime of his intellectual powers, tingling with the consciousness of ability, he found that he had become suddenly solicitous in small matters of social precedence; he experienced a pained deprecation of the presence of wealth; he winced with a sensitive realization of poverty; he had acquired a wavering yet proud self-assertion, consciously futile.

The change had been wrought in a time of grievous tragedy, full of poignancies scarcely to be adequately appreciated by the practical world. For less sensitive men have suffered more bitter woes. It was a trite tragedy, with no traits of dramatic potentialities. On the sudden death of his father ensued the revelation of a shattered estate, the usual frantic, useless effort to avert total wreck, final defeat culminating in the forced sale of an old home with all its appurtenances. The memories, the dreams, the traditions, the broken hopes that had hallowed the old chattels were too immaterial even for the cormorant-like comprehensiveness of the inventories, and these sanctities were all that was left for the heir.

His friends, however, took an optimistic view. When the struggle was over,—brief, but hopeless and conclusive,—they found solace in the completeness of his equipment; his education was at length finished; he had returned to his Maryland home only the previous June from an elaborate course of study abroad; the world was before him. As to the profession of the law for which he had been destined, they cheerfully argued that the preliminary training and the necessary library would be expensive, success uncertain,—and he must needs live pending its delay,—the tardy emoluments disproportioned to the labor and ability involved. Since there seemed no vacancy in the professorial ranks of the small western colleges, where they had hoped he might find a chair, they spoke of him as having fallen upon his feet when the unusual brilliancy of his scholastic record brought him the offer of the tutorship of the three sons in a wealthy family, dwelling in the isolation of a secluded Mississippi plantation, the opportunity coming at the ultimate crisis of the painful financial emergency. For although the salary was small, in comparison with the allowance which the generosity of his father had heretofore afforded an only son, his prospective earnings would have abashed the honoraria of a fledgeling lawyer's professional labors, even had he already attained admission to the bar. Thus, followed by few regrets, the last month of the year found him arrived at the scene of his pedagogical work.

"It is Mrs. Faurie's chief desire that her sons shall be adequately prepared for college. She is a great believer in individual instruction by a thoroughly competent educator, who can discern and—ah—strengthen the weaknesses, and—ah—develop special capacities in the mind of youth,—ah, yes! She fears that our frequent and extended tours abroad have cultivated their powers of superficial observation and love of travel at the expense of their love of study, and—ah—capacity to absorb theories and to concentrate their thoughts, and to take an interest in books, and—ah—that is the reason,—*one* of the reasons,"—with a bow and smile,—"why we esteem ourselves so fortunate,—so *very* fortunate to have you with us." Nothing could be more suave than the old gentleman beaming upon him from the foot of the table, but Edward Desmond, after an effort at a receptive and grateful smile, looked down at his fork and turned it aimlessly in his hand, without a word in response.

He had had full range of the pastures, and the harness galled him. Yet logically he could not find aught of fault in this smooth courtesy and tone of appreciation. It so became even a quasi-employer, though conscious of his magnanimity and sense of *noblesse oblige*. The fact that Desmond had grown gradually aware that Mr. Stanlett was but basking in the reflection of his niece's splendors, and, although having some indeterminate income of his own, was content to spend the evening of his days in her embellished entourage, scarcely mitigated his secret displeasure. He felt that the old gentleman assumed a patronage which he had no right to exercise. Yet this resentment was inconsistent with his own theory that mere money had no title to homage from him. Thus Mr. Stanlett's patronage, poor, should not have been less acceptable than Mr. Stanlett's patronage, rich. Mrs. Faurie had not hastened to make Desmond welcome, but indeed he had been in the house only for an hour or so, and Mr. Stanlett's urbanity was surely expansive enough to atone. He gave the newcomer his choice of excuses in Mrs. Faurie's behalf: first the fatigue of a long drive, and again he mentioned a sore throat as her reason for not joining the group at the dinner-table. "She will see you later in the evening," Mr. Stanlett promised.

If the lady did not choose to appear at her own board for any reason which might seem to her good and sufficient, Desmond was in no position to cavil, but the old gentleman's inadvertences in the matter gave him an impression of insincerity about the methods of the household which grated on his exacting and sensitive mood. Even the manners of the domestics, smooth, and deft, and obsequious in the extreme, were incongruous with the veiled scorn of the stranger, as a man of scant means, which he subtly detected in their eyes, for, the servitors of wealth and large pretensions, they had slight toleration of poverty out of their own rank of life. He perceived, too, the relish which Joel, the antiquated negro butler, took in the elaboration of the details of the daily dinner service, especially the old-fashioned custom of removing the cloth with each successive course, which was so deftly accomplished, revealing the fresh one spread below, that it seemed a prandial miracle. Mr. Stanlett, however, apologized in some sort.

"We keep up the old style, you see. My niece says she despairs of ever inducing Joel to condescend to one cloth for the table at dinner, though she brought some very fancy centrepieces and such gimcracks from Paris expressly to stimulate his ambition for novelty."

Desmond felt little drawn toward his prospective pupils, one seated beside him and the other two opposite. They were of a type with which he had scant sympathy. They were younger, too, than he had reason to expect from the amount of the salary and his own scholastic pretensions, and his consequence seemed further diminished in that he should be called upon to teach in effect mere children. While they were not handsome of feature, they were extremely handsomely built and tall for their respective ages; but he perceived with disapproval that they lacked muscle. They were very apt and delicate in all the usages of the table, and in their elegant nicety of attire "mamma's darling" was writ large. They all had good eyes, and they held up their heads in a frank, gentlemanlike way; but their cosmopolitan air, their easy assurance, their ready phrasings far beyond their years, though evidently the superficial result of their travels and their precocious relations with the world, did not serve to commend them to one who loved a boy for his crude boyishness. These seemed little men of the world, and they sat smug and silent and looked at their great-uncle with faces of filial gravity when, under the influence of too much old port, he began to show traits of the ridiculous, albeit in a genteel and refined fashion. Yet Desmond admitted to himself that he would not have thought it becoming that they should laugh. The clear pallor of the old gentleman's lean face grew delicately flushed. His white hair was sparse on his long head, showing its bony structure. He had a white mustache, and a factitious idea of youth was suggested by the gleam of a very natural set of false teeth beneath it. Presently he began to hum, as if absent-minded, and at length he sang out:—

"My girl so fair, my friend so rare,
With these what mortal could be richer?
Give me but these,—a fig for care,
My sweet girl, my friend, and pitcher."

It was the echo of what had been a very pretty tenor voice in its prime, and its resonant vibrations reached and roused a parrot asleep in a cage, hanging in a broad, deep bay-window. The bird suddenly fluffed its feathers and sent out a sharp, harsh cry; then, twisting on its perch and swinging inverted by one claw, it sang with a painfully realistic imitation and with all the taunting effect of mockery:—

"My sweet girl, my friend, and pitcher."

It was too much for the decorum of the youngest of the three boys. He broke into an irresistible puerile cackle, and the old man, catching suddenly to his senses and his sobriety, flushed deeply, the crimson stealing through his sparse white hair and all along his polished white scalp.

The eldest of the boys, a lad of fourteen, came at once to the rescue with the tact of a Chesterfield, as smooth as cream.

"The idea of Polly remembering your old 'pitcher-song,' Uncle Clarence,—that's quite a compliment. And after so long an absence."

"Very true,—very true," said the old gentleman, readily reassured. "Pretty Polly,"—smiling blandly at the accomplished fowl. "Want a cracker?"

"My pitcher," repeated Polly, as if with the intention of prompting the nature of the refreshment.

"Why, we have been away—let me see—my memory fails me about these little details. How long were we in Europe this time, Reginald?—how long is it since Polly heard that song?"

"Eighteen months, Uncle Clarence. I shouldn't have thought Polly capable of such an effort. May we be excused, sir?"

"Certainly—by all means." Then, turning to Desmond, "I don't care to see young boys linger at the table after the cloth is drawn and the bottle is stirring over the mahogany."

The disaffected Desmond thought a continuance here might prove a salutary object-lesson as to the pernicious effects of vinous indulgence, and his eyes followed with no great favor the little gentlemen as, prettily bowing, they nattily made their exit. Somehow he was reassured to hear a clumsy shuffling of feet in the hall as, to judge by auricular evidence, they engaged in a scuffle outside the closed door. Suddenly one of them was thrown with a great bang against it,—then an abrupt and awe-stricken silence ensued.

"Eighteen months," Mr. Stanlett repeated. "I did not realize the length of our absence. In truth," he added, with a spark of mischief kindling the wine in his eyes, "we stayed as long as we could,—as long as our money held out. My niece, Mrs. Faurie, said that she had run the full length of her tether. You see, Mr. Desmond,"—his voice had a confidential intonation,—"by the provisions of the will,"—he spoke as if it were the sole and singular testamentary document in human experience,—"Mrs. Faurie has a large income,—a very large income,—but she cannot go beyond it,—she cannot touch the principal."

Desmond flushed haughtily. He had had such close dealings with debts and financial distresses and sheer poverty of late, nay, of rivings and wrestings of possessions that seemed so inalienably his own as to give their seizure the taint of robbery, that he had scant appetite to digest the prosperity of others, and he was devoid of the vulgar vice of curiosity which might otherwise have stimulated his interest. His dark blue eyes were on the vast, murky spread of the Mississippi River, seen through the window beyond a group of pecan trees, and the Arkansas bank opposite, a dim line of dark gray against the fainter gray of the low and clouded sky. His closely cut chestnut hair showed the contour of his shapely head. His tall, strong figure, for he had a record in college athletics as well as less esteemed branches of learning, had a supple grace that lent an air of distinction to the well-fitting suit of gray he wore, for at Great Oaks Plantation no one affected evening dress for daily dinner. So quiet was Desmond that his attitude expressed an attention which he did not really accord,—in fact, it was divided by a fear that in Mr. Stanlett's garrulity he was liable to trench too far on the private affairs of the family. However, the old gentleman occupied the position of host or employer, according to the viewpoint; he was treated with filial deference by the youthful Fauries; he had received the tutor with a happy blending of hospitality and authority, and Desmond hardly knew how he might decorously evade disclosures of bibulous candor which he was neither entitled nor expected to hear.

"No, sir," Mr. Stanlett repeated, "by the will she cannot touch the principal, but she has a large income,—a fixed sum, thirty thousand dollars chargeable on the whole estate, and in addition the yield of this Great Oaks Plantation, which varies according to the season,—a very large income,—*so long as she remains a widow*. Yes, sir!—a widow she is, and a widow she must continue! Mr. Faurie was a very arbitrary man in point of temper—where are those boys?—and had a grudging against any other man's getting a chance to spend his money. Notwithstanding the losses occasioned by the Civil War and the various fluctuations in values since, Faurie was worth little short of a million dollars when he died. He had a very level head. He made a remarkable will, a good, safe, sound, able document." Mr. Stanlett had an evident relish of the provisions of that will,—a great respect for it.

9

"She could dissent,—she could break it, I suppose." Desmond forced himself to speak. He was not to have the typical tutor's mental privacy, apparently. By reason of the magnanimity his employers intended to affect, treating him according to his former worldly station and as an equal, a friend, an honored man of letters, he was to have the trial of participating in their social life as at a Barmecide feast, really sharing naught, a mere figment of fraternity and festivity.

"Break the will!" Mr. Stanlett skirled in dismay. "Impossible!—after nearly seven years' acquiescence. But if she could, she would only get what the will gives her anyhow in the event of a second marriage,—simply her dower rights in Tennessee,—one fourth of the personalty, a life-interest in a third of the realty situated there, including his town residence in Nashville,—just what the law would allow her had he died intestate,—and in the Mississippi estate a child's part in fee simple, for 'dower,' you know, is abolished in this State, and the law always follows the location of the realty. But, in fact, she has seemed perfectly satisfied with the arrangement,—as indeed well she might be! I fancy, too, that she has had about enough of matrimony. She likes her own way, and Mr. Faurie was a self-willed, proud, dictatorial—are those boys gone?—And what are *you* doing there, Joel?" glimpsing the butler, standing stiffly near the sideboard. "Gimme the brandy decanter. Have some cognac, Mr. Desmond. Light those candles, Joel,—and take yourself off. Want to wait on the table *all* night?"

Then as the door closed noiselessly on the accomplished old servant,—"That nigger has got ears as long as a mule's," Mr. Stanlett commented in parenthesis, quaffed from his glass, sucked in his thin lips with extreme relish, and continued his confidences.

"No,—my niece's position under the will cannot dispose her greatly to a second experiment in the holy estate of matrimony. Mr. Faurie was considerably her senior,—in fact, he was quite an old bachelor, you might say, when they were married. How much older he was *I* never knew, for *she* would not tolerate any mention of the disparity in years,—though Faurie himself, who was a very stylish, impressive man, was too vain and arrogant to care one whit for it. Why,"—lowering his voice sepulchrally,—"when he died, I couldn't mention his age in preparing the newspaper announcements because *I never knew it.*"

He looked hard at Desmond and nodded his head significantly. "Now, don't you know that people thought *that* was funny?"

He paused to light a cigar, having pushed the tray over to Desmond. "Yes," he resumed puffingly, "as my niece says, we stayed in Europe as long as our money lasted. We had a fine time, went everywhere, saw everything, were fêted and made much of to our hearts' content,—could have married into the nobility more than once, for"—the candle-light illumined the

10

freakish slyness and glee in his senile smile—"people over there don't know how the will is fixed in regard to a second marriage. No! pledge you my honor! They only saw the royal way in which Mrs. Faurie *can spend* money. Now," he broke out into a chirping laugh of relish of the incongruity, "my niece says that she doesn't know how she can make both ends meet till her next year's income begins to accrue. Ha! ha! We are to stay down here in the swamp till the hot weather runs us out, and then we shall go down to the Gulf coast, find some cheap little place near Biloxi or Pass Christian, and ah—ah"—he waved the cloud of cigar smoke from above his venerable head—"and I for one wish that time were come. You see plantation life is a sort of syncope at best,—that is, hereabouts. Further down the river, though, things are livelier. In Louisiana, now, the people are of a different disposition: they go about, visit each other; they make festival occasions; they are of French extraction; they have the light heart and the happy hand. Nothing can subdue the old Gallic *gaieté de cœur*, not even the swamp country. But all this upper region of ours was settled by people from Tennessee, Virginia, and Kentucky,—about the time that the mania for raising cotton in the bottom lands of Mississippi took hold on the progressive planters of the Border States. We have got our inherited English temperament to reckon with, our seriousness, our stolidity, our inability to be amused by a trifle, like a kitten with a string, or a Creole. And, too, it is a matter of neighborhood,—we are only a few hundred miles from Memphis, counting by the crankings of the river, all our associations are with the Border States, and we are out of earshot of the lively Creoles. I am afraid you will find it very dull here, Mr. Desmond, way down in the swamp." He had evidently forgotten the fact that his companion was not a guest.

"I am not here for pleasure, you know," Desmond reminded him.

"True,—oh, yes,—very true,—the boys,—their education. But you are so like"—Desmond thought that he was about to say "one of ourselves," but perhaps he was supersensitive—"ah—so very like a collegian yourself, that I forget you occupy the reverend position of tutor. The boys have a good start in the modern languages—that is, they can gabble fast enough—their mother's wanderings made them regular polyglots—they had native teachers at every stoppage; but I reckon you will find them poor shakes in the rudiments of natural science, mathematics, rhetoric, Latin, and so forth, and I suppose that in spite of their colloquial glibness, they know little of the construction of the foreign languages. Mrs. Faurie is very anxious for their solid advancement. And she is determined to make this enforced quiet recruit both her fortune and their education. So glad to have you here, Mr. Desmond,—so glad to have you with us."

He hesitated, waved the smoke from his white head, and once more filled his glass from the decanter. It was a small liqueur glass, but its size was not commensurate with the potations to which it ministered, for it was easily replenished, and of course he drank his Cognac neat. Desmond began to have a shrewd idea, partly because the tiny glass had been intended for a mere sip of Curaçoa, that had Mrs. Faurie been present at dinner, the bibulous exercises would have been much curtailed. He was experiencing some embarrassment in thus lingering over the potations, for he had arrived only that afternoon, and had never met Mrs. Faurie, having been employed by Mr. Keith, the guardian of her sons. Desmond was solicitous lest the breach of etiquette and good manners be imputed to his connivance. Perhaps Mr. Stanlett's proclivity was known to his niece, but he must seldom have such complete immunity from remonstrance and caution. While the old gentleman's vinous indulgence and senile impairments would suggest that his preferences might with impunity be set aside in such an emergency, the evident appreciation and deference with which he was treated implied that he was a person to be reckoned with. Desmond dared not himself propose to quit the table: the gaucherie would undoubtedly offend the old gentleman as an intentional disrespect. Yet the tutor really felt that by thus lingering he jeopardized all his prospects with that far more important personage, the lady of Great Oaks and the head of the family. Distasteful as was his position to him, he valued it exceedingly the moment it was threatened, as the only opportunity that had offered at his utmost need. He had been positively penniless at the crisis of his disasters. Even had he completed his law course, he must have had means to live while he waited for a practice to accrue. He had no commercial experience or aptitudes. He had no available business connections. Perhaps few people realize the difficulty of leaping into a paying position at a vault, instead of growing and climbing up with it from the ground. All values seem accessible only *per ambages*. A moment earlier he had been recoiling from the employment, the situation he liked so ill, and now he was asking himself if he were desirous of standing behind a dry goods counter in a village store, that he could afford to make his entry into Mrs. Faurie's household under circumstances so inauspicious,—carousing over the dinner-table with a man, not his host, obviously superannuated, in a sort irresponsible, unable perhaps to justify his own dereliction, much less the infringement of decorum by the tutor. The village store,—quotha! No refuge awaited him there. He did not know insertion from indigo. He had fallen into his niche, his proper place, and with a sudden sense of prizing its values, he quitted his chair. Not to leave the room abruptly and at once, however. The crisis had called his tact into play. He walked toward the mantelpiece as if to scrutinize the picture above it and thus pave the way to an easy withdrawal.

"Take the candle to it,—take the candle to it. That is Faurie himself when he was about sixteen,—do not know how long ago it was painted, though! But the length of that rifle is a dead give-away," cried Mr. Stanlett, from the table, his glass in his hand.

As Desmond lifted one of the candles, the light revealed a large oil-painting executed in the florid portrait style of the middle nineteenth century,—a crowded canvas it was, showing a fair, vigorous young stripling leaning on his gun, a horse and foliage in the distance, a deer, with only the fine head visible, gray and antlered, lying at the sportsman's feet;—the frame, inclosing all, very handsome. There were some other pieces in the room, which was large, square, and high-ceiled, all suggestive of game, and the fact that the late Mr. Faurie may have been a bon-vivant. One, a dainty water-color sketch of a piscatorial subject, the catfish of the Mississippi, bore the marks of the hand of a clever amateur.

The wall-paper was dimly pictorial, after the style of even an earlier day, a mélange of forest boughs and boles of great trees through which a shadowy outline of the figures of a chase sped, with deer, hounds, horsemen, huntsmen, and horns, of "elfland faintly blowing." A great, dark, mahogany press showed through small diamonded panes rows of silver vessels, glistering in the dusk, which neither the flicker of the candle nor the twilight glimmer from the great windows could annul. Several of the large cups bore inscriptions, and he thought they looked at the distance like trophies captured by some winner of the turf. As Desmond turned to ask the question, he perceived that the old man had sunk back in his tall armchair, his delicate face, still in slumber, keenly outlined against the cushion of its head-rest in the clear, refined light of the candle close at hand, his white hair gleaming frostily.

Desmond stood uncertain for a moment. He saw through the bay-window that the night was falling fast without. But for the flicker of the moon, he might not have known how the great Mississippi rippled and sparkled under the currents of the wind. The passing of the first steamboat that he had yet seen he marked by her chimney-lamps, red and green, swinging high in the air, and their reflection, ruby and emerald, gemming the water. As she sheered, she showed the long line of her side-lights, like a string of yellow topazes. She did not turn nor approach, but sounded her whistle as if for a landing, and he wondered at this. The boat was saluting the place by way of compliment, for it was known that the queen was in residence, so to speak, and Mrs. Faurie shipped much cotton from the contemned and avoided plantation in the old way by water, for the almost omnipresent railroads were still distant from Great Oaks Landing. Presently the lights were quenched, the craft had passed beyond his view, the moon was overcast, and only the gray night was visible from the window. Desmond seized his opportunity for escape. He placed the candle he held upon the table, and with a noiseless step and a furtive, apprehensive eye, as if the exacting old gentleman might rouse to displeasure and reproach at a mere rustle, he quitted the room, leaving his companion, his empty glass still poised in his hand, asleep in his chair.

The mansion at Great Oaks Plantation was as ill-lighted by night as are most residences dependent still on candle and kerosene. Unless, indeed, some festival occasion demanded extra brilliancy, only the gleam from the chandelier in the main hall guided the exit from the dining-room through a cross-hall, the entry, so called. Desmond had not the necessity for wariness that might have befitted the steps of Mr. Stanlett, but he paused in the dim entry, marking the subdued glow at the intersection with the main hall, then carefully directed his steps thither. Even thus he ran over the "bike" of one of the boys, inadvertently placed where it might most opportunely trip the unsuspecting pedestrian in these glooms, and threw it upon the floor with a tremendous clatter. To his vexation he heard a door open in the hall beyond and a feminine voice call out unintelligibly, whether in inquiry or warning or commiseration he did not accurately discern in his confusion. He hastily set the wheel out of harm's way against the wall, and with a swift, prompt step advanced up the lighted hall toward the open door, which he perceived led into the parlor where he had been received earlier in the afternoon. A large lamp on a high, old-fashioned pedestal stood on a round, marble-topped centre table; a wood fire blazed with a white light in the great chimney-place, and the brass andirons and fender glittered responsively; an old-fashioned crimson velvet carpet was on the floor, and long crimson satin damask curtains hung over lace draperies at the windows. In the midst of this atmosphere of glow and warmth the lady of Great Oaks stood with expectant mien, awaiting him.

Somehow she was so different from his mental image, from what he was prepared to see, that he was disconcerted for a moment. He had imagined a middle-aged frump favored by fortune, portly, puffy, rubicund, overfed, overdressed, bursting with self-importance, smiling in creases, of husky voice and fixed opinions, and laying down the law. This was a woman seemingly as young as himself; tall, slender, regal, with rich brown hair in a high pompadour roll, an exquisitely white, delicate complexion, luminous gray eyes, with a marvelous capacity for expression, a clear, coercive glance delivered from beneath long black eyelashes, and finely drawn black eyebrows, perfectly straight. She wore a gown of thick, creamy lace, some fabric rich of effect though not of commensurate cost, one of the pretty fads of the day, and about her slim waist was twisted a soft, silken sash in Roman stripes of pink and azure and amber, the long ends hanging knotted at one side. The sentiment of youth that clung about her presence was oddly incongruous with her assured address, replete with authority and the manner of seniority.

"This is Mr. Desmond," she said, in a clear, dulcet, vibratory voice, as she advanced and held out her hand. "So sorry not to have met you at dinner! But I am sure the rest did what they could for you. We are all so glad to have you here."

He seated himself in the fauteuil she indicated, and she sank down into one on the opposite side of the table in the blended light of lamp and fire. She fixed her disconcerting eyes full upon him, as if utterly unaware of their bewildering beauty, gravely scrutinizing him, evidently "sizing him up," taking her impressions of his mental quality and personal fitness for the position.

"There are many places on the river which are very attractive. But we are differently situated. We are so far from any neighbors,—quite isolated. It really seems a godsend that you are willing to come to us in the swamp."

As she talked on her homely themes, he was irritated to be so tongue-tied, but somehow he could not reconcile the situation; and as she looked straight at him from beneath those level brows, he gazed spellbound at her.

"My three big babies are too old for the nest, I know, and in fact they are toppling out. But I can't bear to send them off as yet, and I have great faith in home influence and individual teaching."

Desmond thought if he could but shut his eyes for one moment; he could see the kind of frump whom her sage, staid discourse would befit.

"I think they can be prepared here for college, right here in the swamp with me,—and then—why, we shall see what we shall see. And now, good-night. I will not detain you." She touched a bell, and as the brisk young footman's black face appeared in the door,—"See that the lamp is lighted in Mr. Desmond's room, and that the fire is burning well."

CHAPTER II

D esmond, dismissed, felt cut through and through. It was no failure of courtesy, but the note of indifference, of complete self-absorption, impressed him; yet how could he expect Mrs. Faurie to be interested in her sons' tutor except from her own viewpoint. To his apprehension it was as if in some psychic magic he had shifted his identity. He did not recognize himself in this null, unassertive personality. So lately he had been the centre of fond hopes, the pride of his father's life. He was an object of mark at his university; his scholarship had been worthy the respect of the faculty. He recalled the words of their glowing commendations with a sort of pained wonder that they had ever been addressed to him. The president himself had not deemed it ill-advised to say, "With your equipment and your fine talents, we must expect great things of your future. Your name will reflect credit on our Alma Mater; I confidently believe it will stand high on the scroll." His classmates rejoiced in his exceptional record, so far removed he was from envy or detraction. His popularity was unbounded, for he had an attractive personality and all the effervescence of cheery youth and good-fellowship, and his notability made him a lion in the social circles of the college town. His reputation followed him wherever he and his multitude of young friends had a connection; and he had enjoyed all the prestige of actual achievement, so amply did the flowering promise herald the rich fruition.

How small was that microcosm of college life, how far removed from the actualities of the great uninstructed, prosperous world, blundering on in suave content, with its crass ignorance of all but money values, he learned only when the blow fell and he must needs have work, and work at once, for his daily bread. He might look in vain for market quotations on Greek. There was no corner in Old Saxon,—modern slang could better turn the trick on 'Change. The opportunities that lay in the line of pedagogy were already overcrowded; and thus instead of that road to the stars, to worthy achievement, for which he had so long and so laboriously prepared, for which he was so preëminently fitted, he was to trudge the by-paths of hopeless poverty; to be the drudging, futureless stipendiary in a rich, frivolous household, teaching three mollycoddle boys, buried in the seclusion of the Mississippi bottom lands, as if translated to another sphere.

With these thoughts Desmond lay long awake that night. He mechanically watched the flicker of the fire on the light paper of the walls of the large, airy room, giving out here and there a sparkle of gilt from the scroll design, till it dulled gradually, and at length faded to a pervasive dusky red glow. He was not used to a bed with the old-fashioned tester and four posts, and when he was about to fall asleep, he was roused by the unaccustomed sense of something poised above his head, or standing solemnly sentinel, surrounding him as he lay. He was not sorry when the room grew too dark for aught to be seen but the gray night looking in between the long white curtains at the tall windows. Yet the hours brought incidents even in the monotony. He was apprised that he was on the side of the house nearest the river when he saw through the small panes the sudden distant glare of a steamboat's electric search-light, making a rayonnant halo in the dim glooms of the riparian midnight, and heard the husky, remonstrant tones of her whistle, and the impact of "the buckets" on the water as the wheels revolved. He was not yet sufficiently familiar with the plan of the house to have otherwise known of his proximity to the bank; but after the boat had passed and the last vague echo of the stroke of the paddles on the water had died away, he was impressed by the silence of the night and the absolutely noiseless flow of the swift currents of the great river. It dismayed him in some sort, the sense of that mighty, irresistible, mute, moving force of nature out there in the still night, as changeful as life, as inexorable as fate, as ceaseless as eternity. He had felt small, reduced in worldly esteem, robbed of every prospect, and he had no heart to hope. With this expression of silent, majestic immensity brought to his contemplation, he seemed infinitely minute in the scheme of creation. So long had it rolled its waves from the far north to the Gulf; nations had risen on its banks and passed away, and strangers had come anew to die and be succeeded in turn by foreign faces still, and what mattered it what an atom such as he might suffer, or hope, or grieve to lose.

He could not sleep; he had desisted from the conscious effort; he had resigned himself to the wakefulness embittered by such thoughts as these. It had grown dark, quite dark,—the windows, vague parallelograms in the gloom, more distinguished by his memory of the features of the room than by actual sight,—when he heard a sound that somehow thrilled his every nerve. Hardly a sound,—it was rather a sibilance. But for the intense stillness of the house he could not have noticed it,—a mere rustle.

"What is it?" he asked himself, intent and curious. For when it vaguely came again, it conveyed the sense of motion; it suggested a varying distance. Once more his straining senses caught the sound,—very soft it was. Furtive, was it, he wondered, for he had identified it as the lisping note of a sliding foot on a velvet carpet. At first he thought it within his own room, but as it receded at regular intervals, he realized it as a step on the stair without. He began to appreciate that the head of his bed was against the wall, on the other side of which this stair ascended to the upper story, for his room was on the ground floor of the great, rambling house. He thus caught the vague vibration of motion, as well as the susurrus of the impact of the step on the pile of the carpet; otherwise he might not have distinguished so cautious,

17

so very silent a transit. It had peculiar features of mystery. It receded into absolute quiet, then, approaching anew, seemed to pass.

A long interval ensued while he lay still, the interest of his surmise, the doubt, the surprise, solacing his wakeful mood. Suddenly he started with a thrill that sought out some nerve of superstition which had contrived to coexist with all the logic of his mental training. It was coming again, softly, very softly, its sibilant passage scarcely to be discriminated even in the silence of the night, ascending once more the padded velvet stair. Then Desmond fancied that he heard a long-drawn breath, a stifled sigh. He lifted himself on his elbow, listening intently. The furtive step receded and yet receded, till it had won the distance that the ear might not reach. A long interval of absolute silence once more ensued. Then abruptly, again, a muffled step descending, softly, secretly.

With a sudden thought Desmond sprang to his feet. His first idea of the passing of some member of the family to the upper regions of the house on some domestic errand, for extra coverings or for medicine or lamps, was annulled by the amazing silence and secrecy of the recurrent demonstration. Its repetition implied purpose. Its furtiveness suggested malignity. He reflected that, so far as he knew, the inmates of the house, with one feeble old man and three young boys, were all inadequate to cope with the intrusion of burglars or other marauders. He flung the door of the bedroom open and stood in the hall, his pistol in his hand.

"Who is there?" he called out, his voice ringing through the darkness like a clarion.

There was not a sound in response, not a stir.

"Speak up," he threatened, "or I'll fire." The metallic click of the weapon as he cocked it was of coercive intimations.

Still not a sound, not a stir. No scurrying footstep to be out of harm's way,—no premonition of the attack for which he was prepared, shifting his posture each time after he spoke, to escape a shot that might be aimed at the sound of his voice in the darkness. Nothing—the hall was absolutely vacant, silent.

He stood irresolute for a moment. He scarcely dared turn to secure a light lest the lurking intruder escape in the interval of his absence. Yet when he heard a stir in a room farther down the hall, the sound of bare feet bouncing out of bed, the opening of a door heralding a trickling of candle-light into the gloom, he was all at once ashamed of the commotion he had aroused and its apparent lack of justification.

As the light advanced along the hall, he was pleased to see that it was held in the hand of Reginald Faurie, the eldest of the three boys; the old man was too feebly irresponsible to be trusted, and he was glad that he had not aroused Mrs. Faurie. But as the young fellow held the candle high in his hand, the light showing his tousled auburn hair and his pink and white striped pajamas, the expression of his face, distinct in the glow, was not such as to ingratiate the future pupil with the tutor. It was of half-repressed mirth; yet Reginald paused once, and looked over his shoulder into the shadow with the half shudder of a qualm of cold fright. He showed no disposition to search for the cause of the disturbance, however, and he cut short Desmond's excited attempt at explanation as of no importance.

"Let me in here with you for a moment," Reginald said. "Don't want to wake up the kids! Yes,—yes,"—with a mature air of patronage,—"I know exactly what you heard,—old Slip-Slinksy, as we boys call him, going up and down stairs."

The coolness with which he shut the door, placed the candle on the high, white, painted mantelpiece, and sought to stir the fire was proof positive that there was no intruder to be reckoned with. Desmond yielded reluctantly. But it was the house of a stranger, and he was unused to his surroundings. He stood in his bath-robe, which he had flung on at the first alarm, and leaned on the high back of a chair, while Reginald set the blazes to flaring in the great fireplace, then dropped down on the rug and put the pointed toes of his bedroom slippers against the brass fender, evidently preparing to elucidate the mystery.

"I know you'll think I'm loony,—I hate to give myself away! But you are one of the solid, scientific, investigating kind, I'm sure. You will make inquiries, I know, and I don't want mamma to learn that old Slip-Slinksy is at his queer tricks again. She is not a bit superstitious,—no sort of a crank,—but it is a creepy, inexplicable kind of thing that one doesn't like to have in one's house, and it would make her hate the plantation worse than ever; and as she has got to stay at Great Oaks for a while, I think she had better not hear about this demonstration to-night."

"But who is it?" asked Desmond, mystified.

"Nobody,—just nothing at all!"

Desmond walked around the chair, and, seating himself in the renewed radiance of the fire, drew the folds of his bath-robe close about him. He bent the brows of prospective authority upon Reginald, and the lad sought to explain.

"What is a ghost but nothing at all!—its emptiness is what gets on your nerves. You can take your gun, as you did to-night, to the wicked man when he gets gay or out of place,—as long as he is alive. But once a deader, and he *has got you*. I'd like to hear your learned chemical analysis of a ghost. It is compounded of a winter night's imaginings! It's an untimely shiver! It's the tremors of hearing a storm coming down the Mississippi River and making all the boats tie up for the night! It's old Slip-Slinksy doing nothing but going

19

upstairs and coming down again. I don't know what on earth started it, but that is our ghost, and we have got it for keeps."

"Fudge!" exclaimed Desmond, contemptuously.

"*You* heard it," said the boy, significantly. "I did not."

Desmond *had* heard the strange manifestation, knowing naught of it hitherto. He remembered the unearthly thrill its first intimations had sent through every startled fibre. "But it must have some natural explanation, of course."

"I am sure I hope so," rejoined Reginald. "But the natural explanation has defied us so far. We have done our little possible to solve the mystery. We have examined the walls and roof; we have taken up the carpets; we have lurked in wait for it, and rushed out upon it as you did to-night,—and found nothing,—as you did. I, for one, would take mighty kindly to any sort of a natural explanation. A ghost—no matter how much you give him the cold shoulder—doesn't make for happiness in the home, and"—he shuddered—"he is apt to give you the cold shoulder."

"Is it an old affair?" asked Desmond.

"We can't exactly fix just when the manifestation began. It *always* butts in immediately after we come home. Then there will be a long interval. Presently it starts up again,—every few nights. Then we may have another long exemption. You would think this old house like any other happy old home. But in the midst of the preparation for departure it is sure to begin again,—if anybody is fool enough to lie awake to listen for it. Of course I don't know what the ghost may do while we are away,—in our long absences he may run riot all over the place. At all events, we can get no caretaker to sleep in the house. I shouldn't be surprised if its reputation of being haunted protects it from depredators, river pirates,—and such cattle. Anyhow, we leave only the ghost in charge, and there is not a thing stirred when we come back. Only the dust over all, and a sense of mystery."

"Of course there must be some natural explanation," Desmond protested anew.

"So glad you think so," said Reginald, politely. "But you will not mention it to mamma."

"Certainly not; but is the demonstration always the same?"

"Always the same,—a step going up and coming down the stair;—going up and presently coming down the stair, just as you heard it. It is up to you to explain it. It is no tradition as far as you are concerned; you were all unconscious and without expectation."

A sudden wind had sprung up without. It came down the great channel of the Mississippi in chilly gusts, with a thrill of dawn in its reviving stir. It shook the silence. Myriads of undiscriminated voices were rife in the air. The boughs of the great oaks of the grove without clashed and fell still again. The evergreen leaves of the Cherokee rose hedges, fencing the place for miles, kept up a rippling stir in the section close at hand. A draft became perceptible at the nearest window, and Desmond, looking toward it, saw through the parted curtains that the clouds were riven asunder and a clear, chill star was scintillating in a deep abyss of darkness. The night was wearing on,—not far from day—not far from a frosty dawn.

"And nothing has ever been seen," said Desmond, drawing the cord of his robe closer.

Reginald stirred the fire; then resumed his easy posture before it, his eyes upon the blaze. "I beg pardon," he rejoined, somewhat unwillingly; "but I did not say that."

"I misunderstood you, then," said the tutor. He sought to laugh, but he had himself heard too much that he could not explain to make his ridicule effective. "But there must be some natural explanation."

"Well,—we can't get at it,—that's all," said Reginald, somewhat nettled by the ridicule. "You see I am not stuffing you. I have not the least disposition to trot out our ghost to—to lord it over you. I do not expect you to bow down and admire him. I am not trying to make prestige on his account. You and he struck up an acquaintance without any introduction from me. And the apparition on the stairs is so logical and in keeping that it bears out the sound of the step,—and that is what troubles us,—especially mamma. She is not superstitious, but she is a very sensitive organization,—and she always hated this dull old plantation, and this gruesomeness that it has developed does not recommend it the least little bit."

"But about the apparition?" Desmond asked eagerly, even while he was ready to rally himself that he should entertain so primitive a curiosity.

"Why, it came about the most natural way in the world," declared Reginald. "There was a wedding over at Dryad-Dene, Colonel Kentopp's plantation,—Mrs. Kentopp's sister, I think,—a great wedding, all in the old style. The Kentopps are up-to-date people,—make a point of keeping up with the procession, unless some fashionable antique craze takes hold on them. Just at that time the imitation of the big old country wedding was all the go. So instead of having the ceremony at our little neighborhood church, and taking the next train or packet for the wedding tour, the marriage was at the mansion, in the style of fifty years ago. They invited the country; and the relatives and the friends came in their dozens, if you please. Of course the Kentopps couldn't put them all up, so some of the guests were entertained by their neighbors, and there were many dinners and dances and such functions in the vicinity—houses five miles apart, mostly—to compliment the happy couple. We took our part, of course. We were just returned from Europe, Asia, Africa, and Oceanica" (with a pert little fling), "and the house was

21

jammed. I don't know if you have noticed that there isn't a regular second story to this old bungalow. The rooms above are in a half story,—mighty near *all* dormer window. We don't use those rooms unless we are hard put to it. But on this occasion they were full,—even cots and pallets on the floor. Well, in the bedroom on the left hand side as you ascend the stairs were a lady and three children. They were nearly related to the bridegroom, but strangers to us,—they had never been here before—and one of the kids took advantage of the opportunity to make himself conspicuous by getting exceedingly ill. My mother suggested that, to have help near at hand in the night, the nurse should sleep on a pallet in the hall. The nurse was cheerful and agreed; there was a big, bright moon, and all the dormer windows were very festive. About midnight this lady was awakened by the nurse, who came and asked leave to draw her pallet into the bedroom, because she could not sleep for the continual passing up and down the stairs,—tip, tip, tip,—slyly slipping up and slyly slipping down." He paused to listen apprehensively, then recommenced. "The good lady's nerves were racked with anxiety, I dare say, for she declared that it was very ill-bred in the other guests not to let the house get quiet, when there was illness and a chance that her child would die. Then she told the nurse to return to her pallet,—that the room was too crowded already with herself and the three children, and the sick boy needed air. After a time the nurse, an intelligent, patient, reasonable woman, came back, declaring that she was afraid. There was something strange in this passing. It was not the other guests. The people were all still, asleep; the house was as silent as death; but yet—slip, slip, slip—something shuffling along so silently, so slyly,—she was fit to scream. She was once more rebuked and sent to her place. Presently she did scream! The moon had traveled over the house and the beams began to fall through the window over the staircase, and there she saw what had been going up and down the stops,—a man in fancy dress, she declared,—my uncle thinks it was some antique costume—"

"Did he see the apparition, too?"

"Sure! the whole house came running, scared to death,—in just what they had on,—a beautiful lot they were, too! but the thing had vanished. Only the nurse and her mistress, who, being awake, had run out instantly upon the alarm, saw it distinctly. They both said that it was a man in fancy dress, with powdered hair. My uncle had just opened his door on the lower floor, and, looking upward at the landing, his view was indistinct, but his impression was the same."

Desmond pondered for a moment. "Did it never occur to any of them that it was some wag of the house-party frightening the nurse for a freak."

"I have heard of making a long arm, but I can't imagine making a long enough leg to keep a footstep going up and down a staircase, when none of our guests have been in the county, or even in the State, for four or five years."

"It is strange," said Desmond, at last. "But all the same I am sure that there must be some reasonable natural explanation,—if it could be found."

"I wish I shared your belief, or disbelief," said Reginald. He looked up doubtfully at the candle burning low now on the mantelpiece. It was not the regulation bedroom light, but in a tall, silver candlestick, that offered no protection against the drops which its guttering state sent dripping down its sides. The fire was sinking; the room had taken on a shadow and a sense of gloom; the wind suddenly rose in a shrill skirl; then one could hear some slight débris of leaves or twigs skittering across the grass as if in a weird dance without. Any suggestion of uncanny footsteps was in jeopardy to the maintenance of equilibrium. Desmond, fatigued from his journey and his vigils, was growing heavy-eyed and disposed to slumber. For some time he had been sensible of the increasing chill of the air, and was beginning to canvass the propriety of himself terminating the interview, and in his character of tutor authoritatively bidding the boy to betake himself to his own bedroom instead of awaiting his exit as a guest. But Reginald suddenly resumed. "I wish I could agree with you that there is a natural explanation,—if we could light upon it. I believe in its supernatural quality enough to wonder how I mustered the courage to come through the hall when I heard you call. I was afraid that if you spoke again, mamma would be roused. I don't see how I am to get back. I am something of a man in the daytime, but a regular baby about it at night,—and—if you don't mind—I'll just climb over there in the back of the bed and stay with you till the rising bell. Oh, thanks, muchly. You have saved my reason, if not my life. Suppose—oh, just suppose—I was to meet old Slip-Slinksy in the hall,—and he was to—to—to blow out the candle."

CHAPTER III

The breakfast-table showed little correlation to a haunted house. It was surrounded with bright and smiling faces when Desmond, to his chagrin a trifle tardy, opened the door. The sunshine lay among the potted plants blooming in wire stands at the two casements opposite the great bay-window, and through its broad outlook one could see the immense shining expanse of the king of rivers, with a golden glister on its ripples, and in the distance a line of tender brownish gray to denote the growth of cottonwood fringing the farther banks against the blue sky. The sylvan hunt on the wall-paper, in the medley of scrolls and fantastic tracery, had a realistic effect of motion as the sunshine and shadow shifted over it through the stirring boughs of the great live-oak tree close without. A fire of light wood glowed on the hearth, more it might seem for gladsome cheer than needed warmth, this balmy day of the southern winter, and old Joel, the butler, was holding on a silver tray a large, low basket of ripe figs and brilliant hothouse flowers, while Mrs. Faurie read a note that had come with the fruit. She paused for a moment and glanced up as the tutor entered.

"Good-morning, Mr. Desmond. I hope you rested well." Then, rustling the missive, she read aloud: "'Congratulations on the date'—what the mischief is the date, Uncle Clarence?—the 5th of December?—Heavens and earth! The cruel woman! She is reminding me of my birthday." She tossed the note aside with a gesture of mock desperation. "Let me give you some coffee, Mr. Desmond,—I can swallow my mortification later,—or will you have chocolate?"

As she sat at the head of the table, moving the pieces of the large old-fashioned silver service, that glittered with polish, but showed here and there an indentation that bespoke the battering proclivity of years of daily usage, the light from the several windows was full on her face. Her complexion was more than ever like a white rose in its softness and delicacy thus displayed. Her fine, long throat was shown by the surplice cut of her plain white lawn blouse, of which the sleeves reached only to the elbow of her softly rounded arms, with their slim, dainty hands; her skirt was of plain pleated black voile, and her brown hair was rolled straight up from her forehead. Nothing could be more homelike, more simple; but the effect of her eyes as she looked at him from under her long lashes, her level brows slightly drawn, had a vaguely bewildering effect on Desmond. He had seen charming women heretofore, but none to parallel her loveliness. His mind was acclimated to the idea, the tradition of incomparable beauty, but not in these close relations. To breakfast with Helen of Troy, to receive a cup of chocolate from the hand of Diana herself, to reply to a word of simple inquiry and assured authority from the embodiment of the ideal that poets have sung and painters have limned in all ages, was disconcerting. Had she seemed herself more aware of her preëminent endowment, had she been self-conscious, he could have better adjusted himself to its continual contemplation; but he had the sentiment of a unique discovery, of perceiving somewhat unknown, unnoted.

"I can't see any cause for mortification; it seems to me a very pretty compliment, mamma." Reginald had taken the note up with some anxiety and was perusing it with a clearing brow.

"A compliment!—to be reminded of my dreadful age."

"Ah, Honoria, you are absurd, my dear," Mr. Stanlett protested, with an air of concern. "Thirty-four is still young,—still young, my dear."

"Oh, how can you mention it, Uncle Clarence? Let me forget the exact number! I feel one foot in the grave! I am the prey of time!"

She cast up her beautiful eyes in an affectation of distress; then, catching the serious regards of the youngest boy fixed upon her, dubiously, uncertain of her mood, she looked at him intently for a moment, and burst into a ripple of smiles, to which, reassured, he responded with a callow chuckle, infinitely alluring.

"But we will have the basket in the centre of the table," she continued. "All of you who have the heart can eat a fig. I'll bet there are just thirty-four of them."

The two younger boys strained over the table to count.

"Dead to rights, mamma," said Rufus, the tenyear old, who enjoyed the preëminence of "baby." "Just thirty-four figs."

"A very pretty compliment, mamma," protested Reginald again. "For my part, I am obliged to Mrs. Kentopp, and I am ashamed that I did not remember the date myself."

"Oh, ho! You bet I did!" said Rufus, with a triumphant nod.

Mrs. Faurie put down her spoon, and cast a look across the silver service so replete with maternal affection, so embellishing to her proud beauty, that it seemed indeed a pity that the face on which it was bestowed should be so round, so freckled, so jocosely creased, so facetiously winking.

"What have you got for me, Chubby?" she asked. Her look was angelic.

"You'll see,—you'll see!" He smiled widely. The dentist had been at work on that smile, and had eliminated two teeth, and the interval interfered with the happiest expression of filial affection.

The other two brothers, though manifestly disconcerted and deprecatory, looked at him with the quizzical contempt with which an elder boy cannot refrain from tormenting his junior. "Chub, don't be such a chump," Horace admonished him. "You ought to be ashamed to give mamma a birthday offering of some of the trash that you have collected in your European *towers*,"—with a leer to emphasize the taunting mispronunciation,—"a last year's calendar or a cigarette tag."

"'Tain't no old European bibelot!" Chubby declared, his round cheeks no longer distended with happy smiles. His eyes were grave and flashing fire,—he was consciously on the defensive. He breathed hard and deep.

"Oh, to be sure,—some of his chiffons from the Rue de la Paix,—souvenir de Paree," Reginald twitted him, with a nettling laugh.

"'Tain't,—it's brand-new," Chub protested.

"Where did you get it?" the other two asked in a breath.

"I bought it with my own money,"—there was an intonation of pride in this assertion.

"But where?—bloated capitalist!" asked Reginald, really curious, for there was scant opportunity to spend money at Great Oaks Plantation, forty miles distant from any town larger than a hamlet or a railroad way-station.

"Where do you reckon?"—with temper. Then with a gush of pride, "From the trading-boat,—that's where!"

Desmond could not understand why the two elder boys stared at each other for a moment, then collapsed into inextinguishable laughter, scarlet in the face, nerveless, well-nigh helpless. Even Mr. Stanlett laughed with merry relish, and Chub looked from one to another, pitiably crestfallen. A "shanty-boat," that had been tied up at the landing, was not of the usual type of trading-boat, offering provender and provisions and assortments of merchandise in localities remote from railway and packet connection, but a mere travesty on this mercantile craft, hardly more, indeed, than a raft, drifting with the current, bearing a little cabin in which the owner lived, and from which he sold a medley of stock,—pins, needles, stale candies, tobacco, whiskey, snuff, ribbons, plated jewelry,—such as might meet the needs or strike the taste of the humbler dwellers about the river-side, or the backwoods population among the bayous, along the sluggish current of which it was sometimes poled.

"Oh,—oh, mamma,—the *trading-boat*!" cried Reginald, barely recovering the power of speech.

But Horace was altogether beyond words.

"It *is* a trading-boat!" Chub protested. "Anyhow, they have lots of things to sell. They pole and row along the bayous and lakes, and they get towed by a steamboat once in a while, and go up any of the rivers they like. Then they drift down again. They have been selling along all the rivers in the State of Mississippi,—they *told* me so."

"They must have been well able, then, to pay the considerable privilege tax to the State," Mr. Stanlett commented dryly.

"Did it occur to you to inquire into that question, Chubby?" asked Reginald, still gasping with merriment.

"Ha! I'll engage that the very word 'license' would make that boat's crew cast off in a trice!" exclaimed Mr. Stanlett, with a significant nod. "That 'trading-boat' would be swallowed up from sight in the twinkling of an eye."

"But we have no right to take that for granted, Uncle Clarence," Mrs. Faurie remonstrated. "Their trade along the bayous and bogues and lakes, where no other boats come, may be considerable and aggregate enough to justify the tax. The swampers in such out-of-the-way places have no other way to buy goods."

"Ah, well,—perhaps so,—I'm not a collector. We will be charitable and hope for the best. And they may have some exemption from the tax."

The proud Chub, suddenly brought down, was near to tears.

Mrs. Faurie, all unmindful of the ridicule, was looking at him with eyes aglow. "With your money, Chubby,—your own little money?—and you always so hard up,—you dear little spendthrift! And you really remembered my birthday, and bled your precious nickels to commemorate it! Where is my present? I can't wait to see it! I'll value it above everything I have in the world. I'll always treasure it as beyond price,—my lovely Chubby's gift."

And then it developed that "lovely Chubby," intent on surprise, had been seated throughout the meal with the present in a paper bag poised on his knee under his napkin. He was reassured in some sort by the cessation of the laughter of the fraternal torments. He was too young and too ingenuous to realize that it was only a momentary respite that they might better view the pomp of the presentation. Their physical condition might have alarmed one unused to view the ecstasies of adolescent mirth when the paper bag parted to disclose a large, round, wooden apple, highly tinted with the colors of nature, the upper section of which opened to reveal within an assortment of needles, pins, a cake of wax, a brass thimble, a bodkin, and an emery masquerading as a realistic strawberry.

"An apple,—oh, ye gods and little fishes!" cried Horace.

"An apple,—presented to mamma,—my prophetic soul! Didn't I say it must be a souvenir of Paris,—to the fairest?" exclaimed Reginald, convulsed.

"Ah, ha,—very good,—classical allusion," said Mr. Stanlett, appreciatively. He cast a glance of pride at the tutor, as if calling his attention to this point of precocity.

Mrs. Faurie silently examined every detail with deliberate gravity, while the two elder sons went from one spasm into another of mute laughter, deeming the episode too funny for words, and the breathless Chub looked seriously and expectantly at her.

"Very useful, no doubt," said Mr. Stanlett, taking his cue from the gravity of her manner. "Valuable,—always ready,—needle-case."

But when Mrs. Faurie lifted her eyes, Desmond could but note how brilliant they were with unshed tears.

"Come here, Chubby," she said, with a break in her voice. "I can't wait to hug you!"

He was a big boy for ten years of age, and looked bigger in his mother's lap. She had pushed her chair a trifle back from the table, and as he sat enthroned and cherished beyond his fellows, some qualm of jealousy terminated their convulsions of mirth.

"You have not touched your plate, mamma," said one. "I have heard of people living on bread and cheese and kisses, but I never saw its demonstration before. Sweet Chub,—lovely breakfast food!"

"You two must quit that thing of calling Rufus 'Chub,'" remonstrated Mr. Stanlett.

"Yes," said Chub, whisking around in his mother's lap, and facing the party from behind the silver service; "makes me feel like a fish,—chub and dace always mentioned together."

"Chub is a first-rate item on a bill of fare; serve him out, mamma," suggested Horace.

"I am coming down myself," said Chub, with a final exasperating hug and kiss.

"And—quite a coincidence!—the waffles are coming in," jeered Horace.

"And now," said Chub, once more settled in his place at table, and feeling in fine fettle and high favor, "I move that, being mamma's birthday, we have a holiday."

Desmond was altogether unused to being so set aside and passed over and made of scant account. He was aware that he could not expect aught else in a family life in which he had no part; nevertheless, he felt all the uneasiness incident to a false position and a new experience. He had scarcely spoken a word since he had entered the room. He could not expect the conversation to be guided with a special consideration of him in this circle of family privacy, and he had submitted to eat his breakfast among them, but not of them, with what grace he might. Chub's last remark, however, trenched upon his own peculiar province, and he spoke uninvited and to the point: "And I move that we have no holiday."

Chub glanced up, his eyes both grieved and indignant. "Oh, why?" he said,—a phrase that is in more frequent use in remonstrance than any other in the English language by all American youth under twenty years of age,—a plea to which Desmond then and there resolved that he would never reply. There ensued a moment of awkward silence.

Horace suddenly answered for him. "Because, Chub, we have to be classified, you know. Mr. Desmond might be expecting you to read Greek, if he started you without examination, you know."

"Don't look so downcast, Chubby," said Mrs. Faurie, with a caressing intonation; and Desmond was aware that, but for the pose of supporting his authority, the coveted holiday would have been granted without another moment's consideration. "Mr. Desmond is not such an ogre."

Chubby wagged his head with a sorrowful monition of experience and forecast. "Tutors are all alike—when it comes to ogreing."

Despite her partiality, Mrs. Faurie evidently thought this hardly civil. She came hastily to the rescue. "And we have all the preliminaries to arrange; this must be a busy day." Then, obviously with a lingering hope for Chubby's release, for his appealing look was very touching, "But perhaps it might be best to begin to-morrow. I should think it would be well for you to look about you a little before going to work, Mr. Desmond,—familiarize yourself with your surroundings." She ended with a rising inflection that required an answer, and her evident bias would seem to dictate its import. It was short, succinct.

"Nothing whatever is gained, Mrs. Faurie, by the waste of time," he said, "and much is lost by the bad precedent."

She was rising from the table. "Then we will at once consider the choice of a schoolroom," she said, as she preceded the party out of the dining-room. At the intersection of the entry with the main hall she paused; here was an outer door which opened on a broad veranda, from which the glittering Mississippi could be seen through the vistas of the trees. This veranda ran quite around the front portion of the house, and passed through it, dividing the main building from the two wings. At one point this airy structure widened, the flooring extending into a roofless circular space, built around the great trunk of a live oak, that made a dense canopy of evergreen boughs above it, and let fall drooping shady branches all about it. The balustrade of the veranda was fitted with a circular bench, and one could scarcely imagine a more attractive bower.

"This would make a fine schoolroom," suggested Chub, and Desmond was irritated to observe that Mrs. Faurie actually seemed to consider it.

"The less there is to distract the attention, the better," he said promptly.

"The passing of a steamboat,—or a squirrel, would put Chub out of the game for the day, I suppose," she conceded, with evident reluctance.

"We could come in if it rained," persisted Chub.

"We could if we had enough sense," said Horace; "I have always understood that it required sense to know enough to come in out of the rain."

Desmond was feeling more interest in his unwelcome vocation as he followed Mrs. Faurie into the main hall. He was apprehensive lest some puerile folly of his pupils and the facile leniency of their mother jeopardize the practicability of his mission, and his vocation be riven from him when he had come to depend solely upon it. He looked about the place critically, noting facts that might have escaped him otherwise in a cursory, uninterested survey. The house bore little or indeed no token of the extensive wanderings of its inmates in foreign lands. There were a few good paintings on the walls, but their frames were old and tarnished and in several instances marred, and he fancied they were trophies of the travels of previous generations. Other canvases were devoted to the portraits of the family, some evidently painted by brushes of distinction, and others only redeemed from the imputation of being daubs by the facility and freedom with which the likeness had been caught, the art subordinate to the lifelike portrayal. The ornaments, clocks, vases, were rich and represented the expenditure of money, but were obviously the haphazard aggregations of years and successive owners, and with no system of collection or interest of suggestion. He divined that Mrs. Faurie cared too little for life in the mansion house of the hated plantation to spend time, or thought, or money on its decoration. Hence, in lieu of rich oriental rugs and polished floors, the old velvet carpets still did service, being of good quality, seemingly imperishable, covering every inch of the wood; the old satin damask curtains, with lace beneath, draped the windows as of yore. The furniture of carved rosewood, and especially that of ponderous mahogany, was better in countenance in view of the modern craze for ancient relics, but its owner valued it no whit more for the fashion. There was nowhere the museum-like effect to be seen so often in the home of a traveled proprietor. Except for a casual mention, no one could imagine that any of the household had sojourned in Japan, or journeyed on camels in remote deserts, or voyaged on the Nile and the Ganges. It was an old house, distinctly of its locality, in a fat, luxurious country, replete with the suggestions of decorous antecedents; and one might seem ungrateful to be so loath to come to it, and so eager to be gone again, as was Mrs. Faurie. The sons had evidently lost all sense of preference, small citizens of the world. Home was with each other and their mother; and it hardly mattered if it were in Rome, or in the light of the midnight sun, or on the banks of the great Mississippi.

Desmond had felt himself somewhat expatriated in surroundings so foreign to the world of letters, of art, of public interest, of intellectual activity, until he came into the library. Unconsciously he drew a long breath of relief. On every hand he knew were friends. He was not sorry to see that the books were old and evidently long undisturbed. They bore the marks of some previous owner's loving care. They were all under glass, the shelves built into the walls; below, extending up three feet from the floor, were solid doors betokening cabinets, fitted with locks, and doubtless containing treasures of old files of newspapers, pamphlets, magazines. These were all collections of elder members of the house of Faurie, and little troubled by the present generation. Two big globes, one terrestrial, the other celestial, could indeed give to the experienced young travelers of to-day only the information how very little was known of the world at the time of the construction of these microcosms.

There was a great fireplace, vacant now, the room being out of use, with the usual glittering brasses of andirons and fender. The sun streamed in at the tall windows at the eastern side; on the other,—for the apartment was in one of the wings separated from the main building by the veranda,—one could look out through the vistas of gigantic trees at the great embankment of the levee in the foreground, the splendid scroll of the Mississippi emblazoning the middle distance, and far, far away the low line of the forests at the horizon meeting the blue sky. The windows were draped only by some old-time lambrequins, short and of a grape-blue, and below were suspended the slatted shades called Venetian blinds. A heavy mahogany desk, with innumerable pigeon-holes, and a wide writing-shelf, covered with grape-blue leather, looked tempting and scholarly. A long table with drawers was in the centre of the floor, and on each side some chance hand had arranged chairs high and stiff and ready for writing or reading.

"This seems made for us. Could you spare this room?" Desmond asked, feeling nevertheless the assurance of the demand.

She hesitated. Though she cared little for Great Oaks, the incongruity struck her. This was indeed a fine room to devote to the uses of pupils and pedagogue, and it might be that all that Chub would ever learn would not be worth the wear and tear that his acquisitions here would cost it.

"But why not?" she asked in turn. "Certainly the parlors are ample for so little company as we see here."

"And we shall keep regular hours; the room can be at the service of the family in the evenings"; he rather pressed the point. "The library is separate from the rest of the building, and less liable to interruption, out of earshot of anything that may be going forward in the household; the books are all at hand; the atmosphere is inspiring."

"By all means, then," she assented.

But later, when she mentioned the decision to her uncle, he looked dismayed, and she half regretted her compliance.

"He selected the library as a schoolroom!" exclaimed Mr. Stanlett. "Well, he *is* moderate!"

"He showed the first vestige of emotion that I think it is possible for him to entertain when he saw the books," she said. "I want him to be satisfied at Great Oaks,—if anybody *can* be satisfied in the Mississippi swamp."

"What sort of impression does he make upon your mind?" asked Mr. Stanlett, solicitously.

"I think he is an iceberg; he lowers the temperature whenever he approaches."

But the value of the library as an educational influence was not immediately apparent, and Desmond, who had never taught, was destined to find that there is far more requisite for success than the equipment for instruction. The poignancy of the relinquishment of his dear ambitions, his sensitive appreciation of his reduction to an unsuitable, subsidiary position in the esteem of the world, the tingling sense of personal isolation, of humiliation in a sort, as of an unwelcome, disregarded, yet necessary supernumerary in the family circle, so apart themselves as to render his presence always felt,—he thought these elements of his poverty a sufficient handicap on satisfaction in the present and hope for the future. He might have been still further dismayed at the outset to realize that education is a cooperative function, and the receptivity of the student is as essential as the radiation of the professor. He had been himself so eager in the acquisition of knowledge, so earnest, so alertly intelligent, his mind assimilating as by an involuntary process the pabulum that the curriculum set forth in courses, that he did not readily grasp the idea of a different point of view. He was totally unaware of the luxury of mental inaction, the atrophy of the industrial muscles, the dead levels of the lack of ambition, of supine content with the least achievement compatible with the least exertion. He had given his instructors no occasion to seek to stimulate his aspirations to the goal of his best possibilities, and he had not even turned the eye of casual contemplation upon their labors as they herded their unwilling and loitering flocks along the dusty approaches to learning, fain to be content with such progress as their charges could be prevailed upon to make.

Even in the preliminaries for instruction in the big, luxurious room, friction supervened. A fresh fire blazed on the hearth, the places at the table were assigned, the box of schoolbooks was unpacked, and the stationery deposited in appropriate drawers. Chub's joy in the acquisition of a fountain pen it was necessary to moderate, and his plea to inaugurate his scholastic labors by experimenting with a writing lesson was tabooed.

"You are not here to do what you wish, but what is best for you," Desmond said finally, and Chub cast the pen from him on the table with an air of permanent repudiation and a sullen pout of disaffection.

For a time Horace, with the puerile mania to be stirring something, must needs turn in his chair and with a meddlesome finger revolve again and again the terrestrial globe that stood near by, contemplating not its charted surface, but merely its pleasing semblance to a big ball, and its satisfactory poise that so slight a touch would compass the revolution of the earth. Twice Desmond politely requested him to desist. Horace was still for a little while, but soon his careless mood had lost the memory of the command, the world was briskly awhirl anew, and in his lazy consciousness he was scarcely aware of his own agency in the fact.

Desmond hesitated. He gazed at the forgetful Horace for a moment, then he commented: "I hope that you are fond of the study of geography. If you turn that globe again, you shall map out every country on it and chart every body of water, working all the afternoons while the others are out of school till you practically own the earth and the boundaries thereof. Are you a pretty expert cartographer?"

Horace, amazed and insulted, grew round-eyed and red. "Mamma would not permit it," he said stiffly.

"We shall see. This is *my* schoolroom, and what I say here—goes!"

"Now, Horace, I hope that you have got it!" Reginald exclaimed in reproach.

Horace was motionless, mutinous in dubitation. Then with a fling he turned his back upon the allurements of the world and joined the silent and pouting Chub in fixedly regarding the grape-blue leather cover inlaid in the table, and spotted here and there with the ink of old-time chirographers.

Desmond himself had his distractions. He was interested in the old sand-box, full of metal filings, formerly used instead of blotters to dry the ink on the page. He was surprised when a bronze bust on the table revealed an inkstand, as the helmet of the head of Pallas was lifted,—a series of inkstands, it contained, for different tints, and his set and joyless face relaxed as he refilled them. "This is a quaint fancy,—this inkstand," he said.

Then he must needs be quick to check Reginald's intention to throw into the fire a bundle of carefully made quill pens of a bygone date. These came from a small drawer, evidently long disused, that had a trick of sticking. There were also some wafers here, for the sealing of letters, and a stick of sealing-wax.

Desmond sought to inaugurate a more agreeable topic than had hitherto distinguished the incidents of the morning. He took these relics of the past as a suggestion. He said that it ought to be peculiarly pleasant to them to work here, where those of their own blood had read, and written, and thought out the problems of their day; and that this was home in the truest sense, a oneness of mind and heart and effort. They should have a sentiment to retain the inkstand, sand-box, and bunch of quills, these tokens of the mental activity of their forbears, hallowed by their usage; and the stiff, unnoticed, forgotten drawer of the table, where these writing-materials had been found, might cause them to think how yesterday always leaves a trace on to-day, and to take heed that it is not a vain regret nor the disaster of the waste of time.

They listened in blank silence and unresponsiveness. Desmond, somewhat taken aback, for he had had a purpose of talking to his pupils to mould the form of their thought, to fashion their habit of phrasing, to direct their outlook and give the values of viewpoint, to accomplish their improvement insensibly even in their leisure hours, felt a disposition to recur to the line and rule of the text-book. "Let them learn, then, just what is set down for them," he said, disappointed with the first experiment.

But even thus his expectations were so suddenly dashed that he had a sense of helplessness,—an incapacity to reach that volition of mind that makes it a motive power. Words were all ineffective, argument thrown away. Already he began to perceive that he might teach in vain if they would not, and therefore could not, learn. His heart sank within him as he noted the look of dull disinclination, desolation indeed, with which Reginald turned the leaves of the Greek Reader.

"What is the use of the classics, Mr. Desmond?" he asked in a tone of dreary protest. "Nobody speaks the languages any more. Why, when I was in Greece last winter, even I could see that what I had learned of ancient Greek was miles away from modern Hellenic. And I spoke Italian, not Latin, in Rome. As to Greek literature,—why, we have the finest translations,—better than any I can ever make. Now what gentleman ever sits down to read Euripides in the original? Now, honestly, Mr. Desmond, what good has Greek ever been to you?"

This was indeed a home-thrust,—the contrast of his splendid and complete intellectual armament and the field of its employment.

"It has given me the distinguished opportunity of teaching you."

There was dead silence for a few moments as the group sat around the table. The two sullen youngsters, apprehending rather the tone of the retort than its full significance, lifted their lowering eyes and looked in blank wonder from one of the speakers to the other. Reginald continued to turn the volume listlessly in his hand, but a scarlet flush was suffusing his face, and stealing to the roots of his auburn hair. Presently he said, with the air of venturing a suggestion, "It must be a language particularly rich in satire; it must cultivate the faculties for sarcasm, at all events."

The work got under way at length, and perhaps progressed as satisfactorily as if there had been a more genial understanding. Each faction was cautious, being uncertain of the other, and hence experiments were not in favor. There was much of the genuine gentleman in Reginald; he was averse to occasioning needless inconvenience or annoyance to others, and had he no further reason, he would have exerted himself to curb the vagaries of his wandering attention, so little accustomed to concentration. But he had, too, a proper pride. Without the opportunity of cramming for the examination, the disadvantages of his erratic training and the irregular development of his immature mind were to be discerned without palliation. This, however, gave token how solid an intellectual endowment he possessed. As he struggled with the questions and bent every faculty to the endeavor to do himself as little discredit as he might, Desmond felt somewhat encouraged. There was good material here, if it could be disengaged from the tangle of puerile folly, superficial observation, false standards, and a total lack of the habit of application.

The other two promised less well, and Desmond had with them far less sympathy and less patience. Horace, still swelling with wrath for the indignity of the geographical threat, was merely biding his time, and temporizing with his tyrant till the close of the diurnal session should permit him to bear his tale of woe to his mother, who he doubted not would avenge him summarily. But Chub had capitulated. He adopted propitiatory tactics. Now and again he quitted his place and came around and stood beside Desmond's chair, with a plump and pleading hand on his arm, and explained carefully that he could not really hope to master fractions because they had a peculiar effect on his head. He thought it would be much better to review long division, until his health was fully confirmed,—he was a crackerjack at long division. He would like to show Mr. Desmond what he could do; he could cover a slate with figures to beat the band. And would Mr. Desmond make those two boys quit laughing at him, and agree that he might skip fractions altogether. He had heard people say that fractions were of no use,—upon his word of honor, he had.

"Some small people like unto yourself, I dare say," Desmond retorted.

Chub was always so disappointed and surprised when he was sent back to his place, his errand fruitless, to bend the round integer of his head over the tantalizing fractions on his slate, so eagerly abounding in renewed hope as he came out again with his plump paw to be laid persuasively on Desmond's arm, as he stood by the tutor's chair, advancing his enlightened views,—all of which tended to eliminate study from the scheme of things at Great Oaks mansion,—that it began to be very obvious that this was the pupil most difficult to contend with and for whose idiosyncrasies Desmond would have least toleration. For scholastic attainment was a very large and noble endeavor in Desmond's mind, despite the reasons he had latterly perceived to minimize its worldly utilities. And to this effect did Mrs. Faurie express herself that evening at dinner when they were all grouped around the table.

"I should judge from the children's report, Mr. Desmond, that you have all had a rather serious time of it, to-day. And that is just what I desire,—that you should maintain your authority,"—she cast her beautiful coercive eyes on each of the youthful faces, shown in the candle-light intently regarding her—"and that they should exert themselves to do their duty."

They seemed to accept the fiat as law according to their several interpretations of duty,—Reginald with a sort of manly serenity, Horace as reduced to order, and the little Chub as so distressful and helpless and a-weary of the world that Mrs. Faurie could not refrain from reaching out her long fan, and with its downy tip touching him playfully under his chin to bring out his dimples and win from him once more a smile.

CHAPTER IV

The insubordination of the youthful students at Great Oaks was happily at an end, but their educational problems remained. These promised Desmond food for much thought for an indefinite time, and roused him to an ingenuity of expedients to secure the best efforts of the young scholars themselves. For a time success swayed in the balance indeterminate. Sometimes it seemed impossible to break to habits of application, to harness the attention of these wildly roving minds. He did not love the spectacle of wounded pride, but the heroic treatment of bluff ridicule had the happiest effect.

"For a fellow to have passed through the Suez Canal, to have seen the Assouan Dam, and the Sault Canal, and the Segovia Aqueduct, and the Ganges Canal, and the Solani Aqueduct, and have no more conception of the principles of hydraulics than a mule shipped in a stock-car has of the motive powers of a steam-engine! You didn't notice?—neither does the mule."

Reginald was letter perfect the next day in such elementary exposition as the text-book on Natural Philosophy afforded concerning locks, dams, jetties, and the varied utilities of controlled waters; and Desmond, with a touch of self-reproach, called him into the library that evening after dinner, and made himself very gay and entertaining with stories of college life, details of hazing, rushes, athletics, such as had but a bitter flavor to his memory now, though likely to please the fancy of a destined collegian. Once or twice afterward Reginald dropped in again, his eyes bright and expectant; but the tutor had no immediate cruelties to atone for, and was dreary and sad himself, and of no mind to lacerate his sensibilities with reminiscences of happier days. He gave himself up to such solace as he could find in a book, and Reginald, quick of apprehension, sat on the other side of the table, a book in his own hands, albeit his attention wandered now and again to the black panes of the windows, where he could see the moon in the sky and a brilliant and shattered luminary fallen below, which he knew was the lunar reflection in the Mississippi River. The very touch of a book Desmond considered salutary, and thus he did not rebuke Reginald's failure of attention.

In truth, Desmond felt that he needed his evenings apart. He worked so hard with his difficult and unmalleable material during the day that he was likely to forget his disappointments, his perverted destiny, his many feuds with Fate. But he had not ceased when alone to set them in order before him, to canvass futile ways and means for a counter-stroke, to ponder with rancor on men who had made settlement of the financial difficulties impossible, and others who had found profit in pushing him to the wall. He would have his revenge, he resolved; he would pay them back in their own coin, some day,—some day,—and suddenly he would feel the sting of his own sharp ridicule as he would bitterly laugh aloud and demand of his utter helplessness how this might betide. Though it was now little more than a year since his father had died at the critical moment of a business enterprise of magnitude, which wrecked in its collapse his other interests, it had been already demonstrated that, had he lived, it would have succeeded signally,—indeed, in the hands into which it had gone, it was more than justifying the confidence of its projector. Desmond, who could not retain a single share for the lack of means, meditated ruefully on the sums spent in completing his course of study according to his father's directions, before the condition of the decedent's estate was definitely ascertained, and how these funds might have been applied to more utilitarian purposes. He was often too depressed, too distrait, too irritated by the untoward results of the day's labor, to care to read; but a book in the hand was a protection from the intrusion of the family on the polite theory of not seeming to exclude him from their social life. He had been sent for once or twice in the evening to join a game at cards with Mr. Stanlett, Mrs. Faurie, and Reginald; but afterward, when he saw the boy's figure appear on the veranda without and flit away softly from the library window, he was glad that the report that he was busy with books and papers had protected him from that irksome interruption. His leisure was not of pleasant flavor with his embittered memories, but it was his own bit of time with himself, and if he had come to be not a merry man, he could make no compact with a new identity. Sometimes he had a sudden thought, an abstract thought, as unsolicited, as unexpected, as beneficent as an angel's visit, and he wrote. So late the light burned from the library windows night after night, so consecutively, that the pilots of the river craft came to reckon that stellular gleam among their nocturnal bearings betokening the Great Oaks mansion.

Desmond soon began to take little note of other interests save indeed his pedagogic duties. He had begged off several times when guests, strangers of course to him, had come to dine. He was writing something, he once told Mrs. Faurie, confidentially; then he was offended by the eager alacrity with which she had excused his presence at the table, and the promptness and deftness with which the brisk waiter had served his dinner alone in the library. He did not write at all, that night. He smoked pipe after pipe of his own strong tobacco, instead of Mr. Stanlett's fine mild cigars sent in with the dinner tray, although he esteemed it in the nature of "breaking training" as much now as when he was a star "half-back" on a crack Eleven. He meditated much and long over the bitter problems of the various degrees of want and woe expressed in poverty absolute and poverty relative, and in what actual wealth consists, and if the rich are not often paradoxically the poor, and if the poor,—but he felt that the converse was a more difficult proposition to be maintained, to demonstrate that the poor are ever by any fortuitous circumstance to be considered the rich.

The winter was wearing away,—the passing of time marked only by the gradual development of approximate symmetry in the minds of the pupils; the slow budding of the trees of the grove, that had been the favored haunt of deer some fifty years earlier, before the marauding currents of the river had carried away the point called formerly "Faurie's Landing," amounting to near a thousand acres, thus bringing the mansion house forward on the banks of the stream, within half a mile of the levee, indeed; the adding of page after page to the record of the thought that had come to him in the deserted library in the midnight;—when there suddenly befell one of those incidents in which he played an important part, that were as links in a chain of events, fettering the lives and fortune of all in the house and many besides. This, the first of these significant happenings, came about in the simplest way, its importance all unrecognized at the time.

It was morning, and in the library his pupils sat at their books, when there sounded a sudden tap at the door. Desmond turned, frowning, and looked over his shoulder. In response to his summons the footman entered, his face irradiated by subdued excitement; he presented formally, however, the compliments of Mrs. Faurie, who would be glad to see Mr. Desmond and his pupils in the parlor, Colonel and Mrs. Kentopp having arrived.

Chubby sprang up with a whoop. It would be difficult to say whom he would not have welcomed with like enthusiasm to rescue him from the grisly lessons.

Desmond rebuked him sternly, while the young servant looked on in amaze.

"Say to Mrs. Faurie that Mr. Desmond and his pupils beg to be excused, as the hours for lessons are not over."

It is impossible to describe the look of wall-eyed remonstrance with which the footman hearkened to this message, and to emphasize his own opinion of it he closed the door so slowly that Desmond was sorely tempted to bound up and kick it to after him.

Chub, on the verge of tears, was tempestuous in argument,—his mother had sent for him, he plained, and he was not allowed to go,—in the midst of which a second tap at the door heralded the footman, with a change of face if not of heart. Mrs. Faurie begged Mr. Desmond's pardon for the interruption, but would be glad if Mr. Desmond would shorten the study hours by ten minutes in order to meet Colonel and Mrs. Kentopp in the parlor before luncheon.

"Hi, Bob, they goin' to stay to lunch?" cried Chub, hilariously. "Did the children come?"

Bob's grin of assent was petrified on his face.

"Take your seat, Rufus," said Desmond, sharply. "You must want to do some extras for penance." Then to Bob, "Shut—that—door!"

A great gush of talk and laughter issued from the parlor as Desmond approached it before luncheon. It scarcely seemed as if so limited a coterie could keep astir so cheery a conversational breeze, but Mrs. Kentopp was vivacity itself. She was about thirty-eight years of age, of medium height, but very slight. She impressed him at first as somewhat haggard, but he soon perceived that this was the effect of the dye or blondine, which heightened the natural tint of her light hair to a golden hue, that required special freshness of complexion to accord with this embellishment. This disparagement was obviated when she laughed, for a becoming flush came and went in her cheeks, and her light blue eyes danced. She was handsomely gowned in pastel-blue cloth, heavily braided, with a hat of the same shade trimmed with the breast of the golden pheasant. She wore long tan gloves on a hand so small and soft that Desmond almost thought the fingers boneless, for despite her air of condescension, she shook hands with him in the cordial southern fashion on informal occasions.

"You have not given us the opportunity to welcome you earlier to this benighted region, Mr. Desmond," she said, laughing always. "Misery loves company!"

Her husband was tall, portly, fair, and flushed, with a bright, round, brown eye, dark hair, and a clean-shaven, square face. He was dressed in sedulous conformity to the dictates of the most recent fashion of gentleman's garb, and this dudish suggestion was queerly accented by his peculiarly open and genial manner and his ringing, hearty voice. He strode quite across the room, and most cordially clasped the stranger's hand. But Desmond appreciated that it was a very keen, searching, and business-like glance that Colonel Kentopp bent upon him, singularly unrelated to his jovial, haphazard manner and joyous tones. Desmond felt that it held an element of surprise, and that he was altogether different, for some reason, from what Colonel Kentopp had expected to see. Mrs. Kentopp, too, turned after a moment and seriously surveyed him through her gold-handled lorgnette, as he was replying to the civilities addressed to him by her husband. Concerning the newcomers Desmond made his own cursory deductions, almost mechanically, for they did not interest him in the least. He fancied that Colonel Kentopp rather valued himself upon his amiability and popularity, and was even prone to make it evident that his two children, a girl and a boy, were fonder of him than of their mother. They came in ever and anon from the veranda, where they raced and chased with Chubby, to acquaint him with some juvenile news, some change of moment to them, such as they had fed the parrot, or that Chubby had a Shetland pony, and they hung upon him, one on either side, their cheeks against his hair, their arms around his neck. Their neglected mother seemed no whit disconcerted by her supersedure in their affections, and talked on blithely to Mrs. Faurie and Mr. Stanlett—especially to the old gentleman, with whom Mrs. Kentopp exchanged many compliments and affected to hold a very gay flirtation.

At the lunch-table Desmond would have felt quite apart from the occasion, since they were all old friends and had many subjects in common of which he knew naught, but that Colonel Kentopp, with his genius for geniality, persisted in drawing him out, making him talk, appealed again and again directly to him, and would not suffer him to be ignored by Mrs. Kentopp, who seemed disposed now to flaunt her condescension and now to give him the cold shoulder, albeit ever and anon she fixed upon him a surprised, contemplative gaze that temporarily stilled her brilliant, laughing face. Desmond could not imagine and he did not care in what respect he did not meet their expectations, and although he responded in good form to Colonel Kentopp's lead, he was not sorry when the meal, unusually prolonged, was over at last, and he was free for the afternoon.

He betook himself, as soon as the party had scattered sufficiently, to the library, where he sank down in one of the easy chairs to rest, not his bodily frame, but his tired mind and heart. He had not wished to seem to hold aloof from the family by withdrawing to his own room, yet he felt intrusive with them and their friends, who were no friends of his. He found the library a neutral ground; in some sort it befitted him and his calling. The quiet solaced him; the atmosphere of the books was always friendly; the traces of the scholastic labors were all effaced, shut up in the deep abysses of the drawers of the table; the fire glowed upon the hearth. He was more and more at ease as he rested, and the slow hours of the afternoon wore on. The shadows began to slant on the level reaches of the long vistas under the oaks; the sunlight had that dreamy, burnished splendor that embellishes the southern winter; it loitered slow, content, its progress imperceptible. All was still; not a sound reached his ear save the distant chatter of paroquets flitting about the pecan trees as if still in search of nuts. He could see from where he lounged in the great armchair the long stretch of the Mississippi River, the light reddening the hue of its murky floods, the ripples tipped with a sparkle like gold; he noted as often before the peculiar conformation of its surface, the curving centre rising apparently so much higher than the margins, which slanted downward still toward the interior after the manner of the banks of deltaic rivers; the opposite shores were merely distinguishable as a line of soft, tender green. Here and there a trio of white sea-gulls poised, then winged away, and again darted down toward the water, evidently roving hundreds of miles up from the Gulf intent on fishing.

He was not reading; his mind seemed quiescent, blank. The intensity of his emotions, the dull discouragements of his position, had worn on him more than he was aware. He was mentally resting. He had no conscious thought, no recognized intellectual process, when suddenly he gave a start to perceive a figure standing at the French window that came down to the floor of the veranda. It was Mrs. Faurie. She opened one of the long sashes from outside, and entered without ceremony.

"Why, how cosy you look in here!" she exclaimed. "'There are none so deaf as those who will not hear.' No wonder you did not answer."

"Were you calling me?" he asked, with an apologetic cadence. He had started to rise, but Mrs. Faurie had herself sunk into a chair, and he resumed his seat.

She was looking about her with an intent, bright interest. "I think that we never quite appreciated this old room. What a scholarly look your rearrangement has brought into it! That old telescope,—why, you have mounted it again! How nice to put it in the centre of the bay-window—it is just the right height for observations of the sky, and can sweep it in three directions. Somebody yanked it off its stand long ago to read the names on passing steamboats from the veranda."

As she leaned her elbow on the arm of the chair and turned her beautifully poised head, he could not keep his eyes from her. She embodied to his mind the poetic ideal of all the beauties of fable or history. She was as a flout to the commonplace aspect of the day, to her associates, her surroundings, her own words and identity, and to himself. He could not accustom his eyes to such peculiar and preëminent perfection. Her charms seemed heightened at the moment by the embellishments of dress; for since luncheon she had made a toilet for the afternoon, of a richness which she had not hitherto affected,—a note of compliment to her guests. She was younger of aspect; her face seemed that of some radiant girl, though proud, assured, dominant. Her gown was of gray silk, quiet in tone and not heavy of texture, the brocaded pattern being a plume shading from darker gray to a tip of white. She wore on her richly tinted brown hair a velvet picture-hat of the same gray hue, with a line of vivid white about the brim, and apparently the ostrich plume of gray, that the brocaded gown simulated, coiled about the crown, its white tip drooping to her shoulder. And against this neutral background the splendor of her beauty glowed, her complexion so exquisite, her lips scarlet, her gray eyes so full and fine and lordly in their expression, and with those imperious brows so delicately drawn above. Somehow he could not hold his own before them. Never heretofore had eyes challenged him that he dared not meet. Her evident unconsciousness of the impression her beauty must make upon him added to his embarrassment. It was like talking to one in a mask or under a disguise. He could not speak to mother of hobbledehoys, householder, butterfly of fashion, while these incongruous characters were blended into the personality of Juno, or the ideal of the moon, or a muse of poetry. He was glad that she busied those radiant glances in scanning the sombre old room, and his chance bedizenment of it with such cast-off gear as had come to his hand.

"Are the lenses of the telescope all right? Well, that's a blessing! And you have brought out that old geological cabinet."

"It contains some quite valuable specimens," said Desmond. He deprecated his tone; it seemed to him as if he were making excuses. "A few are genuinely rare."

Mrs. Faurie nodded her comprehension. "So I suppose; an uncle of Mr. Faurie's had quite a fad in that direction."

"Mr. Stanlett?" asked Desmond, surprised.

"No,—Mr. Stanlett is my uncle. This was a relative of Mr. Faurie's, with quite literary tastes; and oh,—that old screen!—I had forgotten it completely,—skeleton leaves mounted between plates of crystal."

"There is nothing so symmetrical, to my mind, in all nature as the various tree-forms," Desmond commented; "those outlines are grace itself, both in the denuded shape of the leaf and the tracery of the veins. Their preparation is exquisitely done."

"They look like lace!" she remarked. "If you are fond of tree-forms, you ought to have a beautiful time in the woods at Great Oaks"—she drew a deep sigh. "We have little else to offer as entertainment; but we are long on wilderness! Will the children study botany?"

"Perhaps,—as a reward of merit,—when they shall have learned something in the indispensable branches."

Mrs. Faurie hastily changed the subject. "I am glad that you find enough interest in these things to resurrect them. I remember now that they were in that big old mahogany press in the alcove."

She rose suddenly, opened the door of the press, and looked in, her head poised inquiringly. There seemed nothing to attract her explorations, and she returned to her chair.

"That's where you found the frames for those old steel engravings; the arrangement of them is very inspiring, much better than that ragged old portfolio, which I see you have relegated to the press, where it ought to be. I wonder what used to be in those frames; but they are the very thing for steel engravings." For between the bookshelves and the row of cupboards below, a blank space of paneled wood had received a series of small framed portraits of the great men in the world of letters and scientific achievement. The pictures were unharmed by time, save for spotted and yellowed margins, but the suggestion of antiquity better accorded with the old and worn fittings of the place than fresher equipment.

"What did you find of interest in the cupboards of the bookcases?"

"They are locked," said Desmond, a trifle out of countenance to have tried doors obviously closed against intrusion.

"Why, how odd! There must be lots of things in them which would interest you." As if she could not trust the vigor of his experiment, she rose once more and flitted across the room, trying first one, then another of the small doors. They were without knobs, and only a key that might fit could open them. She had evidently broken a nail in her efforts to draw the doors ajar by the moulding, and she was looking somewhat ruefully at her dainty fingers as she returned. Not to remain seated at ease while she labored to open the obdurate cabinets, Desmond had followed her about the room, making similar efforts wherever the door seemed a less close fit; and as she took her chair by the fire he resumed his place near her, listening attentively as she talked on. "I remember that there are many old English periodicals there,—the 'Gentleman's Magazine,' the 'London Magazine,' the 'Annual Register,' all from the beginning of their issue, and a thousand old scientific and literary pamphlets. Why should they be locked up? Perhaps Uncle Clarence may have the key; if not, we may find one about the house that will fit, or on that little trading-boat where Chubby bought my apple, don't you know?"—with an animated glance. "It has been off on the bayous and lakes since then, and it dropped down the river to-day and tied up at our landing—it may have a bunch of keys among its treasures of junk. We must try that expedient, at all events. I know you would enjoy exploring those nooks, and you might find something that would interest you. What are you writing?—something for publication?"

He drew back in surprise, embarrassed, half flattered, protesting. "Oh, no,—only jotting down a few thoughts that struck me,—of no value to the public,—for my own entertainment, or rather my own satisfaction,—a sort of argument, pro and con, on some questions of political economy that were never clear to my own mind, never justified to my own point of view. It is in a sort a dialogue, thoughts that, expressed otherwise, would bore the life out of any interlocutor."

"But why don't you arrange to write something for publication while you are here, Mr. Desmond?—not history, for of course this library is too general in selection to afford you the data requisite, but—something else; why won't questions of political economy do? something—I don't know what,—but something for publication and permanent interest."

"Why, I couldn't," said Desmond, flushing painfully, so close had she come to his grief for the relinquished ambitions of achievement. "I am not capable of that kind of thing. Besides, I came here to teach—"

"Surely you don't have to sit up o' nights to prepare for Chubby's lessons! And you can't work the boys all day; you have to let them stretch their muscles in the afternoon. You think that more consecutive time would be necessary,—more concentration—well, perhaps,—I am not up to such things myself. Such ideas as I have are originated in the twinkling of an eye. At all events, you have made this a mighty pleasant place to read and rest and jot down any vagrant ideas that may be roaming around when your day's work is done."

She lay back in her chair and let her eyes rove smilingly about the changes in the aspect of the room. "I shouldn't be surprised if you will have to share the library now. I dare say that all the rest of us will want to 'butt in,' as the boys say." She laughed with a mischievous relish of the grotesque phrase and its unseemliness on her dainty lips.

On the low marble mantelpiece were figures in bronze of two of the muses, Clio and Calliope, evidently costly and of some artistic merit, and Desmond had crossed on the wall above them two long swords, that had stood in a corner of the room, genuine relics of warfare that had seen grim service, and in their way carved out records in both history and poetry. An oil painting, a spirited battle-piece, was still above, the scarlet uniforms giving an intense note of color among the prevailing tints of grape-blue with which the room was furnished. Desmond had not inquired as to its subject, and the signature of the painter was not familiar to him. Its execution did not rise above a respectable mediocrity, save for the central figure, a commanding officer, who, with raised hat and mounted on a white charger, seemed galloping down the line of troops and straight out of the picture at the spectator.

All these details did Mrs. Faurie successively scan as she sat languidly pulling on a pair of long gray gloves; all were brought into new significance, into added harmony, in the readjustment of the room. She seemed at great leisure, and it was some time before she spoke again.

"You give a very beguiling aspect to scholastic labor. I don't think that I should mind learning a thing or two, myself, from you here."

She looked at him with a smile touching the curving lines of her lips. His cheek flushed. He lifted his head as he returned her look. It was a fine head, and was well poised on his broad shoulders. That wonderful magnetic smile of hers was addressed to him, and he must needs have been more than human had he not responded to its subtle, unconscious flattery. He had been so reduced in pride, in the esteem of the specious world, so thwarted, agonized, deprived, humiliated, that this look of interest, of rallying mirth, of alluring charm, was singularly suave to his sensitive perceptions. For a moment his face was as it used to be; his dark blue eyes had a serene light, confident, spirited; they were smiling in their turn. His expression was lifted out of its wonted cold constraint,—it was earnest, ardent; and he seemed to Colonel Kentopp, pausing at the window on the veranda, as handsome a man as could be found between Lake Itasca and the Balize; he was stricken with amaze by the mutual expression of the two.

"It would be my place and privilege to sit at your feet, Mrs. Faurie," said Desmond.

Perhaps because she was acclimated to the language of admiration and missed it sorely at Great Oaks, perhaps because she was so genuinely pleased with the tutor as a tutor that she could but approve him as a man, she cast upon him a warm radiance from her beautiful eyes, and broke out laughing and flushing as a much younger woman might have done.

"What a pretty speech, Mr. Desmond,—and how pitifully insincere! What under heaven could you hope to learn from me?"

He had not seen before that exquisite dimple in her cheek, for she seldom laughed with such exuberant mirth, or perhaps he might not have answered with such definite aplomb.

"I should learn those higher things beyond the ken of books," he declared.

Before the fire was quenched in Desmond's eyes, the pose of his head shifted, the flush on his cheek faded, while yet the whole changed aspect of the man was patent, Colonel Kentopp conceived it beneath his dignity to stand on the veranda and look in the library window at what seemed to him singularly like a flirtation between his hostess and the tutor of her sons. He forthwith laid his hand on the window-catch, and as it clicked in opening, Mrs. Faurie turned and burst into a peal of silvery laughter while he slowly and ponderously entered.

"How funny!" she exclaimed. "Where is our walk on the levee? Have all our party fallen by the way or dispersed? I took upon me the mission to find Mr. Desmond, and I suppose the rest sent you to find me."

Colonel Kentopp could not smooth out the frown that would gather and be dissipated to corrugate his brow anew as he listened. She seemed all joyous unconsciousness and insouciance, yet this might be affected. He could not judge whether she was merely carrying off the awkwardness of having been so absorbed in the tutor's conversation as to forget her waiting guests and her own errand, which was to invite him to join the party in a walk along the levee, or whether she was genuinely interested as she called Colonel Kentopp's attention to the changes by which Mr. Desmond had so enhanced the attractions of the library. Colonel Kentopp, who was as far removed from the possibility of the appreciation of any literary point as a man of intelligence and education can well be, surveyed with blank assent the details which she indicated to him.

"I thought," he could not refrain from saying, "that you always declared that you did not care *un sou marqué* how things look at Great Oaks Plantation."

"But this is not 'things'—it is thought; it was done with an idea,—an inspiration. There never was a duller and a dowdier old room, and now it is replete with suggestion, with charm, with all the allurements of learning; and miracle of all, without the expenditure of a cent of money."

"Take care, Mrs. Faurie," said Colonel Kentopp, laughing in that mirthless, rallying way in which privileged friends give themselves the pleasure of saying a disagreeable thing in the guise of jest; "after all your open-handed career, you may become a miser yet."

"Heaven send the day!" she exclaimed. And long, long afterward Desmond remembered the phrase and her look as she uttered the words. "It might be better for me and mine if the open hand had been always the close fist." Then she broke off suddenly,—"Why, there is Mrs. Kentopp."

For that lady was coming in, laughing very much, which always started her pink flush to justify her blonded hair, and declaring that she had almost gone to sleep on the sofa in the parlor, while they neglected her and kept her waiting. If Colonel Kentopp had had scant appreciation of the esthetic value of the changes that Desmond had wrought in the aspect of the library, Mrs. Kentopp's glacial, superficial glance at its details implied absolute disregard. It might have been a lesson to reduce the vanity of those purblind insects denominated men of science, who grope about the hidden meanings of the universe, who seek to "unclench from the granite hand of Nature her mighty secrets," to bring near the stars, to revive the dead life of the rocks, to discern the brush that paints the flower and leaf, to descry whence comes the fashion of the cloud, to find out the paths of the trackless oceans, could they have appraised the degree of Mrs. Kentopp's contempt for their objects as her eyes rested upon the insignia afforded by the telescope, the geological cabinet, the skeleton leaves, the epitome of history and poetry above the mantelpiece. Her flout of intentional inattention was so patent, her air of minimizing, almost ridiculing the importance of the tutor and all which to him pertained, that it became obvious to the other two that the afternoon walk was in order, and they were presently sauntering down the veranda, while Desmond ran for his hat.

To Desmond's surprise, he was not in the slightest degree mortified, nor intimidated, nor crushed by Mrs. Kentopp's manner, as she had doubtless intended he should be. He was noting the fact that, despite their apparent intimacy, these people did not call each other by their Christian names after the manner of their sort elsewhere. It had never been the custom in this region, where a certain formality of the old regime still lingers, and he felt a kind of special gratitude that he was not called upon to endure to hear Mrs.

Faurie address Colonel Kentopp as "Tom," and his wife as "Annetta," and their responsive familiarity to her as "Honoria."

The four walked abreast along the winding avenue under the boughs of the dense trees of the grove, which was perfectly clear of undergrowth and as level as a floor. Now and again the colonnades formed by the great boles parted to show beautiful open, grassy vistas amongst the gigantic growths that had given the place its name; but the eye could reach no limits of the forest, save on one side where the river had come "cranking in and cut a monstrous cantle out." The party struck off presently into a byway, which at length brought them into the road at the base of the levee. Here they climbed the great embankment covered with Bermuda grass. The short, dense growth was evidently feeling the spring of the year in its thick mat of roots that held the earth together, being an almost impervious network of innumerable, interlacing fibres, and of special utility because of its imperviousness in times of "fighting water." As they took their way along the broad path upon the summit, they could view from the elevation, of peculiar advantage in so flat a country, a vast circuit of the surrounding landscape. The water was high and the river was still on the rise. The space outside the levee seemed to Desmond to have shrunken very perceptibly since he had seen it a few days before. This strip varied greatly in width; now it looked at the distance as if it might measure a mile or more, and at certain points it showed only a few hundred yards, with here and there marshy intimations and disconnected pools where the water stood and reflected the light like oval mirrors. The sun, down-dropping, vermilion red, had turned all the currents of the great stream to crimson, and as it sunk lower and lower the shadows began to gloom in the dense woods on the hither shore, albeit there was still a line of gilding sunlight glinting along the forest summits.

It was all very quiet; not a craft was visible on the currents; the vast river was absolutely mute. Despite the fact that this is one of the great highways of the world, a natural channel from boreal to subtropical climes, designed, one might fancy, to bring man near his brother man, without reference to his own ingenuity of device,—in conquering the wilderness, harnessing the steam, annulling time, and obliterating distance,—it could have seemed no lonelier were theirs the first of human eyes to rest upon it. There was no trace, no suggestion of man's presence, save the great embankment of the levee along the river-side, now and again receding so far inland as to elude the sight, and the newly arrived "shanty-boat" lying at the landing.

This craft held the degree of comparison with the usual trading-boat of these waters that a junk-shop bears to a warehouse. Desmond's attention was first attracted to the humble and grotesque nondescript vessel when Chub, nimbly footing it in his trim little knickerbockers and well-filled stockings and natty Paris shoes, to overtake the group, joined his mother; he began to bang upon her, his arm about her waist, his head lolling against her arm, begging and pleading with her to buy him a bicycle,—a beautiful second-hand wheel,—which the amphibious trader had assured him was as good as new.

"But you have your own wheel," she remonstrated. "You actually want another? You would have to be a quadruped to ride both."

"And a long-eared one at that!" Colonel Kentopp declared, somewhat nettled; for his own small son had come up on the other side, casting up lustrous, anxious eyes, beseeching that if Chub did not secure this treasure, dear, *dear* papa would open his heart and purse and bestow it upon him; for woe to tell! he had no bicycle whatever,—he had only a tricycle, and a bitter blow it was to his pride when Chub rode a safety and he could only accompany him, bowed to the earth, as it were, on a humiliating three-wheeler.

"My wheel?—Gracious! my wheel is all out of whack!" cried the tumultuous Chub. "Just look at it, mamma,—that is all I ask. Just go down to the trading-boat and look at the wheel,—a—beautiful—second-hand—bike!"

"But, Chubby, it would be out of the question for you to own two wheels and both already used—"

"Mine's got a punctured tire," wailed Chub.

"Gimme second choice,—if Chub don't make it; lemme have it, papa dear," beguiled the Kentopp hopeful.

It had been Desmond's firm determination, rigidly observed so far, that he would have no concern with his pupils other than scholastic. He would consider the trend of the conversation in their presence, as indeed is necessary always in association with young persons, that the equilibrium of their moral, political, or religious convictions be not shaken till they are of sufficient age and discretion to exercise a sober and independent judgment. He would direct their thoughts to subjects of value in their general reading. He would impart information or correct mistaken impressions in the course of casual chat. He would in moments of recreation narrate details of special interest or amusement, and thus further incidentally the judicious development of their mental faculties. But with the problems of their control outside the schoolroom, their sports, their manners, their moral training, he would not tax himself. This was in a manner interference, however salutary, and might be resented by those in actual authority, resulting in anarchy for the youths, and their last estate would be worse than their first. He thus argued that he did not stand in *loco parentis*; he was simply a machine for the furtherance of learning, a paid purveyor of wisdom, and when his day's work was ended his responsibility ceased for the day. Therefore he was surprised at himself when he stepped forward briskly, as Mrs. Faurie, with a somewhat doubtful and disconsolate air, yielded so far as to agree to examine the treasure, and turned to the descent of the levee on the outer side.

"Let me go and examine the wheel, Mrs. Faurie, and report its condition to you; I understand these machines better, probably, than you do."

She turned back with a wave of the hand,—a fine, free gesture at arm's length. "A rescue!" she exclaimed. "I was just wondering if I could survive the unmitigated boredom of the tires, and the bell, and the handle-bar, and the pedals, and the saddle. Is the date set for your canonization, Mr. Desmond? Go, by all means, and add another to your deeds of grace."

But Chub emitted a disconcerted whine. "I don't wish you to go, Mr. Desmond," he plained, with the unwitting insolence of juvenile sincerity.

Desmond was not out of countenance; he even sustained the furtive sneer in Mrs. Kentopp's face. "Just as it happens, I don't care in the least what you wish."

"Now, there it is, mamma. I want the bike, and Mr. Desmond doesn't care what I want; *he says so.*"

"It ought to be little trouble to teach the logical ideas of the clever Chub to shoot straight," commented Colonel Kentopp.

"Well, then," Mrs. Faurie could not resist, "suppose I go, too. Mr. Desmond can instruct me as to the perfection of the tires and the bell and the handle-bar, and the tumbling guaranty, warranted to give the best headers in the market,"—she was looking down with her gracious maternal smile at Chub, as in his tumultuous callowness he clamored and clung about her skirts ("Oh, rats! mamma, it's got no tumbling guaranty," he interposed),—"and in the mean time I can meditate on the price."

"But, mamma, it is cheap, it is dirt cheap, it is dog cheap."

"What is the price?" Desmond demanded.

When Chub responded, the tutor might have had a salutary monition of the discretion of his resolution to keep apart from the affairs of his pupils outside the schoolroom. "You just wait and see," said Chub, sullenly.

"Come!" cried Mrs. Faurie, her foot poised on the verge of the outer descent of the levee, her skirts held daintily clear of the grass with her left hand, her right about the shoulders of the enterprising Chub. She looked back with bright expectation at the Kentopps as they stood motionless.

"Thank you, no," said Colonel Kentopp. "We will await you here. I shan't put myself in temptation's way. To be dragooned into buying a crippled bike from such a trading-boat as that would be the final blow to my paternal authority."

He and his wife looked gravely after the pedestrians while standing together on the summit of the levee. The sparkle and suavity of their countenances, addressed to the exigencies of society, were dying out. They both seemed years older in a moment. Mrs. Kentopp's haggard pallor was unrelieved by the flush that was wont to come and go as she laughed, and a certain pendulous effect of the cheeks became noticeable in the immobile contemplativeness of her expression. Her husband was more saturnine than one could have imagined from his arrogations of bonhomie. He had a spark of irritation in his eyes, too sharply flashing to have been kindled merely by the persistence of his little son, now picking his way after the group bound toward the trading-boat, now pausing irresolute.

"Mr. Stanlett is certainly in his dotage!" Colonel Kentopp exclaimed acridly. "I never could have imagined him guilty of such folly as to bring that man here."

"Why, what is the matter with the man?"—his wife had a short, crisp tone, level and direct, and all devoid of the little aspirations and sudden rising inflections and exclamatory interludes which interspersed the tenor of her usual discourse.

"The matter,—why, he is as handsome as a picture! He has the dignity of a lord, and I never saw a man who seemed more highly bred."

"Well,"—she drawled, "don't you consider those facts advantages? A stranger in one's house is always a nuisance, but it is better that a tutor or governess should be as genteel as possible."

"Great Scott! Annetta, how can you be so dense? He is a man whom Honoria Faurie might very well elect to fall in love with and marry."

Mrs. Kentopp laughed in derision,—not her breathy, flushing, becoming laughter, but a simple cackle of scorn. "Why, he is young enough to be her son."

"He is ten years younger,—that is all."

"*All!* Ten years is enough. No doubt she seems an old lady to him."

"You wouldn't think so if you had caught a glimpse of his face as I saw them talking together in the library. They would make a very comely married couple."

"Why, Tom Kentopp, you are wild! She would have to give up that big income if she married, thirty thousand dollars of it every year are as certain as taxes, chargeable on the whole estate, and the Great Oaks crops besides,—and take instead only her dower rights in Tennessee,—just a life-interest in a third of the real property, with that old Nashville residence, in a locality that is awfully unfashionable nowadays,—she has never lived there since Mr. Faurie's death,—and a fourth of the Mississippi property. And such a sacrifice for such a man,—a penniless tutor! Why, if it were not way down here in the swamp, he would seem hardly of more consequence than a courier."

51

"Exactly; it is a mighty lonesome country for a pretty widow, and he is a mighty fine man."

Mrs. Kentopp grew grave. "I never was more surprised than when he came into the parlor. I expected to see a little lean, wizened body, like the man they had last,—little Mr. ——, Mr. ——, I have forgotten the little animal's name. This man is not at all what a tutor should be in appearance; he carries himself as if he owned the world. And his look of cool, assured gravity is positively insulting. I don't think that he gave himself the trouble to fetch out a smile throughout luncheon."

"He was not amused, perhaps," Colonel Kentopp suggested.

"But he should be amused when his betters choose to be merry," the lady retorted.

"It would be a deuced unpleasant thing for us," her husband resumed the matrimonial speculation. "As long as Mrs. Faurie is in the world among her peers, and the value of that large and certain income is forever in her mind, with the bliss of spending it, and living like a princess, I am not afraid. Besides, the lords and counts would back out the instant the settlements would reveal the awful trap that Faurie set for his successor. But this man, this Desmond, would be mighty well satisfied with the division that gives her a life-interest in one third of the Tennessee real estate and a fourth part of the personalty there, and a fourth absolutely of everything in Mississippi. It would be a long sight better than tutoring. He would be mighty glad for another fellow to be hired to teach Chub,—especially with Chub's own money. Mrs. Faurie is at no expense on her sons' account—except such as is voluntary; she gives them those costly foreign trips, for instance."

"But *she*,—she wouldn't be satisfied with that provision;—she would not give up her income for any man living."

"This is a very exceptional man, and this is the jumping-off place of all creation," persisted Kentopp.

Mrs. Kentopp's shallow eyes scanned the far reaches of the Mississippi. The sun was no longer visible, but the vermilion reflection was still red upon the rippling waters, for the afterglow was in the sky. "I don't see how Honoria Faurie manages so badly as to come to the end of her income in this way; it is positively ridiculous," she said, with a sort of petulance.

Colonel Kentopp bit off the end of his cigar and spat it forth with an expression that suggested it might be bitter, but his thought was wormwood. "Oh, she even anticipates her income as far as she can,—she spends at such a clip! She bought her steam yacht with her *savings*, Chub told me." He smiled derisively. "It is in dock now; it ought to have been chartered while she is on dry land."

"And her automobile is another extravagance; why couldn't she hire a touring-car for the little time that she is rusticating while abroad?"

"Princesses don't stoop to such economies, that is, abroad. Economy befits the swamp. I have nothing to say against the diamonds, although I think she might well have been satisfied with the Faurie family jewels,—nor yet those wonderful emeralds, for such 'savings' have an intrinsic value. But it does seem a most mischievous mischance that she should have to *faire maigre* here in the swamp just at this time, with such a hero of romance as Mr. Stanlett has introduced as tutor."

"Mr. Stanlett never saw him till he was engaged and had arrived. I heard him say that the whole matter was arranged by correspondence through Mr. Keith, the boys' guardian. It seems that he and the tutor had some mutual friends. I understand that this fellow has an exceptional collegiate record,—though if he has, I should think he could get a better place. But why should his presence here concern us, do you think?"

"Because if there were a prospect that the Faurie property might come on the market for division, as the result of her marriage, at any reasonably early day, we should never be able to sell Dryad-Dene Plantation to Jack Loring. He evidently much prefers Great Oaks."

Her face lowered heavily. "I was just beginning to think of that," she said, now dully out of sorts.

"There are actual advantages," he argued. "Dryad-Dene Plantation is subject to overflow, and Great Oaks rarely goes under unless their cross levee breaks. Our lands are cut up with bayous and sloughs, while Great Oaks has thousands of acres as level as a floor and as dry as a bone. And then the old house, the groves and the glades. Loring is as new as yesterday, himself, but he wants a place reeking of ancestors and aristocratic traditions."

"I don't see why; it is his one merit that he grew in a single night! It is Jack that has shot up so surprisingly this time, and not the beanstalk," said Mrs. Kentopp, sourly.

"He isn't going to stay new. That is the reason he does not locate somewhere else. The Great Oaks air of the *ancien régime*, its shabbiness and out-at-elbows look of romantic poverty, the ruin of princes, on account of that woman's grudging neglect, when it is really bursting with richness and luxury, would fill his bill exactly. Loring would be furnished with all manner of aristocratic hereditaments, and in ten years people would forget that he was not born at Great Oaks. His people were natives of this region, and his name is familiar in Deepwater Bend; he would rather own Great Oaks than anything else his millions can buy. Let him once hear of that prince-in-disguise-looking tutor, of fine family and exceptional cultivation, in constant association with the beautiful Mrs. Faurie! He is not precipitate at best. He will wait till the division of the Faurie estate consequent upon a second marriage puts Great Oaks up at auction to the highest bidder."

Mrs. Kentopp's face seemed in anxiety to suffer somewhat of a collapse. How, it might be impossible to describe, but now her blonde hair showed that much of it near her face was false, when its naturalness of arrangement had rendered this suspicion impossible hitherto. She was one of the women not pretty, but who contrive to compass that reputation by assuming the pose, the conscious attire, the bridling expression. As she looked now, the coquettishness of her equipment was a painful commentary upon her appearance, haggard with disappointment and foreboding. For the Kentopps had scant affinity with this secluded life in the Mississippi bottom, and they had not had such resources as Mrs. Faurie for shaking its mud—one cannot say its dust—from their feet for indefinite periods of absence. The sale of Dryad-Dene Plantation, with its elaborate industrial equipment and beautiful modern residence, would make possible the dream of their lives,—its transmutation into a handsome town house in New Orleans and a summer cottage on the Gulf coast, with lands enough somewhere at the minimum price to rent out to tenants to make cotton, as lands are created to do, to furnish an income for the absentees. But purchasers for a property of such value as Dryad-Dene are rare, and the *ci-devant* swamper, Loring, who had grown very rich by speculation, was one of the few men who cared to invest in so inconvertible an asset as a fine house and large plantation in Deepwater Bend. A species of self-assertion it was to him, perchance. Here where he was born, as poor as poverty, though of genteel and respectable parentage, he could, as a bit of luxury, own the finest estate around which the river curved, and in the scene of his early privations have its magnates in hot competition to place their splendid holdings in the best light for his somewhat supercilious appraisement.

"It would be idiotic,—it would positively be ridiculous—and she ten years older," Mrs. Kentopp declared bitterly.

Suddenly, like the lightning-change effect of a performer on the stage, she resumed her wonted aspect as if by magic. Her cheeks rounded out; her flush came and went; her lips were again curving and plump with distending smiles over her white teeth; her eyes were all a-sparkle; and she was waving the end of her long feather boa in a response of exaggerated mirth to a fancied greeting from the door of the "shanty-boat" far below. Mrs. Faurie was issuing thence, lifting one of her delicate hands, gloved to the elbow in gray kid; but the gesture was one of protest. She was not looking at her guests, but after a loutish, grotesque, thick-set man, of amphibious suggestions, who was springing with great leaps up the bank with an open knife in his hand. With this he so swiftly cut die rope that held the boat to a gnarled old tree, that the craft, feeling the impulse of the current, began to move from the shore before Mrs. Faurie could step from the gang-plank of the deck to the ground. As it was, the ripples ran over her feet, and she exclaimed aloud in agitation and sudden fright. She was safely on the bank when Desmond, still on the deck, sprang lightly across the ever-widening interval of water, now almost impracticable, swinging Chub ashore with a hand under each of the boy's arms. As the boatman came running down the bank Desmond paused, and meeting him at the margin, struck him between the eyes a blow so fair and furious that the fellow was weltering saurian-like in the water before he scarcely realized that he had been felled. Perhaps the deficiencies of his craft, with no propelling power, constrained his attention; perhaps the vigor of the blow tamed his rancorous rage. He made no effort at reprisal, though Desmond lingered on the bank, but struck out swimming after his boat, and turned, only when once more safe on deck and out of Desmond's reach, to gaze lowering and askance across the water, with a look at once vengeful, amazed, and dismayed.

"What can have happened?" exclaimed Mrs. Kentopp, watching the scene from afar with wondering eyes. "Mr. Paragon is a muscular Christian, it seems."

"He is very injudicious," said Colonel Kentopp, gravely. "These water-side vagrants are often dangerous rascals,—river pirates. Their good-will is safer than their grudges."

CHAPTER V

The errand within the cabin of the shanty-boat had not proved swift or easy of dispatch. When Desmond and Mrs. Faurie had approached the dingy and plebeian craft along the muddy bank, he once more urged that she should wait without and permit him to make the preliminary examination.

"The boat is clean!" cried Chub, on the defensive. "It is as clean as any other old place. Mr. Desmond is so particular. It *isn't* damp. Its smell is just doolicious."

Chub continued insistent, and Mrs. Faurie once more yielded.

Oakum, tar, and the peculiar and distinctive odor of junk were the blended perfumes thus lauded which floated out to them from the open door of the cabin. The boat was gently oscillating on the current, teetering as if with the instinct of dance, for the river was at flood height, and even thus close to the shore the encroaching waters were deep. As Mrs. Faurie and Desmond made their way along the gang-plank to the deck, she glanced over her shoulder at the great cable that held the craft to the bank, passed again and again around the girth of a tree. "I hope she is tied up fast and hard; I should object of all things to go floating down the Mississippi River, the involuntary guest of such a trading-boat, impossible to land except by the uncovenanted grace of the current."

The cabin seemed dark at first, by contrast with the pellucid atmosphere without. A formless hodgepodge of barrel and box, of bunk and junk, it presented, until the eye was sufficiently accustomed to its comparative obscurity to discern such degree of symmetry as informed its arrangement. One end was dedicated to the domestic life of the proprietor; holding the cooking apparatus, expressed in a monkey stove that furnished heat as well, a tier of bunks on either side, a few broken-backed chairs grouped around a table, a gaunt, pale woman in a tattered gray woolen skirt and a man's ragged red sweater, with a mass of dull, straight brown hair "banged" across her freckled forehead and hanging unkempt down upon her shoulders. She held in her arms a wan, puny baby, bent on sucking its thumb, and giving the universe only such attention as it could spare from that absorbing occupation. Knowing this habit to be an infringement of juvenile etiquette, the woman had tried to effect a diversion the instant she saw the flutter of Mrs. Faurie's gray silk gown at the door. But a house cannot be set in order for distinguished inspection on the spur of the moment, and still less can a neglected infant's conduct be immediately brought up to standard. A piercing, heart-rending wail made the air hideous, and as the released thumb, all curiously translucent and blanched and reduced in size, went back into the child's mouth, Mrs. Faurie, entering, whirled around and saw both the effort to save appearances and its failure.

She shook her head in indignant rebuke. "That will never do!" she said imperiously. "You ought not to let the child spoil its hand. That is a bad habit, and keeps it from being bright. It just sogs away over that old thumb, and you don't care so long as it is quiet and doesn't worry you."

The woman rose with a belligerent toss of the head. "Mighty easy to talk!—mighty easy! But you just wait, young lady, till you gits some childern of yer own, an' see if you won't be sorter lax todes anythink that will keep 'em from yellin', when yer head is achin' fit ter bust. I been havin' chills and ager all winter."

"*Some children of my own!*" Mrs. Faurie drew herself up, majestic and boastful. "I have *three* of my own,—nearly as tall as I am—*three*! This"—pulling Chub forward—"is my baby,—and doesn't suck his thumb, and never did. And that reminds me," she continued, as the forlorn river nymph stared amazed at this rich and brilliant apparition of health, and wealth, and beauty, and transcendent youth that might have seemed immortal, feeling the contrast God knows how poignantly, "there are a lot of baby clothes left over up at my house—I am Mrs. Faurie and live close by;—they will fit that fellow out for a year or two to come. I will send them down to you this evening if you will promise to put some pepper on that child's thumb to keep it out of his mouth."

The woman murmured her thanks, but she did not feel her gratitude so acutely, rags and dirt being the natural concomitants of her life, as her interest in this resplendent personage, and the error as to her age and state of life. "Lord!"—she smiled broadly, showing the devastations of a mouth whence many aching teeth had been "rotted out with bluestone" in default of a dentist's care—"I thought you was just a girl,—turned twenty, mebbe; and this"—she pointed at Desmond—"was your courtin' beau."

Mrs. Faurie for once looked embarrassed. "Oh, no," she recovered herself swiftly; "I'm getting middle-aged now. And where is the bicycle, Chubby?"

The other end of the cabin was fitted up as a store, with shelves about the walls and a sort of counter. Here were displayed toys and gewgaws of imitation jewelry and beads, some bolts of coarse cloth, a glitter of tinware, some earthen and wooden bowls, an assortment of candies and canned goods, tobacco, fine cut and plug, snuff, and some boxes of cheap cigars. Incongruously enough, among these things was a fine, fresh bicycle, with pneumatic tires, evidently perfectly new.

Desmond looked sharply across the counter as the sodden, amphibious, nondescript animal that the raftsman seemed, hardly frog, hardly fish, hardly water-rat, yet partaking of the characteristics of all three, eyed the party furtively from his place among his medley of wares. His straight red hair was pulled forward in wisps on his brow as if it had been wet in a ducking and matted there. His big black hat was on the back of his head. His freckled, red, mottled face had a sort of soaked, bloated suggestion. He hesitated for a very perceptible interval before he named the price, and Mrs. Faurie exclaimed in surprise:—

"Ten dollars! Why, Chubby, you told me that the price was five"; for Chub had waxed confidential with his mother as they had approached, her opposition withdrawn.

Chubby's earnest, eager countenance scarcely showed above a pile of cigar boxes on the counter over which he peered. He was genuinely surprised, yet not willing to seek to take advantage of any mistake that he might have made.

"I understood you to say that you would sell the wheel for five dollars"; he addressed the boatman directly, with a sober but unflinching gaze.

The trader's broad face did not change, but there was a furtive gleam in his quick, sharply glancing, rodent-like eye, which sought to measure Chub's simplicity. "No, sport, I said ten," he declared, with a smile showing teeth singularly sharp and closely set together in his wide mouth, appearing as if he had more than the ordinary complement.

Another man in the background, big and raw-boned, but young, leaning against the door of a cubby-hole at the rear, which from some obstruction, apparently hastily thrust within, would not shut fast, seemed to bear witness to this statement. He grimaced affirmatively at Chub with the familiarity of previous acquaintance. He had a large face, which seemed somehow out of drawing, as if swollen here and there, and with uninflamed red spots. One eye and one eyebrow were higher than the other, and he had a half-witted or mentally weak appearance, suddenly confirmed when he abruptly licked out a large red tongue in grotesque triumph in the conclusion of the dicker, as Chub responded:—

"Well, ten dollars is cheap anyhow,—dirt cheap,—dog cheap. We will buy it at ten, won't we, mamma?"

The proprietor had taken Desmond's measure the instant he entered the cabin. Silently gazing at one another across the counter, both knew as well as if the fact had been put into words that the price had been doubled to meet his scrutiny. It would have been still further advanced had the trader better understood the quality of the wheel.

"Why, ten is *very* cheap," Mrs. Faurie began.

"We cannot buy it at ten," Desmond interrupted swiftly,—"in fact, not at any price."

Mrs. Faurie turned toward him in angry surprise, her eyes blazing. He met them without flinching. "You must take my word for it!" he said sternly. "Chubby shall not have it! It is useless to discuss prices."

Desmond had laid his hand on Mrs. Faurie's arm and was about to lead her forth, when the flatboat-man in sudden fury flung the machine down behind the counter with a great clatter of the spokes and pedals.

"No, no!" he vociferated to Chubby, the insurgent, who was hopefully emptying his pockets and counting his cash; "*you* can't buy it at any price. Clear out!—the whole bunch of ye. I'm about to cast off. I'll souse any stowaways in your old Mississippi bilge-water. I'll cut the rope and see how ye'll get ashore then! I'll land you all in the Gulf of Mexico!" As he voiced his frenzied, disconnected, incoherent threats he suddenly ran past the group, sprang from the deck, and with deer-like swiftness sped up the bank, his open knife in his hand.

Within the cabin Mrs. Faurie started back in dismay as the half-witted creature left the door he had held closed, now showing within the cubby a glimpse of coarse bagging, intimating a surreptitious cotton bale, the corner of which had prevented the slipping of the bolt. He jumped up and down before the group with a capering step and a wild and foolish eye, now to the right as they pushed toward the door, and as they turned aside, now to the left, evidently with the intention of preventing or delaying their exit. Even the woman pushed a chair in front of Mrs. Faurie so suddenly that her knees struck painfully against it. "Take a seat, lady," she said mockingly. "Oh, *do* take a seat!"

Desmond scarcely could credit his senses. It was like a disordered scene of a dream. His logical faculties grasped but the one idea of flight. "Make haste," he cried out to Mrs. Faurie. "Get off the boat even if you jump into the water." For he felt that the craft was already loosed and moving from the bank.

"For God's sake, hurry!" he adjured her.

Then as the great gawk of an idiot sprang again in front of them, Desmond seized him, with an effort to sway him back and forth and fling him from his feet; but the river man was as strong and heavier, with a stolidity and lack of expectancy that seemed to add sensibly to his weight and immovableness; and when he was finally thrown, it was after a series of struggles that carried them locked and swaying together around the room, both coming down at last with a tremendous crash, bringing with them not only the stove-pipe but the monkey stove itself. This spewed forth a cataract of live coals over the floor, and as the clouds of soot and smoke circled about the rafters, obscuring still further the dingy quarters, the woman exclaimed loudly and resentfully her fears of fire in notes of woe and injury, and left off such schemes of hindrance as she had furthered to run for a bucket of water from the shelf. A coal had touched the gigantic idiot, and he was bleating like some great calf in a wide open-mouthed blare of sound till admonished by her to lend his aid in extinguishing the fire.

In the midst of the confusion Desmond seized Chub, and though doubting if he could compass the space as the current swung the boat ever farther and farther from the bank, he leaped ashore. The flatboat-man was at the moment running down the bank for the purpose of reëmbarking. Despite the limit on his time which the receding craft imposed, he suddenly swerved from his intention, and made a swift lunge at Desmond, intending to stab him in the back. The attack was not altogether unexpected. Desmond, on the alert, sprang lightly aside, and, being unarmed, struck the boatman with his clenched fist, the blow landing between the eyes.

It was a short, sharp fracas and an easy victory. Desmond was a trained boxer, and here he had light and air and elbow-room, which he had lacked in the wrestle within the cabin. There was not a word spoken between the two; but after the boatman had dragged himself out of the water where he was tossed, to his jeopardy of drowning in the suction, and regained the deck, Desmond, breathless and agitated, took his way up the bank to rejoin Mrs. Faurie, muttering to himself, and now and again pausing to look back over his shoulder at the progress of the boat.

"He ought to be apprehended. If Kentopp had a pistol and had been nearer, we might together have held them both. Perhaps the miscreant might be stopped by a shot if we can get a rifle at Great Oaks mansion; but no,—he'll be too far down the river by that time. The boat is crossing in the current; he is going to try to get screened behind the towhead, and then the boat will hug the Arkansas shore, and it will be too dark and far to risk a shot. Is there no chance to overhaul him? Is there no telegraph station nearer than Fairglade, Mrs. Faurie?"

But Mrs. Faurie, pale and bewildered, did not reply directly. "Why, Mr. Desmond, that man tried to abduct us all! What could have been his object?"

"Nefarious enough, no doubt; but I don't understand it at all." Desmond's eyes had now a more definite expression of heed, yet she was aware that she only shared his attention.

"And upon my word, Mr. Desmond, I don't understand your high-handed interference," she exclaimed. "What was the matter with the bicycle? It seemed a very good wheel. It was your refusal to allow us to buy it that made all the difficulty."

"The wheel was too good," said Desmond,—"too good entirely for the price. It was perfectly new and obviously stolen. It was worth fifty dollars at least, and was offered at five. Chubby is no fool to mistake a price. The trader doubled the price when he saw me. But the rise was not enough."

"Oh, how fortunate that you were with us! I know nothing of the value of these things. No, Chubby, you must never buy from a doubtful source an article far below its value; it implies that you profit by a fraud that you understand." Then looking over her shoulder, "How distant they are down the river. Mr. Desmond, *look* how fast the current is running. Do you suppose they were afraid that we would report the suspicious bargain bicycle?"

There was something evidently more than this. No mere effort to avoid the imputation of receiving stolen goods would justify such violence, Desmond was reflecting. The Great Oaks party were to be drowned, as if by accident, before the eyes of their friends; or they were to be carried off by a similar unlucky chance apparently, and among some trackless network of sloughs and bayous and lakes of the swamp country, of which such craft is the only voyager, the rickety flatboat would be sunk, with all on board save only the murderous crew, surviving not to tell the tale, and disappearing without a trace,—or was the whole demonstration the expression only of the wild, ungovernable rage of the miscreant, that such a clue to some terrible and heinous crime had been thus fortuitously discovered?

Desmond could not judge, and he looked with a sense of baffled mystery at the craft as it swung along in midstream, smoke issuing not only from the stove-pipe, evidently once more in place, but from the windows and door as well. There was in this obviously no menace, for the proprietor was seated upon the deck at large leisure, manipulating an old violin in a style of very jaunty bravado. The strains floated far on the transmitting medium of the water, and the tune was easily distinguishable as again and again the catgut reiterated "A hot time,—a hot time in the old town to-night." Desmond was of the opinion that the incident should be forthwith reported to the authorities. But Mr. Stanlett, hearing the details with some concern, demurred to the proposition.

"You cannot be certain that the bicycle was stolen,—at any rate, by that particular flatboat-man. He may have bought it among a lot of stolen stuff, to be sure, but offered it for sale again, not knowing its value or suspecting its history,—a *bona-fide* purchaser himself."

Desmond listened in surprise, for Mr. Stanlett had not impressed him as of a particularly charitable nature nor lenient in his judgments.

They were sitting around the hearth in the front parlor after dinner; the fire was blazing in cheery wise, more in accord with the chill of the night and the record of the calendar than the springlike atmosphere of the day just closing in. The Kentopps were staying overnight, and the topic had been for some time up for discussion, after the manner of those whose lives are leisurely affairs and of little distraction. It had come in with the cigars, for the gentlemen had been sociably permitted to bring them into this sanctum after the service of the coffee.

"We want to hear you talk," said Mrs. Kentopp, with a pretty *moue*.

"Yes, indeed," cried Mrs. Faurie; "a man never has an idea in his head unless he has a cigar in his mouth. There is some obscure psychological connection between facility of cerebration and blowing rings, and some day when I am not too busy, I'll think it out."

"As to the boatman's casting off in that hasty way," said Mr. Stanlett, pursuing the subject, "that is not an infrequent trick with better craft. Why, in my time I have been inadvertently left at a wayside landing ten miles from a habitation,—no joke in this country way back in the fifties,—and I have been carried off halfway to Vicksburg before I knew that the boiler had steam up. It is a pity that you floored the men. You overrated the provocation. Rough river rats can't be expected to show drawing-room manners. That is one disadvantage of college athletics,—it makes a gentleman as handy with his fists as a professional bruiser."

When Mrs. Faurie interposed to protest her fright and danger, the temper of the party who did not participate in the turmoil within the cabin made it seem as if she were ambitious of the pose of heroine.

"Why, my dear," Mr. Stanlett reasoned with her, "you said yourself that the man who danced about and sought, as you supposed, to detain your party was a poor simpleton, a weak-minded creature; he doubtless meant no offense, though perhaps they were all nettled at Mr. Desmond's refusal to buy the bicycle when he had heard it priced."

"I should have asked no questions about the bicycle, and therefore should have been told no lies," said Mrs. Kentopp, with airy recklessness. "I should have taken the bicycle at the very cheap asking price, and in my innocent ignorance suffered no qualms of conscience. A little learning of the law is a dangerous thing."

"Quite right, quite right, madam," commented Mr. Stanlett. "Really, I feel that we have no obligations in the premises, and our riparian situation here, so isolated, renders it peculiarly necessary for us to be on our guard against collision with the rougher river element."

Colonel Kentopp waved away the smoke that had thickened about his massive head. "Very true, very true!" he said, with a definiteness of assent welcome indeed to the old gentleman, who had spoken with some hesitation, for no man likes to express a fear that others may decline to entertain. Relieved of the imputation of timorousness, Mr. Stanlett went on with decision:—

"These water-rats, many of them really river pirates, enjoy such immunity that I wonder that they are not more daring and enterprising than they are.

I should not like to provoke personal animosity and possible reprisal for injuries, real or fancied, among them."

"That is just how our house at Dryad-Dene is so much more safely situated than you are here at Great Oaks. Why,"—Colonel Kentopp leaned forward with dilated eyes and lowered voice,—"a handful of marauders could loot Great Oaks mansion any foggy night; and once an oar's length or two off the landing, they would be as completely lost in the mist and their pursuit as impracticable as if they were in the desert of Sahara."

Mr. Stanlett looked uncomfortable.

"Yes, indeed," declared Mrs. Kentopp, dimpling, "a bit inland,—as Great Oaks mansion used to be in the old time, before the bank caved in and the river carried off the whole point,—and this place would be Paradise! I sometimes wish that the river would make another grab at it and take it off—off—away down to the Gulf of Mexico!"

"Thank you for your very queer wishes," began Mrs. Faurie.

"Only that you might move inland and rebuild near us,—we are *so* far apart as it is," said Mrs. Kentopp, with her head askew and her sweetest smile.

"Never because of river pirates. What are our peace officers for, if we are not to take our ease under our own vine and fig tree?" retorted Mrs. Faurie.

"Ah, but evil is inherently stronger than good. Hence the difficulty in the administration of the law and the conservation of the peace," said Colonel Kentopp, magisterially. "Otherwise, of course, the cause of right and justice would have a clear walk-over. It is unfortunately far easier to conceal a crime than to detect it,—though skill and practice and persistence in ferreting out misdeeds go a long way and ultimately triumph in most instances, no doubt. But then, think of that affair last fall at Whippoorwill Landing,—nefarious business,—the malefactors still at large! Two men killed inside a good trig house,—big, healthy, hearty fellows. I knew Patton well,—used to keep a store in Arkansas;—and not a sign nor a clue yet as to how or why,—both wiped off the face of the earth,—touched off as lightly as the ash of this cigar," suiting the action to the word, then shaking his head solemnly.

"Oh, oh! raw head and bloody bones! Not another word! You will give the whole house awful dreams," cried Mrs. Kentopp. "Come, Mr. Stanlett, let us show this worshipful company what bridge whist really is."

She rose with a great rustle of silk skirts and whisked away to the centre table, where she opened a drawer with an affectation of busy and sly peering, and thence produced a pack of cards. Desmond could not understand why Colonel Kentopp should look so disconcerted and annoyed. He had an air of positive concern as he said with pointed emphasis, "Choose some other game, Annetta, that perhaps we play better,"—with a heavy attempt at mirth. "We are too many for bridge. *I* would sit out willingly, but I know that Mrs. Faurie will not permit me in my quality as guest,—distinguished stranger!—and Mr. Desmond being 'home-folks' here."

"Bridge mote it be," Desmond responded lightly, perceiving that Mrs. Kentopp, usurping the initiative of her hostess, had arranged the party expressly for his exclusion as if he were of no consideration, and caring little or naught what the tutor might think or feel; and to his surprise, Desmond cared naught for her demonstration. "I have letters to write,—I hear the packet passes near daylight to-morrow. I was just about to ask to be excused."

The straight, level brows above Mrs. Faurie's fine eyes were drawn into something like a frown. It was inconsistent with her high-bred sense of courtesy that this exclusion should have been suggested. She would not willingly have ignored the gentleman, poor and proud, whose dignity should have been the more jealously regarded because of its jeopardy in his subsidiary position. As Desmond, on his way to the library, passed on the veranda without, he glanced through the window at the group, now settled at the table, a cheery scene, with the glow of the old-fashioned crimson curtains and velvet carpet, the sheen of gilt-framed mirrors, the elusive flicker of the fire, the rich dresses of the two women. He could but note that the frown was not altogether effaced from those level brows, somewhat formidable of expression in their *rapprochement*, and he discerned that Mrs. Kentopp had found it necessary to be even more resolutely alluring in her sparkle and flushing laughter and insistent gayety than her wont.

CHAPTER VI

Desmond's conviction that the matter of the bicycle was eminently fit for report to the authorities was shared by the party who was most intimately concerned, the flatboat-man himself. The jovial pose which Jedidiah Knoxton conserved that afternoon while he sat on a coil of rope on the deck and sawed on the fiddle, as the friendly current carried him farther and farther toward the centre of the stream, had no relation to the attitude of his mind. It was dismayed, intimidated, as he now reflected upon the episode and its possible consequences. He did not welcome the realization that his thought was shared by his wife, as he noted that she was standing with the child in her arms, staring with a sort of dull, apprehensive, quelled contemplation at the receding scene, for it seemed to move instead of the craft,—the bight of the great river bend, where the roiled water gave token of the path of the boat; the strip of level territory outside the levee; the immense, green, serpentine embankment where the group of "quality folks" stood dwindling till they seemed but a bunch of bright-hued fabric; the heavy, tangled growths of a stretch of swamp country to the north, and to the south, with no apparent limits to their extent, the seigneurial groves of Great Oaks.

And here could be seen the mansion itself, with its score of red chimneys, its long, low white façade, each remove showing its many appanages,—now a wing and then, swinging into view, an ell, and straggling away the kitchen and offices, and dove-cote, and dairy and bell-tower, and stables, and orchards and vineyards; farther still was the village-like cluster of buildings for hired hands and tenants, formerly the "quarter" for slaves; and yet beyond appeared the steam-gin, the saw-and-grist mill, the potato-houses, the sheds for cows, and the work animals, mules, and horses; then thousands of acres of cotton-fields, orderly and neat as a flower border, already ploughed and bedded up, ready for the planting of the great staple,—a principality indeed, the realm of the rich and powerful and learned;—and was it wise to excite the just wrath, and the dangerous suspicion, or even to court the notice of those whose stake in the country was so large, whose hand was so heavy, whose ascendency was so complete!

"Mighty fine folks, Jedidiah," she said at length, still staring at the moving landscape. Her voice reached him even amidst the discordant sawings and scrapings of the horsehair and catgut. His hat was thrust back; his red forelock tossed to and fro as his head wagged in unison with his raucous performance. He did not speak, and presently, still eyeing the receding scene, she said, "Mighty rich folks, Jedidiah!" Her voice was pitched high, and its penetrating quality made itself insistent throughout the hubbub of the "hot time in the old town." The discordant strain ceased suddenly. The bow, still held after the fiddler's fashion, was shaken at her in emphasis as he drawled malignantly:—

"Ye-es,—an' if this fallin' weather in the upper country holds a week longer, I can take a cool thirty thousand dollars outer that sucker's pocket with three strokes of a spade; an' by gum, I'll do it, too!—if I gits a chanst."

He lifted his hand to the abrasions of his bruised and swollen face, which he had hitherto disregarded with an assumption of hardihood as naught. The last building of the "quarter" was disappearing in the distance, glistening with whitewash,—it was said on the river that the manager at Great Oaks whitewashed all creation when he was informed that Mrs. Faurie was returning from abroad, *even the under side of the horse-block*!—but the flatboat-man's wife still stood staring, some vague premonition of trouble in her mind. Jedidiah, the frog-like suggestions of his face emphasized as he crouched his body forward, his legs doubled up among the coils of rope, stared, too, blinkingly. The light in the sky was a keen saffron gleam now; it dazzled his eyes; he was thinking hard, eagerly, fearfully, maliciously.

The next moment the whole world seemed resonant and rocking with a wild, pervasive turbulence,—a steamer was rounding the point, and the little helpless, drifting leaf of a boat lay directly in her course. How he should not have heard the respiration of her engines, like that of an immense breathing creature which she resembled, he never knew, or how he had not felt the vibrations of the water pouring like a cataract over the great wheel at her stern,—for formidable as she moved upon the currents, loftily as she towered in her white, glistening presence, her chimneys seeming to vie with the forest heights of Great Oaks, she was not one of the fine packets plying between the cities. She was destined for one of the smaller tributaries, and the Mississippi made only a part of her course. But she looked to the flatboat-man like the scourge of God. She was materialized Fate! She was Terror, Doom, and Death in one to the wretched man whom momently she threatened to run down. He could never have described what he felt as now and again she lifted anew her frightful voice and spoke to him,—he could only feel,—spoke of warning, of smug and exact compliance with the law, of due notification of the death that she must presently mete out to him. He seemed all apart from the straining wretches that toiled, one at the pole and two at the rowlocks, as the two men and the woman strove against the current to bring the raft aside from the path of the domineering monster that bore straight down upon them,—for as far as consciousness was concerned, he could not have moved a muscle. It was a matter of instinct which controlled his labor, a mechanical effort, with which heart and brain had no part. He began to tremble when he perceived that the steamboat was slightly sheering to the left. Then for the first time he was sufficiently in command of his faculties to realize that the pilot's bell was continually jangling, that the throbs of the engines were disjointed, feebler, that there was a desperate effort making to back, to sheer, to change the course.

It was all useless,—too late! He saw as his frenzied muscles still strove against the impossible that the guards were filled with people, passengers, calling out undistinguished words of commiseration, of encouragement; the roustabouts stood on the lower deck, scarcely higher out of the river than himself in his humble craft level with the surface, and roared out advice.

Suddenly with a wild scream the woman despaired. She rose, dropping her oar, and held up the child at arm's length, with a gesture of appeal, toward the captain, who was standing on the hurricane deck. He waved his hand in encouraging response, and then the sheer was sufficient for Jedidiah to see that the yawl was unslung and sliding from the davits, and that the Flora F. Mayberry proposed to have the credit of humanely picking up their carcasses, after she had sent to the bottom their floating home and all their pitiful store of goods and chattels.

For this was the aspect the episode took to his mind when, almost within the suction of the steamer, the flatboat struck a swift swirl of current, made, heaven only knows how. Some obstruction on the bottom may have caused it,—the smokestack of an old sunken boat, long since forgotten; a tree of former swamp growths, too deeply whelmed to be known to snag-boats or river charts, barely sufficient to turn a ripple. With the vast strength of the Mississippi River currents the deflecting ripple swung the flatboat around like a leaf in an eddy, and, as safe as if he had miles of sea-room, Jedidiah Knoxton stood on his raft, with his face corrugated and lined with rage, and his mouth stretched wide and distorted, and shook his fist at the towering steamer, and called out frenzied curses upon the craft and her captain, and passengers, and crew, and consigned them all to hell, a deep and fiery hole in his version. Meantime the passengers, their sympathy reacting, laughed and sneered; the deck-hands yelled out gibes of derision and responsive defiance; the captain shrugged his shoulders in silent contempt and ordered the yawl once more to its place.

The woman, her arms akimbo, the baby, wailing unheeded now on the dancing, teetering floor, looked bitterly after the greater craft as she passed, the water playing in cascades of white foam over the wheel at her stern, her moving chimneys seeming to describe scrolls of mystic import among the clouds, punctuated here and there by the faint spark of a star.

"It is allus the way, Jedidiah," she said. She could scarcely get her breath as yet, and her voice had a catch like a sob. "It is allus the way! The big folks is safe, an' high, an' dry, while us pore folks take water, an' skim the edge of hell."

His pride, if he might have claimed such an endowment, his self-sufficiency, had been grievously cut down by the incident; but since it had not culminated in death or disaster, it had seemed to resolve itself into a flout, an injury, a wanton insult. This view was confirmed in an illogical sort by the evident revulsion of the sentiment of the passengers and crew, their sympathy naturally enough checked, however, by his rage and futile venom as he volleyed his curses at them.

"Not *allus* so safe an' sound," he protested, "the rich folks ain't. Them galoots up there at Whippoorwill Landing didn't skim the edge of hell,—that's true; they went teetotally in,—kerplunk!"

The woman had been wringing out her hair and shaking out her skirts, all damp with the spray of the stern wheel of the steamer and the churning wake of her passage in which the raft yet rocked. An awed stillness though fearful delight came over her face at his words, and she softly drew near, and sat down on a coil of the ropes with the baby in her arms. The child had ceased to cry aloud bewailing his desertion, but as if silence were too great a boon to accord, he kept up a sort of absent-minded whimpering or crooning, reciting in some sort a theme of woe, learned by rote, the significance of which had been forgotten or was uncomprehended.

"Yes, sir!" Jed Knoxton exclaimed with hearty satisfaction, "*they* got the butt end of the club, sure! Providence was right after them at a two-forty clip!" He sneered as he laughed. "I tell you the way it was meted out to *them*, you might have thought they was pore folks, fur sure."

"I never could make out how 't was they never suspicioned nothing,—how it was so easy done," she speculated.

There was not a soul within a mile of the boat, yet he glanced fearfully over his shoulder before he answered. His brother, the idiot, had gone back into the cabin, and now and again a long-drawn snore and at times a sputtering gasp told that he had sought his bunk for the night. The broad Mississippi stretched silent and deep, vacant on either hand, so broad that they could only see the line of the hither shore a mile away as they drifted along on the swift current. There was no other craft in view; no motion save the long, elastic undulations of the waves, here and there crisping into ripples when a flaw of the chill night breeze struck the water. Sometimes they were tipped with a shifting scintillation, the reflection of a star, and again only a sense of a dark, transparent lustre betokened the depths. A world, it was, and all to themselves; yet he looked over his shoulder, fearfully.

"They got into the store by purtendin' to be customers,—that's how."

"But stores don't keep open past midnight," she remonstrated.

He ducked his red head and chuckled into the bosom of his checked hickory shirt. It seemed so funny,—so very funny! "Of course 'twas outer business hours; but they was ailin'—oh, my, how ailin' they was! Becburn give out that he had ptomaine pizenin';—when they landed in the skiff, an' came up the bank, Danvelt told me that they hallooed the store bold as brass, same as if they was in earnest. An' them two, the proprietor of the store and his clerk, they took it all in, for gospel sure. Becburn *had* swallowed something mighty nigh as bad,—a power o' ipecac,—and he was jus' a-vomitin' an' retchin' as he come,—an' sure enough them suckers opened the door, to give him something to ease him off!" He paused again to laugh silently, holding his head down. "That light-haired, slim fellow, Oscar Patton, the clerk, he said that common kitchen sody was the antidote; an' all bar'foot as he was, he run into the back room to git a box,—they dealt with him there."

The child still crooned its plaint, though forgetting its sorrow; the woman's face was illumined by the light of the moon, only a mere segment of pearl, but all else was so dark,—the silent river running like the stream of Time, the glooms of the forest crowning the nearer banks towering dimly into the night, the opposite shore lost in distance,—that its lineaments were easily discerned by one familiar with them. Even one not accustomed might have noted the peculiar slant of the eyes, the snake-like contour of the countenance, the long, serpentine curve of the throat,—she seemed not out of place clinging to the slimy timbers of a raft in the midst of the murky Mississippi. She listened in cold-blooded interest to this tale of a deed of dread, but now and again she shuddered.

"The t'other fellow, Ackworth, was harder to kill, they say. He got his chanst and fit. He got on to the game, whenst he heard Patton yell out 'Oh, my God!' an' drap to the floor. Ackworth made a break for the drawer of the counter then,—he had just been pourin' out a glass of whiskey for the sufferer from ptomaine; Becburn declares now he ain't responsible for nothin' 'bout it all, for he done nothin' but turn himself wrong side out with that ipecac!—an' when Ackworth laid holt of the knob of the drawer, they knowed there was a pistol in it, an' they jumped on him. Ben Danvelt jes' held him by the nape o' the neck, an' though he got the drawer open, they pushed him down an' shut his head up in it. He couldn't git a purchase on himself to pull his head outer it. Tom Turfin stabbed him twicet, while the t'others held him thar with his head in the drawer,—stabbed him twicet in the back just under the shoulder-blade. He wasn't dead, though, when they let the drawer loost an' he drapped,—he died hard. Tom say that he wriggled an' writhed on the floor like a wum. He only spoke once; he lifted up his voice an' he says, says he, 'My blood shall be a testimony against you.' An' his mouth was full of it, then. But Ben Danvelt he spoke up,' Incompetent testimony in this court.' He's a funny feller, full of his jokes! Then he let Ackworth have the knife agin,—right in the throat, this time. An' they got no more o' his jaw then. A slick job, it was,— done right."

The progress was swift down the great, pulsing river; they could see the dark forests upon the bank all a-journeying northward as so elastically, so noiselessly, they swung along toward the south. Now and again the braided currents carried the craft close in shore, and they could smell the dank, rich vernal odor of the earth, the pungent tang of herb and tree; once in a deep, oozy tangle where a bayou went sluggishly forth into the woods, an outlet from the Mississippi, they heard a sudden resounding splash in the water. The woman started nervously, and with a sharp exclamation let her snuff-brush drop from her mouth into her lap.

"Shucks, Jocelinda," the man sneered, "don't you know a 'gator takin' to water yit?"

The ripples of the great saurian's stir as he swam along the marge were perceptible now in the moonlight as the boat shot past, down and down the stream, and they seemed far away and faint the sound when they heard the alligator's resonant call to his mate in the lagoon, and presently another roar hardly more than some dull blast of a distant horn, so fast the river swept them on.

"It ain't seemin' no slick job to me," Jocelinda commented at length, "else it would never have been found out."

"Oh, *you*'d have done it mighty different, wouldn't you, now?" he sneered. "*You* are up to all sorts o' tricks."

"I can kindle a fire that won't go out," Jocelinda declared.

"But the fire didn't go out; 'twas *put out*,—that's whut! The light gin the alarm so denied quick. That old hussy, the Swamp Lily, came scootin' down the river a full day behind time; an' headin' for the landin', the pilot seen the store afire. He sounded the whistle fit to wake the dead,—waked all the swamp country for miles around. The old boat jes' sot there on the water a-pipin' an' a-blowin' as if she'd bust. Then all the galoots round about got inter their breeches an' boots an' run to the landing to help put it out. The Swamp Lily sent out all the deck-hands, an' the Mississippi River had a leetle water to spare,—no reason why they couldn't throw the water on the fire an' put it out. *You* couldn't kindle a fire that the Mississippi River can't squench, hey, 'smart Aleck'?"

"But then the folks found the bodies right there," she objected.

"Ye-es," he drawled. "They had their own reasons for not having walked off."

"An' so the folks found the bodies fresh killed, an' seen that the store had been stripped of mighty nigh all the goods an' all the money in the cash drawer."

"Ye-es, the boys loaded up all they could kerry on the steam-launch an' set the shebang afire. But for the accident of the Swamp Lily comin' along out

70

of turn, the whole caboodle would have been ashes and cinders before the sun had riz. They would have thought the proprietor an' his clerk was burned by accident, or in tryin' to save something, or was drunk an' didn't wake. I 'member Danvelt said he thought that Ackworth had the name of takin' a glass too much once in a while."

"'Twas a big fire," she remarked, as if making a concession. "It lighted up the whole country. The river shone like a stream of flames in the fog,—just seemed to split the world in two."

"'*Twas* a big fire—an' a slick job, too," he protested. "They got away with the goods an' some cash,—consid'ble spondulix,—an' nobody ain't 'spicioned 'em yit. 'Twas way last fall, too."

"Them bodies ought not to have been found," she argued dolorously. She felt that it was the one disparagement to the artistic achievement.

He did not reply. They were now passing between a small island and the shore. The water, thus compressed in volume, ran with still more turbulent rapidity. He was not sure how their voices might carry on the still air and the transmitting medium of the silent river. They were too near the land on either hand to risk such words as might phrase the thoughts of their dark hearts. The island was in progress of swift building. At no distant day it would be the shore. The great, restless river—now sweeping away hundreds of acres, that melted into nothingness in the floods; now cutting channels through points of land in an inconceivably short time, transmogrifying them into islands far from their ancient affiliations—was here filling up with silt the shallows and rifts and chasms into solid continuity with the bank. This island was what is locally called "a towhead," a spit of white sand, sparsely covered with brush; and one might imagine so desolate a loneliness could shield no human being who could lend the ear of comprehension to a chance word floating over the water. But Jedidiah Knoxton and his wife Jocelinda kept their dubious counsels, till once more they swung along between distant banks of the deep and lonely river below and the unpeopled skies above.

"Jed, warn't that bicycle one of the Ackworth stock?" she queried, in a mere whisper.

"Ax me no questions an' I'll tell you no lies," he retorted gruffly.

"I allus believed them was 'spensive things,—heap mo' 'spensive than you knowed. I b'lieve Danvelt let you have 'em jus' to let you git tracked by 'em," she suggested, "ter keep s'picion off 'n him."

"Shet yer mouth, Jocelinda," he vociferated furiously, "else I'll break it in."

"Why, *you* had nothin' to do with thar trick," she expostulated. "I ain't taxin' *you* with nothink."

She was quiescent for a time, as if knowing that her silence would stimulate him to speech. The surest way to reopen the discussion was paradoxically to close it. The child was sleeping now, and once and again she patted its back, as it lay on her breast, with a fragmentary "Bye-oh, Bye-oh."

"Them things ain't labeled," Knoxton recommenced, as if there had been no cessation of the discussion. "They are as common as crayfish. Folks are wheelin' all over the country."

"Not at no five dollars, Jed,—nor yit ten. I tole you that I priced them jiggermarees whenst I was in Vicksburg, an' some was as high as fifty dollars."

"An' I tole you that the store folks was stuffin' you," he cried, with a sort of turbulence that was akin both to rage and woe. "A tacky body like you to go pricin' wheels an' such fixin's!—they was makin' game of you."

"Mebbe so, mebbe so,"—she yielded a facile acquiescence, apparently without sensitive vanity; "but I *did* see this evening that ten dollars was a power too low. That man wouldn't let Mrs. Faurie risk herself with it,—rich as she is! He knowed it war new and stole."

"Well, damn Mr. Faurie,—that is all I have got to say," the flatboat-man cried, his hand going up to his bruised face tingling with pain as his rancor roused at the recollection of the incident. Then tremulous with a nervous rage, that yet contended with a cold chill of fear, "But if this wheel was to be tracked to me, what would ail me not to split on Danvelt and Turfin and the others?"

"I reckon they are too far by this time to be caught; it all happened last October, and here it is nigh the spring o' the year agin. I reckon they think that nobody would believe you. The law would have you safe by the laig, an' the goods found on your boat. 'Twas only a blind if anybody took after them."

There was a long silence. The boat was again approaching the shore of its own accord, it seemed, yielded as it was to the whim of the current. The dark forests were coming down to the verge of the stream with beckoning, sheltering suggestions in their wild, tangled glooms. Her breath was short, so ardently she hoped what she dared not say. He divined her hope, but with that perverse sense of domination, so characteristic of the domestic tyrant, he would say naught to encourage it. He pursued the subject. "If I believed that, I'd sink the wheels in the river without more ado," he declared.

"They are too light," she protested. "I dunno how them cur'ous injer-rubber rims might make 'em float."

Again there were no words between them for a time, while the river clove through the night as silent as the stars vibrating above in the sky. The moon was sinking toward the western bank. A vague sense of yearning, of wistful sadness, pervaded the lunar light that began to suffuse the summits of the great, gloomy, primeval forests. This glister seemed to respond to the slow down-dropping of the weary one who had finished her course through the skies,—no joyous welcome this, but replete with solemnity, with weird silence, with aloof suggestions such as might typify the down-dropping into a grave. The wind had grown more chill. Jocelinda wrapped closer a ragged petticoat of red flannel, which the baby wore about its shoulders like a mantle. The touch of the fabric reminded her of the infant's wardrobe which Mrs. Faurie had promised her,—not that she cared for such comforts and means of tidy array; it would have been far too much trouble to keep the child clothed and tended in many whole and clean garments. The recollection merely brought to her mind a collocation of ideas that had earlier occurred to her. "I don't believe that man was Mr. Faurie!" she said suddenly.

It was an unlucky topic. The very name roused Knoxton's rancor. "What for no?" he exclaimed, in a sudden gust of anger. His knowledge that the bicycle had been instantly recognized as stolen goods; the possibility that his possession of the machine might connect his identity with the miscreants who had plundered the store at Whippoorwill Landing, and murdered the proprietor and clerk; the fear that this was their nefarious intention in shunting off on him these costly wares so easily detected, so rare among the humbler population among whom his trade lay, so incongruous with his stock of goods and character of custom, filled him with a bewildered dismay. His was not a trained mind to think consecutively, to deduce correct conclusions; he blundered upon his convictions; his plans were founded on impulse, inclination. Ignorance is not compatible with a just and accurate foresight. His resolves, taken in a tumult of angry volition, he would seek to execute without due regard to feasibility or perception of sequences, and he had no sense of justice and could maintain no poise of temper. "What for no?" he reiterated, striking at his wife with the rope's end.

Thong-like it curled around her body, the end lashing her arm, bare to the elbow, with force enough to raise a welt. Experience had ripened such wisdom as she possessed, and in self-defense she forbore to exasperate further her brutal husband. She said naught of the smart of the lash, but recanted hastily. "I just took up the idee that he was somebody else. I thought that old man Faurie was dead. Ain't this his widder?"

"Widder?—rats! old Faurie's widder? That slim, handsome, high-steppin' gal! She is his son's wife,—she 'lowed to you that her name was Mrs. Faurie."

"Mebbe so; they hev been gone to Europe so long I lost the run of 'em," the woman meekly admitted.

"Naw, that ain't it," Jedidiah sneered. "Ye are grudgin' her them good looks an' brash, high-handed ways; draggle-tailed vixens like you can't stand for other women to be young an' sniptious." He spat moodily into the Mississippi. "That was young Faurie an' his brand-new wife—the old man is

73

dead long ago. I'm thinkin' the brat mus' be his leetle brother. I remember that there was a new baby at Great Oaks mansion about ten year ago; I noticed it 'cause the old plantation bell was rung like mad for rejoicing, like it had an ager fit, an' the Swamp Lily an' other boats whistled a salute when they passed, though such is agin the regulations."

"I hedn't never been hereabouts in them days," she stipulated, by way of excuse for her lack of readiness to confirm these vagrant and erratic recollections of his wandering experiences as he floated down the river with his store of goods, or poled his craft laboriously in and out of the bogues and bayous. "I lived then over in the Arkansas." She held her head down for a moment. A scene had arisen before her mind best discerned with eyes closed: a little cabin in a bit of clearing in the dense, dark woods; a filthy, miry dooryard; the fowls and hogs and lean old mule, all clustered about the rickety porch; a stationary home on dry land,—all seemed paradise at this instant to the amphibious nomad, for the rope's end stung, and her indurated sensibilities had yet some nerve a-tingle to the coarse taunt and the bitter fling.

"Why, any fool but *you* would know. Didn't *she* say that she was Mrs. Faurie? And didn't he tell the brat he shouldn't have the wheel at no price? And didn't he tell her she must take his word for it? And didn't he grab the woman by the elbow and the cub by the collar, like they belonged to him, an' start them off the boat, him looking as fierce as Judgment Day? An' ain't that the Faurie plantation, Great Oaks, where we was tied up? Answer me that,—answer me,—answer me,—ye tongue-tied slut,—or I'll cut yer tongue out."

"Oh, laws, Jed," said Jocelinda, her nerve shaken and very near to tears. "I 'lowed that she was a widder lady. She spoke of her kids. I 'lowed that boy was one of 'em. I hearn her say that—"

"Ye *'lowed* an' ye *hearn* like a dod-rotted fool. That man is Faurie and owns Great Oaks! An' ye can bet yer immortal soul I'll give *him* somethink to think about soon that'll make him forgit he ever seen a bike or a tradin'-boat, air one."

He had risen from the coil of rope and was stepping about elastically on the deck as if he intended to pole the craft in to the shore. She silently followed his example, first placing the child in the centre of the coil of rope, and taking her turn at the work with strength and activity as muscular as if she were a man. Perhaps an infusion of cheerfulness aided her exertions, for they were making for a bayou that the river sent sluggishly wandering down with scant impetus from its currents through the swamps and the heavy glooms of a cypress slough, and she welcomed the sense of added safety in the deep seclusions of the wilderness. Before the Faurie party, with the utmost expedition which the isolated situation of Great Oaks

Plantation permitted them, could contrive to notify the authorities of any suspicion they might have entertained, the shanty-boat would have quitted the thoroughfares of the river, leaving not a trace. The story of the imminent danger of being run down by the Flora P. Mayberry would suggest some similar disaster as a reason for the disappearance of the flatboat-man and his craft. The bicycles—there were only three—could be hidden, destroyed, buried in the deep, murky, marshy tangles of the lagoons. Here it would be scarcely possible that the fugitives should be seen or followed,—a succession of cypress brakes, of swampy pools, a network of bayous and sloughs with scarcely a dry acre for miles, the land of no value and impracticable, the locality the deepest solitude, the aquatic growths of an impenetrable density. She had not expected to sleep that night with so grateful a sense of security, for it was not long before the boat was tied up in a jungle of young cottonwood trees, awaiting the passing of the hours till dawn should bring the light necessary for the navigation of such tortuous ways. But she was up and ready at the first glimmer, her energies recruited as much by the surcease of suspense as by the physical rest.

As the gray day began to break, dim and clouded, it might seem to a sophisticated sense a desolate scene, for even such symmetry as the sluggish bayou possessed was obliterated; and now the boat was poled along a stream-like channel, and now it threaded a series of lakelets connected by narrow straits, full of half submerged growths, and again it seemed almost aground in a slough where the medium was mud rather than water. These lakelets were of an inky blackness, and in their midst stood forlorn forests of gigantic cypress; upon the dark, mirror-like surface of the water the white boles of the trees, long ago deadened by a permanent inundation from some freak of the changeful river, were reflected with weird distinctness and a spectral effect. The boat was as if afloat in a world of dead vegetation, the duplication of the lifeless trees below, the ghostly white forest towering above. Now and again a sharp bit of steering became necessary to keep the craft clear of the cypress-knees, as the conical, protruding excrescences of the roots are called, rising considerably above the surface of the water. Hanging moss depended in vast masses and heavy festoons from the bare white boughs far, far above, and served to deepen the gloom of the eerie effect of the scene. More than once the voyagers saw an alligator lying half embedded in ooze and mud, looking as lifeless as the log it resembled; but one had awakened apparently from the period of hibernation, and was swimming down the centre of the black lake. Jedidiah Knoxton, watching his approach, was dubious which course he might take, in meeting the boat, in the narrow passage.

"He don't understand the code of signals nohow," he demurred. "'Twouldn't be no good to whistle if I could."

The alligator solved the problem as far as he was concerned by diving suddenly, and doubtless embedded himself in the refuge of the mud. The question as to where he might come up again presented another doubt to the mind of Jed Knoxton, but he prodded boldly with his pole, and presently they had passed, the huge saurian still invisible.

There were other tokens of the spring besides the awakening of the alligators from their wintry torpors. Birds were flitting through the air; frogs were all a-croak about the logs; the slimy, nondescript medley of vegetation and muck was here and there pierced by tender spears of delicate yet intense green, the folded leaves and shoots of the swamp lily. Suddenly the first ray of the sun struck upon a wide expanse of silver sheen in the distance,—it was a lake evidently miles in length, of the peculiar horseshoe contour characteristic of the lacustrine waters of the region, surrounded by dense and gloomy forests, and fringed with saw-grass. This thick, prickly growth, so heavily notched as to suggest its name, caught Jed Knoxton's attention. It was a keen glint of green at this season, almost as intense as light itself. Jed Knoxton stood still and held his hand above his eyes as he gazed; then he turned to scan some landmark which he identified toward the west, and again he shifted toward the east.

"I done los' my bearin's somehow in the swamp," he muttered. "I been polin' todes the north 'stead o' south. An' damn that old corkscrew of a river. We drifted thirty miles las' night to make five miles o' distance."

He still stood absorbed and pondering when his wife issued from the little cabin on the deck. "What's the matter, Jed?" she asked apprehensively. Smoke was curling from the stove-pipe thrust through the roof, and the sizzling of frying pork came with its pungent odor from the open door. She held in her hand a long iron spoon coated with meal batter while she fixed expectant and anxious eyes upon him.

"Jes' as well, jes' as well!" he muttered.

"What is it, Jed; what you studyin' about?" she persisted.

"We made no distance las' night scarcely on that twisted sarpient of a river," he said. "It is blamed like that old joke of the fool drummers,—travel fifty mile down the Mississippi, an' then take your gripsack an' walk half a mile back to where you started from." He grinned in surly mirth. "Then I done shortened it some more by missin' my way in the swamp." He looked about in dull speculation, as if he were wondering anew how this mischance should have betided him, and she dreaded lest he might fail, in considering this problem, to disclose the intention evidently slowly forming in his mind. But for him its interest was paramount. It struck her as a blow in the face might have done when she heard it voiced anew, for she had hoped that time and distance had combined to obliterate it, and it boded ill, she knew. "We ain't more'n five miles from the edge of Great Oaks Plantation,—I know it by the earmarks o' that old White Deer Lake. An' it's just as well,—*just as well*—p'intedly convenient, in fac'. I'm goin' to give Mr. Faurie of Great Oaks Plantation something to study about that will make him forgit there was ever sech a thing as a bike or a tradin'-boat, air one."

CHAPTER VII

The ensuing days were bland and soft, and the Faurie family life gravitated insensibly to the wide verandas of the Great Oaks mansion, where much time was spent in futile chat, and where one could take the air without the exertion of exercise and be out-of-doors without the trouble of quitting the house. It was a fine illustration of the best method of *dolce far niente*. The favorite rendezvous was beneath the canopy of live-oak boughs on the extension of the veranda just outside the library windows, and here Desmond often joined the group, saying to himself that it had an air of churlish avoidance to hold himself aloof when they were all so near. In these days he heard no little of Mrs. Faurie's plaints of the limited capacities of Great Oaks for rational entertainment.

"Nothing to do,—nothing to say,—nothing to see. 'Oh, give me to drink of mandragora, that I may sleep away this gap of time!'" she exclaimed, as she reclined languidly in her garden chair.

There was something to see in the Great Oaks avenues,—the sward was rich and fresh, and all the vague, sparse, spring foliage of the trees sent out a glitter now of gold and now of green. Hyacinths, pink and white and blue, shook their fairy bells in a parterre near the house, and the trellises in the old-fashioned garden were delicately sprayed with green, lace-like leafage. There was much to see in the vast, murky floods of the Mississippi River; the opposite banks had wholly disappeared in the encroachments of the water on the swampy Arkansas shore, and as its limits were beyond the reach of vision, its aspect was that of some great inland sea. When Desmond remarked on the phenomenon, Mr. Stanlett stated, with the pride which the dwellers on the banks of the river take in its arbitrary and monarchical exhibitions of power, that sometimes here, in high water, it measured sixty miles wide, and always in the Bend its average depth was not less than one hundred and eighty feet.

"And just beyond the point the lead-line often marks scant four feet on the sandbars," Mrs. Faurie interpolated iconoclastically.

The words suggested a lurking danger to the larger craft visible, the possibility of getting aground even in such a vast welter of waters. A great tow of coal was in midstream, bound from Pittsburgh to New Orleans, the steamboat pushing before her a score of broad, laden barges, ranged elliptically about her prow, and gliding slowly and majestically down the current. Seen above the summit of the dense forests in the distance, against the bland, blue sky, a whorl of black smoke uncoiling from lofty chimneys announced the approach of the steamer of the regular packet line rounding the point; and the upward course of a snag-boat had its own suggestion of yet another of the jeopardies of the navigation of the great, lawless river.

"Talking about something to drink," said Mr. Stanlett, a bit uneasily, "I had a queer experience yesterday. I was out riding, and when that sudden shower came up, I was pretty far from home and got soaking wet. And—you know my rheumatism—I stopped at the first house I could reach; it was Jessop's shack, and I went in to dry off by his fire. Well,—Jessop is a friendly fellow, and would have me take a drink to keep from catching my death of cold. You know he is only an Irish wood-chopper,—makes a scanty living by furnishing wood from anybody's land who will give it to him for the clearing, and selling it to anybody who will buy it; but I accepted because I don't like to refuse a civility from such a person,—and, bless my soul! it was French brandy,—good sound Cognac. He was mightily surprised when I told him so. He said he knew that it was a tipple to which he was unaccustomed, but it cost the same as 'bust-head whiskey'; he said it was all the same to him so long as it fired up all right,—'made drunk come.' He bought it from that shanty-boat."

Desmond looked up significantly at Mr. Stanlett, who resumed: "You are right, sir,—stolen, no doubt! I fear from the Whippoorwill Landing stock. I remember that though Ackworth kept a general assortment of goods, he had a limited class of fine custom. Some rich people live near Whippoorwill Landing, and they preferred to give him their orders instead of dealing elsewhere. Ackworth was of the gentry himself,—came of good people,—broken up by the Civil War. He put what he had left into this store; he had been in the Confederate army, though one of the youngest veterans—distinguished himself—was very popular—and as the planters round about gave him all their custom instead of sending to Memphis or New Orleans, he kept in stock such choice grades of articles as they would require. I fear this brandy was stolen and that bicycle also; I wish that I had taken your view and given notice of our suspicions to the police authorities."

"To be quite candid, I did not think it prudent to abide by the theory of non-action," said Desmond. "I wrote that evening,—and the mail-boat took the letter next morning."

Mrs. Faurie sat up straight in her chair and looked about her with widening eyes,—that a tutor in her house should take the initiative in its direction! Mr. Stanlett's delicate face flushed. Even through his sparse silver hair one could see the polished scalp, all roseate. He said nothing, however, looking down at his cigar as he flipped off the ash.

Desmond noticed their evident attitude of mind both with humiliation and indignation. Then he roused himself,—for his paltry salary they did not buy his identity, annul his personality.

"The responsibility was mine," he said icily, more in self-assertion and in response to their offended silence, their mien of rebuke of his presumption, than because of any sense of obligation to give account of his motives. "It was I who discovered the quality of the article offered at a mere fraction of its value. Knowing that it must have been stolen, I did not feel justified, as far as I was concerned, in remaining silent."

"There is a grave responsibility in unwarranted interference," remarked Mr. Stanlett, dryly.

"And in bringing down suspicion on innocent people, perhaps," Mrs. Faurie said, with cold reproach.

"If the proprietor of the trading-boat came honestly by a wheel, perfectly new and a favorite make, which he is able to offer for sale at five dollars, he will have no difficulty in making the fact clear. It is not my prerogative to judge."

"I should be sorry to provoke the enmity of a rude, lawless man such as that, by putting upon him an unnecessary affront and hardship," Mr. Stanlett coldly urged. He had no longer his genial drawl of leisure and luxury. His intonation was crisp, clear-cut.

"As I understand it, a heinous and brutal murder was committed only last fall at Whippoorwill Landing," Desmond said, his pride pulsing in his temples, his own restiveness under expressed displeasure showing haughtily in his flushed face. "To have knowledge—or such grounds of suspicion as amount to knowledge—of stolen merchandise being vended through the country at fantastic prices and yet say nothing, in my opinion comes perilously near conniving at the escape of the villains,—accessory after the fact."

Mrs. Faurie turned and surveyed the tutor with wide eyes and a look of such affronted amazement that even he quailed before them. Desmond was impressed with the fact, noted by him for the first time, but doubtless often perceived before by others, that the very rich are fearless of the ordinary operations of disaster. The ægis of great possessions overshadows them. The law is their ally, for their protection; the imputation that by their negligence, or assumptions, or bravado, or inconsiderateness it could be arrayed against them is in itself a ridiculous impossibility, a sort of grotesque parody on fact, a distortion of the powers of established order. All other menace is likewise abated in their favor. The dangers of travel are minimized for them; the distresses of sickness are mitigated; every ill that flesh is heir to is softened and alleviated and embellished till they are scarcely to be identified with the woes, savage and hideous, that rack the multitude; and death itself is so bedizened and beautified and exalted that it ceases to be the great leveler. Mrs. Faurie's astonishment that anything that she or hers thought proper to do could be liable to misconstruction, to question, to disparagement, was beyond words.

Mr. Stanlett, however, stared at him with a sort of dawning comprehension in his watery blue eyes. "Upon my word, I never thought of it in that light!—ridiculous aspersion—impossible, though, as far as we are concerned; but, I believe,—in respect to the law, the bare facts of the case,—silence might aid the murderers, shedding the goods of which they stripped that store among the flatboat-men, woodcutters, ditchers, and niggers."

"Then Mr. Desmond was right?" asked Mrs. Faurie, seriously.

"Yes,—yes,—though I deprecate anything that tends to draw upon this house the enmity of the wretches."

"The law is its best protection," declared Desmond. "To make them feel the power of the law is the real resource. To let them and their fences and pals get away with impunity is to invite depredations."

"Yes, yes,—true, true!" said Mr. Stanlett. "But you take a good deal on yourself, Mr. Desmond."

"It was imposed upon me by good conscience and good citizenship."

"Ah, well, now,—I don't know about good conscience," said Mr. Stanlett, drawing hard at his cigar, but with renewed satisfaction. "Batting the eye is necessary sometimes. It won't do to see so much, and deduce so correctly, and act so promptly. Let sleeping dogs lie."

"Do you call these sleeping dogs?"

"So far as we are concerned they are. Quiet, peace, security,—we have them all at Great Oaks."

"And a dullness that has no parallel outside the grave," declared Mrs. Faurie, once more falling back in her graceful reclining posture. She had never seemed to Desmond so beautiful as to-day. She wore the daintiest of afternoon dresses, of delicate lavender broadcloth, and the dazzling purity of her complexion was even more radiantly asserted in the full light. Her gray eyes, with their dense, long black lashes, seemed more expressive in their petulant, slumberous disaffection. From her white brow her hair rose in the usual pompadour effect, but its rich brown tint was heightened by the broad illumination of out-of-doors, and her lips had all the lustre of wet coral. Into the meshes of the lace of her high "transparent collar" and chemisette, that showed the gleam of her snowy white neck and throat, was thrust a set of stick-pins of amethyst. She held some wands thickly studded with pink almond blooms in her hand. "Great Oaks leads the field for monotony," she said disconsolately. "It might be a gentle distraction to be called upon to defend the mansion against river pirates."

She suddenly sat up straight, her eyes dilating and brightening, her infrequent flush, an incomparable tint, mounting into her cheeks. "Think how it would sound in the deep midnight,—if the old plantation bell should boom out on the air, up the river and down the river, and across the Bend, calling on all who ever stood on the pay-roll of Great Oaks Plantation, or owed it a good turn, or wished it well, to lend a hand at its utmost need. I can hear it now! It would sound so far! It would shake the moss on the cypress trees in the White Deer Swamp, where ghosts have been seen. It would rouse the gangs at the engineering work who are trying to raise the river on jackscrews, or sinking a revetment mat, or building a dyke at the point, or whatever they are up to over yonder in the chute. It would even start up the loafers from the card-tables at the old Shin-Plaster Landing, way down on the Arkansas side, where everybody says they gamble half the night. And the Swamp Lily would be climbing up the current, and old Captain Cleek—who dropped me into the Mississippi River once when I was a baby and he was a mud clerk, and my parents were leaving the steamboat in midstream to make the landing in a yawl, and who has always declared he owed me indemnity for a ducking—would signal to head for the shore with every pound of steam that his engines can carry."

Mr. Stanlett moved uneasily, and now and again cast a furtive, anxious glance at her sparkling, girlish face. This badinage was far from appealing to him. He had sought once or twice to interrupt, but in the very desperation of idleness and lack of interest she found a sort of entertainment in the picture that she had conjured up, and persisted:—

"What would you two do? All out here in the grove where it is so egregiously dark of a moonless night—we shan't have this function on till the moon changes—there would appear occasionally a sudden, funnel-shaped flare of light and a sharp report,"—she put her hands over her ears for a moment as if to shut out the sound,—"and Mr. Desmond would be winning his spurs, and Uncle Clarence would be wanting to show how worthy he is of his, already won, and the babies would be telling each other, and everybody else, how wrong and wicked and purblind I was never to let them learn to shoot so that they might now fill the marauders full of lead; and I—why I—would just open the door a bit ajar, and—'Gentlemen,'"—with the most gracious bow and an airy waving of the hand,—"'the goods and chattels in this house are somewhat antique, but with a lot of wear in them yet. They are racy of the soil, and the trail of the European serpent is over none of them. They are all at your service. As to the people,—Mr. Stanlett is a man wise in counsel, gentle in manner, and a genial companion at dinner; Mr. Desmond will teach you "to speak Greek as naturally as pigs squeak"; and you are welcome to *both* of them until I can ransom them, which I will do as soon as I can save something from my next year's income!—all for the slight consideration that you will give me and my squabs a free passage down to Natchez on the Swamp Lily,—and no questions asked!'" She paused breathless, triumphant. "Now, Uncle Clarence, don't you think that would wake us up?"

He turned to throw his cigar stub over his shoulder into the grass. The wind was stirring the long, drooping branches of the live oak above their heads, and little, fluttering ripples ran through the folds of the skirt of her gown. "I think that we may have yet something to disturb us, not so sensational, but sufficiently perturbing. There is no necessity to 'raise the river on jackscrews.' Colonel Kentopp thinks we are going to have an overflow in Deepwater Bend. The river is at flood height, and in several localities above, the water is standing against the levee. There have been recent rains all through the upper country. He says that since the rise, the work of the River Commission on the other side has had the effect of throwing a water of overwhelming weight against the levee above his place, and if it breaks at Ring-fence Plantation, where it was always liable to crevasses, considerable territory in the Bend must go under too."

"So poor Colonel Kentopp makes his moan! We never go under on account of the cross levee. I am mighty sorry for his anxiety; an overflow, especially if it were not general, would hurt the sale of Dryad-Dene, and he has been negotiating that place so long with that rich Mr. Loring. For my part, I believe that man will need only so much land as he can lie down in,—he will be dead before he makes up his mind to buy," Mrs. Faurie prophesied.

She gazed silently out for a time at the tawny sweep of the Mississippi at flood height, beyond the vivid variant tints of the bourgeoning spring growths. "I wish the Mississippi River were drained. Such a torment as it has been. What a queer thing its channel would be, though. Just think of it! Boats unnumbered, of all sizes and pretensions, from the first little stern-wheeler to the floating palaces of the days of the Robert E. Lee and the Great Republic. Then the bones of all the people that have gone down in the fires and collisions and swampings and sinkings to their watery graves! The nations, the races, they are all represented there, and who knows what prehistoric people! And in modern times the English, the French, the Spaniard,—De Soto, himself, must be there yet. He could not be swept with the current down to the Gulf, for he was buried in his armor, encased in a hollow log, and he must be lying still, oh, very still, the great wanderer! bound to one restricted spot,—the great explorer! under tons and tons of the ooze and mud of the Mississippi, that he came so far to find, and that has held him fast so long! Yes,—the bottom of the Mississippi River must be a strange sight indeed."

"Might try a diving-bell; that would put an end to the dullness!" suggested Reginald, who had come up and was leaning over the high back of her chair as she talked. Now and again his eyes wandered to the tennis-court at one side of the house, where Horace and Chubby were playing a match, running very nimbly, but serving the balls badly enough from the standpoint of his superior expertness. Mrs. Faurie did not reply. Her eyes were fixed on a mounted figure approaching through the grove, presently identified as a groom from Colonel Kentopp's place. Dismounting at the foot of the steps, he presented a note with the request for an answer.

"An answer?" said Reginald, who had run down the flight of steps to receive it. "Then you had better ride around to the kitchen and wait."

As the groom rode off and Reginald turned to ascend the steps he remarked: "From the Kentopps, mamma," holding up the envelope, showing the elaborate crest. Then, as she extended her hand, he continued in the accents of an extreme but half-suppressed surprise: "It is addressed to Mr. Desmond."

The tutor looked up in blank amaze, the expression deepening on his face as, after a request for permission, he read the contents. The note was from Mrs. Kentopp, in a tone of the suavest urbanity and the most friendly and informal cordiality, begging that he would give Colonel Kentopp and herself the pleasure of his company at Dryad-Dene for the week-end. "We have some very charming young friends staying with us whom we wish you to meet, and especially we wish to give them the pleasure of knowing you. I have selected the week-end, thinking that this will not much conflict with your schoolroom duties with the little Faurie torments. So I beseech you to let us have you Thursday evening, Friday, Saturday, and Sunday. We will return you, with no disparagement of your wisdom, early Monday morning, though we don't intend to be very serious and staid at Dryad-Dene either."

He could not command the muscles of his face in his surprise as he read, and his disconcerted doubt and dismay were so patent that Mrs. Faurie cried out gleefully:—

"Have mercy on our curiosity! What are the Kentopps doing to you?"

Without a word he handed her the note. Her brilliant eyes scanned the lines with a brightening interest over all her face. "Why, how perfectly delightful! A dance after dinner Thursday evening—Mercy! in Lent?—oh, I remember,—it is Mi-Carême. Will they have enough?—Yes, with Miss Allandyce and the Mayberrys and Miss Dennis and Rupert Regnan and those two young gentlemen who were landed from the Primrose last night, and Miss Kelvin, and she suggests others whose names she does not mention,—and a camp hunt on Friday and Saturday,—'the young ladies are wild to go!'—Oh, I know they are, and I will bet everything that they do go, and spoil the fun for the men.—No shooting Sunday,—but only the sylvan pleasures of the camp; for if the ladies don't go earlier, they will then join the hunters for a day in the woods. How delightful! How perfectly delightful! But,"—a shadow crossed her face, quizzical, but nevertheless a shadow—"how very strange that she doesn't invite me!"

"I was thinking of that," Desmond remarked. "It must be an oversight."

"How can it be?—'Cordial remembrances to dear Mrs. Faurie.'"

"I don't understand it," he said helplessly.

"I do," Mrs. Faurie declared; "she is relegating me to my proper place as an old woman. This entertainment is given for the young people; 'gay youth loves gay youth.'"

Desmond flushed. "I think it an extreme impertinence on the part of the Kentopps."

"Well,—in a way. I shouldn't take up much room,—and oh, how I should have enjoyed it,—the days are so long!"

"If you will excuse me, I will step into the library and answer the note," said Desmond, rising slowly from his chair.

"Do; and I am sure that you will have a charming time,—it will be a delightful break in the monotony for you."

Desmond stood aghast. "I have not the most remote idea of accepting." He had his hand on the back of his chair, and he leaned slightly upon it as he looked down at her. His expression seemed reflected upon her face.

"But, my dear child, you must accept," she exclaimed in dismay. "I wouldn't have you miss it for any consideration."

"I don't think an acceptance is appropriate—with you excluded."

She laughed lightly. "Can't you see that it is a party of young people, and that it is only my incurable frivolity that makes me frenzied to go to it? You are the only member of the household of the appropriate age for such volatile amusements. The children are too young for society such as this, and Uncle Clarence and I are too old. I insist upon it. I will not have it otherwise. Go write your acceptance, or I will do it for you."

Still he leaned on the back of his chair, and still he looked at her doubtfully. Rarely indeed since his advent at Great Oaks had his face shown its natural lines of expression. It was frank, gentle, almost appealing now, without the cool constraint, the aloof dignity, the critical reserve, it generally wore. "The Kentopps did not particularly attract me,—and, to be candid, I think that I perceived that I was not acceptable to Mrs. Kentopp. It would be distasteful to me to go."

Mrs. Faurie remembered suddenly Mrs. Kentopp's pointed exclusion of Desmond in her proposition for a game at cards, her manner of airy, unseeing indifference.

"But you must perceive from this note that there was nothing intentional,—it is cordiality and consideration itself. Mrs. Kentopp's manners are so affected and she is so self-absorbed that it is easy to take her amiss. One should not be too exacting; we must take the people in this world as we find them."

Obviously, however, he was not placated, and she resumed with a note of decision: "Now, I make this a personal matter. As a favor to *me* I hope that you will accept this invitation. The Kentopps are exceedingly civil to you,—and you have no excuse. They would think a declination very strange. And, besides, I want you to have the little bit of entertainment that you can get from a neighborhood visit, while you are consigned to this slough of despond yclept Great Oaks Plantation. I only wish I had an invitation, too,—" She dropped her hands in her lap with a gesture of mock despair, then she laughed out gayly at herself.

"Couldn't you go without it," he suggested. "There seems such an established friendship between the families, formality might be dispensed with."

"If the note had been addressed to me,—perhaps. If I had been charged with the transmission of the message to you, I might have stretched a point and interpreted it as inclusive. But no!—I am expressly and of set purpose excluded. I am out of the game! There is nothing for me but to sit down in the chimney-corner and just be old."

She turned her radiant face up toward him, the most apt interpretation of beauty in its fullest expression he had ever imagined, the bloom of perfect development upon it, the rare ripe fulfillment of the promise of first youth. She was apart from the idea of time. There were more lines about Chubby's eyes, from much crinkling with laughter; her fair, smooth lids showed naught but the form of their perfect design. Reginald had a vertical crease between his brows, from a frown of perplexity he sometimes wore in moments of cogitation; but his mother's face was as free from the trace of care as of age, and morning itself looked out of her eyes.

The point of exclusion was so preposterous an incident,—it was so jejune, and lacking in social tact and appropriateness, that Desmond, try as he might, could not interpret it. He did not give over his impressions of Mrs. Kentopp, for all her fair words now; he did not easily forgive or forget, but the ground of offense was untenable. It was infinitely unpalatable to accept, yet it was not practicable to decline, and he was as little in a holiday mood as ever in his life when, two days later, the Kentopps' phaeton, which had been sent for him, rolled up to the porte-cochère of the mansion at Dryad-Dene Plantation.

If Great Oaks were reminiscent of the past, it might seem that Dryad-Dene was a respecter only of the morrow. It could hardly be said to be up-to-date,—it was an earnest of the future. Certainly it was the most modern house in all that portion of Mississippi; and but that the surrounding woods, with the peculiarity of harboring no shoots nor underbrush, betokened the locality, one could scarcely have identified the vicinage. The river was out of sight; the levee, unseemly, utilitarian, suggestive of jeopardy in its promise of protection, held its serpentine course far beyond the range of the windows of Dryad-Dene. There were no forest trees immediately about the house; the grounds were laid off in the formal Italian style, with conventional walks in the midst of a fine green turf embellished with cone-shaped evergreens and other ornamental shrubs, white stone vases, terraces with stone copings and steps; and pleasing though the effect was to the eye, it was as foreign to all suggestions of Mississippi as if it had been hundreds of miles from the dominant old river. Only when its beauty might compensate for its old-fashioned savor was aught brought into use of merely domestic suggestions. These walks were covered with tiny, fine white shells, brought up by steamer in hogsheads from the Gulf coast; and charming as was their aspect, this entailed not more expense than ordinary gravel, which must needs have been imported also, for there was not a pebble to be found in all this stoneless region. A crystalline glitter from one side betokened the slanting glass sashes of the conservatory, and great ornamental plants—palms and Japanese tree-ferns—were ranged on either side of the stone flight of steps of the main entrance, as well as the porte-cochère. The house was of brick, with stone facings, the roof of fantastic device, of many peaks and gables; a tower was at the eastern corner; a deep loggia, an oriel window, a balcony, embellished the façades elsewhere, breaking up every suggestion of regularity in the architectural effect.

The large reception hall, into which Desmond was ushered, had a fire blazing in a deep chimney-place, so huge as to be of mediæval suggestion, and a grand staircase in massive oak, descending in devious turns, with here a landing below a great, stained glass window, and here a niche in which was a marble bust on a tall pedestal; on the lowest step was lolling a young lady, a cup of tea in her hand and a riding-crop across her knee. There were several other figures turning at gaze as he entered; in fact, the apartment seemed full of people to Desmond, coming into an unaccustomed entourage from the brighter light without. It was a moment or two before his dazed sight disintegrated the group. Most of the party were sipping tea, as they stood about, their whips under their arms, for they were in riding costume. Two ladies sat chatting in the high-backed antique chairs on either side of the fire. A little beyond, in a deep bay-window, was a tea-table, a rich gleam of color with its choice ware and lustre of silver, where Mrs. Kentopp, in a blue-and-white striped silk tea-gown, long and flowing, was handling the sugar-tongs, while a tall, blond youth was holding out his cup toward her, apparently facetiously dickering for an extra lump. She suddenly caught sight of Desmond, and sent the sugar-bowl falling to the tray and scattering its treasures as she rose precipitately.

"There, now!" she exclaimed, "I said I heard horses' hoofs, and this greedy thing said I didn't,"—for the young man had possessed himself of the tongs and was sweetening his tea to his own taste. "I can't hear the phaeton's wheels for the rubber tires."

She swept toward Desmond, the skirt of her gown trailing behind her, and the white lace which veiled its front from yoke to hem all shimmering above the broad blue-and-white stripes of the silk foundation. "Mr. Desmond," she cried, "how good of you to come!" She pressed his hand cordially, and turned about to the group with her most coquettish air, her fluffy flaxen curls above her forehead somewhat more deeply tinted in the glow of the fire and the light through the ruby "jewels" of the stained glass window. "This is the Mr. Desmond with whom we all fell in love over at Great Oaks," she exclaimed joyously.

"Is it the regulation thing to fall in love with Mr. Desmond?" one of the young ladies asked, as Mrs. Kentopp, having concluded her flaring collective introduction, began to mention the names of the guests nearest at hand.

Miss Allandyce was standing beside the tall newel-post, and he noted in surprise that she wore the dark cloth "cross-saddle riding-breeches" affected by progressive horsewomen, with boots to the knee and a riding-coat, in lieu of the habit in which he was accustomed to see fair equestrians. The costume was not utterly unknown to his observation, but never should he have expected to see it here, and affected by a lady with the unmistakable southern accent. She was tall and thin, though of a large frame, and wore her masculine gear as successfully as a big, bony boy might have done. She was not without charm; her gauntleted hands were small, her boots were shapely and slender and displayed a high instep. She had a Derby hat in one hand, while she held her crop under her arm, and nibbled at a sandwich from the other. She had a fair, frank, freckled face; her auburn hair was packed high on her head to be well out of the way of the Derby, and amidst the mass two or three fleecy short curls escaped from a richly tinted tortoise-shell comb. She seemed much at ease, and moved about with great freedom among the petticoats, though there was no other costume similar to her attire. The delusive draperies of a divided skirt, which one of the party wore, came to the floor, and were even fuller and much less graceful than the familiar riding-habit of the girl who sat upon the step, and who was of the type so usual in that country,—the woman who looks like a white rose, with dark eyes and hair and very fair, delicate skin; who spends the summer-time resting indoors, with a novel, taking care of her complexion; who would as soon consign herself and her complexion to Tophet as bathe in the sea, or climb a mountain, or walk out without a veil or a mask of chamois after April. She had an oval face, her lips were red, and her high silk hat had all the chic which the contrast with exceeding femininity is expected to afford.

"Can I bow upward?" she asked, with a ripple of lazy laughter. "Is it polite to bow when you are sitting on the floor?"

"You are perfectly horrid, Gertie,—the idea of pretending to be so worn out as all that by a little horseback exercise!" Mrs. Kentopp declared, with an assumed air of pettish displeasure. "Please don't speak to Miss Kelvin, I beg of you, Mr. Desmond. Remember that I haven't introduced you."

"I am saving up for the dance this evening, Mr. Desmond," the young lady declared. "You ought to be glad that you did not get here in time for the drag-hunt. We have had a run after an old bag, that we made believe was a fox,—and I never knew before how many bones I had to ache."

"Would you ache any less if you had had a fox instead of an anise-seed bag?" Mrs. Kentopp reproached her. "Let me give you some tea, Mr. Desmond"; and with all her silken train a-flutter she whisked back to the tea-table.

"Yes, indeed,—glory would have sustained me," Gertrude Kelvin declared. "I was ahead of the hounds, Mr. Desmond," she protested, still in her soft collapse on the lowest step of the stairs. "The field was nowhere. I can't say that I was in at the death, for there was nothing to die; but if I could have had the brush, I should have been forever happy. Nobody could call me lazy any more! I can't say that I captured the bag—Is that sportsmanlike, Mr. Desmond?"

"Did the hounds run well?" asked Desmond, seeking to seem interested, now equipped with a cup of tea and a sandwich, and free to stand about at a distance from Mrs. Kentopp.

"Oh,—they did that!" exclaimed Miss Gertrude Kelvin, wagging her head and widening her eyes to express great speed; "and I was in—with the bag to hold!"

"Oh, the hounds make me mad,—they are so easily deceived! I hate a fool!" Miss Allandyce came up in a gentlemanly fashion near Desmond and Miss Kelvin, looking down at that young lady, who was secretly a bit out of countenance at her proximity in this novel attire. She said no more, and Miss Allandyce went on presently, moving one of her handsome feet with a heel and toe alternation, to which she was accustomed with her skirts, but which now had a style of brazen indifference in the mind of the young lady clumped up in her habit at the foot of the stairs. "It is a pretty good pack, though."

"Colonel Kentopp's kennels, or do they belong to a neighborhood hunt?" asked Desmond.

Both girls opened wide eyes to horrify and impress him.

"Neither!" replied Miss Kelvin, significantly.

"Isn't that ridiculous?" exclaimed the strong-minded Allandyce, whirling half around on her heel. "The pack belongs to an old wood-chopper named Sloper,—and 'the quality' *borrow* his dogs."

"Isn't that low?" Miss Kelvin cast up her dark eyes from her humble posture. "*He* is all right—for a wood-chopper! Is he Irish,—or Scotch? He has a queer accent."

"Plain Mississippi,—without any foreign frills," replied Miss Allandyce.

"He lives all alone,—got no relatives,—and keeps such a lot of dogs for company, he says. They are just friends of his,—guests, a permanent house-party, and oh!—think of it!—when they all ask together to be helped first at breakfast."

"And the neighborhood planters object to it, for he won't take a cent, and they don't want him in the run; but if they borrow his dogs, they have to invite him and treat him as a guest for the time being. So about a year ago they thought they would make up a good pack—" explained Miss Allandyce.

"Went at it in great style—" interpolated Miss Kelvin.

"Imported dogs,—English—"

"Colonel Kentopp bought some beauties—"

"Great price—"

"Oh,—oo—oo—!" said Miss Kelvin, but beyond that enigmatic syllable she could not express her sentiments.

"Oh,—oo—oo!" echoed Miss Allandyce.

Their eyes filled with tears of laughter, as one looked down and the other looked up.

"Well, how did they run?" asked Desmond.

Miss Kelvin in her lowly posture took refuge in the safety of silence. She began to manifest renewed interest in her sandwich, and proceeded to eat it up on both sides of its bit of encircling ribbon.

Perhaps even the assumption of manly attire imparts a degree of courage. Miss Allandyce chose a bolder course. She walked first to the tea-table and put down her cup,—Desmond realizing too late that the influence of her boyish aspect had prevented him from offering that service. As she came back, her Derby in her hand and flecking her boots with her riding-whip, she looked over her shoulder once or twice to make sure of Mrs. Kentopp's distance. Then she said: "I'll tell you, but you must never mention it to her, and above all things never to the colonel,—he is a sweet dear and I love him! His English hounds ran like fun; they gave tongue like a bell,—the most mellow, searching, thrilling, musical sound you ever heard,—and the first staked-and-ridered rail fence they came to—"

"They could as easily have climbed a tree, the poor foreigners!" giggled Miss Kelvin, sly in her corner.

"Such a fence as our swamp dogs would just scramble over," explained Miss Allandyce; "but the imported English hounds ran hither and thither, squeaking and wheezing, and Colonel Kentopp—"

"They say his language was awful!"—Miss Kelvin had crumpled herself up very small.

"I never see him so decorous in church without thinking of it," said Miss Allandyce, and the two exchanged a glance of extreme relish.

"The hounds climbed the fence at last?" asked Desmond, impatient for the sequel.

There was a moment of silent and speechless mirth. Then Miss Allandyce said, in a husky voice and with eyes full of tears, "Colonel Kentopp and the huntsman dismounted and *lifted* the imported English hounds over the fence,—and by that time the fox had run to Issaquena County!"

"Why, what a gay time you are having over there! What's the fun? Don't keep the joke to yourselves," called out Mrs. Kentopp, in the midst of their laughter. But she did not approach the group, and presently the two recovered their composure.

"I wonder,—I have often wondered what did ever become of those imported hounds," speculated Miss Allandyce.

"Perfect dears, too."

"So handsome! But they were seen here no more, and whenever 'the quality' have a run, they borrow old man Sloper's house-party, and put the old wood-chopper up on as good a horse as there is in the county."

"They don't indulge in riding to hounds about Great Oaks, do they, Mr. Desmond?" asked Miss Kelvin, still resting her bones.

"Not since I have been there," replied Desmond.

"How long will you be at Great Oaks?" asked Miss Allandyce.

"Why, I hardly know," replied Desmond, slightly embarrassed.

"Oh, they make it so delightful to guests, I don't wonder you can't say when you will get your visit out," Miss Kelvin remarked.

A sudden illumination broke in upon Desmond's mind. Mrs. Kentopp had not acquainted her house-party with their fellow guest's vocation.

"But I am not a guest at Great Oaks," said Desmond, quickly. "I am the tutor."

An appalled astonishment was on the face of both young girls for an instant. Miss Kelvin remained silent, but Miss Allandyce rejoined in a tone which obviously sought to keep the key of the previous chat, "Oh, yes,—Mrs. Faurie has three children,—what a charming household it is there!" Then she drew a tiny watch from her fob and said in a low tone to Miss Kelvin: "I wonder that Mrs. Kentopp doesn't let us go and dress. I shall be a fright if I don't have at least an hour."

"We have to dance, too, in our dinner-gowns," Miss Kelvin murmured a trifle absently.

Desmond silently upbraided his folly in yielding to the insistence that had brought him here. Despite his gentle breeding, the position of his family, the opportunities of wealth that he had hitherto enjoyed, his culture, he felt that he was at a disadvantage in general society. His poverty, his station as a private tutor,—to small boys, mere children,—rendered his presence an incongruity among frivolous people who could not know and could not appreciate him fairly. He had no opportunity to make his value and quality felt. It was only in some cultured coterie capable of going deeper than the shallow appraisement of fashion that he could ever hope to find again his level. He could not forgive himself that he had laid himself liable to this misapprehension, and for his life he could not imagine why Mrs. Kentopp had given her guests no intimation of his position, to avoid such a contretemps as he had encountered. For their own sake, and for hers, they would have been civil in any event. Had she intended to pass him off as a man of their world, of wealth and leisure and luxury? And why, indeed? For his own part he had no desire to pose in a guise that must coerce their respect. But the malapropos incident had made him feel out of place, as if he were a presuming aspirant, patronized by the Kentopps, and foisted upon their guests' society without warrant. Neither of the young ladies had spoken again, both apparently absorbed in their eagerness to be off to dress, and the negligence of Mrs. Kentopp, still flirting at the tea-table, to give them the opportunity.

Suddenly Colonel Kentopp entered and rushed forward with an enthusiastic extended hand. "Why, my dear sir," he exclaimed heartily, "I didn't know that you had yet arrived. Glad to see you! How well you are looking! The sight of you is good for sore eyes." His left hand had crept up to Desmond's shoulder, which he patted affectionately as he spoke. "Wish you could have been with us on the run to-day,—great time!—But what are you all dawdling around here for? It is time to dress for dinner. The Mayberrys and Timlocks will be here long before you are ready. Joyce, keep those sweet nothings that you are whispering into my spouse's ear for a season of more leisure." And he advanced upon the tea-table, where Mrs. Kentopp was mildly carousing, so to speak, in a flirtation with a man almost young enough to have been her own son. She broke out into a peal of her affected, coquettish laughter, and Desmond in their midst looked on with as unresponsive a pulse, with as alien and unrelated a mien, as if among some mystic crew of Comus.

CHAPTER VIII

The room to which Desmond was assigned was never intended for an unimportant guest. As he looked about him, he could not understand the incongruity. The Kentopps were neither of them such people as value a man for his own sake, regardless of wealth or station; they had no fine perceptions that could discriminate the higher attributes; they were devoid of that gift of generosity which belittles self to make the more of greater worth; they could not even understand a lofty poise of mind, and it amazed him that they should seem to strain after it,—to ignore the trivial incident of the vital fact.

It was a spacious, airy apartment at one of the corners of the building, and the sharp angle was decorated with a dainty oriel window, though large enough to hold a fauteuil, a writing-desk, and a shelf of books; from this outlook one might see down a deep bosky dell artificially beautified, with a tangle of vines and interlacing shrubs, amongst which was visible here and there an elusive face, with the pointed ears of the fauns and elves of garden statuary. There were no trees of tall growth, and hence he caught a repeated glimpse of jets of leaping water among the leafage, and in the stillness he could hear the splashing of a fountain. At the end of a pleached alley was a rustic pavilion, evidenced by its conical roof, and in the opposite direction a life-size figure in marble on a pedestal had suggestions befitting the classic ideal of sylvan nymphs. The new fad of an old dial was illustrated in a shadowy nook where the sun might make scant register of time. This, Desmond was sure, was the "dene" which gave the place its name. The preciousness of its design affronted him, despite its prettiness. In his unconsciousness he did no homage to the ingenuity of Kentopp, who, after the burning of his simple farmhouse, inherited from his father, at the other end of the place, had utilized this desirable building-site despite the proximity of an old "bear wallow,"—the swampy depression thus drained, civilized, and made ornamental and even poetic. Any declivity or acclivity was rare in this level region, and the "dene" was greatly admired; its original status was wholly forgotten in the success of the landscape gardener's achievement, save when some blunt yeoman neighbor sought a rift in the armor of the Kentopps' satisfaction and the relish of a crude joke by directing a note or other paper-writing to "Kentopp Bear Wallow" instead of "Dryad-Dene."

As Desmond turned from the window and again surveyed the room, he was struck anew by the elaborate aspect of its appointments. A reclining-chair invited to lounging, with foot-rest and book-holder. There was the daintiest of toilet tables draped with lace, instead of the heavy old mahogany bureau such as the gentry of Deepwater Bend were accustomed to use; and in place of the immemorial mahogany four-poster was a brass bedstead, also canopied and covered with lace, and furnished with a duvet of delicate, embroidered blue silk. The polished floor had rugs in which this azure hue predominated; an open door gave on a bath-room tiled in blue and white, and the cut-glass candlesticks among the other crystal accessories of the toilet table held faint blue wax tapers,—never intended for use, however, for a flood of gas-light illumined the room, and made his preparations an easy matter, in contrast with the usual labors of dressing in the country for a festive occasion by the light of a kerosene lamp, however decorated.

Desmond had earlier experienced a natural youthful gratulation that his evening clothes, relic of his London visit the previous June, seeming a thousand years ago and in a different state of existence, were so fresh and unworn, and a specially handsome garb. He could at least appear to personal advantage and be no discredit to his entertainers. Now he did not care! He fretfully adjusted the diamond studs, a gift that he had not parted with in all the exigencies of the financial stress he had known, and the choice and fine sleeve-links, also mementos of happier days. He would as soon wear jeans, he said to himself, as he stood, tall and conspicuously imposing, before the long mirror, tying his cravat with a touch that grudged its practiced deftness, for in his undergraduate days he had been something of a dude, despite the roughening influences of the "Gridiron." He called out in a peremptory tone when a tap fell upon the door, and as it opened admitting a young gentleman, one of the guests of the house, the leisurely drawl with which he entered upon his mission received an impetus from the imperious gravity and challenge of the eyes fixed upon him.

"Mrs. Kentopp requested that as I was going by—Great Scott! they do you immensely proud." He was young, and blond, and of slight figure, and had already a tendency to baldness. He was not tall, but very erect, deported himself with conscious chic, and spoke with a superficial, negligent enunciation. It was with an air of surprised amusement that he paused to look about the room. "They haven't put me up half so fine. I feel slighted," with an airy laugh. "Well,—Mrs. Kentopp asked that as I was going by I would stop for you, to—to"—he was beginning to feel the influence of Desmond's eyes—"to show you where the drawing-rooms are located."

"Lest I should lose my way without chart or compass," Desmond commented.

"Well,—they seemed actually to try to twist things when this house was planned,—nothing is where you would expect to find it," said Mr. Herndon.

"I am beholden to you, then, for towing me to a safe harbor," said Desmond.

Young Herndon had recovered his equanimity. "Kentopp is such an incorrigible dawdle that she dare not trust him. But I have a special virtue of promptness,—among my many other virtues. My friends say that I will die some day twenty minutes before my time comes."

Notwithstanding this vaunted promptitude, there were several gentlemen already in the large drawinging-rooms when the two entered. The glitter of gas and crystal from the chandeliers, the gloss of the floors, the richness of the oriental rugs, the gilded chairs and sofas, upholstered in cream and terra-cotta satin brocade, the glow, deep yet delicate, of costly pictures, the scattered ornaments, vases of Venetian glass and choice porcelain, tall urns of Persian ware, Chinese curios in carved ivory,—there was not a suggestion of home but the great fire blazing behind a brass fender and andirons, and this was so bedizened by a modern "high-art" mantel, that the leaping hickory flames had much ado to make the domestic note heard in the bizarre medley; and indeed the fire itself was a mere matter of ornament, for the house was heated by a furnace fed by Pittsburgh coal, even more convenient in this riparian locality than wood which must be hewn, and incredibly cheap by reason of the low rates of water-carriage as compared with railway freightage. Neither of the Kentopps had yet appeared, and as Desmond entered the room, though maintaining his manner of proud composure, he was grateful for the fact. Their overwhelming cordiality daunted him in the realization of its superficiality. He fumbled vainly for his identity in the midst of their soft deceits and unimagined intention, beyond his ken, but unmistakable. He could meet their guests, to whom he was not even conventionally beholden, on a level as man to man, and he would make no concessions. He would maintain his sense of his own dignity.

In the sensitiveness and self-consciousness incident to an unaccustomed and in a degree a false position, he did not reflect that beyond his name he was wholly unknown to the party, and that the momentary interval after his appearance was instinct only with uncertainty and a preliminary effort to "place him" in evolving some suitable phrase introductory to conversation with a stranger. He interpreted the silence as cool, critical, not to say supercilious, and he had no mind humbly to await his adjustment to such place in the coterie as the sense of the meeting, so to speak, might consign him. He walked to one side of the hearth, and stood for a moment as if in contemplation of the group. Then singling out one, a man of mature years, conventional of aspect, with a long, thin face and a most unenthusiastic expression, he remarked, "I think I have not met you earlier."

"And what of that?" was in the countenance of all the amazed group, as Desmond held the centre of the stage,—even in the impassive, wooden countenance of the gentleman whom he had addressed.

"Mr. Loring, Mr. Desmond." The youthful Herndon was no reluctant scholar; as he often remarked, when he had had a thing demonstrated to him forty thousand times, he had learned it. He had now mastered the fact that the tutor, for whatever reason placed in the position of Colonel Kentopp's guest, was by no means disposed to interpret this as patronage, nor to capitulate to good-fellowship on anything short of the full honors of war. "Mr. Loring has just arrived," Herndon further explained.

As they shook hands Desmond's next remark brought a sudden gleam of expression into the wooden grooves of Mr. Loring's immobile face. "I have heard you mentioned at Great Oaks Plantation," he said, recalling vaguely Mrs. Faurie's account of the dilatory methods of the prospective purchaser of Dryad-Dene.

"Great Oaks? Are you visiting at Great Oaks? Charming old place."

"I am living there. I am the tutor of the Faurie boys."

Mr. Loring could not control the surprise in his face, for this princely presence was not to his mind the way the tutor of unlicked cubs should look. It was no intentional discourtesy, for he said with more animation than an article so apparently manufactured might be expected to show: "Do you intend to make teaching your regular profession?" He could but think that there must be something unexplained. This was some friend of the Fauries, perhaps taking a pose for a freak; there was some lure that had induced a pretended lodging in a humble position at Great Oaks.

"My present intention,—certainly."

Nevertheless, Mr. Loring did not for one moment relegate this imposing personage to the situation of a mere pedagogic drudge for small boys, because, if it were true, what did he here? The Fauries, with their ancient traditions and high standards, might annul and obliterate all worldly differences in their intercourse with a poor gentleman, refined and intellectual, but never the recent and purse-proud Kentopps.

And here suddenly they both were, overflowing with cordial greetings and exclamatory apologies and with elaborate rustlings and bows. Colonel Kentopp showed such a glittering expanse of white shirt front over his broad bosom that the sight of so much linen suggested undress; and his wife showed so much collar-bone and sternum independent of fabric and almost of flesh that she suggested no dress at all. She wore, however, a ruby-tinted brocade, and a fine pendant of rubies and diamonds swung from a delicate chain about her throat. Her hair had a deeper hue of blondine than usual, and she wore in it a cluster of ruby-tinted ostrich tips, at the base of which a very large diamond scintillated.

But diamonds were all at a discount in comparison with those that glimmered like dewdrops in the dark masses of Gertrude Kelvin's hair. They were not many nor of great size, but they were set artfully to quiver and glitter at every movement of her head, and the midnight of her hair gave them a stellular brilliancy. She was attired in a gown of delicate green tissue over silk of the same shade, and the exquisite whiteness of her shoulders and arms and face, heightened by the dainty tint of the dress, seemed worth some deprivation of the garish light of the summer sun and outdoor joys.

"Come, Mr. Desmond, you will take out Miss Kelvin," said Mrs. Kentopp, busied in arranging her party. Then in an aside to Mr. Loring behind her fan of ruby-tinted ostrich plumes: "He was just dying with suspense!" She played her blue eyes at him significantly, and Mr. Loring was thus given to understand that Mr. Desmond's lure in Deepwater Bend was Miss Kelvin.

"But how old man Kelvin will cut up if there is really no money," he thought sagely.

In slow and stately wise they filed out in couples to the dining-room; and even if the predilections of Mr. Loring were already engaged by the traditions of the *ancien régime*, he must needs have admitted to himself that the entourage at Dryad-Dene was most attractive, embellished by this glittering company, which set off the house in its gala aspect to the greatest advantage.

The dining-room was large, and its appointments betokened that its owners gave serious heed to the problems and the pleasures of the table. "My house was built around my refrigerator," Mrs. Kentopp was fond of saying; and Colonel Kentopp might have added, with a significance not altogether literal, that his house was built over his cellar. For the Kentopps, though not sages of wisdom, were quite indisposed to depend largely upon the attractions of their personality and the feast of reason and the flow of soul to commend their entertainments. The wines were choice and had been long in bottle, and distance and inaccessibility worked no impairment upon the menu. All the delicacies of the season, and many out of season, graced the successive courses, and the decorations of rare exotics—the spring flowers were left to bloom in their thousands out-of-doors—had indeed scant affinity with the backwoods.

"These are from our own hothouses," Mrs. Kentopp was saying, in reply to a comment. "Yes,—we have the world at command at Dryad-Dene. This is the newly discovered site of the Garden of Eden, between the waters of the Mississippi and Bogue Humma-Echeto; they used to be called the Pishon and the Gihon rivers, you know." She held her head down and looked up under the rims of her eyelids to emphasize the felicity of her remark. "If there is any little item that we haven't got, the Mississippi River on one side and the railroad on the other will bring it to us."

Mr. Loring sat at her right hand and was subject to all her beguilements. Opposite at a little distance was Desmond, between Miss Kelvin and Miss Allandyce, with Herndon on the farther side. Desmond had been presented to the Mayberry and Timlock contingent, but he had taken only a vague impression of pink and blue draperies and blonde hair and roseate smiles, with the usual complement of attendant cavaliers; for in the place to which he had been assigned he was absorbed in an effort, more or less successful, to explain to Miss Allandyce a reason for not recognizing her that should be something less blunt than the statement that her riding-costume had quite disguised her at their earlier meeting in the afternoon.

"I have heard that the cultivation of the powers of memory is considered important in modern education," she twitted him. "I should think your pedagogical laurels would wilt after this. How can you urge upon Chub Faurie the value of such discipline of the faculty of—of—"

"Observation," suggested Miss Kelvin, on his other hand.

"Yes,—observation and—and tabulation of traits as to enable you to recognize an object—"

"In the landscape—" prompted Miss Kelvin.

"Yes—in the landscape—an object with a red head, after the lapse of an interval of time,—an hour, say—"

"Arithmetically, sixty minutes, to be exact," Miss Kelvin urged her on.

Desmond had no sense of amusement as he realized that he had tabulated her equestrian garb in his mind and would never forget it. The predicament he was in was far too critical for that. He made a gallant struggle for a diversion of interest. "I saw no object with a red head," he stipulated. "I should never tabulate it as red, but auburn."

"Then you would be most discourteous; for red heads are very fashionable, and mine is treated with chemicals at stated intervals to make it seem redder than it is," she said gravely, assuming an air of staid and offended decorum.

He wondered in his desperation whether it would be permissible to tell her frankly that she was not half so gentlemanly in her gown of white silk. A necklace of seed pearls of fantastic device hung about her delicate white neck. Her short sleeves had a fall of lace that met the tops of her long white kid gloves, which she had slipped off her hands without disturbing the upper section, tucking the fingers beneath her bracelets. She wore a comb of seed pearls in her auburn hair, and she looked very handsome. He had an idea, curious enough to him, that she did not in the least grasp the reason of his failure to recognize her, his apparent lapse of memory, but that Miss Kelvin had divined it in an instant, and had a mischievous delight in his plight. Although Miss Kelvin would not have alluded to the riding-costume her friend affected,—for she thought it a horrifying, strong-minded notion, worthy of the woman who wants to vote, who engages in business, who preaches, who practices medicine and law, and its adoption by a southerner an apostasy, abominably uncharacteristic,—her eyes dwelt upon him with a luminous mirth, and now and then, as she caught his glance, she burst into a ripple of involuntary laughter.

Her recurrent observation of him, her smiles in response to his glance as oysters and soup, and fish and entrée, successively filed past him, almost untouched, were remarked by Mr. Loring, and these apparently tender passages between the two were interpreted to further Mrs. Kentopp's plan even more than she had anticipated. She had expected to artfully give Mr. Loring such an idea of mutual interest as their propinquity might suggest, aided by some crafty phrases of her own. But she had not dared to hope for these bright glances from Gertrude, for her half-suppressed delighted laughter, for the attitude of the girl, leaning half across Desmond to whisper and prompt Miss Allandyce to further jocose upbraidings of the mischance. Gertrude seemed, indeed, throwing herself at his head; and to her demonstration he ardently responded, now and again turning to take her counsel in a low voice how he might best plead his excuses, often misadvised to his detriment and setting Selina Allandyce off on a new score of rebukes and reproaches. For they found the tutor great fun. After the first shock of disappointment, they resigned themselves with a good grace to his impecunious state and ineligibility. He was too handsome a man to view with indifference, and too interesting, for his manner attracted no less than his presence. There was something, too, below the surface of his talk, and while they did not discriminate its quality, they were aware of its submergence there.

As the gay chat grew in interest and animation, Mrs. Kentopp in her elation could not leave the aspect of the trio to produce its own impression; she must needs give it a nudge.

"Love's young dream," she murmured sentimentally to Mr. Loring, her head held down, the iris of her eyes under the upper lids. "'There's nothing half so sweet in life.'"

Mr. Loring for some time had seemed quite attentive to the champagne and the roast, but he was not altogether absorbed.

"Not so young, I take it, as far as the gentleman is concerned," he replied discerningly.

"Oh,—oh,"—Mrs. Kentopp could hardly contradict this conclusion fast enough. "Why, *he* is just a boy,—a collegian,—graduated last June,—just twenty-four."

"Rather old for a collegian," commented Mr. Loring, dryly.

"Took a very elaborate course, all sorts of elective extras as well as the regular curriculum. Has a degree from *two* great universities."

"One is more than enough," sneered Mr. Loring, who had matriculated with much brilliancy on 'Change.

"Oh, yes,—he is a mere boy!" Mrs. Kentopp emphasized her insistence.

"He looks fully thirty," said Mr. Loring, wondering why olives were not always "pitted,"—otherwise it seemed more decent to swallow the pits, if the possibilities of appendicitis did not hinder.

"Oh, he has had so much sorrow,"—and Mrs. Kentopp conjured an appealing sadness into her eyes and shook her flaxen head as she bent it to look down in token of sympathetic woe.

"Hasn't turned his hair gray," said Mr. Loring. "He is the finest-looking man I ever saw."

"Oh, do you think so?" asked Mrs. Kentopp, with a surprised and negative tendency.

"Certainly; he has a noble head, and a very fine and impressive face. They must be long on looks at Great Oaks. I always thought Mrs. Faurie the most beautiful woman in the world."

"'The most beautiful woman in the world!'"—one of the Mayberry group caught the words and tossed them back. "I know just whom you are talking about."

The attention became concentrated. Mrs. Kentopp sought to divert it. "I want you to observe the mould of the sorbet," she interrupted, bespeaking notice for the red ices. "Somebody said that this looks like a melon and ought not to be striped this deep red. Do you think it is a melon?"

"Why, no," said Desmond. "It is a pomegranate."

"There,—what did I tell you?" She clapped her hands in juvenile glee, as she spoke across the length of the table to her husband.

"The first time I ever tasted a real pomegranate was down at Great Oaks," said Miss Mayberry. "They have them in their old-fashioned garden yet. You have got the flavor, too," she added, as she daintily tasted the ice.

"And who do you say is the most beautiful woman in the world?" queried Mr. Loring, his inelastic countenance reluctantly crinkling in his smile, sure of her answer.

"Mrs. Faurie, of course! I have always heard her called that, and everywhere as well as at home. I remember when we were at Vevey we met some Italians,—high-class people who knew the Berkeleys,—oh, they were very agreeable,—and one day we were talking at random of pictures and pose and elements of beauty, and one of the gentlemen, who was quite an art connoisseur, said that he believed he knew the most beautiful woman in all the world. He had met her in Chamouni, doing Mont Blanc, and that sort of thing; and when he said that she lived in Paris, Madame Honoria Faurie, we all screamed! He didn't even know that she was an American."

"But she has gone off a good deal in her looks of late," Mrs. Kentopp suggested.

"I hoped that I would meet her here to-night," said Mr. Loring, without even ordinary tact; everything connected with Great Oaks, the embodiment of his ideal, for which his soul sighed, was interesting to him. "Is Mrs. Faurie not well?" He fixed his eyes on Desmond and asked the question directly across the table.

"Oh, yes,—quite well," Desmond replied, a trifle embarrassed.

There was a pause. The general attention was apparently required by the game course, which was just being served. The inference was too plain. Mrs. Faurie, it seemed, had not cared to honor the diversion at Dryad-Dene with the distinction of her presence. For who could imagine Mrs. Kentopp's purblind folly in failing to invite her!

The tact of all the party seemed to have suffered a collapse. "I suppose that Mrs. Faurie has gone so much, and seen so much, and had so much, that she does not care for our neighborhood gatherings," said Gertrude Kelvin at length.

"She finds Great Oaks as dull as the grave," snapped Mrs. Kentopp, the pendulous tendency of her cheeks reasserted without the dimpling breadth of laughter. "Doesn't she, Mr. Desmond?"

He was a little at a loss. "She complains of its monotony," he said.

"The idea!" exclaimed Mr. Loring, indignantly; "one of the finest places in the whole Mississippi River country. From Memphis to the Balize you couldn't find its superior. To my mind it is the loveliest place I ever saw. I wish it was mine! Monotony! I'd like to own that kind of monotony."

From the foot of the table Colonel Kentopp, in all his pose of geniality, with his glass of Chambertin in his hand, lowered upon Mrs. Kentopp.

The woman rallied first from the contretemps. "The land I know is fine and there is a deal of it, and the outbuildings are good and stanch, but the old mansion is a rattle-trap,—so out of repair, and built on any kind of an old plan. It has no style about it, no modern improvements and embellishments and—"

"It simply crystallizes the past," Mr. Loring declared solemnly. "It is an epitome of the old South,—its comfort, its space, its disregard of ostentation; its broad acres about it can keep the tally of its values; it takes you back a hundred years; it has yesterday in every line. I wish it was mine!"

He talked on and on, the taciturn man, over the salad and the sweets, the theme unvaried, throughout the service of the dessert with the notable ancient Madeira, till at last his voice was lost in a silken rustle. Mrs. Kentopp had given the signal for rising, and the young girls were presently flitting along the big square hall, still visible from the dining-room, making a picture that enhanced the charming setting which should have appealed to any man with an eye for beauty, who did not cultivate a distorted squint backward toward the exploded past instead of the sophisticated present.

The ballroom was in the third story,—another intimation of the intensely modern spirit of Dryad-Dene. There was all out-of-doors to build on, and surely there was scant reason to economize space when the value of land was contemplated by the quarter section instead of the running foot. The destined use and cost of building materials alone might limit the size of any structure in Deepwater Bend. But though there was no need to climb stairs, there was much that was picturesque in this airy ballroom, and it was indeed a great contrast to the long, low wing devoted to the same purpose at Great Oaks, with its green shutters closed, the spiders weaving in the corners, and the wide, smooth spaces of its polished flooring devoted to the humble purposes of miscellaneous storage; for there was not a dance at Great Oaks mansion in all the quiet years while Mrs. Faurie had been the admired cynosure in palatial assemblages in many foreign capitals.

Here the decorated ceiling had a fine pitch, and all the architectural embellishments of the house below culminated on this level; the cupola of the tower gave a circular alcove to the ballroom, and on the opposite side the French windows issued upon a long, flat roof that, furnished with a balustrade, offered a charming promenade between the waltzes for the young people under the white, palpitating stars and in close familiarity with the gentle night wind. It offered also every opportunity to the overheated dancers for pneumonia and influenza; but as they gave this fact no heed, it might scarcely be considered one of the choice advantages of the ballroom. The hothouses had sent hither their offering of palms and banana trees and ferns for a tasteful scheme of decoration, and an Italian band, brought up from New Orleans for the occasion, tossed lilting melodies from behind a leafy screen. The stringed vibrations found in Desmond's heart a thrilling response of poignant memory, reviving in contrast with the present all the happy past, the cherished prospects, the vanished faces, the hallowed home. But he was young, and his pulses were astir with vitality and vigor. The rhythm, the motion, the sweet, swinging melody, imparted their own jubilant effects, and he could but enjoy with his muscles all the buoyancy of his stalwart young frame, while with a curious duality his heart's sorrows were unassuaged and his mental indifference and aloofness were no self-deceit. It was perhaps the mental attitude of many a reveler in joyous scenes that awoke no sense of mirth, but it had no parallel among the dancers at Dryad-Dene. The young ladies were all a-weary of the dull season spent at the

103

abominated plantations; it was too late for New Orleans, being mid-Lent, indeed, and yet too early for the White Sulphur Springs or the Gulf coast.

"How delicious!" Gertrude Kelvin exclaimed. "I should have thought I had forgotten how to 'two-step,'—I have scarcely stood on my feet since Mardi-Gras." For it was with the charming white rose that Desmond found himself chiefly awhirl. He danced specially well, and more than once, as the music recommenced, she looked from a chatting group toward him, with so bright and expectant a smile that he was fain to ask the pleasure once more. And indeed it was no great constraint. She was as light, as airy, as poetic of movement, swinging as rhythmically as a blossom on a bough, with as little suggestion of effort. Her delicate green tissue draperies floated diaphanous in the breeze of their motion; her white arms and neck were fairer still in the moony gleams of the shades of the gas-jets; her ethereal pallor took on no unbecoming flush with the exertion; her movement was as devoid of the idea of fatigue as the flitting of a butterfly or the noiseless winging here and there of one of the white moths that, allured by the lights, came in, now and then, from out of the night. The sparkle of the diamonds in her hair flashed into his eyes occasionally as her head was poised so close to his shoulder, for she was tall despite her small and feminine ways, and they made a pretty couple to look at, as Mrs. Kentopp did not omit to point out to Mr. Loring when at length he came into the apartment.

He had been loitering at the table over Kentopp's good wine and fine cigars with his martyrized host, although the younger men had earlier joined the ladies, who had had coffee in the drawing-rooms, and together they had trooped up to the ballroom at the first long-drawn, plangent cadence of the violins. Mrs. Kentopp had a freshened, elated mien as she surveyed the scene, standing in the ballroom door beneath the vines of an elaborate hanging-basket, with the most feathery of trailing ferns, and plying her fan of ruby ostrich plumes, though she felt the cool breeze from the widely opened windows.

"A handsome couple; that will be a match," she commented, smiling sentimentally.

"No doubt,—no doubt," replied Mr. Loring. He smelled very strong of tobacco: when the cigars were mild, he smoked a good many of them. He was a self-made man, the architect of his own fortune,—a massive structure on which little ornament had been bestowed. He was apt to consider market prices, potential bargains, possible rebates, and equivalent values, even in social affairs, although his interest in social affairs scarcely seemed actively concerned with an adequate return for the outlay at present. He was bent upon enjoying his money, but he wanted the best article of pleasure that the market could afford. He saw an opportunity of richly rewarding himself at a very great bargain in buying one of the fine old estates in Deepwater

Bend far below its value in the shrunken estimates of post-bellum ratings, where he might retire to enjoy the pose of magnate and millionaire within a few miles of where he had been born of poor but eminently respectable parents. His father, who had been one of the subordinate clerks, "mud clerk" it was called in those days, on a steamboat, had secured for him by favor a place in the office of a broker in New Orleans, and stood amazed by the portentous growth of his scion in that hotbed of speculation. Loring felt always much at his ease, assumed to be as "good as anybody," yet he was very definitely aware that his consequence would be much enhanced in the neighborhood that he desired to dominate by the possession of one of the fine old places, at whose seigneurial splendor he had once gazed as at fairyland, without a thought of entrance. He had little sympathy with poverty,—it was never romantic, or picturesque, or appealing to him. Wealth had been his ambition, and wealth was now his admiration. His study was how to seem not less magnificently endowed than he really was with this world's goods. He was a bachelor, and could not express his riches in the splendor of a wife's equipment. He could not afford to marry when he would, and since he had been able to consult his wishes, he had lost the impulse toward domesticity. His eyes roamed over the charming scene of the decorated room, the whirling dancers, the dark blue night looking in with a myriad stars from the windows of balcony and long, railed promenade, with no fixity of interest and no undercurrent of sentiment.

"Yes," he reiterated, "no doubt it will be a match. Naturally, Mr. Desmond will recoup his disasters by marrying money."

For Mrs. Kentopp had effaced the dullness of his propinquity at table by talking much of Desmond. The matter just now nearest her heart was her scheme to divert Loring from the theory that Mrs. Faurie might become interested in the tutor, and she was sure that the peculiar quality of Desmond's personality would soon set such a rumor afloat, were it not forestalled by one more credible. Mrs. Kentopp was one of those women whose shallow minds are reflected in their talk. She could no more have kept a secret without a word to play about it than she could have emulated the Spartan boy and without a sign held the gnawing fox beneath her cloak. She would never give such an intimation of her plan that Loring might discover and rush in upon it; but she needs must chat of Desmond, his recent history, his father's death, the ensuing financial disasters, his relinquished career, the incongruity of his collegiate record with his humble position.

"Oh,—I didn't give you the idea that Mr. Desmond is a fortune-hunter, did I? Why, I wouldn't have you think that for the world!"

Mrs. Kentopp had a peculiar aversion to the character of a fortune-hunter. As a girl she had been rich in her own right, and Colonel Kentopp had not escaped the suspicion of a lively perception of the side on which his bread was buttered.

"Why not? Are we not all fortune-hunters?" demanded Mr. Loring, dryly. "What else do we hunt?"

"But not in that sense—a mercenary marriage! Oh, no!"

Mr. Loring had a touch of perversity, or perhaps Mrs. Kentopp, with her *arrière pensée* concerning the disinterestedness of her own marriage, had been heavy-handed enough to permit him to feel rebuked. "I can't look on Miss Gertrude Kelvin as such a hardship,—even if she would tack a tidy little fortune on to a wedding-ring," he retorted, his wooden countenance smiling satirically.

"Gertie? why, she is adorable!" cried Mrs. Kentopp, seeking in a frenzy to find her feet in this slough of misapprehension. "Any man would be too lucky to talk about to win her, even if she would not have a cent!"

"Just *my* opinion," said Mr. Loring, as if he had enforced its adoption. "But if Miss Kelvin has not enough money for our gentleman, perhaps his good looks, and his great learning," his lip curled cynically, for Mr. Loring was very short on the classics, "and his collegiate honors, and his interesting dumps and douleur over the fling that Fate has given him, might appeal to Mrs. Faurie,—she will give up that nice income some day for a life-interest in a third of the estate and a husband,—and the third will be a deal more money than our tutor will ever see otherwise."

Mrs. Kentopp suddenly felt a cold chill stealing up and down her spine, to which her dress, cut low and loose in the neck, left her liable. But it was not the inclemency of the wind! Her heart sank at this deliberate wording of the fear which her husband had evolved and she had adopted. If this idea were seriously entertained, the sale of Dryad-Dene was indeed a distant and doubtful prospect, for there were few investors able to compass a purchase of such magnitude, and fewer still with a disposition toward property of this character. And Dryad-Dene was not always gay like this. With half the rooms shut up, and the gilt and brocade furniture in hollands, and the visitors few and far between and always the same, and no excitement, and naught to do, and her eyes forever fixed on a house in New Orleans in the winter and a cottage on the coast in summer,—oh, Dryad-Dene was but a dreary imprisonment indeed in the depths of the backwoods! The crisis was so acute that it imparted to Mrs. Kentopp a touch of dignity.

"You forget, Mr. Loring, how very distasteful such a suggestion would be to Mrs. Faurie were she to hear of it. This man occupies a very humble position in her household,—a paid retainer,—not exactly like a courier—"

"Why no, indeed,—I should say not!" cried Mr. Loring, as indignant with this perversion of his suggestion as with its affront to the dignity of the tutor. "He is a gentleman, of fine family, and a learned man."

"So *I* said; but he *is* a paid and humble attaché of her household, and the idea that she could unbend to consider such a person, ten years her junior,—"

"*That* makes no difference," interrupted Mr. Loring, who took this schooling rather aversely.

"—And sacrifice her great income for a man so egregiously beneath her,—why, the suggestion is belittling, Mr. Loring."

"It is belittling to get rid of money, sure!—and she *may* hang on to her money yet," Mr. Loring conceded.

"Except that we are all so deadly dull down here and value any new face," she began once more.

"Especially such a handsome one," Mr. Loring stipulated, with a knowing grin.

"Yes,—and a dancing man, too."

Mr. Loring did not dance. At the period when he might have had the opportunity to learn the latest Terpsichorean quirks and kicks, he was absorbed in the saltatory vagaries of the stock market and the fandangoes of cotton futures.

"And there is always such a dearth of cavaliers that we have admitted him among us as one of ourselves. Otherwise and elsewhere, as you know, the tutor would be in his place in the schoolroom."

"*Though* a gentleman and a learned man!" sneered Loring.

"Yes,—and I hope that he may marry Gertie Kelvin, and get a chair in some good college, and one day be the president of it." Mrs. Kentopp benevolently smiled.

"And what will old John Kelvin be doing all that time?" asked Mr. Loring, with a sidewise twist of his mouth, of which his wooden face seemed incapable.

"Oh, Mr. Loring, in an argument you always vanquish me—Why, certainly, Mr. Herndon,—I am *dying* to waltz."

And thus, perhaps because she had the only blondined coiffure in the room, was considerably rouged, and floridly attired in her rich, ruby-tinted brocade, Fate maliciously decreed that she should dance with Mr. Herndon, the slightest of spindling young gentlemen, wan of face, thin of flaxen hair, of incipient involuntary tonsure, altogether pallid and fragile of effect by contrast with the artificially heightened charms of his partner, and together they furnished the aptest illustration of "before and after."

Mr. Loring still stood in the doorway, apparently casting the eye of appraisement over the festive scene. He was of so monetary a personality, of so speculative a reputation, that it was impossible to disassociate his presence with a deal. It had a certain incongruity and incompatibility with the remainder of the company, and even Mrs. Kentopp, who had not the most delicate perceptions of tact, was vaguely aware of this with an irritating subconsciousness as she whirled and whirled. She had hoped that, being a single man, Mr. Loring would be at once assimilated in the merry party as one of the beaux, and while she could count with security upon his conventional acceptance, on the footing at which she proposed him, by the well-bred young people, she had not reckoned upon the lack of malleability of Mr. Loring's own predilections in the matter. He was not one of them, he had no pulse in common, no affinity with their tastes, no social ambitions to which their warmth of reception might minister. He made no pretense of being a young man; he claimed naught of the courtesy that thus reckons one scarcely yet of middle age. He was not sensitive on the point; his record on 'Change kept the tally of the years, and he was proud of the events as they totted up. His age was known to people of more importance in his mind than these inexperienced girls just liberated from the schoolroom, and their cavaliers still with a lingering dependence on the paternal purse-strings. He had no response for the graceful coquetry of the young ladies, nor for the jejune opinions of the youths, financially mere cumberers of the ground, for he had no method of rating other than financial. He was too rich a man, too dominant, too self-centred and consciously important, to submit himself unnecessarily to boredom, and he had not that altruistic impulse of high social culture that would constrain him to sacrifice his preference for the sake of his hostess. Hence it pleased him to stand in isolation in the doorway, under the feathery fronds of the drooping ferns, and stare moodily, absently, silently, at the revolving dance, taking no part.

He was never intentionally frank, but the unavowed reason of his presence became very definitely outlined as the evening wore on, and Mr. Loring associated with every appearance of satisfaction with himself. Mrs. Kentopp, now and again, fluttered up to him and made a great show of talk, aided by a waving fan and upturned eyes, and he had then the grace to respond; but to Colonel Kentopp, who must needs sometimes take her place, he had not a word to throw. Being of a festive temperament and relishing the joyous occasion, the host was obviously a martyr, in the long intervals when he felt constrained to stand beside the wooden figure and ply him with artful talk, so constructed as to need no response other than the absent grunt or nod which Loring vouchsafed in recognition of his character as quasi-guest.

"'How doth the little busy bee improve each shining hour,'" quoted Gertrude Kelvin, as she and Desmond, breathless from the final whirls of the waltz, issued into the tower alcove to find already standing there, enjoying the breezes of the open space, Selina Allandyce and Rupert Regnan. He was a tall fellow, with an outdoor complexion suffused with a constant red flush, brightly glancing gray eyes, and dark hair. He had served in the Spanish War, and had acquired, besides the title of lieutenant, a military carriage which would be his proud possession for all time, and which added a certain stiff stateliness to his appearance in evening dress. His father, a veteran of another war, one of the Unreconstructed Rebels, was wont to look askance at him, tabooed his title at home, and had informed him that he could not set foot on the plantation while he wore a blue uniform. But the son cheerfully responded that he had shed the uniform when he had quitted the service, and that the title of lieutenant was too tight a fit for him,—he was out for bigger game! He had developed a sense of his own importance, and he now felt it jeopardized in some sort.

"What is that man here for, do you suppose?" he said to Miss Allandyce. The coterie was quite confidential in the restricted space, which, with the windows all open between the pilasters on three sides, seemed to poise them in the midst of the cool, dark night, the airy roof of the cupola above.

"For the same reason that you are here, I fancy,—for the pleasure and honor of your company," she responded, looking in the dim light very sweetly feminine in her white silk gown and her pearl-crowned auburn hair.

"But there isn't any pleasure in *his* company, I should judge from Colonel Kentopp's countenance, and I should judge from his own that he isn't disposed to confer any honor. I imagine that he has come to look at the house,—people say that he is going to buy it."

"You seem to object; are you a prospective purchaser, too?" Miss Kelvin twitted him with this incongruity in view of his youth and financial inexperience.

"I do object. I may be exacting, but it strikes me that this party was made up to give him an opportunity to see Dryad-Dene to the best advantage. I can't imagine what else he is doing here. He scarcely makes a feint toward the manner of a guest."

"And you object to dancing for a purpose,—how wrong! You know that the reproach of dancing is that it is at best but an idle amusement. You ought to be glad to convert it to some use."

"I object to being made use of without reference to my feelings," he protested, as he wagged a somewhat round and close-cropped head with an emphatic, not to say affronted air.

"And are you not willing to skip and leap like a young lamb to make Mr. Loring think this is a pretty house?"

"I am not! The pleasure of my company was requested, and I came to compliment my hosts, and to enjoy myself, and to see you all,"—he included the whole group with a bow,—"and to contribute my little possible to the general entertainment."

"And you are frustrated!" Gertrude Kelvin averred. "Now, if I were you, I'd take it all back; I'd cancel my services. I'd make the whole thing ridiculous. You ought to go right out there in the middle of the ballroom floor and throw a somersault! Then you would undo all that you have done."

"Oh, do it, Mr. Regnan,—or rather undo it!" cried Selina Allandyce.

He laughed, but did not stir.

"He's afraid!" Gertrude exclaimed. "You know that he must have been a coward in the Spanish War,—for see now, he's afraid."

"I'm sure that he ran at the battles,—I'd be willing to take my affidavit to it," Selina goaded him.

"It's a mere pretense that he got a presentation sword after the war—for he's *afraid*!" said Gertrude.

"He couldn't have got it for gallant conduct, for he's afraid!"

Regnan looked from one to the other, but only laughed.

"He is deceitful, too," Gertrude recommenced, "and he encourages deceit in others. He lets Mr. Loring accredit Dryad-Dene with all the chic and style of his presence—"

"And all the grace and agility of his waltzing," Selina interrupted.

"And all the bonhomie and sparkle of his conversation," Gertrude added.

"Oh, let up on me; I'll be good! I'll be good!" Regnan pleaded; but he made no saltatory intimations toward the required somersault.

"And all the distinction of his military record," persisted Gertrude.

"And all the prestige of his hereditary position," Selina supported her contention.

"And when Mr. Loring buys this house, the title-deeds will call for more than they cover,—oh, poor defrauded Mr. Loring!"

"But now, seriously,—" Regnan began.

"Seriously," Gertrude interrupted, "in fair dealing you ought to throw a somersault in the middle of the ballroom floor, in order that its lack of style and its grotesquerie and awkwardness, if *you* can make it awkward, may condone for your unwitting alacrity in palming off a house, entitled to none of your signal attractions, on Mr. Loring, who will pay a bonus for the grace your presence lends to it!"

"But now, seriously,— doesn't it seem to you that this is not an appropriate time to show off the house to a buyer?" Regnan appealed to Desmond. "I may be exacting, but yet—"

Desmond, who was aware that he himself was here for a purpose he could not fathom, had a monition of caution.

"Don't ask me; I am a stranger here, and—"

"Hesitate to express an opinion, of course. Well,—we are all old friends, and but that it might seem a disrespect to Mrs. Kentopp's feelings, and in so far uncivil, I should be willing to tax her with it myself."

The soft rustling of the treetops below in the bosky, benighted "dene" impinged upon the talk; the freshening breeze coursed through the tower, at this height inclosed only by the slight pilasters which upheld the conical roof. The sense of altitude, the vision of the lonely, starlit sky, and the dark, far-stretching wilderness on every side beyond the plantation clearings, were incongruous with the ballroom scene close at hand, the graceful figures promenading the glossy hard-wood floor with its mirror-like reflections. More akin was the romantic, languorous theme of the waltz, with a sort of melancholy yearning in its sentimental iteration, and presently a high-heeled white satin slipper was beginning to move unconsciously in rhythm as the quartette still stood in the tower together.

"If your scruples against adorning the premises of Mr. Loring's prospective purchase are not too great a restriction on this waltz," Desmond suggested to Miss Allandyce, with whom he had not danced hitherto.

"Oh, I repudiate the responsibility," she exclaimed. "I am neither the bargainer nor the bargainee, and Mr. Loring is popularly supposed to be able to take care of himself financially."

She had lifted her hand to Desmond's arm before they issued from the tower alcove, and as they came waltzing out of its seclusion together, Mr. Loring noted the change of partners. "He is making himself generally agreeable, and probably has no special idea of Miss Kelvin," he commented within himself. "There is no money in his line of business. If he marries it, of course he will marry all he can. He would be mighty well pleased with the Faurie third,—which maybe Madame Honoria's dukes and princes wouldn't look at after they had seen her flourishing around on the income of so much more."

Mrs. Kentopp's spirits were wilting; the lassitude of brain-fag was evident. She looked her thirty-eight years. Her cheeks were pendulous, so seldom did the distention incident to the redeeming smile visit them. She realized she had taken great pains to a doubtful end. She began to think that she might have better commended Dryad-Dene without the house-party. She could have managed Mr. Loring to greater advantage without its distractions. It had not made the excuse and occasion to get him here incidentally without obviously putting the house on parade. He assumed none of the pose and port of a guest. He seemed to consider that he was invited for business reasons only, and this doubtless suited his easy interpretations of the obligations imposed by hospitality as well. And why else should he have been invited? He was no friend of the Kentopps, and he had no desire to be friend of their friends. Why should they ask him here, save to show him the house to advantage? and to-morrow, on the camphunt, he would have every opportunity to see the land. The house certainly did appear to great advantage, but Mr. Loring was a discreet and discerning operator,—he could easily divest it of such attractions as were added to it by the fascinations of Mr. Regnan's two-step and Miss Kelvin's sylphine charms. He was appraising the woodwork, the quality of the plate-glass, the hand-carving on the newel-posts, with their long shafts holding up lily-like sprays of gas-jets. He condemned what he had learned to phrase as precious or Brummagem, and he regretted that it was all so new, so glossy, so like a fine hotel. He was ambitious of the pose of grand seigneur. He had now as much money as any one of the Mississippi princelings in the palmy days of the old plantation times. He coveted their entourage; it represented taste to him; wealth, family, culture, all the majesty of the magnate, as he rated the great in the world. A few modern conveniences kept as carefully as might be out of sight, a touch of modern frugality,—"I'd never throw away money with both hands like those old ducks,"—and this would comprise all the improvements that he thought would befit the domicile of eld. Still it was not to be had, and he addressed himself to contemplating the tower balcony, with the white-draped figures hanging on the balustrade, now gazing down into the dark shrubbery of the "dene," where the fountain splashed rhythmically, and now chatting with the cavaliers while the group discussed the delectable ices. Mr. Loring partook of his selection with a meditative mien. It was of a mint flavor and was stiffly laced with old Bourbon, and a long, fragrant sprig of the newly budded herb stood in the midst of the delicate glass. Very perfect were the beautifully served refreshments, with accessories of daintiest device; but he knew full well that he would not have command of Mrs. Kentopp's deft arrangements here if the house were his, for money itself could not buy good-will to equal her efforts in the interests of getting Dryad-Dene off on him. "Not even here will the larks fall all roasted into one's mouth." He remembered the old French proverb with a sardonic smile. He took no part in the outcry of protest with which, after one more entrancing waltz, the dancers greeted the strains of "Sleep well, Sweet Angel," wafted out from the leafy screen embowering the Italian orchestra, with which the dinner dance was obviously brought to a close.

Regnan followed Mrs. Kentopp here and there, insisting that she should look at his watch, which he had drawn from an inner pocket, and which marked but ten o'clock. She was doubtful for one moment; so little agreeable had she found the evening that she would not have been surprised to know that it had dragged as slowly as this witness maintained. Then she recognized the artifice.

"It is a gay deceiver,—just like you!" she cried. "But if you did but know at what unearthly time you will have to rise, you would have been off to bed long ago. I expect to hear that old swamper's halloo under the windows any moment, and the baying of his pack."

And so presently, reflected in the polished flooring, the procession wended its way through the ballroom and down the many turns of the elaborate staircase, pausing only once, at the first *entresol*, when Mrs. Kentopp called the attention of Mr. Loring to the electric button in the wall by means of which the gas-jets in the upper story were instantaneously extinguished, and the ballroom and the Mi-Carême dance were in a moment in the darkness of the past.

CHAPTER IX

It seemed indeed to Desmond that his head had scarcely touched the pillow when he was roused by the baying of hounds from the stable-yard at the rear of the house. He was on his feet in a moment, for Mr. Herndon did not monopolize the virtue of promptness at Dryad-Dene, and Desmond was zealously heedful that his distaste to the occasion and his entertainers should induce no breach of observance on his part. He was half dressed when the screech of the speaking-tube summoned him within the sound of Colonel Kentopp's voice, urgently asking if he were awake, then with equal urgency if he were risen,—which demonstrated that Colonel Kentopp's brain was not very completely cleared of the vapors of slumber.

Desmond arrayed himself in his equestrian togs, which he considered the most appropriate gear at his command, and finding the halls alight and following the sound of voices, he soon made his way to the dining-room, where a hasty breakfast was going forward.

"Just a snack," Colonel Kentopp was saying to the gentlemen seated at the table, or standing at the sideboard helping themselves to cold mutton or ham as they would. He himself seemed to be breakfasting on brandy, and he went around the table, decanter in hand, administering a nip here and there, willy-nilly, like the Squeers treacle.

"For the stomach's sake," he would insist to youths whose hearty young stomachs could with impunity have begun the day with ice-cold buttermilk. There was hot coffee, but no hot breads, and therefore, in Mississippi estimation, no breakfast. "We shall have a hot breakfast ready for us at the camp. We just want a snack here to enable us to get away. Those girls will be wild to go, and they couldn't keep the saddle half the distance."

"Why, Miss Kelvin rides as well as any man," said Rupert Regnan, displeased; "and Miss Allandyce—"

"Rides just like a man," Kentopp finished, with a laugh. "The truth is," he spoke mysteriously, "we expect a rough day. We hope to get up a bear, and it isn't safe to have ladies along in such a harum-scarum expedition. This is our last chance,—the game laws, you know. Monday is the first of March!"

There was a touch of the *preux chevalier* about Regnan. It was distasteful to him to sneak off and debar the young ladies of the pleasure they had set their hearts upon. If there had been any means of rousing them to the deceits practiced upon them, other than inappropriately appearing at their bedroom doors, he would have availed himself of it. What cared he for such stereotyped fun as was comprised in pulling through sloughs and cane-brakes with a lot of men after a bear, if one could be found! They were not of metropolitan life; the wilderness and its incidents were an every-day story; they were veritable "swampers," as much old "residenters" as the bear himself! Such amusement as the day might offer lay, to his mind, in the incongruity of feminine society, and the enjoyment at second-hand of these hackneyed details, wonderful and new to the young girls' experience. He would fain have afforded them this joy, which they childishly craved.

He realized, however, that it was not his place to dictate, and presently the men had all trooped out to a small room, ambitiously denominated the armory, and were busied over the choice of weapons and supply of ammunition. A great array of antique blades, helmets, shields, more or less genuine or suggestive of the junk-shops of New Orleans, hung upon the walls, with some really interesting specimens of the blunderbusses and cutlasses of the buccaneers of early times on the Gulf coast; of bows and arrows, beaded quivers, scalp-knives, tomahawks, from the date of the Chickasaw and Choctaw occupation of this region; and of the flintlock rifles, powder-horns, and shot-pouches of the pioneer days. Two or three of the party had brought their own guns, but others had depended on a chance furnishing forth from Kentopp's armory. The modern repeating shotgun, holding in its magazine five cartridges, each with a dozen buckshot, permitting the discharge of sixty balls within five seconds, was a prime favorite with the sportsmen in preference to the staunch old double-barreled breechloader; only those who boasted special accuracy of aim were content with rifles; Desmond, not very enthusiastic in pressing forward, found his choice limited to necessity.

"I hope that you are a good shot, Mr. Desmond," said Colonel Kentopp, with polite concern, "for these fellows have left nothing but two rifles for us. First-rate make, though not repeaters."

Desmond's outdoor accomplishments were limited to the "Gridiron." He fancied the swamp game destined to be long-lived indeed, if they were to die from the chances of a single rifle-ball directed by his unaccustomed aim. For he was no sportsman. He did not thirst for victory over the sylvan folk. He accepted the rifle as graciously as if he were a dead shot and confident of his powers, secured his share of the appropriate ammunition, and rejoined the others, who had already repaired to the stable-yard.

It was an animated scene. The gas-jet over the stable-door brought it out in high lights and black shadows. A number of fresh, restive horses had been led out of their stalls still in their blankets; others were bare and shivering in process of being saddled.

"Will you ride with a curb, Desmond, or just with a snaffle?" asked Kentopp, as he bustled about, as busy as any of his negro grooms, who, with shining eyes and glittering teeth, entered into all the spirit of the occasion.

115

The dogs were literally beside themselves, and with their dark, whisking shadows seemed twice as numerous as in reality. Now they leaped in a series of ecstatic gambols as if they could not keep their feet to the ground, and again they manifested strange proclivities not to be accounted for on a basis of human reasoning. One suddenly planted himself in front of a young and spirited steed and treated him to a succession of frenzied bayings and elastic boundings that sent the horse, restricted to a limited space, quite wild with surprise and dismay,—now leaping aside with the hope of evading his queer tormentor, and now rearing and threatening to bolt. Another of the dogs, with a yelp so shrill that it menaced the integrity of every tympanum within reach of the sound, urged the setting forth without more delay, scampering around among the hoofs of the horses and the legs of the men, and so to the gate and away!—looking over his shoulder presently, seeing that he was not followed, and returning to repeat the demonstration, calling "Come on! Come on! Come on!" as distinctly as if he had the powers of human speech.

The horses, sniffing the morning air and the promise of adventure, again and again sent forth neighs shrill and clear and as matutinal of effect as a cock's crow; there was a great stamping and champing; the voices of the stable-men were loud with calls for gear within the buildings, and admonitions to the horses, and adjurations to Mr. Sloper to take some order with his pack.

"'Fore Gawd, them scandalous hound-dogs don't show no more manners than if they were so many rapscallion childern," the head of the stable averred.

The guests discussed bits and saddles and chose according to their liking, and went in and out of the harness-room with grooms and lanterns. Often, in the midst of the turmoil, Colonel Kentopp looked up with apprehensive forecast at the house, which seemed with its three stories and tower very tall and stately in this region of the bungalow preference, expecting to hear a sash lifted and a voice, sweet but imperious, demand a stay of the proceedings. "Wait for us! Wait for us!" seemed to sound in his ears, until with the quick, assured tramp of a body of horse, a frenzied crescendo of the skirling of the dogs, a wild jocose "Yah! Yah!" of the stable-men left in the deserted yard, the hunters were mounted and gone.

It was still so dark that Desmond could not have kept the road had it not been for the horsemen on either side, and the voices of those valiant precursors, the dogs, some of whom, however, now moderated their transports and were trotting silently forward. The tones of their owner, or entertainer it might seem, so honored were they in his domicile, came from the van, where he rode abreast with Colonel Kentopp, who had ceased his attentions to Mr. Loring to ply old Sloper with his courtesies. He really felt under special obligations to the old swamper for the loan of his pack of hounds, though, as in the case of many other politic people, his gratitude included a lively sense of favors yet to come. It was the opportunity for a day of sport preëminently appropriate to the region, which without Sloper's coöperation it would have been impossible to offer to the house-party. Hence Colonel Kentopp had put up Mr. Sloper on the best horse in his stable, well knowing that the old swamper would be keen to discern and quick to resent any invidious distinction in the matter. Mr. Loring rode only the second best, a point which doubtless ministered to the swamper's satisfaction and jealous sense of his own consequence. Therefore in fine fettle he led the cavalcade, continuously talking, his high-pitched voice, with its frequent breaks into a snuffling chuckle of falsetto laughter, coming back on the keen, dank, matutinal air with great distinctness.

He was definitely of the class known as the "poor whites" of that region, and his company was not acceptable to Mr. Loring. The man who rises in the world is not tolerant of lower conditions. It is only the acknowledged aristocrat who can really unbend. Sloper's estate in life did not duplicate or approximate Loring's origin, which was in all essentials distinctly genteel,—in the fact of educated parents, in refinement of early association, in point of social connection; for although his immediate family were of small means, he was related to well-to-do people of good middle-class standing. Sloper, however, distinctly expressed the "common folks" of that region as contrasted with the baronial planter, and as Loring had no affiliations with the latter class, it offended him to be brought into familiar juxtaposition with the representative of the widely different lower order.

Colonel Kentopp could suffer no reduction of personal consequence in hobnobbing as man to man with the old plebeian, but as far as Loring was concerned, familiarity might seem an outcropping of quondam tastes and associations and similarity of station. Hence he said naught as Colonel Kentopp's jovial laughter rang out at the conclusion of one of Jerry Sloper's stories that he had heard a score of times heretofore. As the old swamper's high falsetto cackle punctuated the applausive mirth of the others, one might have thought that he was himself too noisy to distinguish the fact that Mr. Loring had not relaxed his risibles in compliment to the gifts of the raconteur; it was still too dark to discriminate facial expressions, and the lantern, which one of the colored grooms carried, was too far ahead to afford its gleams. There is not always that submission in the minds of the lowly in estate which would seem an appropriate concomitant of that humble condition.

"Powerful glad to see you here, Mr. Loring,—though I don't rightly see you yit," Sloper remarked, holding in the spirited steed on which he was mounted to range alongside the millionaire. "We feel here in the Miss'ippi bottom that you jes' nachully b'long to us. Why, I knowed yer dad way back in the fifties. *Yes*, sir! He used ter run the river in them days. He was mud clerk on the old Cher'kee Rose. I kep' a wood-yard up yander on the p'int, an' Gus Loring an' me had chummy old times when he would come ashore to medjure the wood. That was before he married—considerable looking up his match was, for a mud clerk, ye know! Yer mother was a tidy gal,—plump as a partridge,—and I used to set up ter her considerable myself. He! he! he! She turned me off, though, for Gus Loring! An' she done better, though I do say it myself. She done better to take Gus instead o' me. She had a leetle chunk o' money, an' yer dad quit the river an' bought a share in a store an' set out a-clerkin'. But Lawd! I reckon ye wouldn't bat yer eye for no such stock o' goods as he had. They tell me as ye have prospered considerable down yander in Orleans! I reckon if *ye* was ter store-keep, like yer dad, ye could show forth as good a stock as they had at Whippoorwill Landing,—that would ha' made Gus Loring stare! I don't mean ye could *own* it all—part credit o' course! But I reckon from all I *have* heard tell that ye could get a note in bank,—an' that is mo' 'n yer dad ever could do."

Regnan loved his fellow-man. "For God's sake, pull that old fox off the Spartan's vitals," he said in a low voice to Kentopp. "I can't abide for a fellow to be gnawed like that."

"Then, curse him,—why can't he show some sense!" Kentopp growled *sotto voce* in return. "Who but a fool would try to top old Jerry Sloper with his *nil admirari* millionaire airs. *He* knows what Loring cut his teeth on! I am afraid of my life to say a word."

Lieutenant Regnan had missed his billet as the destroyer of life. His instincts were all for first aid to the injured. He presently began melodiously to hum, and suddenly as he rode in the clump of horsemen he broke forth: "Say, Mr. Sloper, how does the tune go to that old high-water song:—

> "Step light, neighbor,—*don't* jar the river!
> Rising, rising, brimful and over—"

Forthwith the old swamper was blissfully chanting as he rode at the head of the cavalcade, and Mr. Loring had time to readjust the expression of his face and to conceal the ravages of the onslaught on his pride before a certain pallid influence began to annul the darkness. A sense of mist was in the atmosphere, yet great, towering trees were visible, and far along apparently infinite vistas, level and devoid of woodland débris as a royal park, some vague presence shifted continually, never so distinct, so definitely embodied, as to be formulated to the vision, and at last realized as the impalpable medium of the dawning light. Suddenly day was revealed in the woods. The sun was up, not seeming to rise on those infinite levels, but to spring at once like a miracle into the place of darkness. It filled the world with the amplitudes of a glorious golden glow, so fresh, so elated, yet pervaded with a sort of awe, a splendid solemnity. Stillness characterized its earlier moments, but presently, in the chill morning, the spring birds were singing from the branches of the trees, which rustled with the sudden stir of the wind. Through the vistas to the west the great Mississippi was agleam with thousands of wavelets tipped with dazzling scintillations, and the rising mist that veiled the Arkansas shore shimmered with opalescent reflections. Beyond the limits of the forest one could see here and there a scattered growth of cottonwood trees and the serpentine line of the levee, its great embankment covered to the summit with the thick growth of Bermuda grass, the interlacing roots of which were considered of much avail in strengthening the earthwork to resist the action of the current in times of high water. At one point, where the river turned in its corkscrew convolutions, the horsemen could see that the encroaching flood had crossed the intervening space and was beginning to stand against the base of the levee. This premonitory symptom of overflow Mr. Loring was prompt to notice.

"I have a cross levee half a mile back," Colonel Kentopp said, with a jaunty air. "I don't think we will go under, even if that stretch of levee should give. And if we do," still more jauntily, "crawfish and river detritus are fine fertilizers."

"Best crops ever made in Deepwater Bend was after the biggest water I ever see," interrupted Jerry Sloper, exceedingly glib. "Levees broke in March, and water stood sixty miles wide. Plantations were under till mighty nigh May. River was not in its banks till nigh May. Then the crop was planted and—"

"I have heard my grandfather tell about that," interposed Regnan. "The fields were so thick with cotton that they laughed and sang,—and the planters laughed and sang, too."

"Still, I'd rather Dryad-Dene should keep dry feet," said Colonel Kentopp, turning in his saddle to look over his shoulder at the water lapping about the verdant spaces at the base of the levee. Nevertheless, he felt very cheerful. The cavalcade could hear the plantation bell at Dryad-Dene ring forth its strong, mellow acclaim, calling out the hired force to work, as well as the tenant farmers, who were under the same regimen. The broad expanse of fields was now and again visible, all prepared for the planting of cotton,—as carefully laid off and with the earth as thoroughly pulverized as if for a flower-bed. It was impossible for the heart of a proprietor of so fine a plantation not to swell at the sight, and while away from Annetta and her eager fostering of their mutual ambitions toward metropolitan life, Kentopp felt a sort of independence of the millionaire's doubtful attitude. Let the event fall out as it would, he had here a mighty good thing.

In the midst of these more vital and manly interests, Loring's phlegm and pose of indifference could but give way. He knew the country and its possibilities thoroughly, and now and again he made searching inquiries into local conditions, which showed that his mind was genuinely occupied with the proposition, and caused Colonel Kentopp to think that he did not half care to sell at all. Repeatedly the richness of the opportunity was demonstrated. A turn in the road suddenly gave to view a lovely level of pasturage inclosed by hedges of the Cherokee rose, over whose wide-spreading evergreen brambles the horsemen could look upon a green plain, dotted with trees of gigantic girth, and embellished with as fine a flock of sheep as ever wore wool. Three or four black pickaninnies, already absorbed in a game of mumble-the-peg, and several collie dogs were entered upon their guardian duties for the day, and Colonel Kentopp was descanting upon varieties and pedigrees, weight of shearings and flavor of mutton.

"We raise everything at Dryad-Dene, as a model plantation should. The world is within the bounds of Dryad-Dene. We buy nothing but gunpowder, salt, iron, and sugar."

This was, of course, the ancient brag of the great river principalities; but the immense drove of hogs which the horsemen passed after a time, crowding about a gate where swineherds were throwing out as breakfast the contents of a wagon loaded with corn over the high fence of the inclosure, the wide expanse of the potato-fields, harvested long ago, their yield garnered into the potato-sheds that stretched along on one side like the roofs of a little street, the saw-and-grist mill, the cotton-press and steam-gin, with the obeliscal smokestack towering above the plain,—all the appurtenances of the industry, went far to confirm the boast.

And now into the depths of the wilderness, primeval, apparently illimitable, with the wind footing it featly alongside. There were clouds in the densely blue sky, but high, white, flocculent, and lightly floating. The odors of spring vegetation, of early blooms, came on every breath; and when the first of the sloughs was reached, it was so draped in lace-like willows, so full of verdant moss and ooze, so still and dreamy in its marshy pools, mirroring the sky, that one might have accounted it a valued feature of the landscape, but for the experience of fording it.

"We can't hunt bear in a parlor," Colonel Kentopp declared, as he forced Ringdove to wet her dainty hoofs. The rest were soon splashing after, unmindful of mire and solicitous only of quicksands. But on the farther side they were on dry and level ground once more, cantering alertly amidst the great forest trees, the horses scarcely breathed, and the courage of the cavalcade rising to the summons of exertion. And now,—deepest shades, great overhanging, swamp-like growths! The dense cypress, festooned by the gray Spanish moss, rose towering out of ink-black water; a white heron, standing motionless beside a clump of the protuberances known as "cypress-knees," looked as if it might have been sketched into the scene with a bit of chalk; logs, moss-covered and dripping with slime, lay half buried in the ooze; the canopy of foliage was so thick, the boughs of the trees so densely interlacing, that the light of the brilliant day was cut off and the hunters rode as if in a dream-shadow. Lakes presently opened alongside, series of glassy stretches, blue under the azure sky, and connected by a bayou so dully flowing that, gaze as one might, the motion of a current could not be discerned. Once wild ducks were glimpsed, and though old Jerry Sloper protested, he could not hinder the prompt discharge of one of the shot-guns. On the crash of the report ensued the whizzing of wings in the flurry of terrified flight, and two of the birds floated dead upon the water. A handsome setter sprang into the lake, and presently swam out with his feathered trophy; while the dogs of different breeds wheezed uneasily about the margin, and one of them, a famous bear hound of a singular bluish tint, his hide about his jaws hanging in loose folds, sat down and contemplated the feat with head askew, as much as to say, "Now, how did *you* find out how to do that?"

Jerry Sloper was beside himself with indignation. "Now, you fellers air goin' to spile the chances fur the whole day! How fur d' ye think this here piece o' water 'll carry the crack o' that thar gun? Old Pa Bear will hide in the cane-brake an' old Ma Bear will gather the children up in the hollow tree, an' they won't ventur' out 'fore June. An' then the manners of my dogs! I been tryin' ter get it out o' that thar Lightfoot's fool head that he is expected to go arter what I shoot. *I* don't kill fowels with a gun." His lip curled with scorn, showing his long, tobacco-stained teeth. "I go ter my hen-cup an' chop off thar heads with a hatchet. I am a man, I am! An' when I play, I take my sport like a man. I shoot deer an' bear an' wolves an' sech animals. The last time I killed a bear, 'twas by accident. I hed nobody with me but Lightfoot, thar. An' the crittur,—durn his little old cranky soul!—he p'inted. Came to a stand, with his forefoot crooked,—jes' so"—and Jerry Sloper crooked his great hairy paw in clumsy imitation of Lightfoot's graceful instinct—"else I wouldn't have seen old Bruin. I 'lowed a' fust 'twar jes' a hawg over in the brake. An' all of a suddenty, lo an' behold, 'twas revealed to me that thar was a bear! An' I fired,—an' o' course he fell. An' off skittered Lightfoot ter *bring him in*, mind ye! Thar I was hollerin' arter the child, thrown to the wild beast,—I warn't able to stir hand or foot,—I was jes' palsied with skeer. Lightfoot tuk him gently by the ear,—not to spile him with gnawing,—jes' like he done that duck—Gimme that thar fowel, *you* distracted beast!" and the setter, with half-squatting hind-legs and wriggles of delight and pride, and lifted, liquid, shining eyes, relinquished the game into his hand. "An' what happened? The bear warn't plumb dead! And Lightfoot come back tore mighty nigh ter the breastbone. See them scars on his chist? An' ez soon as he was able to stand it, I gin him a beatin' besides ter teach him better. An' now,—ye have set him at his old tricks ag'in. I wouldn't own a dog with sech

121

a mania, if he warn't a present ter me. An' till ye fellers tuk to triflin' with him, I 'lowed I'd got him plumb sensible. You see that duck?"—he looked down sternly at his accomplished retainer, who, discerning the change of tone, began to cringe miserably, thoroughly crestfallen. "Oh, ho! ain't forgot what I told you, eh? Well, then,—want some mo' slipper pie?"

Oh, he did not! He did not, indeed,—his pleading countenance protested. But the threat was a mere feint; and as the old swamper turned to take up the route once more, the setter, with a shrill yelp of delight to get off from the colloquy with no painful sequence, dashed ahead, and was presently trotting nimbly with his companions of various families and traditions, the only bird dog, and the only one whose record comprised the heady effort to retrieve a bear.

"I'd buy that setter, Mr. Sloper, if you'd put a price on him," said Regnan, who sometimes descended to the trifling sport of bird hunting.

"An' *I'd* buy the State of Miss'ippi, if 'twas layin' around loose," was the not too encouraging response.

Sloughs, lagoons, bayous unnumbered! The horses were soon mired to their girths; the men were splashed from head to foot, and those inexpert at swimming a horse when suddenly out of his depth, had their high riding-boots full of water. More than once an alligator was viewed, half embedded in the ooze, only distinguished from the rotting log that he resembled when he would rouse himself to swim slowly a few yards, tempting the knights of the magazine shot-guns.

"Don't ye know that a bullet from a forward shot will glance off as if he wore chain armor!" old Sloper remonstrated. "The only chance is a rifle-ball behind the eye."

"And when did *you* become acquainted with chain armor?" asked one of the Mayberry youths, in merry wonderment and with a twinkling eye.

"About twenty-five years before you was bawn," retorted the old swamper. He paused to spit forth an enormous volley of tobacco-juice against the trunk of a tree, with a seeming solicitude for the accuracy of his aim; then resumed with the greatest deliberation.

"I helped in a jewel that was fought by two tremenjious swells, who got themselves landed by the Great Republic for that purpose. They tuk up an insult to each other while on the boat. They came up to my wood-yard—I used ter furnish fuel ter the packets reg'lar. They said all they wanted was a man ter see fair play an' shut his mouth. They plastered mine good an' tight with a double eagle. One of the parties was tremenjious brash an' overbearin'; I could see that the other looked into death's eyesockets at close quarters. I medjured the ground for them with the Flying Cloud's wood-staff that the mud clerk had left at the yard,—miserable, unshifty, keerless cuss! Bet he needed it himself before he got ter New Orleans! An' these two dandy fellers tuk thar stand an' fired. An' the one that was so cocksure missed his aim, though his hair-trigger was as fine a weepon as ever I see. An' the t'other, that thought he had come to his las' minit, shot straight. But he aimed at the man's mouth, as it 'peared to me. He threw up his pistol at the last second. The ball tuk the gentleman right through the throat. Ought to have seen the blood spurt out 'n his jugular! Mighty nasty way to kill a gentleman, I thought! An' as we both run to the body on the ground, one on either side, the winner's hand shook so he could hardly undo the vest. So I laid back the fine linen shirt, though I knew it was no use to feel his heart, for he was as dead as a buckeye; I seen between it an' his silk underwear a shirt of fine steel rings. 'T would turn a bullet; 't would break a knife! An' the s'vivor says,—his chin shook so that he could hardly talk,—'What do you think of that? I s'picioned from the fust that he would give me no fair chance in a fight, an' he forced it upon me.' An' I say, 'Let's put this murderer in the bayou. Thar's some fierce catfish thar, an' snakes, an' slimy beasts to eat the flesh from his bones. The mud is deep an' will hold him down, an' the mire is fit for his last home! The Miss'ippi is too tricky to trust,—floats things, ye know. The bayou for me, every time!'"

"Why, Mr. Sloper," cried young Mayberry, suddenly grave and aghast. "I should think that you would have been afraid."

"Well, he ain't never got up from thar,—so fur as I have heard tell. What's to be afeard of?"

"Was that *all* you did? To bury him in the bayou?"

"Naw, sir; I went down to Natchez an' spreed away the double eagle, the twenty dollars."

"But I mean about notifying the authorities?"

The old swamper's face had a bewildered look. "Whar was they? What call had they ter meddle? I done nothin' but the heftin'."

"Didn't the Great Republic say anything the next time she passed?"

"Oh, yes! I told the mud clerk that the price of wood had riz, an' he told me to go to hell. That's the last word with the Great Republic."

Suddenly a sound smote the sylvan silence. A keen note of query, a wide blare of discovery,—and all the pack opened on the scent, baying as rhythmically as if trained to this woodland music. The horn rang out its elated, spirited tones, the sound leaping like a live thing along the far reaches of the levels. The horsemen, in a frenzy of excitement, were separating, each taking his own course and riding as if the rout of some swift pursuit were upon his track. Desmond hesitated for a moment, bewildered, the only stranger to the wilderness of all the party, forgotten utterly by his host, by old Sloper, by the huntsman on ahead with the dogs, by the youthful sportsmen.

Presently, however, Regnan bethought himself of the tutor and his imminent danger of being lost in the fastnesses, and paused after an instant of frantic plunging through a narrow bogue that issued from a swamp where there was promise indeed of scant solid ground.

"Come with me," he called. "I am going to try an old stand on a deer path I know. The hounds have got up a buck—I think so from the tongue they are giving. Follow me. Swim your horse when he begins to flounder in the bayous."

CHAPTER X

There was no choice. Desmond had scant interest in this tumultuous sport of coursing deer with hounds, but he was fain to follow. He could not have retraced his way for his life, and to be lost in the wilderness—for every horseman had disappeared—was taking all the jeopardy of disaster and even of death. He congratulated himself that the excellent brute he bestrode seemed to know more about the matter than he. Suddenly Regnan, who had been for a few minutes lost to him, appeared in glimpses through the redundant vegetation about the lagoon, which could be characterized as neither water nor land, consisting now of one and now of the other, and again of a treacherous combination of both, that afforded neither footing nor the medium for swimming. The young sportsman was thrashing through brake and slough at a breakneck speed that presently carried him out of the reach of vision.

The glimpse was sufficient for the powerful red roan that Desmond rode, and he needed no prompting. He sprang instantly into the water in the essay to follow, swimming with great spirit, now and then stretching his legs to gain a firm footing, and, with a splashing flounder that nearly shook Desmond out of the saddle, striking out again to swim with alert vigilance and stalwart strength. Desmond was used to equestrian exercise in milder form and found a need for all the principles of equitation that he had been taught, for the most progressive of mounts can hardly act on his own initiative throughout the incidents of such a drive as this promised to be. Desmond gave the horse his head as to direction, but checked him according to his own judgment at impassable obstacles, and held him up firmly when he threatened to go to his knees. A little later, in a deep quagmire, where he showed signs of sinking, and, losing courage, began to snort in fright, Desmond used bit and heel to such effect as to reinstate his confidence and bring him leaping lightly out of his floundering instabilities to good dry ground.

When the wild, disordered turmoils of the alluvial wilderness gave way on the borders of a fine bit of water, Desmond was surprised himself to note how reassured he felt to perceive Regnan on his swimming horse nearly in the centre of the lakelet. In the swift transit he had scarcely had time to speculate if he were on the right track, but confirmation was welcome. Regnan had evidently felt a doubt, for he was looking over his shoulder; and as Desmond and the red roan galloped down to the margin, the horse sending forth a gleeful whinny at the sight of his swimming comrade in advance, Regnan waved his hand and pressed on to the opposite shore, where the dense shadows of a great stretch of forest gloomed. Here there was good going. Desmond pressed his horse to added speed to overhaul his precursor, and side by side they galloped at their utmost capacity, with scarcely a word exchanged, through miles of level woods, at last reaching the almost impenetrable densities of a cane-brake, skirting the growth rather than striking across it; this was the outpost of sluggish bayous and cypress sloughs, almost impassable, seeming impracticable, till suddenly they stood on a fair sheet of water. The blue sky looked down suavely upon it, and so serene it was that one might have thought the wild tangles through which the way hither had lain were some vision of a distraught imagination. All around the dense woods were silent, primeval. Something of the redundant swamp growths were about its margin and cloaked the approach to its placid waters, but beyond stretched the endless forests.

Regnan was dismounting. "It is too wide to swim with a horse," he said. "I suppose that is the reason the deer take to it. And once get this body of water between them and the dogs, and the scent is lost."

He was hitching his horse among the tangled growths at a little distance, where he would be invisible, and cautioned Desmond to follow his example.

"See that deer path?" he said. A narrow line threaded the luxuriant marshy grasses about the margin,—scarcely a path,—yet a keen eye might discern the imprint of a cleft hoof in the moist ground at the water's edge. "I have shot deer here before," added Regnan.

With the butt of his gun he beat down the boughs of evergreen shrubs to afford an elastic couch; and here they lay them down and rested and talked spasmodically and dully drowsed, while they awaited the sound of hound and horn.

"He's giving them a good run for the money," opined Regnan, as time wore on and brought no change. The placid lake gleamed serene; the dark forest gloomed. But for their own languid voices they heard naught, and sometimes long pauses intervened in the desultory talk.

"Fond of this sort of thing?" asked Regnan.

Desmond was more comfortable since he had taken off his high riding-boots and poured the water from them, being advised by Regnan to put them on immediately, lest they so stiffen in drying that their resumption would be impossible. The amusement did not seem so disagreeable to Desmond as he lay stretched out at his long length, his soft hat over his eyes, and his gloves also dutifully drying into shape on his hands. He was able to answer both veraciously and courteously.

"I am not used to it. I like the violent exercise well enough. But I don't want to kill anything. I am glad I can't."

"Why can't you?"

"Oh, I never shot at anything in my life but with a handful of bird-shot."

Regnan, also recumbent, with his hat over his eyes to be rid of the combined glare of lake and sky, lifted himself suddenly to look about him.

"What a pity! We both have rifles! Kentopp ought to have given you a shotgun. I wish I had mine. I don't know why I should have brought this thing."

Then he lay back once more and shaded his eyes. A long silence ensued. The glare on the lake had dulled; a network of clouds gathered gradually, the meshes weaving continually until dense, dark, impervious to any gleam, it hung unbroken above the lake. The woods had fallen into deeper gloom; only the green of the saw-grass fringing the water-side seemed lifted into an intenser chromatic grade by the lowering of a gray sky. When a sound smote the mute quietude of the woods, it was a muttering of thunder.

"Rain! We are going to have it in plenty," suggested Regnan.

"It has been demonstrated to-day that we are neither sugar nor salt."

"But it will disperse the scent; the hounds will run counter."

"Hallo!" exclaimed Desmond, in sudden excitement, lifting himself on his elbow. He could not have said why it should thrill him; but that sound of a horn, elastically leaping along the distance, so signally clear, so searchingly vibrant, so infinitely sweet, sought out every fibre of the romantic in him. Then rose the melody of the dogs in full cry, rhythmic, mellow, musical, softened by the distance, significant, unceasing, echoing with the sentiment of the sylvan chase of all the days of eld. It was not old Sloper's "house-party" that Desmond heard, but every pack of high degree that ever coursed through the realms of poesy or the liberties of tradition. He was on his feet,—a light in his eyes, a flush on his cheek, his hands trembling, his muscles alert.

"They are coming this way! They are heading for the lake!" he exclaimed.

Regnan listened for a moment. "Right you are!" he cried.

As they took up their position at the stand, ambushed beside the deer path, Regnan insistently waived precedence.

"You fire first. *You* are company! If you miss, I'll fire. Buck ague?" he whispered.

The undulating sound of the cry of the hounds, emitted rhythmically with each bound, came ever nearer and nearer, and suddenly there was close at hand a crashing through the bushes down the deer path. Desmond threw up his rifle, conscious that he must catch the aim as quick as light. To his own surprise he was singularly cool and steady. A flash, the sharp report rang out; something clouded white and brown and gray leaped high into the air, issuing from the brush, and fell dead at the water's edge,—a gigantic wildcat.

"A crack shot you are!" Regnan exclaimed, amazed. The ball had taken the creature just beneath the ear and pierced the brain. "And this cat is the finest ever!"

He bent over the magnificent specimen. "I didn't know such a fellow as this was left in the country. But oh, how old Sloper will swear!"

"Why?" asked Desmond, the excitement cooling only gradually.

"His hounds are to run only deer and bear, no matter what's the purpose of their creation and previous education. He lets them chase a fox, now and then, with a great palaver of explanation, and keeping right up with them. But a cat! He'll be worth hearing!"

When the pack came presently, swiftly loping through the brake, and beheld their prey, it was difficult indeed to reduce them to order; and as old Sloper raged, and fumed, and indignantly rebuked them, their air suggested contradiction as they whisked about their prostrate foe, their gait as if they could not keep feet to ground—lifting them as if it were hot—in the flutter and excitement, and they noisily yelped with delight every time he spoke to them. It would seem that the subtle current of comprehension, the medium of communication, was broken. They so valiantly protested that they had done a fine thing, and piqued themselves so pridefully on their prowess, that he was fain to end the discussion in his own interest in the prey.

"Git out'n my way, or I'll punch the nose off'n ye," he roughly adjured them, as he dismounted to lay out at length the savage beast, in order to take its measure from its muzzle to the tip of the tail. "Thar! I've stepped on your foot, and I'm glad of it!" as a piercing squeak split the ears of the party. But the sufferer was game and hopped joyously about on three legs, participating in the event, despite his plaintive disabilities.

"What you goin' to do with this here cat, Mr. Desmond?" he asked, an added respect for so fine a shot unmistakable in every line of his face and every inflection of his voice. "Better git it off the ground—the dogs mought tear it; they air so durned sassy over it, I can't govern 'em none. And 'tis the finest thing I ever see. My! how handsome that fur is!"

"Why," exclaimed Desmond, suddenly roused to the possibilities of his possession, "I'll have it stuffed and present it to Mrs. Kentopp as an ornament to the armory and a memento of the occasion." He had not eaten much of her bread, but he distrusted the motive of her hospitality, and his pride welcomed the opportunity to make a requital so promptly and in a guise which he knew would be so acceptable. He began to take an interest in the exceptional beauty of the specimen.

"Then it ought to be skun right now, before the critter stiffens. An' I'll do it fur ye and send the pelt to ye."

Down old Sloper went on his hands and knees to the work *con amore*, his sharp hunting-knife gingerly tracing the lines where the cuticle and fur could be separated with least injury to the appearance of the integument. It was a long job and a careful one, but none of the other sportsmen had put in an appearance when it was finished. He straightened up and looked about him doubtfully.

"They all lost out somehows," he said. "Mighty rough ridin' in them slashes. I reckon they've all rid off to camp, mightily interested in that thar barbecued shoat fur dinner."

The mention elicited a responsive interest and a desire to minimize the distance between the hunters and this dainty, time-honored of the *al fresco* feast. The hounds, old Sloper, and the huntsman set out by way of the deer path, as they had come.

"I'll try a short cut," suggested Regnan, "if you don't mind a bit more wading and swimming."

Desmond protested his indifference to a renewal of their amphibious experience, and, mounting their horses, the two rode off through the saw-grass, which fringed the borders of the lake. Suddenly the slate-tinted clouds, darkening and still sinking lower, were cleft by a vivid forked flash; the thunder crashed with an appalling clangor; the horses were snorting in fright and plunging wildly, and the floodgates were unloosed. The rain descended in sheets; there was not a breath of wind, and the torrents fell vertically. It seemed for a time as if they were menaced by a cloud-burst. The quantity of water liberated was incalculable. The swamp which they now threaded was inundated so swiftly that Regnan more than once paused and looked back as if he canvassed the possibility of retracing their way to the solid earth they had quitted. But the rainfall was no translucent medium. He could distinguish naught beyond its opaque curtain. In serried lines in undiscriminated myriads the torrents fell, yet seemed always stationary. It hardly mattered which course they adopted, for each was soaked to the very bones. On and on they plodded, the horses dully drudging in the progress, making special exertion when they needs must, but obviously showing that they were of opinion the fun was at an end, and that there could be too much of a good thing. Like human beings, they found a vastly different animus in going forth full of expectation and coming back exhausted with the day's run. They held down their heads in meek endurance as the rain beat upon them, and when they stumbled in the shifty, marshy soil, there was great danger both to the animal and his rider in the lack of that alertness of muscle to recover a footing or bound with his burdened saddle beyond the limits of the quagmire. Once or twice this recovery was so precarious, so clumsy a floundering, and sinking was so imminent, that both horsemen were alarmed and prescient of disaster.

"We have done this thing once too often, I am afraid," said Regnan.

Desmond, too, had been looking over his shoulder, though not in the forlorn hope that they might be able to see the point from which they had started, for they had pressed the horses forward, against their will, with such energy that they had made it as impossible to retrace their way as to reach satisfactory footing in going on. Some injutting point of land in the irregular outline of the swamp, or one of the ridges of higher ground whereon switch cane grew luxuriantly, and which here and there traversed it, might yet afford them rescue, but if he could have discovered such opportunity in ordinary weather, the tumultuous, blinding downpour rendered it invisible now.

"There is nothing for it but to go on," he said in a depressed cadence, for his heart had a sensation of sinking. He was growing desperate. The rain had in its midst great shifting clouds of thin vapor. Now it so inclosed them that they lost sight of each other. Yet when they called out in alarm, fearful of the disaster of unwittingly parting company, the changing mist gave a vision of the head of the other horse close at hand, though a moment earlier it could not be discerned.

Suddenly as Desmond shifted his position in the saddle, looking straight over his horse's ears, he gave a start and an abrupt exclamation, staring as if he doubted his senses; for before him, in the pallid, hovering mists, half revealed and half concealed by the immaterial investitures of the curtaining rain and the cloaking cloud, like the travesty of a ship under full sail which tantalizes the desperate hope of wrecked or castaway mariners, he beheld as if suspended in the air between heaven and earth the outline of a river craft, a boat of some humble sort, a refuge.

"Look, Regnan, what is that in the sky?" he exclaimed hastily.

Regnan lifted his head and put up his hand to hold away the flapping brim of his drenched hat. His voice suddenly rang out with a thrill of good cheer: "In the sky? Why, it's in the bayou, thank God!"

"It is a flatboat?" Desmond hesitated.

"A flatboat it is!"

Regnan's face had not regained its florid tint; the chill of the fog and the rain, that had not left a dry thread on his body, and the effluvia of the swamp, penetrating his lungs, had turned his lips blue. But he laughed out gayly, although as his lineaments moved he swallowed the rills of rain that ran down his face. "It is rescue, my boy! That's what it is! The boat is half a mile off, and we can just about make it."

"Half a mile! A flatboat!" Even yet Desmond was hardly convinced that it was not a delusion. "What makes it so high!"

"What makes us so low!" laughed Regnan. "Because we are away down in the swamp, and the flatboat is away up in the bayou."

"I should think the bayou would overflow and convert this swamp into a lake."

"And so it would but for the conformation of its banks. And so it will if this cloud-burst keeps on a bit longer and swells the waters of the bayou."

They shifted their direction and pushed on with a good heart, despite the difficulties that increased at every step; and though the horses, with their bent heads and drenched coats and drudging plod, had not seen the craft so high above their own level, now indeed obliterated from all view by the encircling cloud, they obviously felt the recruited hopes and energy of their riders. The revived spirits of the men were subtly imparted to the steeds, and the improved progress caused the distance to seem less than Regnan's estimate when again the cloud lifted so much as to disclose the mirage-like craft, now lower on the limited horizon by reason of the nearer approach.

"To tell you the truth, Desmond," said Regnan,—the two had become chummy, despite the tutor's sensitive reserve and repellent dignity, for there was no justification in holding Regnan at arm's length,—"I thought our hour had come. I thought we were destined to leave our bones in the bayou with the caitiff of the shirt of mail."

Desmond shuddered. "Oh, give me better company!" he cried. "Death is a leveler, but it can never lay me so low as that."

Now and then each looked up from beneath his sodden hat-brim to discern if their approach had been noticed from the craft, but as yet she gave no sign of observation. There was no one on deck, as they soon perceived. The rain beat down heavily upon it, and the water washed over its low gunwales as if it were the waves of the bayou. The stream, however, showed even yet no motion, no current; it was covered by a myriad of tiny bosses, so to speak, the rain being so persistent, the fall so regular, as to make the drops seem to stand stationary on its surface. It had risen several feet, as was evinced by the half submerged vegetation along the banks, the tips fresh and green, with no token of having been long under water. Beneath that black cloud, with the sinister effect of the white trunks of the cypress trees on either hand, deadened by repeated overflows, their weird reflections in the trembling black water, the funereal aspect of the pendent Spanish moss hanging from the high limbs and even festooning the trees from one side of the stream to the other,—the world, the past, life itself, annihilated by the clouds,—the dark and gloomy watercourse might have suggested the river Styx, and the shadowy, visionary, ill-defined boat the craft of Charon. They both felt an averse curiosity as they approached still nearer, striving to disintegrate from the rain and the cloud some individual characteristic or sign of occupation of the phantom craft. Regnan began to think it a derelict, an old abandoned hulk; but he soon saw that it sat the water much too jauntily, a stout, dry hull, tight and serviceable. Presently their keen young eyes discriminated a curl of smoke amidst the vapors that lay on the roof of the cabin. This was little more than a shed of upright boards, very flimsily put together, and a tiny square window along the eaves promised little for light. It served the purpose of a lookout, however. A pale face appeared there. It seemed to scan disconsolately the rain-lost world without, the encroaching cloud, the swamp with its sinking aspect; and suddenly, with transfixed attention, to become aware of the approaching sportsmen, the horse of the one up to the girth as he plodded through the half submerged morass, that of the other out of his depth and beginning to swim.

For one spectral moment the face stared as if confronted by doom. Then the door of the cabin opened, and disregarding the downpour, with skirts lashing about her, with long hair loose and flying, a tall, sinuous young woman appeared, sprang from the deck upon the marshy bank, cast loose the line about a tree, leaped back upon the deck in a moment, caught up a pole, and with a stalwart effort had pushed off an oar's length or two before the man whom her shrill cries had summoned stumbled out of the cabin and stood staring at the newcomers, with little apparent inclination to lend a hand to the effort of clearing the harbor.

It was vain. The horsemen were too close upon them. Such motive power as kept the sluggish bayou on its course from the Mississippi River was too slight to aid the pole to evade the speed of a swimming horse. Desmond, indeed, had boarded the craft while the imbecile face of the boat-hand was still bent upon him.

"What do you mean by this behavior?" he demanded angrily, not as yet recognizing either the man or the woman. "Tie up the boat again, and show us your bar."

"Jocelindy! Jocelindy! ye fool, ye!" cried the boat-hand, striking the struggling woman on the shoulder with his heavy hand. But for this repulsive brutality it might have been pathetic to hear him tax another with his own obvious infirmity. "Don't ye see the gentleman's goin' ter spen' money with us!"

He busied himself in tying up the boat in quick order, and found a place where the two horses could stand on pretty staunch ground under the interlacing boughs of cottonwood, so thick as to afford some shelter from the rain. He had fodder aboard, too, he said.

"Some fodder we had to pack a lot o' chany," interposed the woman, suddenly and shrilly, "becase there wasn't no straw convenient."

Desmond had no mind to linger on ceremony. Without waiting for an invitation, he turned toward the cabin door. The woman, still standing in the torrents, a secret thought in her face, her head askew, her draggled attire dripping with rain, her mouth bent down upon her clenched fist, suddenly asked:—

"Tell me one word,—is your name Faurie?"

"No," said Desmond, frowning at the identification with his employers as if he were of no importance in himself; "my name is Desmond."

"Thar now, Jocelindy, ye told Jed that very word," exclaimed the boat-hand, mowing and laughing with imbecile and extravagant glee. "Ye told him that this very mornin' before he set out with his spade."

There was an incongruity in any mutual utilities between a boat and a spade, but Desmond was new to the river country and did not appreciate this fact. It struck Regnan at once, but he had no reason to place inimical construction upon the acts of the boat's company, and it passed without comment.

Though what is called "not right bright," Ethan Knoxton was discriminating enough to preside very acceptably at a bar when two storm-drenched wights stood before it, and he ranged the glasses with an extra polish and tipped a decanter. It was a dull, squalid little hole, with a permanent aroma of the greasy fumes of many breakfasts fried on the monkey stove at the farther end of the cabin, and the heavy, oily flavor of the untrimmed wick of a kerosene lamp swinging above the bar. The water dripped dismally from their coats and riding-breeches into the already well-filled legs of their high boots, that gave a squashing sound at every step. From their hats chilly little streams trickled into their collapsed shirt collars and down their shivering spines; and as the first drop of liquor touched their palates, the surprise to find that instead of rank, coarse whiskey it was good French brandy was so grateful that they could but look at each other with glistening eyes over the rims of their glasses as they drank.

The boat-hand watched them expectantly.

"My! Ain't that fine!" Then as they set the glasses down, he whooped out his vicarious joy and smote his leg with the palm of his open hand.

Desmond had insisted on paying by right of his discovery of the bar, and he laid down the price of three drinks. "You will oblige me," he said politely to the boat-hand, struggling with his distaste and disgust. One should not despise the poor, and the uncouth, and the deprived, who may have more value in their Maker's eyes than one wots of. Therefore, because the semblance of humanity was not always disdained, he sought to have a regard to the mere image.

"For me?" The protuberant, grotesque eyes of the boat-hand were stretched. "For *me*!" He could hardly realize the rich opportunity. "For ME!" And at last convinced, he exclaimed, "Lord love ye! Lord bless ye! Lord save ye!" and gulped down the French brandy, casting up the gloating eyes of extreme ecstasy at every swallow. He smacked his lips again and again, to be heard in the remotest corner of the cabin, then stood comfortably smelling the glass while the others turned toward the stove.

"Isn't that queer—French brandy?" Desmond suggested.

"Smuggled, I suppose," said Regnan.

"Stolen, I'm afraid," said Desmond, *sotto voce*, mopping the rain from his cold face and shaking the rills from his drenched hat. The jeopardy, the confusion, the exhaustion attendant on the moment of rescue from the sinister menace of the swamp and the cloud-burst engrossed his faculties, but he was vaguely recollecting that he had recently heard of the dispensing of this choice liquor among a class of swampers to whom its market price rendered it unaccustomed and unattainable.

"Well, I was not *particeps criminis* till it was halfway down,—too far to catch it. And it feels just as good where it is as if it was honestly come by," Regnan laughed.

The woman had utilized the interval while their backs were turned, and perhaps the shelter of a curtained bunk, to slip into a dry gown and a clean apron, and she, too, seemed to have determined on a change of tactics. She would fry for the gentlemen some rashers of bacon and eggs, if they liked; and set on a strong pot of coffee, she said.

"Are you afraid of spoiling your appetite for that barbecued shoat?" Regnan asked Desmond, with a rallying eye.

"No; are you?" For the day was wearing on into the afternoon. There were already dulling intimations in the clouds, as if the limits of light in their midst were curtailed. The woman listened intently as she set forth her poor and humble board with its best; and when they were seated on either side and she whisked about serving them, her strange, snake-like face had a more propitiatory and pleasing expression than seemed possible, with her high cheek-bones, her eyes aslant, her long, serpentine neck.

She suddenly addressed Desmond. "You see he ain't quit suckin' his thumb yit," she said, as an infantine babbling caused Desmond to turn his head to perceive sitting bolt upright in a bunk behind him an infant in a red gown with his thumb in his mouth, regarding the feasting with slobbering admiration, but making no effort to partake and no demand to be served.

Desmond recognized her now for the first time. He had given her but little notice since coming aboard, and on the occasion of his previous visit to the shanty-boat, partly because of the dimness of the light in the little cabin, partly because of the sensational development of the interview, he had not sufficiently observed the subsidiary members of the crew—the woman, the child, and the boat-hand—to remember their faces. If Jedidiah Knoxton had been present, there would have been no delay in recalling the personnel of the whole party.

"That lady, Mrs. Faurie," continued the woman, speaking in a very propitiatory manner, "told me how to break him of it, too. She's powerful handsome, sure, ain't she?"

"Yes," said Desmond to this direct appeal. "And she is a very kind lady."

"Sure! She told me she'd gin little Ikey some baby clothes."

"But you left very suddenly," said Desmond, significantly.

Regnan continued to eat silently, surprised at the evidence of previous acquaintance, but comfortable enough that it made no conversational demands upon him, so keen an appetite had the vicissitudes of the day given him.

"I want to tell you about that," said the woman, winningly. "Jed's a mighty techy kind o' man an' he got sorter nettled 'bout that thar wheel. He 'lowed you b'lieved it was stole. An' truth was, he knowed he didn't come by it right straight. A young boy nigh Ring-fence Plantation traded it to him fur mighty little money. His dad had give it to him fur Chris'mas, an' the chile had got tired of it an' had ruther have a few dollars. I begged Jed not to humor him; 'twas wuth mo'. But Jed said a plaything a boy is tired of ain't wuth nothin'. 'Twas a good bargain fur him, an' he gits a heap o' trade 'mongst the young fry. But he oughtn't ter helped the boy sell his wheel unbeknownst to his folks."

Her serpentine aspect was not altogether unjustified. As she charmed so wisely, Desmond's conviction was shaken. She laughed a little, as if embarrassed, passing the hem of her apron back and forth in her hand.

"Truth is, he was mad 'cause it carried out my warnings; an' sorter skeered, too, 'cause he seen how it mought look to other folks. Jed's real helterskelter. He pulled loose and drapped down the river, but he hadn't gone a mile before he was sorry. That's Jed."

The boat-hand, listening, and now quite won to complaisance by the unusual prosperity that had befallen the "trading-boat," here in its cache, echoed loudly, "That's Jed!"

"So I didn't git my duds the beautiful lady promised me."

"Mrs. Faurie would no doubt send them to you if she knew where you would be," said Desmond, mechanically meditating on his suspicions. The story was very glib. The shanty-boaters might have had no complicity with the tragedy at Whippoorwill Landing and no culpability as the receivers of stolen goods,—thus accessory after the fact. But the flavor of the French brandy still lingered about his palate; evidently they did not know its value as a beverage, and this was suspicious. Still, smuggling was comparatively a venial matter, and he had a vague regret that he had been so quick to direct the suspicion of the authorities upon so poor and defenseless a group. But he had had no word how the information had been received, or whether it was to be acted upon. Nevertheless, it would be easy to prove the truth of her story, provided her story was true.

"Just as well she is where she is to-day," Regnan declared. He was leaning back in his chair, having finished his meal with a good relish, and feeling about in his cigar case to make sure that its contents had escaped without injury in the general flood. "Try one of these,"—he held it across the table to Desmond. "They seem to be all O. K."

Desmond selected one, and, leaning over, struck a match on the lid of the stove. "The luckiest thing imaginable for us," he said in jerks, as he held the light to the end and pulled hard to set it aglow, "that we happened to see the boat when we did."

"Fires up all right?" Regnan queried. Then—"You must charge us a good round price for this dinner, madam. We are paying for not being at the bottom of the bayou,"—he laughed. "We have a special reason for not wanting to meet up with something we know is there."

His face changed suddenly; he looked at her in consternation. Never had he seen such an expression as settled upon her countenance. Fear it was at first. "For God's sake, what!" she gasped. Then—anger. "Ye'd better mind yer tongue, now!" Her fingers closed on the handle of a great butcher knife on the meat block in the corner. And now—venom. "Ye're jes' two cowardly, lying rapscallions! Ye dunno *what's* in the bayou! An' ye ain't got no call to know! An' besides,"— with a realization of self-betrayal,—"thar ain't nuthin' thar fur ye to know—ha! ha! ha!—te, he, he!"

Regnan had risen, startled and wondering; but Desmond sat perfectly still, looking steadily at her, convinced that, added to the unstoried crimes and the unsavory detritus that the bayou hid under its black waters and its deep, unstable mire, lay the stolen wheel, and heaven knew what gear besides, from the looting of the store at Whippoorwill Landing by the merciless murderers.

It was a painful moment. He was glad to walk to the door of the cabin and look out once more at the steadily falling rain; at the spurious palpitation that the drops set up on the surface of the immobile stream; at the dark, encompassing forest, the water-side vegetation still in the pallid green of spring, seeming to hold all the light and color of the neutral-tinted landscape; at the slow circling of the vapors about the deck of the shanty-boat. There was a projection above the door like the shelter of eaves, and as he stood, only an occasional drop of water fell upon his head. He was all unprescient; he was conscious merely of distaste, the exhaustion from exertion, a sense of inexpressible boredom, the discomfort of his half-dried garb, and an impatient desire to be through with the whole episode. It met him like fate!—the muffled boom of a distant bell!

CHAPTER XI

It was a strange thing to Desmond. Try as he might, Regnan could not hear it. Summoned to the door, he stood and looked out, and bent his attention to discern only the rhythmic throb of the rain, only the waves splashing across the deck, only the slow drip of the water through a leak in the flimsy roof. He looked curiously at his companion as Desmond, every fibre alert, his eyes afire with excitement, his lifted hand trembling, and the cigar between his fingers dead in its ash, would exclaim "Now!" and stand motionless again, listening acutely as if to an echo.

"I hear nothing but the rain," said Regnan. "But even if there were no rain, we couldn't hear the bell at Dryad-Dene so far as this."

"But this might be the bell at Great Oaks," argued Desmond.

"They wouldn't ring unless they were overflowed. We left Dryad-Dene high and dry this morning, and Great Oaks never goes under until Dryad-Dene is half drowned, hardly ever even then; for the Fauries have a private cross levee that protects Great Oaks, to a considerable extent. Besides, there is no danger yet from high water,—all talk and the usual spring scare."

"There!" The bell boomed again, shaking the mists. And Desmond looked into the face of Regnan in triumphant confirmation, to find his companion fixing agitated, half-compassionate, half-questioning eyes upon him.

"My dear fellow," laying his hand on Desmond's arm, "you don't hear a sound but the rain."

"I must go! I must return at once to Great Oaks."

Regnan remonstrated. They would be bogged down; the continued exposure would kill them; he would not be a party to so foolhardy a hazard. "What good could you do? If they are going under water, they are ringing up the force to bring out the gunny-sacks and patch up the break."

"It might be something else. There!"

Along the dark waters the sound was borne. It filled the fall of the rain with a distant undiscriminated vibration.

"I ought to be able to restrain you by reason, Desmond," Regnan urged seriously. "Don't let me have to appeal to these people for aid."

"Look out," said Desmond, with a dangerous flash of the eye. "They are river pirates. I have cause to know."

"So have *I*," declared Regnan, bursting with laughter. "I saw two bales of cotton tucked away in that closet when that rascal opened the door to get the brandy."

A word, a nod, an inferential phrase, and Regnan was in possession of the story of the bicycle and of the suspicions of the shanty-boat's complicity as a "fence" with the marauders of the looted store at Whippoorwill Landing.

"If you are minded to trust yourself to such creatures, I can only deplore your lack of judgment. If you will come with me, I know they will be glad to put you up at Great Oaks."

"I'm afraid of getting my feet wet," Regnan whimsically protested.

"You had much better come with me to Great Oaks."

"I'm all right here. There is nothing to gain by meddling with me. These people won't dare. If I should be missing, they know that you would give information where I was last seen. I am perfectly safe. I am going to take up my abode on this trading-boat, my ark, as it seems, till the waters subside. The dove is apparently something of the fiercest. And the lunatic yonder sends cold chills down my spine. But I will risk them, rather than that treacherous swamp. So will you, if you are wise."

Boom! Desmond had already paid his score without question, to the surprise of the boat's company, accustomed to dicker on a price.

"Make my excuses to the Kentopps," he said to Regnan, ending the discussion and turning to leave.

"If ever I see them again," cried Regnan. "I feel my feet spreading out in webs. I think my wing feathers are sprouting. I'll be transformed into some sort of waterfowl and never get beyond Bogue Humma-Echeto any more!"

"I'll send the horse back to-morrow," Desmond called out. He sprang through the rain from the deck to the dark and marshy soil. But his horse lifted his head with a glad neigh of recognition, and as he put foot in stirrup and rode off, the animal set out at a swift gait and with a stout willingness of heart that showed his eagerness for a comfortable stall and manger, and his weariness of the detention that had nevertheless rested him well. Under these conditions the inundated swamp proved a less difficult proposition, albeit the water had risen almost girth high and the wading was slow,—the horse splashing along with a distinct impact of the mire, pulling with a sort of suction under his hoofs.

Desmond, prescient of disaster, he knew not what, fired with the ardor of a rescue, he knew not from what, ready to sacrifice comfort, safety, life itself, in this wild, adventurous sort in his premonition that Honoria Faurie had summoned assistance, that the bell had rung for help at Great Oaks Plantation, resolved that no aid should come more willingly, more instinct with protective spirit, than from him. It did not once occur to him that this was a superfluous hazard which it was no part of his duty to encounter. His only care, his only hope, was to reach the plantation safely, that he might reach it swiftly. He took no risks, less with a realization of his own interest than a prudence in compassing his object. He exerted a judgment that might have been thought impossible in one so unused to woodland experience; and though the sense of loneliness settled down heavily upon him when he could no longer see Regnan on the deck of his ark, and at last not even the outline of the trading-boat, rising ever higher and higher in the sky as he went down and down into the swamp till indeed it seemed caught up into the clouds, he kept a stout heart. He resolutely turned his mind from the knowledge of the coming of darkness, only an hour or so distant, the savage animals of this primeval aqueous wilderness, the probable chance that he might lose his way, the indefinite data by which he might keep it, his burning impatience of the slow progress which might yet fail to put him ere benighted beyond the immediate region of slough and swamp and bayou, now infinitely increased in extent by the rainfall. The small compass in his pocket which he had used in a lesson with the redoubtable Chub was of great advantage in keeping him to his direction. Straight to the south, Regnan had declared, and he would come at last to the cross levee which usually protected Great Oaks in time of overflow from receiving a share of the neighboring inundations, backing up as the waters were reinforced. Southward he went, struggling through sloughs, swimming bayous, scrambling up steep banks. On one of these his stout horse fell backward almost upon his rider, and Desmond, throwing himself to one side, escaped but for a bruised shoulder and arm, while the animal was badly shaken. He could hardly endure the delay as he stood on the edge of the water by the trembling creature and they had some conversation, as one may say, over the mischance and the necessity of pressing on. But the red roan was a good plucked brute, and before long they were forging ahead once more, man and horse in perfect mutual confidence.

Desmond could have shouted with joy when at last he saw the great winding earthwork, covered with its green Bermuda grass; and when they climbed its steep slope and gained the path on the summit, the horse of his own accord struck a jaunty little canter, glad of the good going and the sight once more of a civilized landscape; for presently within view were great stretches of cotton-fields. And what was that immense expanse in the distance? Desmond could not distinguish for the rain and the mist, and for a phenomenon of far more import. In the shadow of a stretch of forest a huge gully intervened in the levee,—fresh, the earth on the sides showing a degree of dryness despite the rain, the sod of Bermuda ripped through, and the turf, still green, thrown aside. The levee had been cut, and Desmond received an illumination in the recollection of the boat-hand's words that Jed Knoxton had gone forth that morning with his spade. He began to have an appalling sense of the extent of the disaster even before he came upon a counterpart excavation and realized that the levee had been cut in more than one place. The nefarious job had been thoroughly done, and though in broad daylight, the cloaking fog and blinding rain offered an impunity that a dark and clear night could scarcely have afforded. He understood now the significance of that broad expanse of copper-hued glister of which he had caught but a glimpse through the aisles of the woods and the serried ranks of the rainfall; it was overflow, miles of overflow, submerging the wide tilled and orderly fields of Great Oaks Plantation. And that roar in the air—what was it? Tumultuous, loud, with a petulant dash and a sinister sibilance, blended with episodic crashes and sudden wild clamors, like the frenzied turbulence of savage beasts. It was the voice of the Mississippi River, silent no longer in its deep channel, but rioting in shallow floods over the aghast, despoiled plains, crying out in its license and its mad joy, seeming now and again to smite against the sky.

The wind was rising. The gusts, coming down the great, unimpeded highway of the stream, gave impetus to its currents surging against miles of levee still unbroken, and lashing and sweeping away, melting in a moment, the embankments that collapsed under its force. The water nearest at hand, he perceived, was backing up; it was not long before he had reached it, lapping playfully about the base of the cross levee on which he stood. How long this path would continue practicable he could not compute. The horse, more accustomed to the river and its incidents, was showing evident signs of uneasiness, and in fact he stopped presently, with tossing head and startled eyes and planted hoofs, before Desmond perceived through the rain and the distance a white flashing in the dun evening light, which, had he no experience of the locality, he might have mistaken for a cataract. The inference was obvious. It was the foam of raging waters as they tore through an excavation intersecting the cross levee once more. The great volume of the flood was surging over its summit. It was a question of only a very short time when the levee, along which he had come and where he now stood, would be swept away. Both he and the horse were in imminent danger of death by drowning. His first impulse was to turn back and retrace his way. But at this moment of hesitation his attention was caught by a moving object on the face of the waters, emerging from the fog and the rain, and gradually materializing as a man in a very small boat.

"Hello!" cried Desmond, peremptorily.

The man ceased to paddle and looked about him doubtfully, at first on his own level, only descrying the mounted figure on the embankment at a second stentorian roar from Desmond.

"Fur de Lawd's sake, is dat you, Mr. Desmond!" he cried out in instant recognition. "In de name o' sense, what you gwine do up dar on dat levee?"

"Is that you, Seth?" for the negro was a hostler on Great Oaks Plantation, a very black fellow, looking as he sat in the dugout like a silhouette against the gray rain and the white mist and the yellow water. "I don't know what to think—"

"I does," Seth promptly interrupted. "I think you gwine git yo'se'f drownded, an' Colonel Kentopp's hawse, too."

"How deep is the water?" Desmond had the instinct of remonstrating against this as a decree of fate.

"Six feet along dar, an' risin' every jump. I ain't never seen the contrary old ribber on sech a bender, an' I been knowin' her gwine on fawty year."

Desmond was alarmed at the idea of jeopardizing the valuable horse. He hardly noticed Seth's plaints.

"We-all's levee done cut—'fore de Lawd, dem planters in Deepwater Bend below Great Oaks would be mighty glad if dey could cotch dat varmint dat cut de levee. Dey nachully depends on Great Oaks cross levee to keep the ribber off 'n dem, when Dry'-Dene goes under. Oh, my Lawd A'mighty, dis am a drefful day, shore!"

"I had better ride back along the levee," said Desmond, ponderingly.

"It'll be under water in ten minutes."

"But I must take the horse to some place of safety."

"Whar is dat?" demanded Seth, walling his great eyes, with the whites very prominent as he gazed up at his interlocutor at long range; the distance was constantly lessened, however, for he paddled closer and closer to the base of the levee as he talked.

"What is the safest way to the stables? I will take the horse there."

"What you gwine dar fur? You hatter charter a steamboat. Water up ter de mangers."

"In the Great Oaks stables? Is the mansion flooded, too?" Desmond, in keen alarm for the household, trembled to hear the reply.

These disasters and their concurrent dangers were so new to his experience and even traditions that he could scarcely contemplate their encounter with composure. Seth seemed to him a stolidly unfeeling clod, hardly able to stretch his limited faculties to an adequate comprehension. But indeed, though there was no lack of water hereabout, Seth had contributed a tear or two to the floods in his woe and despair for the destruction of these familiar values by which he lived and in which he had such vicarious pride.

"The stable under water? Why, how about the mansion?"

"De gret house is safe!" Seth snapped out, as if the question were imputatious; even the insubordinate Mississippi River would not venture upon the presumption to meddle with the dignified mansion house of Great Oaks Plantation. "I jes' seen Bob, an' he 'lowed de water had filled de grove, an' air lappin' 'round de underpinnin', but 'tain't riz yit inter de veranda."

Desmond was aghast at this intimation of jeopardy.

"De gret house is on high groun', an' dough dey tuk up de kyarpets wunst, de overflow ain't never been rightly in de mansion house."

"Bob ought to be there; it is the footman's station," Desmond exclaimed, thinking how few the inmates to cope with any unusual danger.

"Dey ain't none o' de house sarvants dar, 'cept de cook-woman. Mis' Honoria sont de rest ob dem ter holp dar famblies at de quarter. Bless de Lawd, boss, ye oughter see de quarter!" Seth's voice rose to a distressful quaver. "'Twas so suddint—the cross levee never gave way before, an' we-all ain't never had no sich water as dis here. Some o' de tenant folks is sittin' on de ridge-poles ob dar cabin roof, savin' nuttin' but dar bedclothes; dar funicher is floatin' 'way like 'twar 'witched an' gone swimmin'. The chillen wuz mighty nigh drownded. One dem pickaninnies ob Liza Jane's war cotched by the tail ob its coat an' hung in a cottonwood tree. Hit hollered! But hit never squirmed. Hit knowed catfish an' yalligator war smackin' dar lips an' sharpenin' dar teeth for hit. Lawd! Lawd! We ain't never had no sech time. Mis' Honoria sont ebery sarvant from de gret house ter holp dar folks, 'cept de cook-woman—an' *she* say she is feared ter ride ter de quarter in de overflow in a dugout."

"That was why the bell was ringing, then; to summon help?"

The darkey paused, leaning on his paddle, and looked up at Desmond with a curious and searching eye.

"Bell!" he exclaimed. "The Great Oaks plantation bell ain't rung since daybreak."

There was a pause. Desmond knew the superstition concerning bells,—the ancient universal tradition of mystic summons. There was no habitation nearer the bayou whence some great brazen casting could send forth that coercive tone; the distance from the river was too great to admit the sound from a passing steamer.

"Naw, sir; if you hearn bells callin' you to-day, they ring in your mind. Somebody in heaven or hell, or somebody in yearth or air, is callin' you, callin' you by spirit bells—thoughts reach furder'n sound. Mighty cur'us, but that's sure true. Bells!" Seth raised himself on his paddle and looked up with a face distorted by query and fear into the rain and fog. "*Bells!*" he said again. Then he lent himself to the work of the paddle, and was soon within leaping distance of the levee.

"You gimme dat hawse, boss, an' I'll take him ter de risin' ground whar we got what we is saved. Lawd! ye ought ter see de cattle drownded! My Gawd! De cows mooin' an' de calves a-blatin', all swimmin' as long as dar legs could work 'em along—an' de sheep! Ef I had time, I'd jes set down an' moan an' weep an' preach dar funeral. Some ob de best head ob our Great Oaks cattle! Dar carcases floatin' down de ribber or cotched in de bushes in de swamp!

Gimme dat hawse. Colonel Kentopp's a perlite man, but I'd hate fur anything belongin' ter him ter git lost on Great Oaks Plantation. *You* couldn't find yer way. I'll take tacks an' short cuts, an' I know whar is risin' ground. You an' de hawse would lose yer way an' both be drownded. You git in de dugout an' go ter de mansion house. You kin find dat, ef ye kin see ter keep ter de west."

The immemorial dugout, peculiar to the Mississippi River country, is a primitive craft, nothing more, indeed, than a log, roughly hollowed out and shaped as to stern and prow. It is quite adequate, however, to the purposes of its creation, for skirting banks, navigating bayous and lakes, rarely venturing into midstream or crossing the great river. It is safe enough in accustomed hands, but it is doubtful if Desmond were not in more danger of drowning thus embarked than returning on his precarious route along the summit of the levee. The dugout wallowed portentously as Desmond stepped within its restricted space, but after a few words of instruction from Seth he righted the craft and presently paddled off easily enough, the darkey standing beside the horse, watching the boat till it was lost to sight in the rain and the approaching dusk and the fog closing down.

"I 'spec' dat ar man is safe in de dugout," he muttered, "dough his kind is used ter de saloon ob a side-wheel steamboat, an' dat's de fac'. We done loss enough cattle drownded dis day, 'dout him ter top off wid." So saying, Seth mounted and rode away into the rain.

Though the dugout was a new proposition to Desmond, he had had some experience with the paddle as a propelling agent. His Alma Mater was situated on a watercourse, and at one time the Indian canoe and paddle was a favorite fad. Thus his progress was swift through the rain and the fog, despite the fact that for the first time he felt the strength of the current of the Mississippi; for he was soon out of the limits of the back water and in the direct course of the overflow. He would have scorned the acceptance of a superstition, but the premonition of a summons was so strong upon him that he stretched every muscle to his task. The glimpse of the wide expanse of water, that might have appalled him, alone and without guidance in the midst of its willful, riotous turbulence, was but limited. The fog shut in, and but for a few boat-lengths he could see naught but the surging yellow current of a restricted space and the pallid curtain of the cloudy dusk. Sometimes a shadowy looming near at hand intimated a building half submerged, invisible in the fog and rain. More than once he thought he heard voices, whether far or near he could not determine. An incident of the high water, on which he had not counted, was the débris aloose and afloat, which invested navigation with undreamed-of dangers, with which he could make no covenant of caution. More than once flotsam shot past him in the gloom on the swift current, with a force as if flung from a catapult; sometimes it was the lumber of a wrecked building; once it was a capsized boat, adrift, telling either of the strain of the current, breaking it loose from its moorings, or of a hapless wight lost upon the turbulent waves; once it was a drift log, which was upon him almost as soon as seen, shooting out of the white invisibilities of the mist and striking the dugout amidships with a force that threatened to send it to the bottom. It rocked so violently that Desmond had much ado to keep it right side up. When the drift log had disappeared and he was once more paddling on in clear water, it seemed so deep, the current was so strong, night was closing in so fast, that he began to fear he had been swept out to the main river; at length, however, the mist gave intimations here and there of vertical, shadowy objects at close intervals, which he only discriminated as the trees of the grove when he came in sudden contact with the bole of a gigantic oak. The dugout rebounded from the collision with a violent recoil that seemed to stir all the fibres of the hollowed log, but Desmond could hardly realize the shock which had jarred his every bone, so rejoiced was he to feel himself near his journey's end. He steered more deftly after this, with more heed, with less effort at speed, perhaps because the mists were lightening, or that now he had his faculties better in hand since his plunging, frantic haste under the spur and lash of suspense was abated, as his object was achieved. Soon he was able to discern that he was surely and swiftly approaching the house, which to his surprise, massive and wide and low in the gloom, showed not a single gleam of light. He saw the live oak at one side, which the veranda encircled, towering up into the air, and suddenly he lifted his paddle and let the dugout drift without a sound. For there, in front of the main entrance, a yawl swung at a distance of a few oars' length, kept from drifting by the occasional stroke of half a dozen rowers. At the bow a man was standing, holding a colloquy with the inmates of the house. Desmond had not heard his words, the husky, gruff voice and defective articulation had masked them, but his heart plunged responsive to the clear, vibrant tones, thrilled with fright, as Mrs. Faurie spoke as boldly as she might.

"But they are not here," she said.

The man gave a sort of derisive chuckle and the oarsmen laughed together. One of them, a thick-set fellow with matted red hair, vaguely familiar to Desmond, sitting crouched in the place of the stroke-oar, spat contemptuously in the water.

"Well, Mrs. Faurie, whar mought you be willin' to say they are?" the spokesman asked.

Another, pale, wiry, hatchet-faced, and evidently a meddlesome lout, intruded a sneer. "I reckon," he said, with a simpering, brisk intonation,—"I reckon ye won't purtend that you disremember whar you put thutty thousand dollars wuth o' emeralds."

"I will not, indeed! I put them into a bank in New Orleans."

Desmond realized that she was standing at the open window of the parlor, and from such shelter as it afforded was holding parley with the villains,—it was doubtless the identical gang of river pirates who had looted the store at Whippoorwill Landing with such signal impunity.

"Then, madam, we will take your order for them," said the flippant intermeddler, airily.

"Keep yer face out of it,—ye're bug-house, Danvelt!" said the thick-set man. "What good would the order do? She would signal the fust steamboat that passed,—she would telegraph as soon as we were gone!—send a nigger in a dugout across the river to the railroad flag station in the Arkansas. Either one would overhaul us."

"Mightn't be ekal to signalin' an' telegraphin'. Might be gagged an' under lock an' key—ef still alive!"

The man in the bow spoke authoritatively. "Sorry not to take a lady's word. But biz is biz! We will search the house, an' if the jools are not thar, sure enough, you will obleege us with your order on your bankers, and the key of your deposit box."

Mrs. Faurie had lost control of her voice. It was high and shrill in the dank, misty air. "I will not permit you to enter. I warn you of the consequences if you set foot on that veranda. You will all bear witness," she added, as if she addressed an unseen group within.

The feint, gallant-hearted as it was, failed of conviction. The spokesman, openly scornful, disdained response other than threats. "The Miss'ippi River is mighty convenient, here."

"Tain't gone dry noways that I can see," said the pert wit of the party, and there was a tumult of chuckling and shaking shoulders in the boat.

"We have a lot of rope handy," the spokesman continued, holding up a coil in his hand, his hard face white and fierce against the gray waters and lowering sky. "Look at them iron vases!"—the rims of the great lawn ornaments, six in number, showed above the surface of the swirling waters, where they stood at the end of the broad walk and at the intersections of the driveways on either side of the mansion. "They will make capital weights, enough to sink every soul in the house,—the three boys, old man Stanlett, yerself, and even that big fat nigger cook-woman, for that is all ye have got in the house,—sink ye, every one; the Miss'ippi River is one hunderd and eighty feet deep in Deepwater Bend, even at low water." He shook his head ominously, and the rills of rain ran off the wide slouched brim of his hat with the sinister energy of his motion. "Never be heard tell of no more,—if ye don't see yer way to accommodate us with the order and the key."

And, sooth to say, if she should! There was no alternative. It was only a subterfuge of inducement. Desmond's blood ran cold. He perceived in aghast dismay the symmetry and perfection of the plan of the miscreants. They had doubtless made sure of the absence from the plantation of the manager, who was in Vicksburg on a business trip, and of the visit of the tutor to Dryad-Dene, before they ventured to cut the levee. The inundation of the plantation quarter with its flimsy low houses menaced its inhabitants, especially women and children, with drowning, and would draw to its succor every available man from the stanch mansion house, which was amply able to cope with floods. When the servants should return, the absence of the family would be accounted for variously in their minds and without apprehension of evil: some passing steamboat might have responded to a signal and sent out a yawl to assist them to a refuge in Natchez or Memphis, there to abide till the overflow should abate; some neighbor, the Kentopps, the Mayberrys, perchance still on dry ground themselves, might have come and delivered them from their inundated domicile. There would be no one among the tenants and servants left in authority, no one fitted to act. Days might well elapse before aught would be suspected. The order upon the bankers would be duly honored; the fence in New Orleans—for doubtless in an affair of such magnitude the robbers were provided with a respectable seeming *deus ex machina*, some shyster at the bar, some trickster of a loan agent, some defaulting bank official on the eve of detection and flight—would be upon the high seas with the famous emeralds, before the Faurie mystery, as the disappearance of the family would be called, should set the river country agog with horror and baffled wonder and impotent despair.

Desmond's strong head was dizzy; his stout heart fluttered as he realized the peril and the tenuous possibility of succor,—a single hair to which he might cling, the fraction of a minute of time! If only he could enter the house first! From without he could hope for naught. He could not cope here with six brutal and hardened villains, doubtless the miscreants who had wrought robbery and arson and malignant murder in the tragedy at Whippoorwill Landing. He could not show himself here, for he would only sacrifice his life, worth more at this moment than ever before,—than it could be again. He dared not shoot from ambush; for a failure of aim would result fatally to her, to him, to all in the house. He could not venture to step on the veranda, lest his footfall be heard or even his form be dimly descried from the yawl continually oscillating to and fro.

Oh, for one impulse of courage in that fainting feminine heart! Could she but rally her forces to withstand their demand, to brave their hideous threat, to hold them in parley but one moment longer. His own heart leaped as he heard her voice again. It was full of quavering vibrations, high and shrill and strangely out of tune. But she spoke stanchly and with the poise of dignity. "This is my house. I forbid you to set foot in it,—to trespass one inch on this veranda. I warn you that I shall not be answerable for the consequences. I call you all to witness," she seemed to address the group within. "And I have help at hand."

She uttered the words with such apparent confidence in the midst of her direful extremity that they seemed to carry somewhat of conviction, to stir the suspicion, the cowardice of the marauders. They did not at once move forward, but hung as it were in the wind on the oscillating water.

It was a failure of judgment which induced her on noting the effect of her words to repeat them, for instantly interpreting them as a bluff, the oars struck the water and the craft moved forward. "I have help," she piteously repeated. "I have help at hand."

"You have,—you have, indeed!" Desmond's heart responded, for his plan was perfected in those few minutes of final parley. He let the dugout drift away while he caught the drooping branches of the live-oak tree that swept the surface of the water. The stir of the foliage, as with his rifle he clambered through the boughs, was not to be distinguished from the rustling of the wind. He lifted the sash of one of the dormer windows and was safe in a room he had never seen. A wan gleam of the twilight fell through the glass, barely enough to disclose the surroundings, for the window was curtained with some floriated opaque stuff. An unused room it apparently was, with an unfurnished bed, a few chairs, a table, and in the jamb of the chimney on either side tall presses built in the wall, one of which stood half open and was seemingly full of bundles of papers. A mere glance afforded these details as he dashed to the door. It gave easily under his touch; he had had one dreadful moment, faint with fear, lest it might prove to be locked. He was still trembling as he groped along the dark hall, his weapon in hand. He paused for an instant at the head of the unfamiliar, vaguely descried stairs, feeling with his foot for the edge of the first of the flight.

He could hardly control his agitation, his wonder, as he heard a strange, muffled stir, that sibilant, lisping step on the stair which he remembered from the early days of his stay at Great Oaks Plantation, the silken sound of the invisible patrol.

CHAPTER XII

It shook his nerve, strained to the tension of breaking. But he rallied his faculties. This was no time for vague terrors, for theories, for hesitation. He moved on swiftly, silently. Nevertheless, as he hurried down the dark flight, he could have sworn he passed some mute presence, some sense of moving.

He burst into the dim twilight of the parlor, but still without a sound. There were two figures at the window, infinitely incongruous of aspect with the scene without, with the frightful crisis, with the imminence of their danger. Both were dressed with some touch of elegance for the evening; Reginald with an incipient relish for his own good points, and in the wan light from the window and the dark shadows within the room Mrs. Faurie was like some antique picture, her gown of a light Pompeian-red silk, of a quasi-Empire effect, a girdle of dark red velvet, and a guimpe of thick, fine white lace to the throat,—yet robbery, arson, murder, faced her at the moment. Reginald, pale with a realization of his helplessness, nevertheless stoutly stood his ground, his arm around her waist.

Without a thought, Desmond passed his arm around her from the other side. "Be quiet, be very quiet. I am here," he said in a low tone.

Her head drooped on his shoulder and she burst into tears. "How I have wished for you! How I have prayed for you!" she murmured.

"I am here! I am here!" he said again and again. He could only repeat these words. The fact filled the universe.

He was cool, confident, triumphant, despite the desperate odds, despite the awful responsibility that hung upon his judgment. He made his preparations without an instant's flutter. He waited the significant moment without a pulse of impatience.

Mrs. Faurie, quieted, reassured, in perfect confidence did as he bade her. She stood well up against the wall under the folds of the long and heavy silken curtains, while he placed himself in front of the window, too far withdrawn for his presence to be suggested in the dim light. Not until the yawl had almost reached the steps, not until several of the men had risen to spring upon the veranda, did he raise his rifle and fire. For one moment the flash, the smoke, the report,—deafening in the restricted space of the room,—were the only elements that could claim attention. The next instant the result was apparent. That accurate aim, that steady hand, that cool nerve, had come to Desmond as gifts, unknown until to-day. The ball crashed into the skull of the red-headed, thick-set man he had recognized as Jed Knoxton.

He swayed to and fro for a moment, then fell like a stone into the water, leaving the yawl violently rocking, and the rowers doing all they could to prevent her from capsizing.

The return fire came whizzing through the window, but Desmond had stepped aside and the ball crashed against a mirror on the opposite wall. The yawl's party seemed to have recovered from the surprise at finding a defense attempted for the house, expected to be so easy a prey. They gave no heed to the welterings and writhings of Jed Knoxton in the water at their very gunwales, not able to recover himself, and yet not dead, until at last the relentless Mississippi drowned out the flickerings of life that the rifle had failed to extinguish.

Once more, as they approached, this time with a heady rush, the rifle got in its work. One of the assailants sank down on the very steps of the veranda, and the blood flowed higher than the palpitant waves. An attack from an unexpected quarter further demoralized them. A charge of buckshot from the window across the hall rattled against the timbers of the yawl—with not the best aim in the world, it is true. Reginald had been stationed there in the short interval with a shotgun which happened to be in the hall, and which Desmond hurriedly loaded, directing him to blaze away at random, being careful, as Reginald loved to tell afterward, to warn him to keep from between the muzzle of the gun and himself!

The apparent demonstration of adequate force to make good the defense of the house was too much for the nerve of the river pirates. The yawl was no longer water-tight; the buckshot had riven the wood, here and there, old and rotten. It was filling fast, and this fact threatened their safe retreat. They had intimations of more pressing personal interests than had centred in Mrs. Faurie's famous emeralds. Suddenly putting about, they disappeared in the mist, leaving one of their comrades drowned in six feet of water at the bottom of the veranda steps, and another lying on the floor, apparently dying, the blood flowing from his mouth and tinging all the waves as they lapped about with a deeper hue than the copper tint of the great river.

It would seem that no cheer of evening could ensue on so grisly a primordium of horrors. Honoria Faurie wrung her hands as she reflected, appalled, that a man had met a terrible doom at her door, and his bloating corpse still lay at the foot of the steps to await there the action of the coroner's jury, and that another had stretched his lacerated body on her veranda to die a lingering death. But Desmond seemed to have no affinity or toleration for shuddering or tears. He came and went noisily, ordering fires to be rebuilt in the library and parlor. When Bob reappeared, having made the transit from the quarter in an old dugout, the footman was aghast to hear the startling news.

"Ought to have been here, Bob; you missed the time of your life!" cried Desmond, cheerily. "Oh, it was great! And Mr. Reginald Faurie is a *man*, all right, and don't you forget it. Equal to downing any kind of pirate! Pretty nearly sunk their yawl for them. They will all knuckle down to Great Oaks, after this. We are the pirate tamers here."

Mrs. Faurie had sunk into a chair before the dead ashes of the parlor fire, her face pallid, her chest heaving, her hands nerveless.

"I wish you would give me a little brandy," Desmond said to her, "and you would be the better for what Colonel Kentopp calls 'a weeny teeny nip,' yourself." She walked with him to the dining-room, where he detained her upon the pretext that he, himself, wanted to order the belated dinner.

"I need a *good* dinner," he said. "I have hardly had a bite since a daylight breakfast."

The cook was summoned, an immense woman, so tall and so fat that she was apparently immovable. She had been in the house throughout the turmoils. If the skies should fall, she would continue to sit in the open kitchen window and await events. She seemed to do nothing but sit on the sill of the kitchen window, but when she did move it must have been to the purpose, for she was a famous expert,—of an unparalleled excellence. So long did they discuss each dish and compare views and criticise sauces that Mrs. Faurie could scarcely compose herself to wait and listen to these trivial details. It was a distinct hint when she sank into a chair at one side of the old-fashioned mahogany table, the cloth not yet laid, and put her dimpled elbows on the glittering dark red surface and supported her chin in her clasped hands; while Desmond, still booted and spurred and holding his brandy glass, stood before the sideboard, and the cook filled the doorway, beaming with smiles upon a gentleman who knew so well how to appreciate the delicate miracles of her art.

When at last the menu was settled, he turned for its approval to Mrs. Faurie.

"Oh, how can you think of such things at such a moment"—and she shook her head to and fro while the ready tears came—"with a man dying at my door and another dead!"

"The dying man is very comfortable upstairs in a nice clean room and a fresh, tidy bed, where Bob and Seth have no doubt put him by this time, as I ordered. And the other man got his deserts, as no doubt Providence intended he should. We are not going to sentimentalize about them. On the contrary, we are going to ask for the thanksgiving for special mercies to us to be said in the public prayers in our little neighborhood church next Sunday, and I should think you would write to the rector at once so that the request may be received in time. Go into the library, won't you? and write the note at my desk,—the fire must be blazing there,—while I dress for dinner."

"Do you have to take the trouble to dress for dinner?"

He spread out his hands in dismay. "Do you want me to come to the table like this,—with my boots full of water and all over mud?"

She still sat at the table and looked at him through her tears, realizing his vital aid, his courageous rescue at the most crucial moment of her life. But his little devices to divert her mind, to sustain her composure, to prevent a morbid reaction of sensibility, all of which she appreciated, touched her in a different way. The one was essential salvation, but the other had so tender, so careful, so individual a thought for her.

"You are so dear!" she said abruptly; "I shall never call you 'Mr. Desmond' any more. What is your Christian name? Yes, Edward. You are my dear, *dear* Edward; like a dear, *dear* son!"

As she sat at his desk in the library, she was surprised to find how she liked to be there. She wrote her note, and wept some happy tears of gratitude over the occurrence which had taken on the aspect of a merciful deliverance rather than a tragedy; she lingered, fingering the little objects of chirographical use that belonged to him—the paper-weight, the pen, the blotter-holder—and thinking of his thought for her. But for the wholesome influence of his sound intellect her nerves would be shattered by the reaction, she would endure agonies of foolish regret and terror; she would not now have this glow of earnest love to God and confidence and gratitude that made her heart so warm. Yet her equanimity was not entirely restored, and she had a sentiment of recoil when Mr. Stanlett brought a very pallid, harassed, and tremulous face to the window and looked in; then entered by the long sash.

"I am hunting for you, Honoria," he said in a strained, husky voice. "I am much worried."

"There is no need, Uncle Clarence." She was surprised by her full, steady tones. "Edward Desmond will attend to all these troubles. See what a miracle he wrought to-day, by the favor of God. We were at the end of our capacity even to hope."

"Yes—but, Honoria," the old man leaned forward as he stood and laid an impressive finger upon the edge of the desk. "This man, Desmond,—I had forgotten his name was Edward, if I ever knew it,—he takes a deal on himself! Without a word to anybody, he ordered this marauder to be put in the blue room upstairs. And there he is now—in the *blue* room!"

She stared at him in amaze. "And why not the blue room as well as any other?"

He shook his head, and with a gesture of despair struck his high, bony forehead with his outstretched palm.

"I forget! I forget! You do not know!"

She looked at him steadily, sternly, for a moment.

"What is it I do not know, Uncle Clarence?"

He had come around the desk and sat down on a sofa on the opposite side of the crackling fire. It was necessary to turn in her chair to face him, and she looked over her shoulder at him as she sat at the desk. He met her eyes miserably, with a detected, hangdog look, but he had closed his lips resolutely; she saw that he would say no more. His face was bloodless, deathlike in its pallor. He looked very old, with his spare frame, his clear-cut, bony lineaments, his thin, silver hair.

There is something infantile in the infirmities of age. It touched her maternal spirit. No one was making enough of Uncle Clarence,—he had been neglected. He, too, was to-day greatly threatened by overpowering odds; and a man disabled by age and infirmity must feel an appalling helplessness, a pathetic shame, to be no longer of force, of availing courage in the face of physical danger, a source of refuge and protection to the weak. And so great had been the peril, of so terrible an aspect, that it might well have touched his intellect for the time being. She did not press for his answer, albeit she was of an imperious spirit and not accustomed to have her will gainsaid or her words set at naught. She rose and advanced toward him, pained to see how he cringed at the idea of her persistence while he yet massed his pitiful resources, his face hardening, his eyes aglow with an excited gleam, yet terrorized lest his steadfastness fail. He watched with doubt and expectancy, like a beast at bay, as she sat down beside him and laid her hand on his shoulder.

"Don't be troubled, Uncle Clarence," she said, in a dulcet tone. "You are hardly yourself, you have been put through so much agitation and suspense to-day."

He glanced at her ever and anon with excited and furtive eyes, and moistened his lips, but kept silence.

"I will ask no questions that you do not want to answer." She passed one of her soft white arms around his wrinkled old neck, feeling it stiff and rigid with his tense resolve. Then she laid her cheek on his shoulder. "I love you so much. I can't endure to see you worried."

"It is just for you, Honoria. Just for you," he protested huskily.

"Don't worry for me, I feel so happy to-night—so happy! as if I had the world in a sling! I think it so strange. To-night—of all the nights in the year! I suppose it is because we had such an escape." Yet when she thought of the escape, she shuddered.

"I am much worried, Honoria. The—blue—room!"

"If you loved me as much as I love you, you would not worry. Think, Uncle Clarence, how much we are to each other,—almost like father and daughter. We ought to stand by each other."

"That's why, Honoria, I have taken my course. For you, my dear! And—the—blue—room!"

"Let it pass for the time, Uncle Clarence,—for the moment. We will ask Mr. Desmond if the man can be moved without injury, and set your mind at rest; though for my life I can't see that the blue room is less to be desecrated by his presence than any other."

He held his lips together once more as if afraid of disclosure, and sat stiff, immovable, furtively glancing about with absorbed eyes; and as she with maternal patience drew her soft arm closer about his neck, her head on his shoulder, the glow of the shaded lamp and the flaring fire on the rich tints of her dress, her beauty embellished by her softened expression, the two were a charming illustration of reverend age and filial youth when Desmond, freshly groomed once more, stood a moment by the window ere he entered by the sash.

Desmond was in no mood for concessions. He had assumed control of the household, and he had a strong if not a heavy hand. He declined at once to interfere with the wounded man.

"It might be as much as his life is worth to move him. I am not competent to judge. I am not willing to risk it."

Her sympathies went out to the old man, inadequate to cope with this masterful, youthful usurper.

"Uncle Clarence seems to desire it," she said, not without emphasis.

"I cannot imagine a reason sufficient to jeopardize the man's life," Desmond rejoined.

"I am not informed, sir, by what theory I am to submit my reasons to you," said Mr. Stanlett, with stately and satiric dignity.

"Oh, Uncle Clarence,"—Mrs. Faurie started up in alarmed remonstrance,—"think what we owe to Mr. Desmond—how grateful we should be!"

"That is neither here nor there," said Desmond, maintaining his placidity. "You are the arbiter of events here, Mrs. Faurie, but you *must* not suffer this man to be moved, and perhaps sacrifice his life—"

"Heavens—no!" she interpolated.

"—Especially before he can be interrogated by the authorities. The information he may give will cause the apprehension and the breaking up of this gang of river pirates, and avoid the accomplishment of such disasters as menaced this house to-day."

He turned toward Mr. Stanlett, who had risen and stood stiffly, a sort of blight on his face, at one side of the low, old-fashioned marble mantel. "I am disturbed to differ with you, Mr. Stanlett, to urge my views against your preference when you have been so kind to me."

"My kindness is returned in a way I had not anticipated," said Mr. Stanlett, coldly.

"Oh, Uncle Clarence, I protest. *Don't* mind it, Edward!" She smiled and, leaning over, patted Desmond maternally on the coat-sleeve.

"I *do* mind it very much—to incur Mr. Stanlett's disapproval. But, my dear sir, it will be only for a short time. The officers will reach here in the morning. I have sent Jacob off in a dugout with an imperative note to the constable and the coroner; they must come. If the man can be moved, he will be taken to jail; at all events, he can't be long dying with that hole bored through his lungs. Then the blue room will be once more at your service."

"*At my service!*" the old man sneered. "You know nothing about it! You only show your ignorance."

The announcement of the belated dinner put an end to the discussion, and as they filed out, Mrs. Faurie's face was pale and drawn and altogether unlike itself. But Desmond seemed in high spirits. He begged pardon for asking for a cocktail before the soup, and he praised a certain different combination so that Mr. Stanlett requested that a glass be mixed for him, remonstrating sharply against any dilution, when Desmond good-naturedly diverted his interest by reminding him of the classical apportionment of water with wine, smilingly quoting "Hail, Dionysus: are you Five-and-two?" The mixture proved sufficiently potent, and sent the blood to the old gentleman's pale cheeks and brought out a gentle dew on his forehead, and predisposed him to enjoy and digest his dinner, to postpone his unrevealed trouble, and to hope for the best.

Desmond developed a spirit of gossip. He recounted the details of the house-party at Dryad-Dene, and Mrs. Faurie and Mr. Stanlett laughed, though slyly, at Chub, who seemed to think that Desmond had committed a great impropriety in mentioning Miss Allandyce's boyish equestrian costume and describing his embarrassment that he did not later recognize her when accoutred in white silk skirts. Reginald and Horace indulged in great hilarity at this demonstration of the prudish Chub, and Mr. Stanlett was immensely "tickled" by the description of Loring's sufferings because of the unwelcome reminiscences of the old wood-chopper, Sloper, concerning the millionaire's family.

"Shows just what a snob Loring has graduated into," said Mr. Stanlett, his face now pink from Clos Vougeot, the blue room forgotten. "His parents were most reputable, educated, respected people, even if they were not well off, and the only reason they were ever acquainted with such a party as Sloper, as every one knows, is that in this sparsely populated country everybody is acquainted with everybody else. But social differences are now and always have been rigorously maintained."

He had a keen commercial interest in Desmond's detail of Regnan's suspicions that the house-party had been made up to show Dryad-Dene to advantage to Mr. Loring, with charming young people in gala attire enlivening all its highly decorated apartments, and how Regnan resented the idea that he had danced not for his own pleasure, but like a trained dog, for a purpose.

Mrs. Faurie dimpled and beamed, and asked him how the ladies looked and what they wore, now and then checking his description with the exclamation "Impossible!" and setting him to rights with apt conjectures as to fabrics and styles.

"If I were mamma, I'd give a house-party that would mash the Kentopps flat," said Chub, sturdily. "I'd have up a lot of swell guys from New Orleans and down from St. Louis and Memphis, and then I'd open the ballroom and dance all one day and one night on a stretch, and have a party supper and dinner and breakfast,—and leave the Kentopps out!"

The older boys collapsed over this truculence of the vengeful Chub and his idea of a fashionable entertainment. Mrs. Faurie checked him, though smiling. "Mustn't bear malice, Chubby. I am too old for a young people's party."

"Prettier'n anybody, ain't she, Mr. Desmond?" said the confident Chub, with his mouth full of salad.

To the tutor's amazement, he flushed to the roots of his hair at this appeal. He felt the blood mounting and pulsing as it rose, but he was ready with the repetition of Miss Mayberry's compliment to the "most beautiful woman in the world," albeit he doubted his good taste in the rehearsal. Mrs. Faurie, however, who had often heard similar appraisements of her attractions, took the remark quite simply, and was absorbed in the interest of recollecting details concerning this Italian count, who was a man of talent and high position, and whom she had often met in notable circles while she was living in Paris. This brought them to a harmonious end of the feast, and when they rose from the table, Desmond proposed a return to the parlor, where Mrs. Faurie countenanced the cigars, and seated herself before the fire in a great fauteuil, her Empire gown of rich yet delicate red enhancing her beauty, her eyes fascinated by the flames, her lovely neck glimpsed through the lace guimpe, her quiet respiration rising and falling calmly, the tumult of fear assuaged that had shaken her heart so few hours ago.

Desmond had taken his station on one end of the sofa, where Chubby also ensconced himself, for out of school hours he had developed a great disposition to loll on his tormentor. The other two boys had seats here too, facing the window, but only the inconsiderate youngest spoke out his sudden surprise.

"Where does all that light come from?"

Mrs Faurie turned her head apprehensively. The verandas were under a steady illumination, and for a distance the murky waters of the overflow showed their constant, sinister palpitation.

"I had those lamps filled and the brackets fastened to the posts," Desmond said coolly. "I found them by rummaging around upstairs. I suppose they must have been used in some entertainment in the house. There were some reflectors, too, in the ballroom."

Mr. Stanlett raised himself in his chair, his cigar held out at arm's length.

"You have no call to go rummaging around the house. It—it—is outrageous! It is—is—intrusive!"

Mrs Faurie had paled. "Do you anticipate another attack on the house to-night?" she asked in agitation.

"No," said Desmond, "for I am prepared for it."

Beneath his gay and cheerful exterior, sustaining the spirits of the household lest the palsy of panic overwhelm them and bring down undreamed-of disaster, Desmond had wrestled with some sombre fears, distressing doubts, troublous paucity of resource. There was no boat due to pass, or he would have braved the maddening floods in the primitive dugout to put Mrs. Faurie on board. He had thought of the neighbors, to ring the plantation bell and summon aid. But the neighbors by this time were struggling with the overflow, or seeking to patch sodden and threatened levees. Their own families were exposed to the manifold distresses of high water, and the very fact that marauders were abroad had homing promptings. Besides, he did not wish thus to advertise to the river pirates that the occupants of the mansion felt incapable of its defense. The garrison had already demonstrated its efficiency; the pirates no doubt believed that they had been misinformed as to the unprotected condition of the house; and though Desmond feared an attempt at the rescue of the wounded man, in order that he might not turn state's evidence, inculpate the gang, and compass their capture, he could rely only on such means as had been equal to the emergency in the afternoon, hoping that this would prove adequate to whatever the night might bring forth. The idea that Mrs. Faurie was the focus of their schemes, the suggestion of wresting from her an order on her bankers and by some nefarious plan rendering her incapable of giving the alarm till it should be honored, filled him with dismay. The possibility suggested abduction, imprisonment, even murder. He had provided against surprise. No boat, no swimmer, could approach the house without becoming instantly visible,—the old ballroom lights playing a part undreamed of in their festive design. He had posted one of the most reliable of the house servants as a lookout on each veranda, and a relief sat in the kitchen, finding royal good cheer in the remainder of the big dinner he had ordered with this view. His rifle was loaded, his pistols at hand, and Reginald had been called aside and, as he protested, given some points concerning the best method of distinguishing the muzzle from the butt of the gun. He had in fact been taught to load, aim, cock the hammer, and pull the trigger, and he had a half dozen buckshot cartridges in his pocket as he lounged on the sofa.

"Won't the lights attract attention and make navigation easy?" she asked.

"Perhaps; but they will show that we are on the alert and ready for all comers," said Desmond. Then after a moment of hesitation, "It was an accident that they did not reach the veranda before I did this afternoon. Now, any approach would be detected at a considerable distance."

Her level eyebrows were drawn. "I had hoped the danger was over," she said, with a sort of plaintive patience.

"But not the precautions," he replied, with a smile.

"Why don't we have up some of the tenants from the quarter? they could spare ten or twelve men."

He did not tell her that he had already attempted a levy from the quarter, and that the tenants had revolted. For the dead flatboat-man lay alongside the veranda steps with a dog collar and chain around his neck, to keep him from floating away while awaiting the coming of the coroner; this Desmond had been compelled to attach with his own hands. The negroes did not so much fear the living as the dead. They would not undertake to touch the floating body and lift it to the shelter and security of the veranda, there to await the coming of the coroner; they would not wittingly approach the house so long as it was there,—nay, until it should be removed to a distance and to an unknown place. They did not believe that the pirates would dare return, and were not actuated by fear of them, but they were sure that Jed Knoxton would haunt them to their dying day! "I think they are perhaps shy of meddling in our feud," Desmond replied to her suggestion. "The darkeys always seem doubtful as to whether they are fairly instructed as to the points at issue in any disturbance among white people, and are afraid of getting into trouble with the authorities. They would merely give the sense of strength in numbers, anyhow. We had enough, to-day, and to spare."

Nevertheless, he had not permitted to depart those whose vocation had caused them to return to the mansion, and who, upon discovering the facts, would have been glad to get away again. They were fain to reconcile themselves to the grim necessity as best they might. The old butler, whose attachment to the family dated from before the war, a man of experience and intelligence, pinned his faith to the Faurie banner in weal or woe. He smartly admonished Bob, his son, to "show some manners," when the footman was

157

insisting upon putting a goodly quantity of the Mississippi River between himself and the locality where such dreadful deeds were done and which harbored such ghastly visitants, and withdrawing to the quarter. It was not merely that the old butler knew that special duty rendered in time of stress received a special and proportionate reward, for he was long past his prime and had no ambitions disconnected with an aspect of distinction in the Faurie dinner service. But a word to the wise Bob was sufficient. Though under constraint indeed, he cheerfully consented to watch in turn with his father on one side of the house, while Desmond and Reginald kept a lookout through the parlor windows from the front. The cook insisted that naught could approach undiscovered from the east while she sat on the sill of the kitchen window, and Seth, the old-time hostler, who dwelt in a world of Houyhnhnms and rated as slight matters any disasters that did not concern the frog and the fetlock, or threaten spavin or sprain, found his sympathy with mere humanity so indurated by disuse as to be able to stand guard over the wounded pirate to make sure that he did not attempt to escape, that he wanted for naught in comfort, and that no shadowy approach was made toward the house upon the waters viewed from the dormer window, from the hood of which Seth continually scanned the expanse.

"Too many people make confusion and get into each other's way," Desmond explained to Mrs. Faurie. "I need only one steady lieutenant like Reginald here. I invited Regnan to return to Great Oaks with me, and I was sorry at first that he did not come. But we are all right without him."

"I wish I could shoot," plained Chubby.

"I am going to put a stop to this mollycoddle business, anyhow," said Desmond, waving away the smoke from his cigar and looking at Mrs. Faurie with challenging, laughing eyes. "Just as soon as we get out of our ark, I am going to have regular target practice three times a week, and teach these boys how to shoot, and then we will borrow Mr. Sloper's dogs and go on a camp hunt of our own."

"Oh, little Chubby," protested Mrs. Faurie, while Chub fairly rolled himself into a ball of chuckling delight, hugging himself as if he felt that he might fly to pieces in the centrifugal force of so much ecstasy.

"Little Chubby is a good plucked one! I was proud of Chub and Horace,—to stand here in the parlor, and hold still without a word, and get in nobody's way, and make no confusion, and face danger without a protest. Oh, this is a great day for the house of Faurie! We have three men here, rather small-sized and callow as yet,—but *men*, for all that!"

"Oh, you make me feel so proud of them!" cried Mrs. Faurie, laughing and flushing with pleasure.

Suddenly a drear sound—knock! knock! knock! at the front of the house.

CHAPTER XIII

Mrs. Faurie sprang up with white lips and a half scream. The old gentleman, who had sunk into a placid doze, was roused from slumber to vague but terrible fright.

Knock! knock! knock! again reiterated at the door. The three boys gazed in questioning suspense at the tutor's face.

"It is not"—Reginald began—he had held the chain while Desmond locked the dog collar—"it is not—it could not be—"

"Oh, no! *Impossible!*" cried Desmond, bewildered nevertheless, and at a loss.

The strain of the events of the evening was telling on the tutor,—even the stress of the effort to sustain the equilibrium of the household was making its impression. Some moments elapsed before his mind could evolve a conjecture, a reasonable solution of the mystery, and all the time the heavy, dull knocking was renewed at ominous intervals.

"It must be—it is—a drift log!" he exclaimed at length. "No, you must stay here," he insisted, as Mrs. Faurie started forward; "Reginald and I will see."

He led her back to her chair, and was not sorry that he had done so when he opened the door into the hall and saw there all the negro watchmen, trembling and agitated, with a look of abject terror shown in the swinging chandelier.

"No, no! Nathan,—I am astonished at you. You know that a dead man cannot knock at the door! No, Bob! You can't have the dugout. I have got it chained and padlocked. If you leave us here, you will have to swim. Seth—you, too! It *must* be a drift log. I am going to see. I might have been afraid of that man alive, but I have got a cinch on him, sure, now that he is dead. Nobody in the house knows that he is there, but Reginald and me. You tell that fat old cook in the kitchen that the Mississippi River hasn't swept him away from here, or that the other pirates didn't take him with them, and she'll die of fright. I should want no ghost of her size after me, if I were you. Keep quiet here and I'll see."

It proved to be a drift log, and with the aid of a stout cane Desmond leaned over the railing and pushed it clear of the entrance to the house. The body of the flatboat-man had not yet risen, and as the log was on the surface, it struck against the floor of the veranda. Unluckily, as it floated down a little farther on, it caught in the angle between the flooring and the projection of the steps, and there it swung on the oscillations of the current,—knock, knock, knock,—and there it was destined to hang and, as if it were the dead man clamoring for admittance, knock, knock, knock in a dull monotone at intervals all the livelong night.

Desmond could not rally his energies again for a show of cheerful spirits. He could no longer direct the trivial conversation and evolve ebullitions of satisfaction and pleasure. Despite his gratitude for the crowning mercy of his rescue of the household, he had a sentiment of infinite repugnance for the taking of life, necessary, justifiable, even laudable though it was. That dull knock, knock, knocking at the door where lay the man he had killed beat upon more sensitive nerves than he had yet known he possessed, and set them all a-quiver.

When Desmond induced the negroes to return to their posts, old Joel made a great show of self-ridicule and abasement that so little a matter should have shaken his equilibrium. "'Fore Gawd, boss, I done turned fool, fur a fack! *Drift log!* Gawd A'mighty! I wuz cradled in a *drift log!* I been paddlin' in dugout hollowed out'n *drift log* dese six or seben hunderd years. I been loadin' up an' firin' powder fur Chris'mus in de *drift log*—Lawd! eber sence Noah fust went a-wadin' in de overflow. An' now—done took a skeer ob a *drift log!* Ye-all will have ter hire somebody to wait on de table at Great Oaks besides a *dee*stracted ole nigger whut is afeard ob a *drift log.*"

Seth was retreating up the stairs, chuckling at the causeless fright, and Bob was mightily entertained to see the old butler at fault, who was so rich and ready in caustic reproof to the young and flighty. Desmond and Reginald turned from the servants and repaired to the parlor, where the tutor was able laughingly to explain the cause of the sound to the group waiting by the fireside, and to apologize for having awkwardly towed the log into the angle of the steps so that it could not shake free, and thus the melancholy iteration of its oscillations against the flooring would probably continue all night. "But I move that we pay as little attention to the sound as possible, and adjourn for the present," Desmond continued, looking at his watch.

"I feel as if I could never sleep again," said Mrs. Faurie, pressing her hands to her temples.

"What a pity that you sent your maid down to the quarter. She could have a cot in your dressing-room and be company for you so close at hand," suggested Reginald.

"Yes, she is afraid to come back. She made all sorts of excuses, but *that* is the truth," said Mrs. Faurie. "I sent her to help her people save their things; their household furniture and bedclothes are so important to them,—hard to come by and difficult for them to replace,—the accumulations of many years."

"Suppose you let Chub have a cot in your room," suggested Desmond.

"I won't," said Chubby, stoutly. "I won't sleep in a room with a lady!"

The collapse of the two elder boys over this demonstration of Chub's delicate modesty was shared in less degree by the others, while Chub sat gravely on the edge of the sofa and ejaculated—"The *idea*!"

"He'd be no good, anyhow. He is a perfect dormouse," said Reginald.

"Leave him alone in his propriety," added Horace.

"Let things be as usual," said Mrs. Faurie. "Anything different might get on my nerves and make me wakeful."

Desmond was rummaging in a drawer. "There is a hammer here. Will you let me nail up the window-shutters so that the room can be entered only from the hall?"

That idea of a coerced order on her banker operated on his mind like an obsession. Should the pirates return, in view of their peril by state's evidence, to attempt the rescue of their comrade, they would have the opportunity for a renewed effort to secure the paper with its rich guerdon in case of success.

"Nail up the windows!" exclaimed Mrs. Faurie. "Heavens! I feel like a pampered lunatic."

"It would do no harm except to the shutters, and would mightily set my mind at rest," urged Desmond.

"Work your will on the shutters, then, and peace to your mind!" she said, laughing a little at his impetuous haste, as Reginald caught up a lamp to light him and the two made off together.

When they were through with the windows, it would have been as easy to tear down a section of the house as to effect an entrance there.

As the group stood together in the hall for the last few words, the knock, knock, knocking was renewed, as of solemn clamors for admittance. None of them mentioned the sound, and presently they were all gone except Desmond and Reginald, who seemed to linger, but really intended to wait and watch all night.

"The lights are better out," said Desmond, reaching up and extinguishing the swinging lamp in the hall chandelier. "If they should come, which God forbid, they could not so easily get about the house in darkness, and we could fire at better advantage from the shadow than in the full glare of the veranda lights."

They closed the window-shutters of all the house as they patrolled the verandas. The width of these was great enough to limit the light sent across the rooms, but thence through the slats one could look out almost as with the distinctness of daylight on the great brown welter of water palpitating with the rainfall and undulating with the current.

"You had better lie down for a while in the parlor," Desmond said to Reginald. "No—you will play out long before day, if you have no rest at all. You will be well within call here, with your gun beside you, and you can watch through the slats for any approach from the front of the house."

They had arranged that one or the other should remain in the hall outside Mrs. Faurie's door—unknown to her, however, lest this precaution excite her alarm anew—throughout the night. Reginald was in a tremor of terror to perceive that it was she against whom the schemes of the marauders were most directed. He had earlier thought of the family silver and the scattered valuables about the house, and had fancied that these had allured them hither, but that most appalling suggestion of a coerced order on her New Orleans bankers and the extremest measures to insure its being honored was of far more sinister import. The silver in its present form was easily identified; melted down, it would be mulcted of half its value in the loss of the rich chasing of the ornamentation and the fine workmanship. Moreover, the water-rats might well fear their own discrimination between what was real and what might be a heavy plate and for their purposes worthless. But there could be no possible doubt as to her order on her bankers. Without question they were in communication with fences and graduated rogues in New Orleans of such a quality as to be able to present such an order without fear that it would not be honored. Truly, the possibility invested the menace that hung over the house with a terror which he could scarcely contemplate without a complete collapse of all his faculties, and which drove every impulse of sleep from his heavy eyelids. He sank down obediently on the sofa, however, and sought to compose his mind, his eyes staring into the gloomy waters, his gun on the floor beside him within arm's reach, his ears acutely discerning every sound within the house, and the splashing of the water against the foundations as the rain fell and the currents of the overflow rose ever higher and higher, and now and again the sombre vibrations of the knock, knock, knocking at the door before which the dead man lay.

Desmond had thrown himself at full length on the long, old-fashioned, mahogany hall sofa, that he, too, might find some repose for his exhausted limbs,—now beginning to ache and stiffen from the stress of the day's exertion,—if not solace for his racked and anxious mind.

The dark house had grown still—so still that the silence seemed sinister, as if some portentous crash must break this unnatural hush. The lapping of the water had become monotonous, the ear so accustomed to it that it scarcely impinged upon the sense of silence. The ghostly knock, knock, knocking had its sombre echo, and the interval relapsed into muteness. There was no stir of whatever sort from the bedrooms; the inmates were all lost in slumber. The house might have seemed tenantless, when suddenly Desmond became conscious of a sense of motion. He raised himself on his elbow and stared about him.

The hall was absolutely dark. The glass half-moon above the solid panels of the double front door, and the panes in the long side-lights on either hand, were covered with some quilled stuff that tempered the light to gloom by day, and utterly excluded the glimmer of night. He could not have said how or when it came, but something was astir, he knew, even before he heard that lisping sibilance of the ghost of a step on the padded velvet carpet of the stair. Again and again it sounded, sometimes regular for several steps; then silence; once more the sibilant tread, sliding on the silky pile of the velvet. Farther and farther it receded, unmolested; he thought it was gone! And once more—the impact! And now all was silence; he listened in vain. As he laid himself back on the sofa, the cold touch of the haircloth with which it was covered caused him to withdraw his hand with a jerk and start violently. Then he composed himself anew and sought the rest his fagged-out system so needed.

At another moment he would have sprung up to challenge the presence, but in this juncture he remembered the alarm a sudden commotion in the hall would rouse. Mrs. Faurie was aware of the peculiar jeopardy in which she stood. The demand for the emeralds, for the order on her bankers, had apprised her that she was the special mark for the enterprise of the marauders. So extreme a terror as a sudden awakening to more turmoil and suspense might prove too much for her nerves, for her overstrained heart,—might, indeed, be fatal. This demonstration marked no intrusion, no new menace; it was only the old unexplained, inexplicable spectral mystery which he had encountered when he first reached Great Oaks Plantation,—almost forgotten until this afternoon when he had sprung into the window and rushed downstairs, hearing a sibilant descent and passing an unseen presence.

In the midst of the lull induced by the uncanny associations, he felt a rush of impatience that this fantastic demonstration should be forced upon his attention now,—at this time, when any slight lapse of vigilance on his part, any failure of judgment under circumstances so strange to all his training and experience, might cost the life of every one in the house. He believed that there must be some natural explanation for the manifestation; but since it baffled reason and conjecture, it mattered little to the fact that he did not fully accept it. He had as distinct a thrill quivering icily along his spine as if he had no philosophy whatever, and as he placed his hand on his brow, he felt that cold drops were standing there.

Suddenly he sprang to his feet. There was a commotion upstairs, not so much a tread or a movement, but a husky, half-smothered voice crying out. In the tremendous crisis that the moment was to him, he remembered

163

to open the front parlor door, and with a whisper he motioned Reginald to take his post on the hall sofa while he bounded noiselessly up the stairs, three steps at a time. He burst into the room where the wounded man lay—expecting he hardly knew what. It was the only chamber alight in the house, yet full of distorted shadows. The kerosene lamp had been extinguished, and the dim illumination came from that primitive contrivance known as a button lamp,—a bit of cloth tied over a button, the end lighted and set afloat in a saucer of lard, giving a clear, tiny flame peculiarly adapted to a sick-room. Seth had placed this on the fireless hearth, and thus shining upward, all the furnishings cast gloomy shadows on the wall. They seemed curiously out of proportion,—out of drawing, so to speak, because of the slant of the walls of the half-story structure and the deep recesses of the dormer windows.

In the middle of the room Seth stood staring, evidently just roused from slumber; his starting eyes were on the wounded man, who had struggled into a sitting posture, wildly gesticulating toward the door, every fresh exertion sending the blood spurting over the bosom of the white night-shirt furnished him, and trickling down the white coverings of the bed.

"Who is that thar guy?" he exclaimed huskily. "An' what's he comin' after me fur?"

He fixed wild eyes on Desmond, who marveled whether it was yet time for the delirium and fever attendant upon a gunshot wound to set in.

As he spoke in a soothing voice, the incongruity of the situation could but strike him. He had sought to kill this man and had nearly compassed his object; but now he was laying the gentlest hands on the marauder's shoulder, and trying to place him back in his recumbent posture. The danger was all gone out of him, but the semblance of kindness seemed strange.

"Nobody is going to disturb you. Take your night's rest. Lie down and be quiet."

The marauder grasped Desmond's arm with a sunburned hand garnished with broken nails. "But—say—*who* was he? Oh, my! he looked comical! What's he want o' me?"

"There's nobody here," protested Desmond. "Lie down."

"Can't stuff me! Ain't slep' a wink ter-night." A shadow crossed his face, which was young and broad, and with a "bang" of straight sandy hair, a square jaw, and a long, thin mouth. "I got too much to study 'bout."

"Don't do it now," Desmond kindly admonished him. "You have started that wound to bleeding. Lie down."

"That man looked comical; he didn't look like folks hereabout! He had on a three-cornered hat."

Desmond gave so palpable a start that the wounded marauder noticed it. "Ai-yi! *You* know him," he said with significance. "Is he after me?"

"Did he have powdered hair?" Desmond asked, surprised at his own temporizing, and remembering Reginald's description of the nurse's vision.

"Gunpowder on his hair!" the man said wonderingly. "Naw, 'twuz white! An' Lord! he didn't expect to see me lookin' at him. He flipped in—an' when his eyes met mine, he flipped out. Say—I be 'feard o' him,—he looked so comical! Say—is he *alive*!"

Desmond turned to the attendant. "Seth, who is this man?"

"Gawd A'mighty, boss, I dunno!" Seth gasped, the whites of his eyes distended and their pupils wildly rolling. "Ter tell de trufe, boss, an' shame de debbil, I jes' batted my eye one minit, an' dar war dis man shyin' an' plungin' an' 'lowin' dat he done seen—I reckon 'twuz dat ar Slip-Slinksy what de chillern talks about wunst in awhile. Lawe-a-massy, Mist' Desmond, lemme go home! 'Fore Gawd, I can't stay here no mo'! Lemme go'—leastways, down ter de kitchen, whar *he* ain't neber been seen nor hearn. I can't stay whar Slip-Slinksy—oh, yi! hi-i!"

He was looking in affright over his shoulder at a sudden movement of Desmond's shadow across the slanting wall. It was clearly demonstrated that the utility of Seth in the offices of sick nurse and lookout was at an end. So charging him to say naught to his fellows downstairs, on pain of being ordered to return to the sick-room, Desmond assigned him to a post on the back piazza within call of the others, and within exchange of cheerful conversation with the corpulent old cook, always a fixture, half a-doze in the kitchen window.

The clumsy descent of the stairs by Seth, used only to the one-story dwelling so common in the region, Desmond thought was sure to advertise his withdrawal to all the house. But when the back hall door had closed upon him, absolute quiet succeeded. All the inmates were asleep,—a much needed rest, obviously. But the continued hush demonstrated how essential was the strict watch, since so turbulent and erratic a transit had failed to rouse the domicile. He reflected that the cautious methods of burglars could never have permitted so much noise. He began to doubt the vigilance of his sentinels. He had no blame for Seth, who had slept at his post. It had been a strenuous day of excitement and labor for the hostler, and indeed for all the household retainers. The exposure to rain and wind is always of a peculiar exhaustion to the physical energies. He began to fear that, thus absorbed by the strange manifestation of the troublous peripatetic spirit of Great Oaks Plantation, worse dangers might have been allowed to approach.

He went swiftly to one of the dormer windows, and looked out upon the great flood as upon an inland sea. Still the rain fell; the drops stood in bubbles, and again coursed lazily along the panes of the glass, and through their corrugations he could see the rippling waters in the wan light of the illuminated veranda; the vague boles of the trees in the shifting mist; the floating débris,—here and there uprooted bushes, logs, fence-rails, timbers of buildings; but never a boat, never a human suggestion. The ark could not have seemed more lonely, more aloof from all humanity in the floods that drowned the earth, than did Great Oaks mansion in that deep and memorable overflow in Deepwater Bend from the crevasse in the Faurie cross levee.

The tiny light of the primitive button lamp burned whitely on the hearth; the fire was dead some hours since, and no coal gleamed through the ash. The room had a comfortable aspect, though the blue and white curtains were still undrawn as when he had sprung through the window there. It was at the opposite side, and without shifting his posture, where he sat in the recess of the other window, he could see through it the sloping roof of the veranda, on which lay the boughs of the live-oak tree towering high above. A table at the foot of the bed held a glass from which restoratives had been administered, a bowl which had been filled with the soup in which the old cook excelled, some lint and home-made bandages from an old linen sheet, ready for use in case they might be needed for stanching the further flow of blood. The floor was covered with a blue and white matting; the woodwork was of the old china-white paint, as smooth as enamel. The white wall-paper bloomed with blue corn-flowers,—it was the blue room! There were presses in the jambs beside the fireplace, and these, too, were of the spotless white of the door and chair-rail and wainscot. The bed was dressed in white, but from the half canopy long blue curtains depended, mottled with some indeterminate design in white. He rather wondered at the freshness of it all, considering its disuse; but there was little dust afloat amidst the densities of the woods and along the expanse of the river, and the traditions of Great Oaks were of famous housekeepers. A single sign of disorder the room showed!—one of the presses was open, and within was glimpsed a congeries of old account-books, bundles of papers, japanned boxes, all in a degree of confusion that implied long neglect or great haste.

When he glanced again at the pillow, he was relieved to see that the wounded man had fallen asleep, doubtless from the exhaustion attendant upon the excitements of the last hour. The breath came with a queer whistling sound from his torn lung, and this gave Desmond a keen pang, notwithstanding the knowledge that the miscreant deserved far worse punishment than the wound he had received. His sunburned face was yet younger of aspect as he slept, and softer; his unkempt yellow hair, his stubbly, unshaven chin and upper lip, and his dirty face on the fine white linen of the pillow-case spoke the limitations of his low station; and the tutor, who had pinned his faith to training, had a reservation in his condemnation,—holding

166

that this man might not have been what he was but for what his circumstances had made him.

Desmond, in the deep, shadowy recess of the dormer window, thus meditating, looked out keenly at every shifting change of the watery expanse, listening acutely to every semblance of sound within the house, hearing even the recoil of the springs of the sofa in the hall below as Reginald altered his position; hearing the water rush futilely against the foundations and turn splashing aside; hearing every iteration of the knock, knock, knocking of the drift log caught at the veranda steps, and he was instantly aware when once more that scarcely to be discriminated impact of a sibilant footfall, so stealthy it was, sounded anew on the stairway of the hall. He could hardly control his impatience,—the inexplicable incident so jeopardized the fidelity of his watchmen, the composure of the rest of the household. He remembered that it was Reginald who had first told him the story of the strange step on the stair. He wondered if the boy heard it now, as he lay obediently waiting on the sofa in the hall below. He wondered that Reginald could hold himself motionless, for not a sound came save that lisping tread, soft, sibilant,—now still, now distinct once more, ascending the stairs.

Desmond had an impulse almost uncontrollable to rush out into the hall, only checked by the fear that he would find nothing. Then, with an effort at self-control, he held himself quiet in the deep, curtained recess of the dormer window. Since the figure had entered this room before the unwilling vision of the wounded robber, perhaps the lure it then followed might again bring it hither. Desmond caught his breath as he heard the step approach nearer and yet nearer. When the footfall was just without, it paused, and Desmond fearfully heard the sombre knock, knock, knocking at the door below stairs before which the dead man lay. The next moment his heart was thumping so loudly that he thought the sound might betray his presence. For there entered slowly, cautiously, with a quick, nervous glance at the bed where the wounded robber slept, the apparition he had described hardly an hour ago,—the figure that patrolled the stairs in the wan moonlight in the tradition of the nurse's vision.

A tall man it was, and spare. He was muffled in a cloak to the chin. He had upon his head a hat, cocked as if accessory to a fancy costume; his hair was white, not powdered; he held in his hand a scroll of paper; his face was one that Desmond recognized instantly, despite the anxious, secret, blazing eye, the tension of excitement in every drawn feature. Mr. Stanlett, with that careful, soft tread, noiseless save for an occasional slipping shuffle incident to the step of age, crossed the room and stood for a moment scanning the face of the sleeping man. Desmond, invisible in the deep shadows of the curtained recessed window, trembled for him lest that peculiar mesmeric influence, responsive to an intent regard, rouse the sleeper to a moment of frenzied fright. But the man still slumbered, the breath still whistling in labored respiration from his torn lung. Mr. Stanlett evidently harbored no suspicion of the shadowed window recess. He was very old, and his age was telling on him in the draughts that this strange secret made upon his powers of endurance. He tottered as he approached the press, its door ajar, and as he paused and gazed at its disorder, he shook his head to and fro in dismay. He pulled the door back, and leaning within, he opened a drawer which Desmond fancied was a secret receptacle. He laid the scroll in this, and then with a cheering face and a brisk satisfaction of manner, his lips set firmly together, he began to push the bundles of papers and japanned boxes back into their places, his nervous, veinous old hands moving here and there with great diligence in his eager haste to be gone. As he forced the door to shut on the crowded shelves, he did not observe what the keen young eyes in the recess perceived, that the corner of one of these bundles so protruded that the door did not compactly close. He shot the bolt and turned the key, unaware that neither had gone home, whirled about with a jaunty air of capability, looked keenly at the sleeping face on the pillow, and went briskly but softly shuffling out of the door, leaving Desmond at once relieved, amazed, and dismayed.

He could not for a time collect his faculties to ponder on this strange chance. He sat silently listening to the stealthy footsteps that had so long baffled inquiry at Great Oaks Plantation. He was remembering that on the occasion when the spectre was declared to have been seen, Mr. Stanlett was one of those first present in the hall below, and could not recognize, it was said, the features of the apparition through looking upward at the landing. The steps retreated farther and farther, and at last their sibilance sounded no more.

In the silence Desmond took counsel with himself. There was something of mystery here, of an importance to justify some risk, of a continuance to warrant years of concealment. What it was, whom it might affect, he could not imagine. He had the sentiment that whatever is secret is wrong. And certainly this was in a keeping neither wise, nor consistent, nor competent. His nettling discovery, for he wished now he knew naught, entailed a certain responsibility. The old man imagined that the scroll was in a secret receptacle, locked and double locked. And, in fact, one man, perhaps indeed two—for Desmond could not feel sure of those half-closed eyes and whistling breath—knew that it was within reach of any deft and groping hand. He revolted at the assumption of responsibility with which he had no concern. Nevertheless, this had been thrust upon him, and in view of the personnel of all concerned, he could not shirk it.

He rose abruptly, crossed the room, and opened the door of the press. He, too, gazed doubtfully at the sleeping man in the bed, who did not stir.

Presently Desmond's deft hands were fingering the outline of the secret drawer. It was constructed after an old and ordinary type, and with one or two efforts his thumb pressed a spring and the drawer shook loose. Taking the scroll, for there were no other contents, Desmond slipped it without examination or a glance of scrutiny into his breast pocket.

As he descended the stairs, Reginald rose from the sofa to meet him. "Such a night," he whispered. "As if we have not enough to bear already, I heard—I could almost swear it—old Slip-Slinksy going up and coming down the stairs!"

Desmond passed his arm around him and gave him a jocose hug. "And this is the fellow I have been calling a man. Afraid of nursery ghosts!"

He was going into the library. The rain had ceased; the mist was lifting. A pale gray light was sifting through the slats of the shuttered windows. The veranda lamps burned queerly out of countenance before its definite, pervasive distinctness. As Reginald threw open the blinds, Desmond was lighting a wax candle that stood on his desk, and sealing in a large envelope a paper at which he scrupulously forbore to look; and as he lifted his head, he saw that the sun was striking long, red, shifting gleams across the great inland sea of the Mississippi overflow.

CHAPTER XIV

The waters had not yet disappeared from the face of the earth when the routine at Great Oaks mansion was reëstablished. Those ghastly events, the coroner's inquest, the identification and removal of the flatboat-man's corpse, the ante-mortem statement of the wounded prisoner, and the subsequent capture and incarceration of the river pirates, followed in a rapid succession that seemed incongruous with their importance. The horrified and superstitious servants now went about their duties with casual cheerful faces; the tutor had resumed his pedagogic struggles with the young idea; Chubby, in the intervals of his labors as a student, sat upon the railing of the veranda and fished in the overflow, his skill being now and again rewarded by the splashing of a finny trophy at the end of his line, whereupon long and serious conferences ensued between him and the cook as to the best methods to prepare certain piscatorial dishes considered of small gustatory value by the epicure, and always served in a single platter for Chub alone. Mrs. Faurie had resumed her plaints against the dullness and general vapidity of Great Oaks, but not her lassitude. For there was much to do. The preparation for repairs and rebuilding incident to the destruction wrought by the overflow to the farm machinery, the miles of fencing, the tenants' cabins, brought the manager of the place, now returned from Vicksburg, almost daily to the house, with estimates and suggestions and discussions of ways and means. There were many problems presented, difficult of solution even to one of his experience, and Mrs. Faurie had come to dread the sight of him, with his perplexities, paddling up to the veranda in his dugout, the glister of the blinding sun on the expanse of waters narrowing his keen gray eyes to mere slits, corrugating his brow, burning his complexion almost to a scarlet hue, incongruous enough with his straight yellow hair and straw-colored full beard, for he wore his straw hat on the back of his head.

Mrs. Faurie had begun to say often, "Let us ask Mr. Desmond," when the alternative propositions of plans and computations of approximate expenses involved them both in doubt and anxiety, and he had found the clear-headed views of a man of judgment, progressive yet prudent, of value in appraising possibilities and reaching conclusions, despite Desmond's inexperience in the questions at issue and need of information in the premises at every step. He was so quick to comprehend, so willing to take instruction, so cautious of precipitate decision, of such keen acumen and justice of reasoning, that Mr. Bainbridge was glad of his counsel and to be able to cease to confer only with a woman, albeit the owner of the interests involved. He broached the suggestion himself one day in his big, hearty voice, "Let's submit the whole idee to Mr. Desmond"; then, abashed, perturbed, he looked up fearfully from under his bushy blond eyebrows, perceiving the many untoward inferences to be drawn from his reference to this arbitration.

But Mrs. Faurie discerned none of them. "The very thing," she concurred, touching the bell. Then as the servant appeared, "Ask Mr. Desmond if he can't come here for one tiny minute. Tell him to lock Chubby up in the mahogany cupboard, or fasten him in the letter-press, or kill him a little,—anything, to get rid of him,—and come here quick."

She, too, relied upon Desmond's judgment implicitly, and sometimes he was disposed to protest. "What will you two say if all this goes wrong? You know that I am as green as a gourd to this business."

"Ah, but it cannot go wrong,—it is instinct with right reason. I couldn't devise it myself, but I can discriminate its value. You have the happy hand; everything you touch is successful."

Mr. Bainbridge sat demurely by, scarcely daring to breathe for the temerity of the thought in his mind, his eyes discreetly downcast. Would the widow really sacrifice her great income for this man of pinched conditions? "Mighty smart man, though!" he was sufficiently just to say to himself when out of her presence, as he flung himself into his dugout and took up his paddle. "Mighty glad he is here. Don't know how in the world I'd ha' made out to git along with all these perplexity fits with just a woman's whims to control things." For Desmond often boldly battled with Mrs. Faurie's preferences and prejudices in the cause of her best interests, and demonstrated what was most worth while, and what was idle and useless expense in the rehabilitation of the wreckage of the overflow; and though she disputed with spirit, she was open to reason, and if convinced, was willing to concede.

There were other visitors at Great Oaks in these days, and mightily surprised to find the trio in one of these heady discussions were Colonel Kentopp and Mr. Loring, rowing in a skiff up to the veranda steps and ushered into the parlor before the wranglers well knew that intruders were upon them. At the sight of the papers piled upon the table, the account-book in Desmond's hand, and the budget of letters that Mr. Bainbridge held from Mrs. Faurie's "machinery man," as she dubbed a great factory, Colonel Kentopp's face clouded.

"You have fallen upon evil days, Mr. Bainbridge," he said, gripping the hand of the manager, for he made it a point to be hearty and cordial with all sorts and conditions of people in the conservation of his reputation for popularity. "You will raise more crayfish than cotton this year," he continued, with that agreeable manner of making a distasteful remark which serves the double purpose of indulging one's ill-humor at an interlocutor's expense while complimenting him with conversation.

"Not at all," interposed Mrs. Faurie, for she had an affinity with success, and resented evil prognostications in her affairs as intrusive. "Mr. Desmond says that if the water recedes in time to get cotton planted properly, the alluvium of the overflow will enrich the land and materially increase the yield."

"Much virtue in an 'if,'" Colonel Kentopp contended, as he came around the table with a rolling step and flung himself into one of the big armchairs. "I did not know that Mr. Desmond is an agricultural authority," he continued with a large air of jocularity as he crossed his legs. "I thought his knowledge of rural matters was contained in the Georgics of Virgil—ha! ha! ha!" And he sent a glance of rallying laughter at Desmond from out his round, dark, glossy, unamused eyes.

"Mr. Desmond knows a great deal about many things," Mrs. Faurie retorted promptly, unaccustomed to contradiction or discipline, and restive under the slur of ridicule cast upon Desmond.

"So *we* found out who had the pleasure of being his fellow guests at Dryad-Dene," said Mr. Loring, who had a very bland aspect for a wooden man, as he sat in the group before the fire. He had a great respect for money in the abstract, and Mrs. Faurie represented large aggregations of wealth and thus commanded his interest. He was disposed to soften to her liking the tone of the conversation, which he thought ill-taken. Moreover, he had not often had the opportunity of meeting her, and the sight of the great beauty was an event of moment. He was not a "ladies' man" in the ordinary acceptation of the term, but he had the successful man's reverence for preëminence in any form, and the splendor of her personal gifts appealed to his appreciation of the predominant. Her beauty was always so striking that whatever she wore seemed cunningly designed to enhance it,—even to-day, when her costume was a sheer lawn blouse and a plain black skirt. Her arms and shoulders were so dazzlingly white through the soft fabric; its absolute simplicity made so undeniable a demand to mark how the lack of effort or ornamentation brought into higher relief and added importance all the fine details of her perfect face, the exquisite tints of her long-lashed gray eyes, the lustre of her rich brown hair rolled up so plainly from her fair brow, the beautiful shape of her hands and arms, shaded only by a simple ruffle at the end of her elbow-sleeves. She was in Mr. Loring's eyes a woman whose wishes were to be considered, whose station and wealth were to be respected, whose beauty was to be worshiped, and he wondered at Kentopp's fatuity when, catching his cue, he said:—

"Indeed, Mr. Desmond was greatly appreciated at Dryad-Dene,—especially by the young ladies!" with an arch glance at the tutor.

Loring thought of the dim, pale attractions of Miss Kelvin and Miss Allandyce in comparison with the resplendent vision before him, and he deemed Kentopp mentally a poor creature.

"Of course Mr. Desmond has not had agricultural experience, but he has a very good article of common sense, and with what mind Mr. Bainbridge and I have left, since the overflow fairly crazed us both, we think we are going to make out mighty well," stoutly insisted Mrs. Faurie.

"I'll be bound you do," said Mr. Loring, admiringly.

"But Mr. Desmond is due at Dryad-Dene," protested Kentopp, now on the back track. "He took French leave of us, and our week-end party is not yet dispersed, though the week has. The overflow gave us that boon, at all events. They haven't been able to get away."

"You are very kind, but it is impossible for me to return," said Desmond, courteously.

"Oh, I'm so glad," cried out Mrs. Faurie, unexpectedly, and in a tone of girlish glee. "I was so afraid that Edward might accept." Then, turning to the amazed Kentopp, she added. "You know that he is the source of all our courage. We were in a state of siege here. We look upon him as if he were as powerful as an army with banners."

"Killed two of the men with your own hands; I believe the testimony at the inquest showed that,"—Colonel Kentopp's lip curled as if in distaste. "Painful necessity."

"Not all,—providential opportunity! Edward and I agreed that we would have no morbid sensibility over it," declared Mrs. Faurie.

"Why, I should smile!" said the wooden man, in hearty indorsement, his slang literal. It was not his place, and he knew it, but he rose from his chair with the intention of himself terminating the visit and taking the malapropos Kentopp home. "You have much to do here; we had best be going."

"If Mr. Desmond will not return with us," said Kentopp, gathering his faculties together as best he could, and perceiving the light of elation in Loring's eyes. Great Oaks Plantation would doubtless be soon on the market. Its overflow scarcely made against its value, though it might be utilized to cry down the asking price, since it was only the result of the nefarious crime of cutting the cross levee, that was hitherto a complete protection. Mrs. Faurie, evidently all unwitting of the future, was herself to defray the immense expense of its rehabilitation. Loring scarcely looked as wooden as was his wont, smoothing down his bristly mustache with a jaunty air, a secret smile behind his eyes, as it were, so confidential, so introspective, so self-communing was its expression. Of all the boons that his money had brought within reach of the millionaire, Great Oaks Plantation was the one he most coveted. Even its semi-grotesque amphibious aspect could not diminish his desire as he paused on the veranda, the water lapping about it, the great trees standing inundated, as if knee-deep, the glistening expanse of the overflow stretching out to the Mississippi proper, its channel only to be now discerned by the course of a steamboat ploughing her way through the illimitable floods, no vestige of a shore within view. He was cheerful in his leave-taking, and turned in the skiff, even after the darkey at the oars had rowed far down the submerged avenue, to wave his hand at the group on the veranda, while Colonel Kentopp moodily pulled his hat down over his eyes with a muttered "Confound this glare," as the sun flashed blindingly upon the waste of waters.

The prominence of Desmond in the lady's counsels was also noticed by old Mr. Stanlett, and he regarded it obviously with jealous distrust. He had been peculiarly favorably impressed by the young man during the earlier days of his stay at Great Oaks, and had taken pains to bestow upon him a kindly consideration and courteous attention, of which the tutor, then fresh to his duties and despondent, consciously out of his element, was very definitely sensible. Now, Mr. Stanlett seldom addressed Desmond, and when this was necessary he used a cold civility, in strong contrast to his former demeanor, and savoring very distinctly of a realization of the inferiority of the tutor's position and a resolute intention of relegating him to his proper sphere. Whenever Mrs. Faurie spoke to Desmond, discussing her affairs and deferring to his opinion, Mr. Stanlett was wont to draw his heavy white eyebrows together in a very definite frown, scanning first one and then the other, an angry flush mantling his face, evidently minded to protest. One day at the table, when she chanced to address the tutor as "Edward," Mr. Stanlett stared as if startled, then broke out with so satirical and frosty a laugh that she looked up in surprise, forgetting what she was about to say. She manifested no confusion nor self-consciousness, but Reginald flushed hotly to the temples, and Chubby paused, his fork in his hand, and remarked in callow affront: "Uncle Clarence seems to have a good joke that he keeps to himself."

"Just so, Chubby,—a very good joke—ha, ha, ha!—and I wish to God I could keep it to myself!"

Mrs. Faurie had so far recovered her composure and the tone of her nerves, greatly imperiled in all the anxiety and jeopardy and stress of the tragic events of the overflow, that Desmond resolved on the evening after the visit of Kentopp and Loring to defer no longer to acquaint her with his discovery of the mystery of the spectral manifestations at Great Oaks mansion, and to surrender to her keeping the paper which he had seen so strangely and significantly concealed. From time to time he had furtively watched Mr. Stanlett, seeking to discern if he had become aware of the abstraction of the scroll from the secret drawer of the press in the blue room.

He was sure that the old man would manifest such disquietude as would be ample evidence that his caution had gone amiss. But Mr. Stanlett maintained a genuine composure, absorbed in the simple routine of his day,—the mail from the packet, or the neighborhood news brought by some amphibian in a dugout scouting on various errands on the face of the waters; his cigars; sometimes humming an old song and looking from his easy chair placidly out on the waste of the overflow. Occasionally he occupied himself in telling one of the boys, or the three in conclave, old stories of war times, the gunboats on the Mississippi, the riders and raiders, the burning of cotton—bales, gin, and all—by the soldiers rather than let the precious staple fall into the enemy's hands; and again he abounded in anecdotes of the palmy days of river travel and traffic, the tremendous loads of cotton the freighters carried, the choice company on the floating palaces, the phenomenally high play of the "gentleman gamblers," the competitive speed of the steamers and details of the exciting races, the horrible accidents and the frightful picture a blazing boat presented, a tower of flames, as she came swinging around Deepwater Bend on her course. No; placidity was the keynote of his life save when his frown gathered as his eye fell on Desmond, and his manner stiffened, and his intonation grew crisp and icy.

To-night, as they sat by the parlor fire, he was busied in a game of chess, the fashion of his youth in which he excelled. He had taught Reginald to play with such skill as to give him difficulty enough to maintain his interest in reaching the finality of checkmate. The other two boys were on the rug romping with an Irish setter, and the dog was most unwillingly learning to sit up and shake hands and make a feint of smoking an empty pipe. Desmond could count on their absorption for some time as he passed the window on the veranda and saw them there thus occupied. The moon was beginning to steer clear of a surge of clouds that had hung in the sky all the afternoon, presaging rain, and as its long, golden slant fell upon the waste of waters Mrs. Faurie rose from her chair, laid her book on the centre table, and went anxiously to the window. As she saw Desmond standing outside, she naturally supposed that he, too, was absorbed in scanning the signs of the skies. With more falling weather the waters would rise anew and postpone, perhaps past feasibility for the season, all the plans for the rehabilitation of the plantation, and all the possibility of making a crop or even a half crop of cotton.

"Don't you think that it looks less like rain?" she asked, slipping the thumb-bolt of the sash of the long French window and joining him at the balustrade.

"The rain has gone around this time," he said. "I am very sure of that."

It was difficult for him to bring his mind back to the weather signs, bent as he was upon the imminent disclosure, canvassing continually its best method. He was sensitive in submitting his own conduct for scrutiny, and eager for her approval. He was solicitous concerning matters of phraseology, knowing how she valued her uncle and cherished his age, fearful lest some unconsidered word offend, or, worse still, wound her. He was afraid that the disclosure might involve some shock to her nerves. He did not know, he could not imagine, what the paper so significantly hidden might contain, and how she might condemn his course in possessing himself of it. Indeed, she might deem that he had exceeded all the bounds of convention, and, declining to look at the paper, require him to surrender it to Mr. Stanlett and make confession of his unwarranted interference. He stood in silence, his meditative eyes on her face so long that she noted his absorption.

"What is it?" she said suddenly. "You look strange, troubled. Surely there is nothing more amiss."

"Let us take a turn along the veranda. I have been waiting for days to tell you something."

She assented in silent suspense, and together they walked along the broad, moonlit veranda, the shadows of the trees now and again falling athwart it, the sheen on the waters striking across the expanse for sixty miles, making a vast roadway of glister to the vague unknown of the shimmering distance. Her lustrous dark eyes with the moon in their depths were dilated, expectant, her face was ethereally white and quietly serious. Her dress was white, of a soft, clinging woolen fabric, with a stripe of satin at intervals, that shone itself with a moony lustre. The square-cut bodice was filled in with lace that rose and fell with the stir of her breath as she waited, intent and a trifle agitated.

Desmond began without preamble. "When I first came to Great Oaks, one of the boys, Reginald it was, told me of the step on the stair."

She laid her hand on his arm, and he felt the quiver in its slim fingers.

"I had then heard the step, once,—it was about midnight; and I heard it again, twice,—the night of the attack on the house."

"Oh, oh,—I cannot abide that idea," she exclaimed, with a quiver of pain in her voice. "You never have heard me mention it. I am sure it must be some fallacy,—some"—She could not speak for gasping. Then she gathered her composure and resumed with dignity: "It is nothing,—it is some trick! It is an insult to the memory of the sacred dead. It was never pretended to be heard in the lifetime of Mr. Faurie."

Desmond felt on difficult ground. "I think that no one has ever associated his name with the manifestation, though it is very natural that you should deprecate that idea. But the step is genuine, for I heard it distinctly twice that night; the last time I waited for it to approach, and it entered the room, and I saw the presence in the light."

"Wait,—wait!" she exclaimed, and he paused, for she seemed unable to advance a step. The waters lapped about the veranda; the shadows of the great trees were weird and strange, falling across the surface of the flood flowing in the midst of the grove; the continual melancholy rise and fall of the voices of frogs sounded from woodsy tangles in lagoons and submerged marshes; the broad lunar lustre quivered on the expanse of the gray waters, and the moon rode high,—high in the dark sky.

"Let me tell you," he urged. "I was standing at the window in the blue room—"

"The blue room," she faltered, as if with some vague memory.

"Yes,—where the wounded man lay. I heard the stealthy step on the stair, as I had heard it twice before; a mere slip and then silence, and again a suggestion of a footfall, coming and coming up the stair; and I waited in the curtained recess of the dormer window,—and the step paused at the threshold; the door noiselessly swung ajar,—the step entered,—and it was Mr. Stanlett."

"Mr. Stanlett!" she cried, standing suddenly erect and strong, her moonlit face showing a haughty displeasure; "why should you connect him with such mummery?"

"Because I had heard the step twice before and recognized it; because as I listened to this step it came straight to the door, and, as I say, Mr. Stanlett entered; because I identified his aspect with the description of an intruder who had silently appeared and disappeared at the door earlier in the evening, frightening the wounded man with a vague terror."

"I am ashamed to listen, I am ashamed to question; but if only to have done with these mysteries, I will ask what action did you observe Mr. Stanlett to take while you lay *perdu?*" As she confronted him a proud indignation burned red in her cheeks and her eyes flashed in the moonlight.

Desmond took umbrage at her tone. His spirit mounted as he felt that his motives were entitled to some consideration on that night of all nights, when he had done so much for her and hers at the risk of his life. It was in his mind in self-justification to tax her with this, and demand the respect for his deeds due to the integrity of his intentions. But he, too, was proud. If she could forget her gratitude, he could waive its cause. He continued to describe, with a certain constraint in his voice, how the old man cautiously advanced to the bedside, and with fantastic cocked hat and disguising, muffling cloak watched the sleeping man to make sure of his unfeigned unconsciousness. She winced as she learned that the swift, skulking step took him straight to the press, in which he hid within an interior drawer a scroll of paper.

Desmond was surprised by her next words. "He locked the door of the press? I know that it has a key," she stipulated.

"He *thought* he locked it; but I saw that the bolt did not go home."

She had every trait of wild agitation. "Did you not speak to him? Did you not warn him?"

"Why should I? Would he not have resented my presence as spying on him? when even you resent my disclosure of the fact that you may give the matter such weight as it deserves."

"Resent it?—oh, no! no!" She laid both her cold hands on his as she stood looking up into his face. "I resent nothing from you; we all owe you too much, far too much! But I am frightened, mortified, uncertain. Can't you see that that paper must be of the first importance to be so secreted—setting such a superstition afloat in a simple, domestic household—by the frankest, the kindest, the most gentle of men? Don't you connect and interpret now the story of the step?—always heard just before we complete our preparations to quit the country, for he carries the paper with him,—always heard just when we return, for he brings it back and hides it again. And last week, that dark and dreadful evening when you say you passed the presence, the step on the stair, he thought that we must quit the house and he was doubtless bringing it down. But after you had rescued us—never, never imagine that I forget it for one moment!—he felt safe again and took it to its hiding-place once more. And oh, Edward, how could you—so unthinking, so heedless!— let him leave the door ajar believing that he had locked it,—an old man, Edward, a very old man,—and make off with the useless key in his simple satisfaction while that scoundrel lay on the bed,—oh, I shouldn't speak harshly of the unjudged dead!—and his suspicions had already been excited, and perhaps he secured it, only having pretended slumber,—and oh, we must see if it is really there still. Say nothing to Uncle Clarence; let us go up first to the blue room and see if it is gone; get a lamp,—let us go."

Desmond laid a restraining hand upon her wrist. "It is not there," he said, looking down into her wild, eager, agitated eyes. "I saw the danger of leaving it there, and I secured it for safe-keeping until I could consign it to your care."

"And what—what—is it?" she faltered.

"Can you imagine that I would so much as glance at it?" he replied sharply. "Stop; here we are at the library. I will give it to you now."

CHAPTER XV

The fire was dully drowsing on the hearth; a lamp on the desk burned dimly with the wick turned low. Desmond had a quick, nervous touch as he stirred the embers into flames, threw on a fresh stick of wood, and set the lamp aglow. His sensibilities, despite his vigor and youth, had felt the inroads of all the agitation to which the household had been subjected. The renewed cheer of the room dispensed, however, its cordial influence. We are at last but animal mechanism, and must needs shiver with cold, and burn with heat, and gloom in darkness, and hope in the glad light. Everything seemed suddenly more facile of adjustment, more possible of optimistic interpretation, and at all events the period of suspense was terminated when, seated at the desk, he turned the key in the lock of the drawer and wheeled in his swivel-chair, the envelope in his hand.

"Here it is, at last,—all safe," he said, in his firm, clear voice.

Mrs. Faurie, who had sunk down on the end of the sofa, almost collapsing in uncertainty and agitation and dubious foreboding, her hands pressed to her eyes, roused herself as the room sprang into its wonted cheerful guise and lifted her head. She did not immediately take the paper as Desmond held it out to her. She adjusted a sofa-pillow under her elbow, and set her dainty foot on a hassock on the floor, and piled up the supporting cushions,—hesitating, contriving hindrance, postponing the evil moment.

"I am afraid of entering upon some hasty action and that I may afterward regret my precipitancy," she temporized.

"I should advise you to be deliberate," he rejoined. "From what we know of the history of this paper, it would not seem to press for action."

"And yet delay might be prejudicial," she said, eager when not opposed. She held out her hand for it, and then drew back, once more doubtful. She had grown calm, and she looked deeply meditative as she leaned forward in her soft, clinging white dress from amongst the dull crimson silk cushions, her slim, jeweled hand extended, yet not touching the paper that he held out to her as he sat near by in the chair before the desk. "But have I the right to examine it?" she argued. "It may not concern me or mine. Mr. Stanlett has affairs of his own, no doubt, into which I am not privileged to intrude."

"His course has been very eccentric," said Desmond, tingling with impatience to reach a conclusion, yet not willing to urge her decision, and weighing considerately her every argument and scruple. "He has carried on for years, apparently, a very elaborate and mysterious emprise of concealing a document which, if it were his own, might be considered safe enough among his valuable papers. His midnight comings and goings have given rise, as he knew, to a theory of spectral manifestation in the house which might be very injurious to young minds, and even, in default of all explanation, to elder people. He went so far as to foster this theory by a semi-disguise as a precaution against recognition should he be unwarily glimpsed."

Then they both sat silent while the freshened fire glowed red in the room, and the lamp dispensed its steady, white light, and the great windows revealed the moon shoaling on the vast stretch of silvery water, with the shadows of the trees on its expanse below, and the dendroidal forms towering high into the pearl-tinted sky,—all seeming some strange, mystic, illuminated tangle of enchanted forest and lake, full of dreams and vagaries, of quivering radiance and yearning melancholy, under a spell, perpetual, somehow, and far away from to-morrow.

"But I feel as you do," Desmond recommenced after a moment of reflection. "From the first I doubted my right to touch it. Still, it has occurred to me that in view of his age and its possible relation to his eccentric actions in this matter, and also in view of your position as the head of this house in which these practices have come to your knowledge, you might justifiably open the package, and glance at its contents sufficiently to discern if they concern you. If they do not, then I will restore the papers to him and apologize as well as I can for my interference."

"I believe you are right," she conceded. She took the envelope from his hand. Even then she drew back. "The seal!" she exclaimed. "I cannot break a seal."

"That is only my seal," Desmond explained. "I put it on to protect the papers from interference."

She leaned toward the desk to catch the light on the papers, broke the seal, and drew out two inclosures, one a document of length, the other evidently a letter.

"It is mine!—mine!" she cried wildly. She gave a gasp, her free hand fluttering nervously. "It is my husband's handwriting," she whispered in a reverent, awed tone, as if consciously in an unseen presence.

Then, as her brilliant eyes scanned the lines, shifting from side to side as she read, the color surged up into her cheeks and her lips curved in a radiant smile. Suddenly she burst into a flood of tears, her words, as she sought to speak, breaking into gusts of happy laughter, her brimming eyes looking into his with eagerness to disclose the tenor of the papers, yet in her agitation her powers of speech failing, inadequate. "It is such happiness,—happiness,—happiness" was all that she could say.

Once more she strove to read, but her voice broke and trailed off into a sob that was yet like a gurgle of laughter. "Read it,"—she handed it to him. "Read the letter—I'd rather have it than all the diamonds of Golconda!"

As Desmond straightened the pages, he saw that it was addressed to a lawyer of Memphis, whom he knew to be the executor of the will of the late Mr. Faurie, and in fact this letter related to that instrument. He desired to alter certain dispositions of this will, the writer said, although mailed so recently as by the last packet, and he stated that he had set forth these changes in a paper that he inclosed, duly signed and witnessed, and which he pronounced a codicil to his last will and testament.

"It is, I doubt not, a poor performance," he wrote, "in comparison with the admirable instrument that you drew with such care and skill; but it will hold, and I cannot hope to have a lawyer to come to Great Oaks in time to take my instructions for the codicil, for I fear that my days are at an end indeed." The writer went on to explain that he had grown dissatisfied with the provision which he had directed to be made in the will for his wife. He had desired that she should enjoy as large an income as practicable, and that she should not be burdened with the management of real estate other than her home place, unless she should herself elect to make such investments with the surplusage of her income. Hence he had thought best not to assign to her the usual one third life-interest in his property, but an annuity of thirty thousand dollars during widowhood, which was a larger income than her statute right to dower in Tennessee could justify, and chargeable upon the whole estate, and he had given her also, subject to the same restrictions, his plantation, Great Oaks, the annual yield from which necessarily fluctuated according to the season. Under these circumstances, the interest of the three sons in the rest of the property was to remain undivided during minority, that the estate could be nursed to better advantage. It was to be partitioned, or sold for division, when the youngest became twenty-one years of age, the elder two, however, to receive a certain sum of money upon attaining majority, for the purchase of business interests, that they might not pass in inaction the years of waiting for the division of the whole and the possession of their respective shares.

"So thoughtful," murmured Mrs. Faurie.

It had seemed to him, the writer stated, that the three sons would be rich enough when they came severally to their majority, and could well spare the aggregations of such portion of the income of the estate as he had assigned to the use of their mother, over and above her rightful share, in order that she might have no reasonable wish ungratified.

"Oh, to be thinking of that in those awful last days!" she interpolated, her flush fluctuating, and once more bursting into tears.

"I should like her to travel, for this she enjoys," the letter continued. "I should like her to see the world, and that others might have the privilege and benefaction of seeing her, as I could wish that no one should be beyond the reach of the sunshine. And with all this in view I directed you, as you know, to draw the will as it stands."

Forthwith he entered upon a systematic defense of his motives and views in the corollaries necessitated by these provisions embodied in the instrument. While he had no crude jealousy, he protested, and would not seek to curb his widow's independence in making a second marriage, he was not willing that the extra income allotted to her should go into the control of a stranger at the expense of the estates of his sons. It was one thing, he argued, to restrict the wealth of his sons for their mother's benefit. It was quite another thing to take from them to enrich a stranger, who might or might not be of mercenary motives, of ungenerous temper, or of undue domestic ascendency, and who might or might not permit her the free use of what was her own. Then, too, the subjection of the estates of the sons to the charge of her income under the circumstances of a second marriage was of discordant suggestion; possibly, in the unforeseen mutations of human affairs, even subversive of their independence, and inimical to family peace. Therefore he had had the clause inserted revoking the allotment of her income should she marry again, and substituting as her provision one fourth of the Mississippi property in fee, and a life-interest in one third of the Tennessee realty including, in lieu of Great Oaks, his town residence in the city of Nashville, the rest of the estate in that event to be sold for division, that the portion of each devisee might be ascertained and set apart.

These were his reasons for such disposition as he had made of his property. Now, however, since he had executed and forwarded the will to his executor, he had begun to fear that this matrimonial clause would be misunderstood by Mrs. Faurie, whose feeling for him it might possibly affect, all unexplained as it was.

"But never!—never!" she sobbed. "I always realized that you were actuated by the best motives for what you deemed the welfare of all concerned. But I am so happy to know *why* you did it!"

Desmond paused, a strange thrill at his heart as he gazed at her. She might have been some young girl in the childlike abandonment to her tears, as she leaned on the arm of the sofa, her long white dress a-trail on the dark carpet, her scarlet cheek against her upheld bare white arm, her lovely hands clasped above her drooping head. Desmond's voice was strained, husky, with sudden breaks as he read on.

Upon further reflection, the writer stated, the provisions he had made in the will for Mrs. Faurie in the event of a second marriage had become obnoxious to him. He had accorded her merely the equivalent of her dower rights, such as the law would allow her were he to die intestate, or were she to dissent from the will. In effect, he seemed to make a point of giving her nothing in the contemplated contingency that he could avoid giving. He had not intended thus to interdict a second marriage, and her right to order her life after her widowhood as she chose, according to her most excellent judgment.

"Oh," cried Mrs. Faurie, with a little irrelevant laugh, not for Desmond, but as if she rallied the writer with the extravagance of his approval.

Therefore, the testator declared, he had revoked in set terms both the dispositions of a life-interest in the real estate in reference to a second marriage, and the imposition of a charge for her benefit upon the realty of the whole estate during widowhood. Instead, he had thought best to devise to her absolutely one fourth of the real estate in fee, inclusive of Great Oaks, which he considered particularly desirable because of its income-bearing values, the other three fourths to be equally divided between his three sons.

He added some words setting forth arrangements for the guidance of the executor in regard to disbursements for maintenance, emergencies, and education of the minors, pending an interval which he evidently anticipated would endure for a considerable time, before the estate could be fairly administered. This depended upon the conclusion of a certain litigation involving some conditional increments, then in abeyance. When a decision should be reached, and these assets realized upon, he directed that the whole estate should be partitioned; and in order that the several shares might be justly ascertained, the portion of each of the minors should be chargeable with such expenditures as had been made for him during the interim, and the portion of the widow should be chargeable with such sums as she had received from the funds of the estate; but she should not be obliged to put also into the common stock for division the profits from any investments that she had made, or accretions of value, of whatever sort, that had accrued from means derived from the estate.

Desmond stared blankly at the paper for a few moments after he had concluded the reading of the letter. "Did the executor win the suit to which he refers?"

"Oh, yes,—in the infinitely leisurely legal fashion. It would go up to the Supreme Court and be remanded on a certain point, and then it would go up on another and come down as before. It was a sort of legal shuttlecock. I was amazed when I heard that the lawyers were through playing with it."

Desmond could not control the cadence of depression in his voice. "How long ago was it decided?" he asked, hoping against hope.

"A little more than a year, I believe."

Evidently, the lapse of time could not be a potential factor in the impending future. The contingent event on which the partitioning was conditioned by the codicil had just fallen out, and the rest of the estate, save for the aggregations of income and the depletion of expenditures, was much as the testator had left it, for the executor had no general powers of sale. Desmond could see no reason why this codicil should not be admitted to probate and at once subvert the existing status. Technically, it was itself a part of the will already in force, though its provisions were *pro tanto* a revocation of the previous testamentary disposition. The indeterminate interval after probate in common form allowed in Tennessee, where the bulk of the property was situated, for the institution of revocatory proceedings; the disability of non-age in the minors, to whom laches could hardly be imputed; the fact that it was manifestly impossible for their guardian to take any action in view of the unsuspected existence of the codicil of which the executor was the proper proponent, would seem to annul all obstacles to its effectiveness, despite any complications with which the conflict of laws in the two sovereign states might otherwise invest the situation, the statutes of each of course controlling the realty within their respective borders.

There was silence for a time. Both looked out from the mellow light of the room through the windows on that pale scape of moonlit mist and water and mystic woods, all in pearly neutral tones, soft, sheeny, white, like some dream scene, full of weird suggestions and dim spectacular configurations. Now there was a floating island, distant, half descried; now a flying, gauzy, vaporous figure, with feet touching the surface of the water, and hands laid against the star-studded gates of the sky; now a phantom craft under full sail, with clouds of tenuous canvas and streaming pennants of mist. She saw naught, busied with her memories; and he, strangely grudging, sought for words to snatch her from them.

"You must look at the codicil," he said, holding the document out toward her.

"I don't care for that—heavens, how I love that letter!" and once more she burst into tears. She rose after a moment to reach for it, and then she read it anew, with sudden gurgles of tender laughter and sobs and gushes of tears.

"I suppose that this codicil will, to this extent, revoke the provisions of the will that has stood all this time," he said. He was no lawyer, but he had a definite understanding of the ways of the business world and the justice of its methods. A very appalling possibility began to open before him. He leaned forward and turned the upper corner of the pages of the letter, still in her hands, to look once more at the date, written evidently only the day before the testator's death.

"It has been a good many years," he said, in dismal forecast.

"Oh, forever!" she exclaimed, the tears coursing down her cheeks.

184

He had begun to understand the quandary of the poor ghost, slipping slyly about the midnight quiet of the house to conceal this bit of paper, potent destroyer of its peace. He doubted the policy of putting into words the fear in his mind. But he must have her attention. He clutched at her thoughts with imperative insistence. Those memories, those gentle, tender memories in which he had no share,—how desolate, how deserted they left him! His jealous reproach was in his eyes, all unnoted. His indignation burned red in his cheek. A figment, a recollection, pervaded the room and annulled his presence. But he would not be ignored, forgotten, denied. He grasped at her attention as a child clutches the skirts of its unthinking mother, and persists in its plea.

"In this division the executor may make a claim on you for the income that you have spent. It strikes me that this will operate as the equivalent of a refunding bond."

"Let them take everything. I have this letter!" and she clasped it to her bosom.

He had a sense of turning aside. He could not move her. He opened the codicil himself and scanned its contents. It duplicated the intendment of the letter, but in more formal and lucid phrase. A very exact and strict man of business Mr. Faurie showed himself to be in this paper. Desmond was impressed with this fact, yet dismayed in a sort, in regard to the accuracy of the accounting which the testator contemplated between the minors and widow at the partitioning of his estate. He even superfluously directed that the difference of age among the children should be considered and the actual outlay for each charged, and not merely an approximation of expense as applied to each of them; since the expenditure for the youngest might for a time be more, in view of extra attendance, elaborate attire, and special liability to ailments, and later less than the disbursements for the elder boys. Desmond might have laughed, yet he could have wept, that the testator, despite his evident astuteness, should have permitted himself the simplicity of anticipating that Mrs. Faurie would have applied any portion of her receipts from the estate to investments of real property or the acquisition of other assets that would yield "accretions of value." As well might one expect the sun to hoard its gold or the bird its song of spring. No! nearly seven years of joyous, open-handed dispensing of all her income from the estate were thus chargeable against the one fourth in fee of realty and of the personalty that formed her liberal portion. How much this might be, Desmond of course was not qualified to judge; but the ravages in this provision which the restoration of that great income for nearly seven years must needs work might well appall the pallid Mr. Stanlett in his niece's interest, and set as talk the storied spectre, the Slip-Slinksy of the midnight stairs.

"Mr. Stanlett must have found this paper in some unaccustomed receptacle," Desmond hazarded.

Mrs. Faurie sat stiffly erect. This phase troubled her more than the fear of the financial loss; it touched her pride. Her level eyebrows were corrugated into a frown. Her eyes were bright, hard, restlessly glancing. But she bent her faculties to the consideration calmly. "Perhaps," she said thoughtfully, but her lips were stiff; they moved with difficulty to frame the words so distasteful to her. "It was understood that all Mr. Faurie's important papers were already in the hands of his executor. He, himself, had them transferred some time before his death,—it was not unexpected."

She was silent for a few moments, looking reflectively out of the window. "I remember that the rest of the papers, account-books, packages of letters, files, and all such things were taken out of the library soon after Mr. Faurie's death and, without examination, placed in japanned boxes and locked in the press of the blue room. It was presumed that there was nothing of real importance among them, but they were preserved on the chance. He must have written this codicil and letter the day before his death,—both are dated on the 18th,—and had the paper witnessed and laid it aside among the other papers in his desk, intending to forward it to Mr. Hartagous in Memphis. The mail packet was due the next day, and passed about dusk; he died just before candle-light that evening, and I dare say this paper was among those in his desk that were packed away in the press of the blue room."

"I suppose that this codicil must have been found some years afterward," Desmond dolefully suggested. "Mr. Stanlett seems to me to be a man of good business judgment. He would never have desired to conceal this paper if a great part of those liabilities had not been already incurred. Of course he had only your interest in view. He has sufficient means of his own. It is nothing to him." She brought herself more willingly to follow his line of thought, since she perceived justification, in some poor sort, in the perspective, for Mr. Stanlett's aberrations.

"I remember," she said drawlingly, as if the recollection had just begun to trail its dubious length into her mind, "that about three years ago the executor called for some old levee bonds, on which the estate was entitled to something, and asked that the papers here be searched for them."

"Who made this search,—do you recollect?"

She visibly winced from the inquiry, but she answered with her usual directness: "I recollect very well that it was Uncle Clarence who made the search; and now that it seems to bear upon the question, I do recall that he was much out of sorts afterward. I remember that his petulance astonished me. He was never a profane man, but he swore violently because the executor had given him so much trouble, and declared that if he had wanted to be set to a clerk's work, he would have asked for a clerk's pay. And he said that the papers were disordered and dusty and devilish, and that he had broken himself down in working amongst them. I was a little hurt by the tone he was taking; and when I said that I was sorry he had put himself out to do a favor for me, he replied very significantly, 'A favor,—for you, Honoria,—for *you*? Why, I would eat off my little finger for *you*.' And oh, poor old Uncle Clarence! We must keep him from ever suspecting that we have discovered his course. It would humiliate him; it would bow him down to the earth with mortification."

Desmond looked dumfounded. "I don't see how we can prevent it. This codicil must be produced, and at once."

"Of course; but will it be necessary to publish all the details, his fantastic masquerades and midnight vigils to protect its concealment?" she argued.

"His course has been very strange, certainly." Then, after a pause, "In fact, I am confident that concealing a document of this sort, a will or codicil, to prevent it from being proved and becoming operative, is obnoxious to the law,—a very serious matter," said Desmond, nerving himself for her storm of protest.

"He has not prevented it from becoming operative," she retorted frostily. "The codicil is discovered and will be sent to-morrow to the executor, who will at once secure the two subscribing witnesses,—the same who swore to the will in force,—both still living, and will offer the codicil for probate. I will have to return the money that I have spent out of the different provision now made for me. I see no sense in telling our little yarn of Slip-Slinksy, and blue room, and secret drawers, for all the world to guy and laugh at, and mortify poor old Uncle Clarence to the soul. Oh, poor, poor Uncle Clarence,—how his discovery of the codicil must have tortured him! What must he have felt for me! It must have turned his brain,—it must have crazed him. That is the explanation of his course,—that is the solution of the mystery."

Desmond did not conceive it necessary to contend on this theory. At first glimpse it seemed to him a remarkably coherent scheme for a disordered brain to evolve, and one which only a strange accident had frustrated. Mr. Stanlett, however, was very old, and it may have been that at first he had withheld the paper in the frantic, senile, foolish expectation that another will might be found, not so destructive to his niece's interest as this codicil, which, by reason of the time that had elapsed in her enjoyment of the estate that was not hers by right, had practically beggared her. Doubtless he had postponed the disclosure from day to day, the disaster augmented by his delay, till perchance the pressure on his brain had resulted in subverting his reason. He had always intended to bring it forth, some day,—some day,—for he had carefully preserved it at great cost of anxiety and suspense and comfort, when its easy destruction would have given him security, and confirmed the existing status which was so happy for all concerned.

Realizing as Desmond did the magnitude of the disaster, that the interests of the widow so tenderly, so richly provided for, had been wrecked by the extreme of the solicitude exerted for her welfare, he was utterly unprepared for the airy lightness and consummate tact with which Mrs. Faurie made the disclosure without revealing the discovery of the concealment of the codicil.

She came fluttering into the parlor the next morning when were present all the family, Mr. Bainbridge, the manager, and Colonel Kentopp, who had been out in a skiff to a passing packet and had paused on his way back to Dryad-Dene to leave some newspapers. "What do you suppose?" she cried. "I can tell you news more astonishing to our neighborhood than anything you are likely to hear from the outside world. You know that of course we had the blue room upstairs, where that wounded river pirate died, thoroughly overhauled, and in one of the big presses in the wall Mr. Desmond found a secret drawer, and in it a later will of Mr. Faurie's,—are you not surprised?—a codicil it is, I should have said."

Mr. Stanlett stared for a moment blankly, rose to his feet, essayed to speak, and sank back very pale and entirely unobserved amidst the excitement of the others.

"Regularly executed?" Colonel Kentopp inquired, amazed.

"A codicil all in his own handwriting," said Mrs. Faurie, "perfectly regular, with the same witnesses as the will."

"To your advantage, I hope," said Colonel Kentopp, his glossy hazel-nut eyes glittering, his eager curiosity difficult to control.

"Oh, I am perfectly satisfied," Mrs. Faurie declared, smiling proudly; and Colonel Kentopp knew as well as if he had seen the instrument that Mrs. Faurie had been relegated to a designated share of the real estate, out of which she would be required to make good her lavish expenditures heretofore. He was not indisposed to rejoice after the manner of men of his kind in the disasters of others, but presently his spirits fell. This change boded doubtless the partitioning of the Faurie property, and with Great Oaks on the market, he knew that there was scant hope of Loring as a purchaser of Dryad-Dene. So ill at ease was he under this theory, so suddenly out of countenance, that he sought to avoid observation, and made haste to conclude his call and get himself away.

He was promptly followed by Bainbridge, dully pondering on the news, half stunned by the revelation, and apprehensive of a change in the ownership of Great Oaks and the jeopardy of his own employment there.

Desmond breathed more freely when both were gone; he felt that he could not have summoned the nerve that Mrs. Faurie had shown in risking the disclosure in the presence of others, although he realized that, had Mr. Stanlett spoken inconsiderately, it would have been ascribed to the vagaries of age and his natural and extreme disappointment,—in effect, the overthrow of his reason in so signal a misfortune to his nearest and dearest relative, who had always been like a duteous daughter to him. Nevertheless, Desmond was glad that surprise and dismay had held the old gentleman silent till only the family group was present. In the disclosure Mrs. Faurie had stated the literal truth, that Desmond had found the codicil in a secret drawer, and Mr. Stanlett accepted it without demur or suspicion of the further discovery of his knowledge of the cache, or agency and motive in its concealment.

"But why, and how, and when, in the name of all that is sacred sir," the old man said, scarlet, trembling, his eyes blazing, and scarcely able to keep his feet, "should *you* go rummaging around into the secret drawers of a locked press?"

"The press was not locked," Desmond said, without looking up, and trifling with the violets in a glass bowl in the centre of the table beside which he sat. "The bolt did not reach the slot."

"And why did you send it off without consulting me, Honoria? Another will might yet be found. I have searched and searched. Another will and a later one is now right among those papers in the blue room. Oh, how many nights, how many nights I have searched!"

"Dear Uncle Clarence, the codicil was written and dated and witnessed on the 18th, and my husband died the night of the 19th."

"Plenty of time for another will,—Faurie was a most expeditious man of business. He was not bedridden, as you know. He even slept in his chair toward the last, as you must remember. That heart trouble would not let him lie down in peace—queer, for a man of his physical strength. He died at last in his chair, in that library. Plenty of time for another will; it could be found! This Mr. Desmond seems to have a nose for game; set him after another will, and see what he can tree this time."

Mrs. Faurie broke in to prevent the old man from indulging in further sarcasm along this line. "And oh, Uncle Clarence, such a dear letter was with the document! I want Reginald and Horace and Rufus, each one, to read that letter, and bless God for a father so good and generous and considerate for us all."

As they sat and listened they had that look so pathetic in children old enough to appreciate their situation in matters of moment, yet realizing their helplessness in the hands of others, and not able to compass a full reliance on the direction of the course of events.

"Do you understand, Honoria, that you will have to refund to the executor, the estate, the expenditures of all these years, the accumulated amount of the income, your annuity,—the money that you have been spending so royally with both hands for nearly seven years? It will certainly sweep away more than half your present provision, possibly the whole, into the craws of those vipers that you have warmed on your hearth." The old man was piteous in his age and agitation, as he stood, lean, gray, wrinkled, half bent in his tremulous emphasis, his arm outstretched, the fingers quivering as he shook them at the group of aghast boys. "Do you understand that, woman?"

"Why, what else, Uncle Clarence? Would you have me rob my children?" She had reached out for Chub when he was denominated a viper with a craw, and was now drawing him into that juxtaposition so unbecoming to his appearance, his fledgeling blond head on her bosom, his hard, round, freckled red cheek against the soft, exquisite whiteness of her neck. He struggled to speak through her tender kisses.

"You will oblige me, Uncle Clarence, by not calling my mother a woman," he said, in callow affront.

"What else is she?—and a most ill-used, unlucky, and poverty-stricken woman."

"She is as 'spectable as any man!" protested Chub; and while the other two boys burst out laughing as usual at Chubby's queer views, they were all three in tears presently, horrified that their mother should be impoverished to make restitution to them, and that they were powerless to hinder the sacrifice.

"Oh, terrible! terrible!" the old man said as he strode to and fro before the fire, literally wringing his hands. "It is the duty of the executor to exact every mill, and he will do it. The executor has no option whatever in the matter. He is constrained by the terms of the codicil."

Then he fell to crying again and again, "Oh, terrible! terrible!" and wringing his hands as he wavered to and fro with his uncertain, senile step.

"Uncle Clarence, why will you not set an example of composure and courage in adversity to these boys? The event must have fallen out this way, at any rate."

"Why?"—he had paused abruptly. "Why, Honoria, why? If the codicil had not been found, you would not have had to refund under any circumstances."

"I only meant that this codicil must have come to light sooner or later," she explained.

But he went on unheeding: "Did you intend to give up the income for a life-interest in the third, under the provisions of the old will? Are you going to marry this man Desmond?"

Mrs. Faurie sat still and amazed for a moment. Then her buoyant laughter rang joyously through the room. "Marry?—a mere boy, like Edward? Uncle Clarence, you are funny,—positively funny!"

"He is no boy,—he is as old as the almighty hills! And if you have not thought of such a possibility, *he has*,—take my word for it, *he has*. He has a keen eye for the main chance. He found the codicil, and now you have to give up the income whether or no. But he had better not be in too great a hurry for the fourth of the estate. Wait till you make good these expenditures. He hasn't seen you spend money as I have done. Wait till you make good your refunding bond, for that is just what this amounts to."

Desmond felt the flush rising to his forehead. His heart was beating furiously. In his agitation he had upset the bowl of violets and the blossoms were scattered over the table, while the water in which they were steeped began to drip slowly, slowly to the floor. He did not lift his eyes, not even when Mrs. Faurie spoke in apology.

"I cannot express to him how grateful I am for his forbearance under these insults," she said gravely. "And, Uncle Clarence, you would never subject him to them and so tax his generosity were you yourself to-day—so scrupulous as you are in every relation in life,—so—"

"*Too* scrupulous! *Too* scrupulous! Scrupulous enough to be such a stupendous fool as not to tear a bit of paper when I had my chance, and save you a gigantic fortune, as fortunes go in this country,—ah,—ah,—when I had my chance!"

He tottered out of the room, banging the door, the three boys staring in dismay after the lurching figure with the feeble impetuousness of gait, and listening to the mutter of his impotent wrath as he went stumbling and cursing down the hall.

CHAPTER XVI

Desmond had never experienced such dejection as now overwhelmed his spirits. He could not rally from it. He could not understand it. He had recovered from the strain of the physical fatigue, even from the stress of excitement. He had permitted little interruption to his pedagogic duties, and the routine of the schoolroom continued in force as regular as if no river pirates had ever assailed the house, and died in the commission of the intended robbery; as if no coroner's jury had ever grimly deliberated on the veranda; as if no codicil of the will had ever been found to reverse all the orderly status with a presage of future financial chaos.

"We will take care of to-day," Desmond had said to his restive, unsettled, agitated pupils, "and to-morrow will take care of itself."

They were docile under his admonition, but he could not so easily press its sage philosophy upon himself. Now and again he struggled with this gloom when he was sufficiently at leisure to cope with it. He had been fortunate beyond any reasonable expectation, considering his status, he argued. In lieu of the position of a tolerated necessity in the house, a tutor to boys remote from schools, he had been treated first with respect and courtesy, then as a valued guest, made as one of the family, and now as the predominant controlling element, from whose decree there was no appeal. More and more did Mr. Bainbridge, with his papers, and a furtive eye, and a deprecating hand laid over his mouth, as if resolved to keep his conjectures from going further than his mustache, come directly to Desmond, to take his advice, as he said, in fact to secure the annulment of some impracticable order, or to obviate unwise dispositions of Mrs. Faurie's in the readjustment of the wrecked plantation interests. He did not directly bespeak Desmond's influence. He only showed the papers and set forth the facts, coughed discreetly behind his hand, and if securing Desmond's promise to place the matter before Mrs. Faurie, would set forth confident and alert, acting on the rescission of the order as if it were received; for whatever Mr. Desmond undertook at Great Oaks Plantation was regarded as *un fait accompli*. The attitude of the servants toward him for some time past was compounded of a deep respect and some real liking, influencing swift feet and dexterous hands and willing smiles in his service. "He is a man, shore!" was the general comment. His pupils first obeyed, then esteemed, and now adored him, using their utmost diligence to win the meed of his approval. Even they, he thought, noted his gloom, which he could not disguise, and which rested upon his aspect as definitely as a pall. He lost his readiness to sleep, which, since he had become content in a measure with his lot, he had recovered—in his youthful health and vitality. Long, long after the house was lapsed in slumber, he would linger in a reclining-chair at his window, the candle burning down to the socket, his fingers in the pages of an unread book, looking out dully at the lustrous scene, now grown so familiar, of the expanse of gray, shimmering water under the white moon and the faint stars, while all the room about him dulled to indiscriminate gloom and the hours wore on and on toward dawn.

What was this obsession? he sometimes angrily asked himself. Why should he wince in poignant pain at the very thought of the tender music in Honoria Faurie's voice as she sobbed amidst joy and laughed amidst sorrow, in the blended ecstasy and woe in reading her husband's letter, so replete with his love and thought for her? Was he jealous of the dead man—dead these seven long years!—the dead man he had never seen? And how did her tears and smiles concern him,—whom she deemed but a boy,—at whom she looked with such sweet, maternal eyes? Sometimes he felt that he was losing his reason. Why should this evidence of her love for the dead man who had been her husband set an exquisite pain a-quiver in his every fibre? Had he thought she had forgotten—that were not to her credit. Did he fear that if the dead still lived so in her heart there was no place in her affections for him? And why had he ever hoped this? And when, indeed, had he first thought of it? There had grown up in his mind so gradually from admiration of her beauty, from approval of her standpoint, from confidence in her principles, from interest in the disclosures of her charming mind, an absolute adoration so complete, so possessive, that he was hardly aware of it until it absorbed him wholly. He had no more identity of his own. He existed only in relation to her. The fact became apparent to him as he reviewed the last few months. He had come here penniless, as a tutor to teach her sons, mere children, to do designated work; he had stipulated and stood stoutly on these limits, defining exactly what were to be his duties, that he might not be called upon to exceed them, to become an overworked, underpaid drudge, with such expenditure of vitality that he might be unable to rise to higher things.

He recurred no more to these limitations. He controlled the boys in school and out, laying commands upon them with paternal freedom, restricting dangerous amusements, interdicting prejudicial reading, requiring salutary exercise, cutting off amusing associates sometimes, for no better reason than that their conversation tended to impair the grammar and parlor manners of his youthful charges,—all of which was out of his contract and beyond the bailiwick of his authority.

He had been inducted into even more exacting occupations. He had become the referee in all matters of dispute about the place, which required some nicety of discrimination; he was often put into a position of extreme doubt and embarrassment in deciding the small property interests between servants or the plantation hands, who had agreed together to abide by his decision, thus exerting, indeed, the functions of justice. Mrs. Faurie consulted him in business correspondence. He had been led, by the turn of events, to risk his life in defense of the mansion and to hold it out in a state of siege. He had kept up the good cheer by his genial arts, and preserved the calmness of all in the house that dreadful night when, but for his stanch composure and his resources of management, they might have fallen victims to causeless fright and ghastly horror in their isolation, and become the wreck of their own nerves in lieu of passing the ordeal with no result but the confirmation of their powers and their confidence in themselves. It was he who had conferred with the county officials by letter and in person when they came to the house. Mrs. Faurie and the younger boys had been spared the ghastly details of the inquest through his representations to the coroner, and were busied in a rear room opening some boxes of potted plants for the approaching summer decoration of the veranda, which had been shipped by the packet opportunely passing on this morning, and which he contrived should be brought off in a skiff simultaneously to the house; thus they were not aware of the event in progress till the inquisition was concluded. His own testimony, that of Reginald and Mr. Stanlett, the confessions of the wounded man, who died later the same day, the corroborative details of the servants as to the subsequent events, were deemed ample evidence, and the verdict of the jury was in accordance with the facts.

He had solved the mystery of the spectral manifestations that had terrorized the house for years; he had secured the cache from its possible wresting away by vandal hands; he was her confidant and counselor in all the troublous forecast of the complications to ensue upon the propounding of the codicil.

Surely these were the services of no hireling. They were the cheerful tribute of love that found danger dear for her behoof, and toil light, and the tangles of perplexity easy of unraveling since she might elude their intricacies, and responsibility a broadening of the shoulders, and his day all too short for its devotion to her interests.

And to her—he seemed but a boy! a mere springald out of college, glad to teach for a time,—to repeat his own lessons recently conned as a stepping-stone to a man's devoir.

And yet—he looked at the long lane of light, the mystic avenue of the moon on the water in the glade between the lines of inundated trees. What alluring dreams, what soft deceits were coming to him along that roadway of shimmering pearl,—coming to him from the moon, the home of fantasies, to which it stretched at the limits of the perspective. Did she know her own heart? She had no mind but his. She adopted his views, and deferred her preferences, and abated her prejudices. He had no need to care for his dignity; she was quicker than he to resent aught that seemed to touch upon it. The whole house, the whole plantation, was relegated to his control. She seemed in a hundred ways to ask his permission,—might she do this? might the boys have that? She said that day,—that dreadful day,—when he and Reginald held her in their arms between them, that she had longed for him, that she had prayed for him. How strange that the bell, which had never rung through all the gloomy day, sounded her signal for him so far away! How was it that his ears quickened to a peal that had never vibrated,—that her wishes, her prayers, drew him from far, through sloughs and slashes, through bayous and lakes, to her side at her utmost, her extremest peril! And why for him had she prayed! She knew that the time set for his return was yet two days distant. The manager was overdue, however, and momently expected. She had not contemplated the coming of Mr. Bainbridge, a stalwart fellow and eminently capable of coping with these familiar conditions. She had not thought that a steamboat might chance to pass and discern and respond to a signal of distress. She had longed for Desmond—for *him*, as the protecting ægis in all her frenzied terror. And love—mysterious love—had clamored at his ears, annulled the distance, shaken the fogs, penetrated the rains, defied, set at naught plain fact, and sounded her summons, her wish, her frantic hope, till he needs must have heed and respond. It was strange, the accord between them. Surely, surely she did not translate aright the tenor of her own emotions.

Suddenly he noticed that the mystic illuminated avenue of pearly, shimmering waters between the giant oaks was dulling: a sort of gloating glister grew golden upon it; vague yearnings were in the air; unseen beings descended continually, their presence demonstrated only by the sense of motion. A wind from out the moon ruffled the surface into thousands of tiny wavelets, like twinkling feet half discerned. Fancies!—fancies hastening down, lest dawn come too soon, cut off communication with the ideal, and leave the poor world the prey, the possession of the prosaic. For, indeed, the light was fading to a glimmering steel, and now to an unillumined gray, and as he rose at last to seek an hour's repose before the household should rouse for the day, he realized that with his griefs and anxieties, his fears and his waking dreams, he had worn the night away.

He did not mistake the character of his emotions—they were strictly paternal!—when it developed in the next few days that Reginald, of his own motion, had written, unknown to all but his brothers, a letter to the executor of the will, Mr. Hartagous, a lawyer of Memphis. The others had signed it, and thus unified the solemn requirement that in the execution of the newly discovered codicil he should make no demands upon their mother for the return to the estate of the funds that she had spent under the provisions of the will as hitherto in force, and now to be charged against her portion. It seemed that they had at first appealed to their guardian, Mr. Keith, who had declined the discussion by stating that the distribution of the property was wholly in the hands of the executor. Therefore they called the attention of Mr. Hartagous to the fact that they were the owners of the estate in his hands, and claimed that they had a right to waive this demand upon their mother, against which they protested, and to impose upon him their command. It would be contrary to the wishes of the testator, their father, they argued, to impoverish for a legal quibble the widow and mother; and even if they should restore to her—as they were fully resolved to do, as soon as the eldest came of age—anything that was taken from her, that was a distant date, and she would spend the best years of her life in poverty, restricted and deprived of the comfort and luxury to which she was accustomed. If the executor should persist in enforcing the codicil, the letter sternly concluded, it would be their resolve to seek to visit their wrath upon him, as his evil deed merited.

This truculent epistle came back to Great Oaks inclosed in a letter from Mr. Hartagous to Mrs. Faurie. Their sentiments did them honor, he declared, overlooking the puerile violence of their menace, and this heralded the coming of Mr. Hartagous to Great Oaks for a conference in the changed state of things.

The Faurie boys were somewhat startled to see their valiant demonstration in the hands of their mother, who kissed and hugged and wept over them till they, too, shed tears as they clung together.

"But will he, mamma, will he make you pay us all that money?" asked Reginald, leaning over the back of her chair and gripping hard the hand that she held up to him.

"Oh, what a pity we are all so young," plained Horace,—"so many years before we can give it back." He knelt by her side and sobbed against her shoulder.

Chubby sunk from her lap to the floor and clung to her, hugging her knees. "Oh, mamma, will you be poor till I am a man? Oh, I will work for you, mamma. I will—I will—I will dig in the garden."

Reginald and Horace had no laugh to-day for Chub's unintentional anticlimaxes, and as Mrs. Faurie sent them away, that she might consult with Desmond, they carried very dreary countenances, and she still pressed her handkerchief to her eyes.

"It is not as if the money were going to strangers," said Desmond, craftily. "It will only advantage those dear fellows. I am so delighted with that letter of Reginald's."

"I didn't realize that it was in him to do that," she said, suddenly smiling radiantly.

"I did," said Desmond, promptly.

"I believe you love him as much as I do," she cried joyously.

"All three," he protested. "I am jealous for the others."

"Poor little Chubby," she said, lingering lovingly on the words.

"Dear old Chubby!" he exclaimed. "So you need not mind about the money. It is for them."

"But how am I to get it, Edward?" She drew her level brows together in her pretty frown. "You have no idea of the clip I went, spending money. I can see now the awful mistake I made; but it seemed not so unreasonably extravagant then, having a large income at my disposal for my lifetime, and my children all independently and handsomely provided for. And now,—to return all that money! And that man is coming! I have been staying here to economize, you know, to get the old place to take care of me till the reservoir fills up again."

"You have something to show for the money, I suppose. Didn't those wretches mention some famous emeralds?"

"Ye-es,—but don't you think it *infra dig.* to sell jewelry?"

"It is *infra dig.* not to have money," he said bitterly.

Ah, how he wished that he were adequately equipped to come to her rescue; to let her relinquish to the Faurie estate all that the name had brought her; to offer commensurate resources.

"I do not agree with you," she said firmly, "*You* have no money, and you can discount the world for dignity."

He had never regarded himself in this light, and he flushed with pleasure. As her eyes rested on him she suddenly exclaimed: "Now you look a little bit like yourself. This torment is telling more on you than on me. I assure you that *I* shall not let myself go off in *my* looks for a few dollars, dimes, cents, and mills."

"About the emeralds?"

"Beauty when unadorned with emeralds is as green as grass. But needs must—let them go! Let them go!"

"Do you love them so much?" he said wistfully.

"You just ought to see them on me!" she bridled.

"They will never be the same on any one else," he hazarded.

"And that is one comfort," she acceded. Her pride in the preëminence of her attractions was like the innocent vanity of a child, so entirely was her beauty acknowledged and a matter of course.

"What will they bring at a forced sale?"

"Thirty thousand dollars, they cost."

Desmond jotted down the sum and then went on. "About the yacht?"

"The yacht? Must it be sold? Why, what will we do in the Mediterranean?"

Obviously, she did not understand the situation. It must be brought home to her. He waved his hand to the waters of the overflow shimmering just outside the veranda balustrade. A dugout was rocking at a little distance. "There are all your facilities for voyaging for some time to come, Mrs. Faurie."

She burst into laughter at the incongruity. Then she said, "I cannot realize that it is so serious as all that. My yacht is a beauty, and ought to bring a pretty penny."

"Perhaps you will also have to give up the title to Great Oaks, which the codicil gives you in fee, to make good the sums which you have received from the estate," he ventured.

Her face fell. "I have begun to love this life," she declared unexpectedly. "I don't want to change. I don't want to give up Great Oaks. I have forgotten the world."

A thrill stole through his heart. What had she said? She did not understand her own heart!

CHAPTER XVII

M r. Hartagous brought with him a metropolitan atmosphere, the manner of one used to good society, a portly stomach accustomed to fine feeding, a handsome gray-streaked beard parted in the middle, and a pair of searching, quickly glancing dark eyes. He landed at Great Oaks shortly before dinner, and it was at table that he made Desmond's acquaintance. It was not he, but the guardian of the Faurie boys who had sought out Desmond, and through the offices of mutual friends secured his services as tutor, when Mrs. Faurie had placed a period to her European wanderings, but Mr. Hartagous, in the general family interests, had been apprised of all the details, and in meeting Desmond for the first time, inwardly congratulated all concerned upon the phenomenal opportunity of finding such a man for such a place. The meal was somewhat more elaborate than usual, in honor of the guest. Mrs. Faurie, in one of her Parisian gowns, was in great beauty. So marked, indeed, was the effect, that it seemed not inappropriate to take some notice of what was so obvious.

"Upon my word, madam," Mr. Hartagous declared, having progressed with great prosperity in feeding through the menu to the dessert, "you must surely lose the tally of the years as you go, else you would not have the effrontery to look younger than when I first met you as a bride."

"I was a skinny bride," she smiled. "The years round out the angles. But they lay on fat and fads and frumpishness, and I feel really like an old country-woman.

He looked at her beamingly, his face flushed, partly from the reflection of the old-fashioned red Bohemian glass finger-bowls, and partly from Mr. Faurie's Madeira, which he had laid down a good many years ago, and which had survived him to delight other palates. Mr. Hartagous was pleased and surprised to find how debonair was her carriage under the changed prospects. He had not thought she could sustain her equanimity in such cruel incertitudes, nothing positively established, but great loss,—financial ruin, more or less complete. He had feared the visit as a dismal experience; but her brilliant aspect, her joyous tones, might enliven even a board at which sat the three downcast and indignant Faurie boys, thoroughly schooled as to their civility, but showing in every facial line how they deprecated and resented his part in the untoward falling out of affairs. The two younger ones asked to be excused shortly after the entrance of the dessert; and as Mr. Stanlett had not appeared at all since the arrival of the guest, sending in by Bob a plea of indisposition, Mrs. Faurie felt some anxiety, and a desire to go and inquire into his malady.

"I leave you in good hands with Mr. Desmond and Reginald," she said to Mr. Hartagous, as she rose from the table with a rich stir of silks and laces; "I will go and see how Uncle Clarence feels now, and meet you later in the parlor."

Reginald, pale and disaffected, and all unlike himself, lingered listlessly for an interval, and presently asked Desmond if he might be excused also.

"What?—are you going to leave us, too?" Mr. Hartagous cried out genially, in a determinedly cheerful and friendly tone.

"I am nothing of a boon companion," said Reginald. "Mr. Desmond does not allow me to drink but one glass of light wine,—I shall not be missed." And with a poor effort at a friendly smile, obviously insincere, he stayed for no more parley.

"Ah, you seem to have the young fellows under good control,—excellent for them. A short tether,—best thing in the world for colts apt to feel their oats."

Mr. Hartagous was now looking about the room with considerable freedom and a sort of disregard of the presence of the tutor, taking *faute de mieux* the part of host. "Everything is just as it used to be: old sylvan wall-paper, in design of tapestry hangings, hunting-scene; old racing-cups in that big mahogany cabinet. Faurie used to have a string of good horses. And there is the family silver,—very fine,—armorial bearings,—all just as it used to be. Can't think what Mrs. Faurie did with her money,—didn't put any of it on Great Oaks, at all events."

Desmond cloaked his failure to respond in speculations on this theme by passing the bottle, and Mr. Hartagous promptly refilled his glass.

"Severe stroke for her,—the finding of that codicil. Pity it didn't come into my hands earlier! There wouldn't be the devil and all to pay as there is now." He lifted his glass and refreshed himself bountifully. Perhaps he was used to livelier company at dinner, for he presently remarked Desmond's serious, not to say dispirited expression, and, possibly because unable to appreciate that the tutor's anxiety could be disconnected with a personal application, hastened to stipulate: "But it will not affect *you* at all. Your salary comes out of the minors' estates. Mrs. Faurie is not at expenses, except such as may be voluntary in their education and maintenance."

Mr. Hartagous was well aware that there had been some difficulty in catching an appropriate man to consign to the remote depths of an isolated plantation in the Mississippi bottom-lands. As Mrs. Faurie was not willing that her sons should be separated from her for their schooling, already much postponed, Mr. Keith, the guardian, must needs secure a college graduate, of irreproachable character, of elegant breeding, and so piteously poor as to be willing, for a small salary, to turn his back on the world at the outset of his career. As by signal good fortune the guardian had captured this *rara avis*, it was no part of the executor's scheme to interfere to set him at liberty again, or to foster restlessness by any suspicion that his financial interest was threatened in the impending changes.

"But Mrs. Faurie will have to pay the piper for the dance that she has had,—a long and a lively one from all that I hear,—and I should think that it would sweep away the best part of her provision under this codicil. I do hope that she won't make a fight for it,—very embarrassing the whole affair is for me, especially considering the attitude the boys take in the matter. Mr. Keith can afford to pooh-pooh it, and say they will think differently when they come to their majority. He is not called upon to sustain their resentment. Yet he would be ready at the drop of a hat to sue me, the executor, in their interest in this very matter that the little fools want to relinquish. As far as their interest is concerned, however, there will be no litigation in carrying out the provisions of the codicil. But I confess I dread the idea of Mrs. Faurie's futile resistance."

"I think Mrs. Faurie has no intention of making a contest," said Desmond, fearing that his silence on the subject might be misconstrued.

The lawyer whirled around excitedly. "Turn over Great Oaks Plantation without a fight,—eh? She will have to lose it to make good."

Mr. Hartagous had a brightening aspect. There had been already sufficiently discordant elements in the situation fomented by the conflict of laws in the two states where the properties lay, a pertinent instance of which came to mind in the incongruity of an indeterminate limit of twenty or thirty years in Tennessee for the revocation of probate in common form, and in Mississippi a prescription, with the statutory savings, of only two years, which had long ago elapsed. Though this was hardly conclusive, by reason of the exception of the statute, in favor of the disability of the minors, and their financial interests in the revocation of the Mississippi probate, it might further be inoperative to render Mrs. Faurie secure in her local holdings, if her interest in Great Oaks, for life or widowhood, as under the will, could be subjected to levy as for debt to satisfy the requirements of the codicil in Tennessee. The guardian of the minors had been alert to perceive another phase of the situation incident to the discovery of the paper, and had indeed averred to Mr. Hartagous that, even could their rights of prescription be defeated, he felt that the long and incomprehensible delay to produce the codicil savored of concealment, and in the event of proof of this, the Mississippi statute allowed two years further for the revocation *pro tanto* of the probate. The lapse of time had wrought such ruin to Mrs. Faurie's interests that, even apart from her high character, which precluded such a suspicion, she could never be supposed to have been a party to such a disastrous scheme of concealment; and the diligence of the search of Mr.

Hartagous among the valuable papers of the decedent was protected by a letter from Mr. Faurie himself, dated a few days before his death, stating that all important papers had been transferred to his keeping, as the executor, in view of the settlement of the estate. Mr. Hartagous had not found it an easy task, with its diversified interests, its complicated litigation, its many details, and he welcomed the thought that perhaps after all Mrs. Faurie might yield at once to the inevitable, and the settlement of the estate might yet go cannily on, including the provisions of the codicil, without raising the issue of *devisavit vel non* and repairing to the circuit court for probate in solemn form.

Desmond was a trifle embarrassed. "It may not be necessary to relinquish Great Oaks," he said uneasily. "Mrs. Faurie has other convertible assets."

The lawyer bent his brows and cast a keen glance at him. There was a significant silence. "So you are in her confidence, are you?"

There was so much receptivity in his aspect as he waited for the reply, he was so evidently ready to discriminate and utilize all manner of subtle and diffusive impressions and information, that Desmond grew unwontedly wary. "Not to the extent of being able to speak for her," he stipulated. "But Mrs. Faurie is very candid, as you know, and I am in a position to hear much of the family conversation."

He came to a dead halt. But Mr. Hartagous had not wrestled with reluctant witnesses for a matter of thirty years to be baffled at this late day by an after-dinner interlocutor with a bottle of choice wine between them. He gave it a push as he said: "And I also stand in a quasi-confidential relation to her, having long been the friend of her husband and herself, as well as the executor of his will. It would gratify me extremely to be able to adjust this difficult matter without contention and the rupture of long-established amicable sentiments." He gazed keenly at the handsome face of the tutor, intellectual and powerful beyond his years and experience, the expression of mental value enhancing the effect of symmetry of feature. He was about to suggest that it might be beneficial to Mrs. Faurie's interests to canvass the matter between them, and from its incidents strike out some middle course of advantage to all parties concerned. But there was something in Desmond's deep, steadfast eyes that admonished him that this confidence could come about only from inadvertence. Desmond would not of set purpose disclose Mrs. Faurie's intentions. The executor began to realize that if he wanted such facts as the tutor knew, he must surprise them.

"Mrs. Faurie would not want Great Oaks at any rate," he hazarded. "I wonder at Faurie for that disposition of the plantation,—cumbrous property."

"It is a fine place," said Desmond, non-committally.

"Looks mighty pretty now,—a full fathom deep in water in the shallowest spot," sneered the lawyer.

"The land is of fine quality,—raises good crops, I am told," Desmond commented.

"Don't need fertile land to raise crawfish."

"Why, even the floods that drowned the world dried off after a while; and Great Oaks is relying on precedent and Providence, and expects to raise cotton here again some day." Desmond's tone was crisp. He had no necessity that he recognized to submit to the acerbities of the executor. It was strain enough on his patience to make allowances for the infirmities and age of Mr. Stanlett.

His tone, the vigor of his argument, shook the self-restraint of Mr. Hartagous. The lawyer's spirit of contention responded. He wagged his head with an aspect of melancholy, not unrelated to his sentiment, when he said: "The overflow will cry down the price. I have a letter in my pocket now from a would-be purchaser, a Mr. Loring, formerly a resident of this county. His offer is low, but as much as the place can command for the next ten years to come." He shook his head and filled his glass anew.

Desmond quickly reviewed the events of the past weeks. Doubtless the news of the discovery of the codicil had been widely bruited abroad, and thus Mr. Loring, aware of the exigencies of the prospective refunding and of Mrs. Faurie's depleted resources, had taken the field with the first offer. He had astutely approached the executor rather than its present owner, whose disposition to sell might be in inverse proportion to the necessity; and as the exacting creditor, Mr. Hartagous, knowing that such an opportunity of sale would not be easily duplicated, might press an acceptance as a ready solution of the emergency, which promised him a world of anxiety and perplexity. Little effort indeed might be requisite to urge, flatter, overpersuade a woman unaccustomed to the turmoils of hopeless debt and annoyed by business complications.

But poor Honoria Faurie! To have unwittingly dispensed her whole fortune as her income, her annuity. To be called upon now to surrender the roof above her head as penance of those years of plenty that had held out to her the deceit of perpetuity. Desmond trembled for her future, for her sons were mere children and helpless. He feared lest she be harassed into precipitancy and clutch at any prospect of speedy deliverance from these troublous toils, willing to concede anything, to relinquish everything, to have peace,—when, alas! there would be no more peace. He realized the immense capacity to clinch tight, to hold hard, of the genus of which Mr. Hartagous was a type,—cool, collected, with no personal interest involved that might affect his judgment, ready to stand on a quibble, to fight for the minutest fraction, to prolong the contention to the uttermost, to the extremest exhaustion of his adversary's slender resources of resistance. And she had not a soul to whom she might appeal, save indeed some lawyer, earning his fee, and appreciative only of the surface conditions of her case,—but no one who cared for her, who would think for her. The realization roused Desmond in her behalf.

"You had best wait till morning to place the offer before her," Desmond said, determined to be the first to acquaint her with the facts, determined that she should not meet her adversary in his guise of friend without consideration of the double identity in which he came. "There is always so much stir in the parlor after dinner,—the children and their dogs make a deal of noise. Mrs. Faurie always gives up her evenings to the entertainment of her sons."

He had no mind to offer the library, which indeed had been assigned to his exclusive use, and he hoped that Mr. Hartagous did not remember its facilities for quiet consultation, so long had it been dismantled.

Mr. Hartagous was one of the most acute of men, and his facial traits were well under control. Few people could have interpreted the sudden cynical uplifting of his bushy eyebrows as he said casually, "Ah, well,—plenty of time,—plenty of time."

But Desmond's perceptions were quickened in her interests and he knew that the hour was come, that before they separated for the night, Mrs. Faurie would be acquainted with the executor's version of the facts,—that they were the most lucky of mortals! for property was slow of sale, plantations a drug upon the market, the labor questions impossible of solution; clouds, darkness, environed them on every side, and they knew not whither to grope,—and here suddenly a flood of financial sunlight was opening upon them in the midst of their night of despondency. Only the touch of her pen,—the title of Great Oaks, which she had always loathed, would be transferred. The millionaire's cash and notes would make good her indebtedness to the estate to that extent, at least; the rest could be "carried"—fatal word!—arranged for a time with liens on smaller properties. Plausible representation!—the sense of a load of debt lifted, the turbulent apprehension of contention averted. She might adopt the executor's conclusions, and indeed from his point of view there was naught else practicable. She had known him long, liked him well, and relied on his friendship. But his duty in the premises was to the estate, to make the most and the best of the testator's dispositions as far as it was concerned. As to the widow, the wreck was her own work, unconscious though she had been, mistaken; he had no responsibility so far as she was interested save to enforce the provisions of the codicil, and to exact the terms of the refunding clause. She might be prevailed upon, in the first flush of relief that any solution of the problem was at hand, to sign at once, to-night, some agreement of sale;

she might not commit herself beyond the possibility of withdrawal, but so far embrace the proposition as to be unwilling to recede from it. And indeed she might be persuaded into a coincidence of opinion. His representations might fix her resolution. Later, Desmond's remonstrances might not avail. He was young, as she knew,—she had called him repeatedly a mere boy. He could not be sure that she seriously valued his business instincts, when he had no business experience. He desired only to put her on her guard, to excite her apprehension, to counsel reserve, above all delay. He could imagine the sequence, and it appalled him. The wishes of Mrs. Faurie, reduced to poverty, to insignificance, would no longer have such weight as when issued from her princess-like affluence and preëminence, and the wishes of the boys were as empty of influence as the disability of their minority would compel. He wondered dolorously as to her impending fate. Perhaps there might be accorded to her, from among the chips and blocks of the Faurie estate, saved from the cormorant clutch of the refunding, some cottage on a side street in the outskirts of Vicksburg or Natchez, some little farm of a few acres regularly overflowed, and raising indeed more crawfish than cotton.

It seemed as if Desmond had intentionally misled Mr. Hartagous when he opened the parlor door and they entered a room of absolute silence and stillness. Mrs. Faurie, in a gown of sage green silk brocaded in lighter tones, the lace at her throat coruscating with the delicate white fires of a diamond "sunburst," leaned back in a large chair, her eyes on the hearth, evidently moody from argument and remonstrance with her sons. Their faces, as they sat in a row on a sofa, were downcast, full of distress, and marked with the distorting trace of nervous anxiety, which they could feel as if they were men, but unlike men could not hope to do aught to abate;—only Chub gazed up at Mr. Hartagous with childish, lowering, resentful eyes and a half-suppressed tendency to pout. Mr. Stanlett, pallid, seeming more lean than usual, shrunken, and very perceptibly aged by the shock of the excitements of finding the codicil, lay in a reclining-chair on the opposite side of the fire. He greeted Mr. Hartagous with courtesy indeed, but with noticeably few words, and protesting that his indisposition had passed, welcomed him to Great Oaks mansion. Desmond felt the future in the instant. It would require but little exertion of Mr. Hartagous's tact to inaugurate one of the old-time reminiscences, which seemed the delight and the resource of Mr. Stanlett's failing life. His eyes would flash, his thin cheek flush, the boys would listen in spellbound silence, and Mr. Hartagous, already seated beside her, would secure an uninterrupted tête-à-tête with Mrs. Faurie; for the tutor, in his subsidiary position and obligatory show of respect, must needs accord Mr. Stanlett's narration his attention also. But even should Desmond so far forget himself as to interpose in the discussion of business in which he had no concern, Mr. Hartagous had arguments which on first view would easily discomfit his crude and inexperienced counsels. Nevertheless,

Desmond resolved anew that she should not hear of the offer of Mr. Loring for Great Oaks first from the executor. He cast about him in desperation. Mr. Stanlett was already replying with some spirit as to the early history of certain localities that Mr. Hartagous had noticed from the guards of the steamboat in coming down the Mississippi River from Memphis, which itself was built on one of the famous Chickasaw Bluffs. Mr. Stanlett's memory reached back to the days before the Chickasaws and Choctaws had generally vanished westward, and he had then gleaned from the chiefs some traditions at first hand which made him an authority on moot points of early history, and he piqued himself on his accuracy. It was easy indeed to engage him in a discussion as to the site of the old Chickasaw towns,—seven of them together in a row, the last called Ash-wick-boo-ma (Red Grass),—where they defeated D'Artaguette and later Bienville, and the details of the battle of Ackia and its famous last charge. The young Fauries' faces had brightened. Suddenly Reginald asked a breathless question as to the boy-commander, the Canadian, Voisin, who at sixteen years of age conducted the safe and skilled retreat of the troops through many miles of wilderness from the field of the battle which his superior officer, the unfortunate D'Artaguette, had lost.

Mr. Stanlett needed no more prompting, nor, Desmond feared, would he heed interruption. Mr. Hartagous presently leaned forward with his elbow on the table at Mrs. Faurie's right hand, and had begun to speak to her in a low voice, when Desmond asked Mr. Stanlett if he knew the ancient French buglecalls, and said that one claimed a Merovingian origin. He declared that he would like to believe that the same strain which had rung from the famous "Olivant," the horn of the Paladin at Roncesvalles, had served to rally D'Artaguette's motley levies of Indians, and *coureurs des bois*, and French soldats along the banks of the Mississippi, and would forever continue to sound down the centuries, to find echoes in the heart of the enthusiast and the metre of the poet.

"Let me see if you find the old calls familiar," Desmond exclaimed, lifting the lid of the piano and tangling it in his haste with its crimson embroidered cloth cover. It was an old piano, with the felt of its hammers worn hard and thin. So much the better, since he desired to drown out the voice of Mr. Hartagous. The martial strain, instinct with its imperative mandate, throbbed through the room and then died away, and as they listened a note was repeated, and still a vibration, as from some vague distance.

"An echo!—an echo!" cried Chub, vociferously. "Oh, mamma, listen to our Mr. Desmond! He can do anything,—how he can play!"

"Now, what do you suppose is the date of that call?" Mr. Stanlett's cheek had flushed; his interest was roused.

"The introduction of this one can be definitely fixed," and once more a spirited lilting strain rang through the room. Then Desmond turned on the piano stool. "Where, Reginald, did you put that old book on the Ancient Military Orders of France? It gives some old calls. I found that rummaging about in the library."

"You find too much, sir, rummaging about!" said Mr. Stanlett, with a bent brow and a fiery eye. "You should curb your talents for rummaging about."

But Desmond had thrust an old folio into his hand, with a recommendation to examine the very quaint and antique illustrations of arms and accoutrements and military costume with which it was embellished. There were some extra inserts of military portraits, steel engravings, and Mr. Stanlett was turning the leaves, his thin mouth drawn in very small, his eye alight with a fervor of interest, his rebuke and its cause forgotten in an instant.

Not by Mr. Hartagous. He made the serious mistake of casting a merry, significant glance at the tutor, expecting it to be returned in like genial wise. He desired to establish confidential relations with Desmond. He might find so accomplished, so versatile, so lightning-quick a fellow of special use here, where diplomatic management might be necessary to smooth the way for readjustments. But Desmond did not respond, and Mr. Hartagous felt the rising surge of anger. He realized that the young man was too observant to have lost the demonstration; he was far too keen to fail to appreciate its relish and its demand for the recognition of Mr. Stanlett's pitiably funny allusion to the tutor's instrumentality in discovering the codicil of the last will and testament of the late Mr. Faurie. Desmond's studied insensibility was a covert rebuke, and the spirit of Mr. Hartagous revolted against this schooling, which he felt might befit some crude hobbledehoy. He would have liked to remind the tutor that he was the guardian's employee and not Mrs. Faurie's, and that the pedagogic office was held at his pleasure; to recall the fact that despite the young man's learning and many accomplishments, it had been already demonstrated to him that one must have foothold, a starting-point, to make these felt by the world. A flood, quotha!—a sorry time a dove or any other fowl would have to find a perch, set adrift from this ark of Great Oaks mansion.

Mrs. Faurie intercepted and interpreted the glance, and for a time she held her eyes down to the fan in her hand with which she seemed gracefully to toy, but Desmond had seen that they were full of tears. She felt that these two men, in the pride of their powers, in the flush of their prime, in the vigor of their health and strength, were ridiculing poor, dear Uncle Clarence for his distress in her loss, for his feeble, inadequate, unreasoning indignation at the officious intermeddling, as he thought it, which had brought the catastrophe about.

But Desmond had begun to sing,—she had not known that he could sing,—and the room was filled with surging waves of melody. A powerful baritone voice he had, of no great cultivation, enough only to temper the crudities of his rendering, but of correct intonation, and it was singularly, lusciously sweet. They were military songs that he sang, with the triumph of the trumpets, the gay clash of the cannikin, the impetuous speed of the high-couraged war-horse, all infused through them. Now they were French and again German, and some were in quaint old English phrase of mediæval suggestion.

"Never, never let me hear you speak another word," cried Mr. Stanlett, in senile delight. "You should go singing through the world like the mockingbirds in spring."

He looked across the room, smiling and nodding, expectant of sympathetic response from Mr. Hartagous, who was as weary of it all as if the evening were spent in that other ark to which Great Oaks mansion was so often likened. Under these circumstances he could have as easily communicated with the ladies of the patriarchal Noah as with Mrs. Faurie,—the terrible Chub chasing continually from the side of the piano and across the room to fling himself into his mother's arms crying, "Ain't it beautiful, mamma? Ain't it beautiful? The grand opera in Paree don't touch Mr. Desmond nowhere!"

So weary, indeed, did Mr. Hartagous presently look that the dispersal of the party for the night was obviously in order, although much earlier than usual.

"Can you find your way back to your room, do you think?" Mrs. Faurie said to the guest, as the group stood at a side table in the hall and she lighted their bedroom candles seriatim.

The house was so large and so rambling in its plan that he was not sure that he remembered his way about it, he replied. He had expected, and indeed so had she, that Desmond would come forward with his readiness for any emergency and officiate as guide. But Desmond, stolidly unmindful, snuffed out and then relighted his own candle, its tiny white blaze illumining his flushed, absorbed face, and after a moment's hesitation Reginald offered to accompany the guest to his room. Thus Mr. Hartagous departed to his night's rest, a little dissatisfied with the situation, and not a little doubtful of the tutor. He resented this incertitude, because it was partly his influence that had placed Desmond here. "And mighty glad he was to come, too," he reflected. He rather wondered that Desmond should not discern his own interests more clearly than to seem to adhere to the losing side, for Mrs. Faurie's power, always limited, was now definitely a thing of the past. "For she is not worth one red cent, as matters stand!" Mr. Keith, he was aware, had begun to doubt whether the redundant maternal coddling was the best thing for the boys, and had only agreed to their persistent retention under her wing in deference to her wish; but Hartagous was sure, did he so desire, that he could easily induce him to insist as their guardian upon packing them off summarily to boarding-school, where they might encounter some of the roughening and hardening phases of boy life. "Make men of them." Although balked of the conversation which he had expected to have with Desmond when he should have reached the room assigned him, and feeling distinctly man-handled, he determined to have a definite understanding with the tutor on the morrow, and apprise him that he was expected to act in the interest of his employer, the guardian, which was identical with that of the executor, in smoothing the way to a pacific adjustment of the troublous toils in which the discovery of the codicil had entangled the household of Great Oaks,—and this signified, in the interpretation of Mr. Hartagous, an unconditional surrender of all the opposing interests.

"It is not late, though you seem tired,—and I must speak to you to-night," Desmond said to Mrs. Faurie, when the young host and the guest had vanished down the cross-hall.

She had her lighted candle in her hand, and the flame threw into high relief against the dull shadows her exquisite face, with the subdued green of her gown, the shimmer of the lace above her bosom, the diamond "sunburst" at her throat. "Won't to-morrow answer?" she replied, stifling a yawn.

"No! Oh, no, indeed! Believe me, I would not insist, but the matter is urgent."

"Heavens! More business!" she remonstrated. "I imagined that with the arrival of Mr. Hartagous all the bother would be over. He can think for us all. What else is a lawyer created for?"

"Your lawyer,—yes! But this man is not acting in your interest. He is acting for the estate."

"It is the same thing,—my sons' interest. He will settle everything."

Desmond could scarcely have feared a more inert attitude of submission than this. How could the woman be so blind! "Come," he said authoritatively, drawing her arm through his. "You shall hear first what I have to say."

She turned back to the parlor with him, dragging a little unwillingly on his arm. "I have always appreciated 'gentlemen's society,' as it is called, and I have to a degree and with exceptions loved my fellow men, but I had no conception until lately that the creatures had it in them to be so wonderfully and fearfully dull and depressing as they are when they talk of their everlasting business. Hereafter, if I have my choice, I shall always prefer 'hen parties' as the lesser evil."

With an elaborate air of patience she seated herself on the sofa while he stirred up the fire and brightened the lamp. As he began to talk, she was inattentive at first, and interpolated irrelevant remarks. "What a lovely voice you have," she said, as her eyes wandered to the open piano. "I shall be wanting you to sing all day."

As he began to recapitulate the details of the codicil and the executor's requirements concerning the refunding clause, she broke out, "Wouldn't you hate to be as chuffy and as stuffy as Mr. Hartagous when you come to be of his age, and look so like a weasel?"

When he disclosed the real mission of Mr. Hartagous, to effect an immediate sale of Great Oaks, a light suddenly sprang into her face, and her voice broke into a sob. He saw that the situation bore far more heavily upon her than she had manifested. She had been whistling, as it were, to keep her courage up.

"How providential!" she cried. "It breaks my heart now to part from Great Oaks, but I see that it is the only way. And oh, for liberation! To be free from debt. The sense of it weighs upon me; I can understand the agony of the old torture of death by pressing."

He was still for a moment, looking at her in sombre thought. "This is what I feared," he said at last,—"your precipitancy. I want you to think, to survey the ground first, to test the possibilities."

He had made out from the will a schedule of the properties, with their approximate values, and the amounts by years of the annual income that must be returned. He went across the room and sat beside her on the sofa, that they might look over the page together. Her face paled while scanning the estimates,—they seemed methodically to set forth financial ruin, absolute, hopeless.

"Then why,—how *dare* that man come here and press Mr. Loring's inadequate offer for Great Oaks?" she blazed out.

"Because he is not acting in your interest, but against you."

She turned and looked Desmond in the face, her beautiful eyes bewildering at these close quarters. He dropped his own eyes on the paper in his hands.

"Mr. Hartagous must distribute the estate according to the terms of the codicil. As executor he is constrained by law to require the refunding of your receipts from it. He is coerced, too, by the position of the guardian, who also has no option, and who will in the changed state of things require this amount to be charged against your portion at the partitioning of the estate and the ascertaining and setting aside of the several shares of the minors. Naturally, Mr. Hartagous is anxious to seize the first opportunity of converting your assets to make good, whatever sacrifice it may impose on *you*."

"What shall I do?—oh, what shall I do?" she cried, in despairing realization of the situation. "But why should I ask? I can only yield."

"You can temporize,—stand out for the full value of the property,—fight for terms. Time is your ally. And you have this strength in your position, that you might give them a contest; a lawyer might find you sufficient grounds,—but, at all events, you are entitled to a fair valuation of your property."

"But even then, Edward," she put her hand on his and pressed it convulsively, "there is not a competence, not a hope from the estate for me."

He did not seek to encourage her by false representations. He was looking the disaster squarely in the eye. "And the boys are powerless for years to come!" he admitted despondently.

Her lips were trembling piteously. "I have not a dollar that I can call my own. I have not a friend in the world."

"You have me,—such as I am," he said, his eyes downcast, still on the papers.

"I never think of you,—you are like another self. But you *are* my friend, and I am not alone! You think for me,—you rescued me at the risk of your life. You think for me,—you care for me,—I am not alone!"

"Care for you!" he broke out, tempted beyond all resistance. "I care for nothing else on God's earth. I love you,—I love you,—I worship you!"

She turned, staring at him in quiet surprise; then, as if she thought he might come nearer, she put one hand against his shoulder, holding him at arm's length.

"Oh, I should have eaten out my heart in silence; I should never have said a word but for this strange change, when you seem as poor as I! But since you feel alone, you may care to know now how beloved, how cherished, how adored you are by me."

"But suppose,—suppose,"—she was still looking hard at him, into his very eyes—"but suppose it might have been grateful to me earlier to know so much—"

"I could not have spoken then; I could not have asked you to make so great a sacrifice for me,—to relinquish your status under the will."

She smiled radiantly at him. "It seems to me now that I might have been glad to make that sacrifice,—for you." Once more her hand pressed against his shoulder to hold him at arm's length. "But it can never be, now," she stipulated, "when I can give you nothing."

"Nothing! You are all the world to me," he protested.

"No, you have your own difficult way to make, and I shall not burden you. It was only a fleeting fancy that came over me,—a sentimental glimpse of what I *might* have felt for you had fortune favored us."

"You shall not decree the future," he declared imperiously. "I shall fashion it for us both. It is not yours to say. You have said enough. I know your heart better than you do,—I believe you love me—"

"Like a son," she interrupted, with a gurgling laugh. "I am older than you by ten years."

"And younger by a century in spirit, and as beautiful as the angels in heaven. If you leave Great Oaks, we go forth together. Life in poor conditions would not be sordid with you. It would always be fresh and deliriously sweet and forever a blessing, whatever hardships fate might impose. I am strong and well equipped, and with this hand in mine I could make my way against all the world. I would have no false pride to hamper my efforts, so truly proud would I be in having the dear privilege of working for you."

"Like Chub,—would you dig in the garden?" The anticlimax was of conclusive import in the stress of the moment. She had not intended to yield, but she laughed in tender recollection of her little son's childish offer of help, and in the instant of relaxation she burst into happy tears. Her head sank on Desmond's shoulder, and his arm was around her.

"Like Chub, I would even dig in the garden," he protested.

CHAPTER XVIII

I t was not yet a late hour when Desmond quitted the parlor, Mrs. Faurie having flitted away, joyously protesting that the consideration of such nonsense as his discourse was undermining to the reason. The evening had resulted in so signal a failure to entertain the guest acceptably that an earlier dispersal than usual had supervened. Nevertheless, as Desmond made his way down the veranda toward the library, intending to smoke and linger an hour or so in his chosen haunt, for with this tumult of joy and expectation and triumph in his brain and heart he knew that he could not soon compose himself to rest, he was surprised in turning the corner to see a light upon the waters at a little distance, in the midst of the dark, rippling expanse that surrounded the mansion.

The night wind blew dank and chill across the damp purlieus of the veranda, the flooring of which was always splashed and reeking from the tossing waves of the recent landing of some dugout at various points, but it brought no other sound than the monotonous voices of the night, so accustomed that they scarcely impinged upon the consciousness: the stir of the foliage of the great oaks, the effect of their stately avenues "queered" by their diluvian surroundings; the iterative batrachian chorus from some insular "high ground" far away; the sudden bellow of a bull alligator; and always the murmur of the widespread shallows of the overflow under the influence of the breeze.

The light was stationary, and though it was now the dark of the moon and Desmond had only the vague illumination of the myriad stars of the clear spring night, he made out behind it the dull outline of a small boat. A lantern was evidently carried at the prow, and despite the fact that the light annulled the suggestion of secrecy, Desmond fancied that the motionless pause bespoke observation. Suddenly he heard the impact of a paddle upon the water, and became aware that the craft was about to turn. The spy, if spy he were, intended to retrace his course;—not until he should have given an account of himself, Desmond resolved, and of his mission, scouting about on the dark waters of the overflow, making his secret observations of Great Oaks mansion when asleep and off its guard.

"Hello, the boat!" Desmond's strong young voice carried like a clarion across the flooded distance.

The answer came, hearty and reassuring: "Hello, the house!"

The dugout swung around once more, and as its prow was presented to Desmond's eye as it advanced in a direct line, its bulk was obliterated, and this gave the man who stood erect plying his paddle in the Indian fashion the weird effect of walking on the water as he approached the house in the clare-obscure.

"God! What *is* that?" exclaimed Mr. Hartagous, looking out from the dark window close at hand. He had been roused by the tutor's ringing call to the boatman, and, apprehending some disturbance, had in the instant's time secured his trousers and his pistol, the two essentials to dignified midnight combat. The light from the lantern of the dugout, which now began to head for a landing at the veranda, was flung far out on the watery gloom, and sent a ray to the long window, illumining a tousled mass of gray hair and whiskers, and a puckered face of most discordant and disconcerted petulance.

"Nare light do you show, Mr. Desmond," said the voice of Bainbridge, the manager, from the dugout. "You are such owels up here at the big house that I made sure o' findin' you up, anyhow. Why, 'tain't quite eleven o'clock."

"And what in hell do you mean by sidling up to Great Oaks mansion in the middle of the night in this enigmatic way without warning?" demanded the lawyer, testily,—he evidently considered Desmond a mere attaché of the household and with no prerogative to speak with authority. Therefore he took bold precedence. "And who are you?—and what mischief are you bent upon?"

"Ah-h-h! It's *you* bent on mischief, Mr. Hartagous! Mischief is the trade of all your tribe!" tartly retorted the manager, none of whose interests could be imperiled by the lawyer, and whose nerves were already exacerbated by the jeopardy of all his prospects in the impending changes.

"Oh, is it Mr. Bainbridge, the manager? Beg pardon, my good man. I didn't recognize you in the darkness,—but you should really let people sleep in peace"; then with an accession of acerbity,—"buccaneering around in the overflow at this time of night!"

It hardly affected Desmond that Mr. Hartagous should take the pas, the air of control in these matters appertaining to Great Oaks Plantation, as if the power of its possessor and her staff were already a thing of the past; but Mr. Bainbridge was not used to such reversals of spiteful fortune. Wind and weather had worked him much woe in his agricultural experience; desperate calamities, such as the overflow, had visited him more than once; but these mischances supervened in his professional conflict with natural forces, and were the dispensations of established authority, the "hand of God," to use the pious commercial phraseology, and he submitted to them with such broadening of his back to the burden and such patience as he could muster. The disaster, however, which menaced the tenure of Great Oaks Plantation, this flagrant injustice, this legalized mischief, was the artifice of man, the deflection of the will of the testator rather than its execution, and he entertained scant toleration of the operations of law that permitted it and the person of its representative. It threw Mr. Bainbridge out of an employment in which he was well satisfied and had given satisfaction these many years, for he had a ghastly prevision of the overthrow of all the existing status which would ensue under a new owner.

"Oh," he said with jaunty bravado, as he ran the nose of the dugout close to the veranda and sprang heavily upon the flooring, securing the trace chain that served as painter around one of the columns, "me and Mr. Desmond go on a 'high old lonesome' most any time o' night. We don't keep reg'lar hours in the swamp, you see, like you cits do in Memphis,—early to bed and early to rise makes you-all so all-fired healthy, wealthy, and wise."

Mr. Hartagous sputtered, but no immediate answer occurred to him, though presently he found cause to admonish Mr. Bainbridge of his heavy footfall. "You'll wake up the whole house,—you tramp like a grenadier."

"And what sort o' animal might that be,—fourfooted?" queried Mr. Bainbridge, affecting deep ignorance.

Mr. Hartagous disdained to reply, but the admonition touching his resonant swinging gait had not been altogether lost on Bainbridge, and to avoid passing on the veranda, thus noisily, the vicinity of Mrs. Faurie's room, he entered unceremoniously at the long French window at which Mr. Hartagous stood, intending to traverse the guest's apartment and thus reach the cross-hall in order to take his way thence to the library, where he could discuss his errand with the tutor. Desmond followed, meditating some lubricating word of apology. But Bainbridge continued in sarcastic ill-humor: "I never *did* pretend to be one of your soft-steppin', Slip-Slinksy sort o' fellows. I could understand your objections to having him slying around the house of a night, but—" He paused abruptly as he opened the door leading into the cross-hall; the stoppage was a sort of galvanic shudder, such as might befit a cessation of steam propulsion. He turned toward the others, over his big brawny shoulders, a face visibly paling beneath its sunburn in the gleam of the candle which the saturnine Hartagous had just lighted.

"Hist," he said, and silence fell. For outside in the distance and the darkness, so soft that one might wonder that it should be so distinct, was that vague sense of an unseen progression,—a step, or rather the impact of a foot with the pile of the velvet carpet of the padded stair, a silken sibilance, then silence, and again a footfall ascending the flight.

It was audible to Mr. Hartagous as he stood half dressed beside the table. A dismayed, protesting question was in the wrinkles and corrugations of his face as he turned it toward the door; a keen, excited gleam shone in his eyes, for he, too, had heard of the furtive spectre of Great Oaks. The blazing match in his hand burned unheeded to the tips of his fingers. When the flame touched the flesh he dropped the match, but without a word or sound. It seemed to have tangibly kindled his intention, his resolution. It was hardly possible to imagine a man of his age and so portly, who was now so light of movement. He had noiselessly thrust his bare feet into his bedroom slippers, great yawning foot-gear, placed his revolver in the pistol pocket of his trousers, while he held in his hand a thing that to the rustic Mr. Bainbridge seemed a pocketbook, but which Desmond recognized as one of the tiny electric lamps that have this semblance. He dropped the conical extinguisher over the newly lighted flame of the candle, and in a moment all was darkness and silence.

Each of the others recognized the lawyer's determination to see the thing out. Bainbridge, for all his bold initiative in matters cognate to daylight, fell behind him as Mr. Hartagous briskly flung the door wide and shuffled noiselessly along the hall. For one moment Desmond felt an agony of indecision. He had an unreasoning instinct to call out and give the forlorn old spectre some warning of the fell forces of flesh and blood that were even now upon his elusive track, that he might craftily compass his disappearance as more than once heretofore. Then he hesitated. He had shrunk from such knowledge as had come to him as to the details in the concealment of the codicil of the will, and he had found its only extenuation in the doubt of Mr. Stanlett's sanity and responsibility. It was impossible to judge how this might have stood in the beginning, but now, when it was so obviously futile and the ghostly step was once more wandering through the midnight quiet of Great Oaks mansion, he became afraid of interference,—discovery could only prove the mental unsoundness that was at last poor Slip-Slinksy's protection. Moreover, Mr. Hartagous was now halfway up the stairs; Bainbridge, sitting on the bottom step, had pulled off his high boots and followed in his stocking feet as noiseless as a cat. Nevertheless, the crafty old spectre had become aware of their approach. Not a sound, not a stir, issued from above. He was still up there somewhere in the darkness. Surely he could scarcely have drawn a breath as the two below stood on the stairs, motionless also, watching, waiting. Desmond, lingering in the hall beneath, one hand on the newel-post, felt a rush of indignation, knowing what he did. The two spies, stalwart, alert, both more than a score of years younger, could easily wear out the endurance of the poor, patient, disappointed ghost, whose lawless mission had always been instinct with beneficent intention. Yet not so easily, perhaps; for presently, when a timber of the stair creaked, Desmond knew that Bainbridge, his muscles stiff and cramping, had been forced to shift his weight.

The house within was absolutely noiseless. The half-moon of glass above the doors at the front showed its presence in a dim gray contour, but shed no light. The splashing of the water of the overflow under the buffets of the wind was distinct in the pause. Once a gust went skirling with a wild, chill voice among the score of chimneys, and passed into the distance, and silence ensued. Suddenly a light cut the gloom like a knife. There, standing on the landing, was the spectre of the tradition, the cocked hat upon its white hair, powdered, alas! only by time, its cloak falling almost to its heels, its eyes blazing with that fierce yet consciously helpless anger of the aged, and its lips drawn close and thin to keep the secret that battered against their reticence.

Mr. Hartagous had crept up the stairs like a panther in his eagerness for his prey, yet at the instant of discovery he slunk back amazed and disconcerted. "Mr. Stanlett," he exclaimed, his finger failing for a moment in the pressure on the button, and the whole scene vanishing into darkness with a leaping suddenness, then as suddenly leaping into view, "I am astonished at you!"

"And I cannot express *my* surprise," the old gentleman said, with a crisp sarcasm that had an unexpected edge. His eyes ran deliberately over the details of the unconventional aspect and attire of Mr. Hartagous: his bushy, tousled gray hair and whiskers; his burly, much wrinkled throat, left bare without collar or cravat; his suspenders, all unadjusted, still hanging from the waistband of his trousers and dangling sashwise almost to his heels; his bare feet and ankles revealed nearly in their entirety by his loose, yawning bedroom slippers. And he had not the wit to take his thumb from the button of the lamp. "I cannot express my surprise to detect you skulking, noiseless, in this unshod condition, about a house in which you are a guest. Fie! Fie! Mr. Hartagous. If you have taken a fancy to any valuables of ours, why, speak out, man, and we will *give* them to you! We have lost too much lately not to realize the vanity of earthly hoardings."

Mr. Hartagous might have seemed of the porpoise family, so resonant were the deep and gusty breaths he drew. "Before God, old man, I have a mind to throw you down these stairs," he cried, in fury and amaze that such an imputation, though forced and satiric as it was, could be cast on his conduct. "I have a mind to throw you down these stairs!"

"Have a care, have a care of your fellow burglar, then," cried Mr. Stanlett, secure in the immunity of his age and his weakness. "Stand from under, my good Mr. Bainbridge."

Mr. Hartagous had never dreamed how much of his acumen as a lawyer, his dignity as a man, his force as an individual, appertained to his usual smart metropolitan costume. He made a desperate effort to lay hold on his wonted identity.

"But you have your own conduct to explain, Mr. Stanlett," he said severely.

"Explain?—to whom?—to you?" the old man flouted contemptuously.

And Mr. Hartagous was aware that this was not the noted cross-examiner whom he had hitherto recognized in himself.

"You surely know, Mr. Stanlett," he began anew, "that your mysterious midnight rovings about this house have given rise to misinterpretations—"

"Strange,—strange that you should think so, and yet go roving too!" said Mr. Stanlett, his eyes burning.

Mr. Bainbridge, a good deal perturbed by the unexpected falling out of the event, yet nevertheless reassured too to find the familiar figure of the old gentleman in lieu of the unimagined spectre, in anticipation of which his stout heart had quailed, suddenly broke out in his burly voice: "Well, I ain't faultin' Mr. Stanlett, anyhows he chooses to do." He had known him since his own early youth, and his veneration had the strength of long habit. "He can have his own way at Great Oaks. If he has a mind to sit up late of a night and loaf about the house, it is his own affair. No curfew here! If I had ha' known that Slip-Slinksy was *you*, sir, I'd ha' been in my dugout and a mile away by now." The tone of respect, of consideration, to which the old gentleman was accustomed, broke down his reserve. He could meet defiance with taunts, and reproaches with sarcasm, but he melted before kindness.

"Oh, Jerry, Jerry Bainbridge," he wailed, holding out both hands and shaking his old gray head, so fantastic in its cocked hat, dismally to and fro, "I was just hunting for a will,—a better will than that poisonous paper that is to destroy us all. Faurie never intended that such a will should hold. Night after night, year after year, I laid it away and hunted for a better one. And I'm hunting for it yet, and I'll hunt for it till I die,—and maybe I'll find it yet." Then breaking off suddenly, with a look of proud and deep offense, "Slip-Slinksy,—that's what they call me! Slip-Slinksy!" He repeated the distasteful word, while a vivid flush mounted to the roots of his silver hair.

"But nobody knowed 'twas you, Mr. Stanlett," Bainbridge urged caressingly, yet with deep respect. "You are more looked up to than anybody in Deepwater Bend."

In view of the tone of this interlocutor, it seemed to Mr. Stanlett not derogatory to his dignity to defend himself. "It was my duty, Bainbridge, my duty. I had promised Faurie. My word was out."

Mr. Hartagous cocked up his head to listen and bent his brows. "What promise was this which you gave to Mr. Faurie, if I may ask?" he demanded, puzzled.

"I recognize no obligation to inform you, Mr. Hartagous, and no coercion in your question," replied Mr. Stanlett, with dignity. "But I would not willingly seem churlish and reticent. I have no objection to answer, now that that unfortunate codicil has been produced—none whatever. Mr. Faurie urged me to search for another will till I found it,—I say a 'will,' but 'paper-writing' was the word he used."

A pause ensued, while his fantastic figure on the landing, with the divergent rays of the lamp full upon him, stood silent and stiff, as he looked down at the brilliant focus of the electric wire in the case, which dulled the dim group about it on the stairs.

"When did Mr. Faurie tell you that?" asked the wondering lawyer.

"Just about four years after he died," the old man replied, quite simply.

A thrill of astonished comprehension quivered through the group on the stairs. Hartagous, accustomed to a sedulous facial control, did not change countenance or speak; his thumb, however, trembled on the button of the lamp, and the scene fluttered back and forth, ghostly-wise, through the darkness. But both the other listeners exclaimed, each after the fashion of his wonted phraseology, though neither could have remembered his own words a moment later. Mr. Stanlett apprehended the amazement in the tones, and his interest, which had seemed but a jaded familiarity with an old experience, pricked up suddenly.

"Very remarkable, wasn't it?" he said. "I remember that it surprised me extremely at the time, though really I don't know that it should. Faurie was always different from anybody else. I was in the blue room up there, where after his death we had packed away all of his papers which he had seemed to consider of no particular account, till *you* sent here, as executor, for those cursed levee bonds." He paused to glare down with sudden wolfish rancor at Hartagous, then resumed abruptly: "I was ransacking the papers again, for in searching for the levee bonds I had found that codicil to the will,—which I wish to God I had never seen or had burnt on the spot. I knew the havoc that four years of Honoria's expenditures would make in her provision if they were chargeable against her portion in the partition of the estate. Four years' income,—one hundred and twenty thousand dollars. It seemed immense then! And *now* it is nearly seven years' income derived from the general estate that she must refund, and in addition all the yield of the crops of Great Oaks Plantation."

He paused, his dreary, sunken eyes lifted suddenly to the upper story opposite the landing, and Bainbridge began to quake so perceptibly for the thought of what might be leaning lightly over the balustrade, a graceful manly figure, which he could see well enough though he would not look toward it, that the stout stair-rail shook responsive to the quiver of his brawny hand laid upon it. He kept instead his attention fixed resolutely on Mr. Stanlett's lean, pallid face, with its fantastic headgear and its fiery eyes. There seemed naught more definite than mere memory before them, for he went on as if he had been only arranging the sequence of the events in his mind. "It surprised me then considerably, but now it seems no great matter. Faurie came in suddenly, as if it were the most natural thing in the world, and he said,—you know that way he had of demanding impossibilities of people and getting them too,—'Keep back that codicil, Mr. Stanlett,—there is another paper-writing; find it and present them both together.' He was pale and eager. He seemed desperately in earnest. He was dressed for riding,—he had come from far. I wonder which horse he had! He held a riding-crop in his hand, and he struck the codicil contemptuously with it,—you remember his tempestuous ways when he was angered, and he had that fine air of scorn that used to become him so well,—he struck the codicil as the paper lay open on the table. And you can see the welt of his riding-crop across it now." Mr. Hartagous was conscious of a vague icy touch that seemed to delineate the course of his spinal column in successive shivers, for he was remembering that he had noticed an unaccountable diagonal indentation athwart the paper when it had been recently produced in court.

The recital had been to Mr. Stanlett a tremendous nervous strain; the old face began to quiver and the voice broke into whimpers, and the thin hands were aimlessly fluttering. "And 'twas just like Faurie to set me to search and never tell me for what nor where. '*Paper-writing!*' have looked—and looked—for the paper-writing,—and I have looked for *him*, too, but I have never seen him since,—though—sometimes"—Mr. Stanlett glanced furtively over his shoulder at the ascending flight of stairs—"I have heard his step behind me as I went hunting—hunting—for the 'paper-writing.' If I had met him once on these dark stairs, I'd have held on to him, dead or alive, till I got some data as to what and where."

As the tall, thin figure wavered to and fro and seemed about to fall, Bainbridge pushed hastily past Mr. Hartagous on the stair and offered a supporting arm to the old gentleman. "Such tiresome times, Jerry Bainbridge, that I have, to be sure. I need my sleep,—I need my night's rest," he plained, looking out of the deep, pathetic, sunken eyesockets of the aged: "to watch, and wait, and listen, and slip, and search,—'twas mighty hard! And then to be heard, after all. To be followed and spied out by this lawyer, and Desmond, and you,—*Slip-Slinksy!*" he repeated with a repugnant mutter.

Suddenly the light went out, leaving the whole in darkness. Mr. Hartagous pressed the button in vain. "The battery is exhausted. It will have to be recharged," he remarked impersonally, as he turned on the stair.

Desmond was suddenly sensible of his position as quasi-host, and he felt the Great Oaks traditions of hospitality had hardly been maintained in the treatment that Mr. Hartagous had received on the stairs. "I will get a candle immediately. There is a fire in the library still, Mr. Hartagous; it has grown quite chilly. Perhaps you might care to have a cigar there."

He addressed the unresponsive darkness apparently, in which, however, the queer figure of Mr. Hartagous was scarcely invisible, so definitely had it impressed itself upon the memory; but it was shuffling along very systematically, for his voice came from out the gloom, far down the hall and near his own door: "Thanks, thanks, very much; I will put on something extra—I feel the change of the temperature—and join you presently."

Mr. Stanlett was not altogether self-absorbed. "Why, Desmond, why don't you offer him a nightcap?" he called out genially, from the darkness of the landing. "Make him mix you a toddy in the library, Hartagous. He hasn't got so little sense as you might think! He knows how to do that, at any rate!" Then with a distressful quaver: "Take something, Hartagous. You ain't used to the Slip-Slinksy business like me. *Slip-Slinksy,*—the very boys call me that!" And now again jocund, though ever and anon his voice broke, "Do a little rummaging around in the dining-room, Desmond, and see if you can't put two and two together,—a sandwich and a decanter."

"But won't you join us, Mr. Stanlett," demanded Desmond, cheerily, for he judged from the diminishing distance of his voice that the old gentleman was approaching on the arm of Bainbridge; but Mr. Stanlett fell anew to whimpering, and said that he wanted to be in his bed, and indeed in his grave, that ought to have been made long ago with him laid at peace within it, for the days had come in which he could take no pleasure and the nights in which he could take no rest. Then he broke off, smartly to reprimand Bainbridge for stumbling, and pathetically averred, "But I have had more practice in walking in the dark. My conscience! I am familiar with the face of the night. Some terrible features it has, too. It is made up of grimaces!"

CHAPTER XIX

When Mr. Hartagous repaired to the library, he scarcely compared in regard to apparel with the point-device Desmond, who was still in the attire that he had worn at the somewhat formal dinner early in the evening, but the guest's aspect was far more conventional than during the episode on the staircase. As he blew a refreshing whiff of cigar smoke from his lips and allowed a second to curl in thin tendrils through his nose, he sank deep in his easy chair and stretched out his slippered feet luxuriously to the fire. They were now encased also in natty black silk socks, which came well up under the trousers and hid the ankles, erstwhile so frankly displayed. His hair had been hastily brushed, and though he still wore no collar nor tie, his iron-gray whiskers, parted and smoothed in his swift toilet, touched the edge of a jaunty smoking-jacket, just donned, of quilted bronze silk faced with cardinal red. He was more bland now than in his demeanor hitherto; perhaps because of the genial influence of the decanter and glasses on the library table, he had reached the conclusion that suavity was the best method to enlist the good-will of the tutor, and throw his influence in the household, which might be considerable, to the advantage of the executor in effecting the sale of Great Oaks Plantation and a pacific settlement under the terms of the codicil to the will.

"Why, I had no idea that Mr. Stanlett had aged so much,—greatly broken!" he remarked confidentially. "He is practically demented. Utterly irresponsible! Did you note what he said about having hidden the codicil? I wonder how long he has had it in his possession,—might approximate the time by the duration of the tradition of the ghostly footfall at Great Oaks."

"He couldn't have had a nefarious intention, or he would have destroyed the paper; yet he must have known how disastrous delay in producing it would be to Mrs. Faurie's interests," argued Desmond, dispassionately.

"You are reasoning like a sane man, but his course is insanity," rejoined Mr. Hartagous. "I suppose that the shock of the discovery impaired his powers of discrimination. There must have been some earlier cerebral lesion, some obscure affection of the brain, to which this incident gave expression. His delusion is very curious,—the apparition of Faurie; great verisimilitude in that character sketch,—I could almost see him myself!"

"What strikes me as amazing is that he should never have shared his secret,—that he could guard his delusion and his search for a 'paper-writing' through so many years with so many narrow escapes from detection," said Desmond.

"Well, insanity is essentially abnormal."

"He is insane in no other respect, apparently," Desmond suggested.

"This is a case of 'the fixed idea,'" said Hartagous. "It is a good thing that he is not legally responsible,—that is, if his possession of the codicil was not also a delusion from the beginning."

"You think that possible?" said Desmond, with raised eyebrows.

"Anything is possible in this connection. But it doesn't matter,—he is wholly irresponsible. Bad thing he has made out of it for Mrs. Faurie! It will leave her practically stranded for life, unless indeed she should make an advantageous second marriage, which I hope to heaven she may."

"That is hardly likely," said Desmond, with his eyes on the fire.

Mr. Hartagous bent his bushy gray eyebrows in insistent argument. "And why not? She is extremely beautiful, and the years literally make no impression upon her. She is as young and as handsome as she was at nineteen. And she is very fascinating, in the best sense of the word. A very charming and delightful woman! Her piteous prospects in this change have worried me no little. Indeed, that is doubtless the one hope,—an advantageous second marriage. Among us we must try and save enough to her out of the estate to put her in a position—temporary, of course—to be able to make it,—go somewhere for a while, Memphis, or New Orleans, or New York. Buried here in the woods, she will never see anybody,—unless—unless—it were somebody slying around trying to buy Great Oaks." Mr. Hartagous paused reflectively. He was essentially a business man, and could have succeeded signally in any line to which he had devoted his energies; he was now unconsciously showing great capacities to conduct a matrimonial agency. He let off a slow, meditative whiff of smoke, holding his cigar in one hand as he looked speculatively at the ceiling. "I wonder—I *do* wonder—whether Loring might not fill the bill! What a solution of the problem it would be, if we could capture Loring!"

"We don't want him," said Desmond, in evident repugnance.

"Why not?" Mr. Hartagous bent his brows in a cogitating frown as he surveyed the tutor. "Loring is a very worthy, honorable man, and agreeable, apart from his money,—and Mrs. Faurie will have absolutely nothing. He is a very brainy man, and of excellent moral character. I should think he could make himself very acceptable. You think that Mrs. Faurie would not marry him?"

"I know she would not. In fact, Mrs. Faurie has promised to marry me," Desmond said succinctly.

In the scope of humane protection there ought to be some restraint on the administration of sudden shocks. The jerk, mental and moral, which Mr. Hartagous experienced was as if a galvanic current had thrilled through every sensibility. Even his physique was not exempt. As his hand on the arm of the chair mechanically flew up, it struck his cigar between his lips with such force as to break it in half, so that it hung bent at right angles in his mouth as he sat upright and stared at the tutor.

Desmond wondered that he should have no qualms of conscience in thus interposing an insurmountable obstacle to the fair haven to which Mr. Hartagous was desirous of steering Mrs. Faurie's future. But he only felt elated, delighted, triumphant. He did not even resent the indignant remonstrance, deprecation, amazement, in the executor's face.

"Did she intend really," he demanded, in a low, tense, excited voice, "to relinquish her fine income during widowhood,—under the will,—for merely what amounts to her statute rights of dower—and *you*?"

The tutor laughed aloud, so joyously, in such gay elation, that Worldly Wisdom could but bend its brows anew. "She never had the opportunity. I could not, I would not, ask her to relinquish anything for me. It was only when she had nothing to lose that I offered my heart and hand,—only this evening, in fact."

Mr. Hartagous leaned forward, the bent cigar still between his lips, to survey the young man who, holding his own cigar between his finger-tips, lightly touched off the ash and smilingly returned the mentor's look. He still smiled in imperturbable good-humor when Mr. Hartagous ejaculated, as if involuntarily, from the depths of his conviction: "You—poor—fool!"

"Thank you very much," cried Desmond, in airy nonchalance.

"My dear boy, she is ten years older than you—"

"And she looks ten years younger,—but that is neither here nor there. I am not marrying her for her beauty any more than for her money."

"Certainly not for that," said Mr. Hartagous, sourly. "But Mrs. Faurie's friends will never consent to this; it would make her ridiculous in the eyes of the world."

"If I may judge by what I have learned in my own experience of friendship, as this world goes, Mrs. Faurie's friends will let her very severely alone as soon as they are informed of the state of her exchequer. As to ridicule,—just as it happens, we do not care in the least for that."

"But you must consider her sons,—the very children will protest."

"And they alone have the right," Desmond admitted. And Mr. Hartagous made a mental note to be early at their ear with crafty counsel.

He again hesitated for a moment, with the bent cigar now in his hand. "I know that you will not thank me for my interference," he said gravely, "but as a mutual friend,—yours as well as Mrs. Faurie's,—a friend of the family, indeed, I must remind you of your financial position. You know that it was difficult to find foothold for yourself,—how can you support an additional burden? I should be glad to advise Keith to continue you in your present employment—"

"I am beholden to you!" laughed Desmond.

"But your common sense must show you that it would be untenable, unsuitable. You know that the learned professions are not paid in proportion to the equipment required and the talent employed. They ought to be—and, in fact, they generally are—filled by men who could at a pinch live by other resources. But what would *you* do if you should find no other opportunity?"

"Snap my fingers in the faces of the Nine Muses and come down from Olympus! I would do whatever fell to my hand. I would not now be so choice, so exacting, so determined on pursuing the course that I had laid out. If 'letters' are not for me, then I am not for 'letters.' I will work at anything. I will dig in a ditch. I will turn wood-chopper. I will 'run the river.'"

"You will make a success of whatever you turn your hand to; but 'run the river'—I hope you ain't talkin' of leavin' us, Mr. Desmond." Bainbridge's rough voice broke suddenly on the colloquy, as he entered, hearing only the last words. "I don't know how we would get on at Great Oaks without you now." Then, bethinking himself of his own insecure tenure of office, his face clouded and his voice fell. "Well, gents," he continued, after a pause, "I have got old Mr. Stanlett resting easy, and I believe I'll finish out my yerrand here and take myself home. Mr. Desmond, do you know if there was any of them sticks o' giant powder left here at the house after we blasted that last tangle?" For a recent development of the dangers of the overflow was the approach of floating débris dislodged from the inundated forests above, now merely drift logs, and again gigantic trees, long since dead and easily overblown in the high winds that had latterly prevailed. Sometimes they came slowly slipping along the sluggish flood of the back waters, sometimes swiftly hurtling, as if flung from a catapult, down the impetuous currents of the mid-channel of the great river. Now they appeared singly, and again entangled with other growths; and these fibrous masses, difficult of disintegration, offered a menace in collision with boats or buildings, which required all the ingenuity of the skilled in "fighting water" to ward off. To climb upon the floating tree, insert a dynamite cartridge in some convenient hollow, and speed off as fast as dugout might skim and paddle ply before the explosion rent the floating mass asunder, setting it adrift in hundreds of harmless fragments, had been found an effective measure, though not without dangers of its own.

Desmond said that he had reserved a few cartridges, which he had deposited in an out-of-the-way place for safety. He laid his cigar on the edge of the ash tray on the library table, searched one of the drawers for a key, and as he left the room, he remarked that dynamite was a commodity with which Mr. Bainbridge could not be too careful.

"I ain't going to set down on it, you can bet high on that!" the manager observed, with the kind of laugh attributed to the horse, with less than fair appreciation of equine manners. He slouched across the room in the big boots which he had resumed, having drawn them over his trousers to the knee according to his wont. His big hat was on the back of his straw-tinted hair, for since Mrs. Faurie was not present, he recognized no etiquette which required him to remove it, and he habitually wore it indoors; he sunk into a large chair of the reclining variety, furnished with a shelf at the side, which was available, turning on a pivot, for either book-rest or writing-desk. As he quietly waited, he began to eye Mr. Hartagous and his bent cigar, which was past all surgery. The lawyer discarded it into the smoking-tray, and spoke to avoid a question concerning it, for he realized that Mr. Bainbridge's curiosity was unrestricted and his tact slight.

"They have made great changes here, Mr. Bainbridge," he said, glancing about the room,—"and yet there is no especial difference when you come to examine,—a mere matter of rearrangement."

"Yes, sir,—yes, sir. The kids recite here now. But Mr. Desmond has a way of putting his mark on things. This room reminds me only of him now, yet I can remember a time when it was as good as a photo of Mr. Faurie. He died here, you know,—and if I don't forgit, it was in this very chair."

"Yes, yes,—of heart failure. Yes,—a good while ago," Mr. Hartagous replied, and fell silent.

The whole house had become silent, too, once more. If Desmond were astir in his search for the stick of dynamite, it was at a distance in the rambling old building, for there was no token of movement far or near. The clock on the mantelpiece was bringing the minute hand into occultation by the hour hand on the dial, and the silver tale of midnight presently rang out. The single log across the andirons, for it had been a bright fire rather than a great one, had charred through by the heat of the day's embers below and presently fell apart, sending up jets of sparks and tendrils of pungent smoke. Mr. Bainbridge rose and nimbly kicked the ends together between the dogs, and as the flames of the dry wood flared up cheerily, he returned to his seat, and seemed disposed to moralize and favor Mr. Hartagous with his views on the mutation of sublunary affairs. "But I useter never come in this room but what I could fairly pictur' Mr. Faurie sittin' in this very chair. Lord! what a power o' pains he did give himself about that will o' his and all his papers, Mr. Hartagous. And to think! it's all turned out as he would have liked least. Not that I blame *you*, sir."

"No, of course not," acceded Mr. Hartagous, promptly, conscious that his position did not commend itself to the manager's favor.

"Being the executor, you have to do as the law requires. But little did *he* think that he was leaving his pretty young wife a share of—river fog, to live off 'n all her days; no wonder it's turned old Mr. Stanlett's brain! She has been like a daughter to him. Well, well,—I don't wonder that he thought he viewed Mr. Faurie up there amongst the old papers in the blue room. Mr. Faurie lived amongst his papers those few last weeks,—every lease, every lien, every mortgage, every promissory note, was examined in expectation of the administration of his estate. I useter look at him and wonder how he had the grit to fix and fix his papers when he warn't able to work, so feeble as he was. He'd send for me as a subscribing witness in leases, and contracts, and such,—me and the trained nurse; we witnessed a power o' papers in those last days. They mostly seemed short,—little matters hereabouts. The important papers had been packed and sent to you in Memphis by that time; but these were some renewals he had promised, and he canceled some obligations he held. Mr. Faurie was not what a body would call a liberal man,—he was rather strict: but he executed a release for old man Tynes, whose debt wasn't more than half paid out, and who was likely to ha' been sold up; and he give a quittance to old Sloper; and he acknowledged a quitclaim deed on that tract o' swampy woodland that that Irish wood-chopper Jessop hadn't paid scarcely any purchase money on—'tain't worth much, but 'twas riches to old Axe-helve; and he relinquished his rights in that steamboat, the Swamp Lily, to Captain Cleek, for old acquaintance' sake; and he remembered the old niggers variously; and he gimme my mule Lucy, finest mare mule I ever see, as good to-day as she was then, and two hundred dollars in gold in a bag,—but *he* didn't care to stand for liberal. He wouldn't ha' put such little extras into his will for the public to know—indeed, no,—not for a pretty! He just settled his gifts beforehand. And every paper was just so!—and they all held together as tight as hell, except that will that he cared for more than all the rest. Things turn out cur'ous, they do,—for a fact!" Bainbridge shook his head drearily, and looked reflectively into the fire. Great Oaks Plantation had been home to him for many a year, and he was a man of scanty resources and narrow experience. He knew naught of the world beyond, and he deprecated change.

"Of course I didn't know the contents of the papers then," he presently resumed his reminiscences. "I just heard about what they were in the gossip after his death, and in fact a good many were put on record in the court-house right away. I wasn't expected to read 'em when he executed them. All I did was to witness his signature." With his unemployed hands he drew before him the writing-shelf attached to the arm of the chair and took the position of the scribe as he meditated, drumming slightly on the wood with his fingers, that showed in their blunt, roughened tips and broken nails the hand of the toiler. "Mr. Faurie was a proud man," he discriminated. "He didn't openly admit that death itself could down him. He only used to remark, 'No man can say that he will be here to-morrow, so I am setting some pressing affairs in order.' He said that to me on that last night, just about a half hour before he died. Why, I hadn't got home,—I was riding one of his horses,—do you remember Indian Chief, and how fast he could rack?—I hadn't reached the willow slough when I saw the rocket go up at the landing to signal the Swamp Lily as she passed to stop and take on the orders for the funeral, you know."

"Yes,—oh, yes," said Mr. Hartagous, hastily, reminded of ghastly details. It was not a cheering subject; he had had a troublous day; he had been awaiting Desmond's return that he might have an additional word with him in continuance of the discussion so suddenly sprung upon him; but the tutor was long away, scarcely sustaining his reputation for rummaging. The lawyer was about to comment with acerbity on the delay, for he felt the need of his well-earned night's rest, when he was struck by the fidelity of the mimicry of voice and manner with which the manager was reproducing the scene so often enacted here, so replete with significance to all those whom these signatures concerned. "'Witness my hand and seal,—witness my hand and seal,'" he repeated more than once. Then, with an imperative intonation, "'Attest, Jeremiah Bainbridge. Sign here.'"

He glanced up with a mirthless laugh, and as he thrust the shelf away from him the elastic strap of a portfolio, attached on the under side, gave way in his rough handling and a flutter of papers slid from the receptacle to the floor.

"Look at me!" exclaimed Bainbridge, in contrition for the mischance. "What's these?—the kids' exercises." He read aloud in a droning voice: "'And when King Xerxes marched to the north he left'—a heap of confusion behind him, I reckon!" he remarked facetiously, gathering up the flying pages of writing, inscribed in a large, boyish hand, stopping now and again to peruse quizzically the inapposite theme with a sort of relish of its incongruity with the scene, the life, and the thought of to-day.

Mr. Hartagous lent his aid. The accident was of a kind peculiarly irritating to his prepossessions, and to his mind suggested the bull in the china shop. He was less animated, however, by the desire to help the worthy manager than to remove the débris and obviate thus any difficulty which might otherwise prevent Mr. Bainbridge from getting himself away immediately upon the return of Desmond with the stick of dynamite; Mr. Hartagous was capable of wishing that this might blow the manager into the Mississippi River, were there no other method of compassing his speedy withdrawal. To preserve the juvenile work from destruction, since several pages had flown within the big brass fender, he reached over it and secured them from the hearth. Then, seating himself in the chair just vacated by Bainbridge, who was now occupied in seeking fugitive papers under the table, the sofa, the globes, Mr. Hartagous addressed himself to replacing the pages in the portfolio.

An awkward, old-fashioned device of desk arrangement, he thought it, for the portfolio attached to the shelf swung beneath, leaving the upper surface free for the writer's needs, and it could only be drawn high enough to receive or disburse papers by means of the elastic strap which Bainbridge had burst. It now showed signs of letting the pages slip as soon as restored; and saying with a note of tense vexation, "Where did these belong, anyhow?—and how the devil does this go?" Mr. Hartagous drew the despoiled receptacle up on top of the shelf to aid his disposition of the collected sheets. As in most portfolios, the two gaping pockets were obvious, but as he was about to stow the remaining briefs concerning the Persian hero therein, another paper from an inner slit in a different handwriting was brought to view. His face changed sharply as he drew it forth, all unnoticed by Mr. Bainbridge, laughing over the crude views of the boy's work as he held a page to the lamp on the table, his big teeth a-glimmer in the midst of his straw-tinted beard, the big hat and broad shoulders thrown in a Brobdingnagian shadow on the wall.

"Will you give me your attention for a moment, sir," Mr. Hartagous said, in a low, repressed voice. "Is this your signature?"

Bainbridge lumbered heavily forward in startled expectation. "By gum, it sure is!" he cried, excited to fever heat. "And that is the last paper which Mr. Faurie ever signed!" he added, leaning over to scan the document. "I am sure of that, because Mr. Dabney witnessed it with me,—'twas me and the trained nurse that always subscribed as witnesses together, except this once. And just before I reached the willow slough I seen the rocket go up at the landing to signal the death to the Swamp Lily, that was just rounding the point off the Arkansas shore."

There were a few other papers with the document, a canceled note of hand, a contract for the erection of buildings, a surveyor's plat of land, all memoranda of completed purpose, which had evidently been returned. Mr. Hartagous was running them swiftly over, while Bainbridge's attention was focused upon his own scrawl as a subscribing witness on the sheet on the portfolio.

"I never thought of it again," Bainbridge resumed; "and I suppose that whoever set the room to rights after he was carried out of it must have laid this away among the other papers in the portfolio and desk. He must have intended to mail it with other inclosures,—that will that Mr. Stanlett found, I reckon,—for see, here is a long, stamped envelope, with six cents postage and an immejet delivery stamp." Bainbridge held it up to the light. "He must have weighed it with the inclosures,—but it has got no address. I remember now that after Mr. Dabney and I had said good-night to him and went out into the hall, I noticed the nigger waiting at the library door, with the bag for

Mr. Faurie's mail, ready to paddle in a dugout to the Swamp Lily just sighted nigh the point off the Arkansas shore."

Mr. Hartagous was once more bending his bushy brows over the names of the witnesses to the document. "And who is this other party?" he asked.

"Mr. Dabney? Richard Dabney?—why, don't you remember him? He used to run a store near Great Oaks. The land it was built on fell into the river not long after that, and he moved away. He was living in Arkansas the last I heard of him, running a sawmill. He had come to Great Oaks mansion that evening to inquire for Mr. Faurie, hearing that he had been ailing,—in fact, he was taken with a short rigor while Mr. Dabney was here. Mr. Faurie was still sitting in this chair when he wrote his name, which he did easily enough, but he seemed very faint when he called upon us to witness his signature, and pronounced the paper a little—little coddle-shell, I think he called it, to his will. I never thought of it since. I jus' allowed it was some of his Tennessee business, because he remarked sorter mumbling to himself, 'twas situated there and that he s'posed this coddle-shell would take effect under the laws there, it being his domicile, so to say, him being a resident o' Nashville, and a regularly qualified voter of Davidson County,—though shucks! we claimed him here in the swamp country; he had been here so much at Great Oaks in the winters, as his health declined. I haven't thought of it since. As he was always busy with his papers in them days, I didn't taken any special notice of the circumstance. Is it any account, particularly,—cut any ice?"

A codicil, indeed, it proved; and while affirming and republishing the main testamentary provisions of the previous codicil, the testator made the single change of giving to his widow all his personal property of whatever sort,—in lieu of one fourth of it,—stocks, bonds, and some hoards of special deposits in Tennessee banks; and though the vital importance of this bequest was altogether unforeseen by the dying man, the crucial emergency being far beyond the purview of his vicarious precautions, it was evident that it would aggregate enough to solve the refunding problem of Mrs. Faurie's receipts from the estate.

CHAPTER XX

It was a joyous household the next morning, and Mr. Hartagous genially participated in the prevailing good cheer. He had very heartily deprecated the hardships to be wrought by the execution of his duty, and was thankful indeed that they were mitigated to the extent of the benefactions of this codicil. Great Oaks under water, with valuable machinery and livestock, miles of fencing and indispensable buildings, to replace, was no boon in comparison with Mrs. Faurie's former rich endowments, but at all events it was not to fall to his lot to turn the widow out of her shelter for the behoof of her young sons. Nevertheless, he resolved to remonstrate very seriously with her against the proposed marriage, and to stint himself no whit in forceful phraseology.

He did not meet her at the breakfast-table, for he was late, owing to the vigils of the preceding night, and when he presented himself to partake of the matutinal meal, he found that she had already departed, leaving him to the vicarious hospitality of Desmond, the jubilant Mr. Stanlett, and the three boys with their shining morning faces. He fortified himself with a good cigar after breakfast and a meditative stroll upon the veranda in the fresh, breezy, summery day, intending that his nerves should be well soothed and his tact whetted before he should enter upon his delicate mission.

The leafage of the wide-spreading grove was green and lush, and waved gilded in the sunlight; hanging baskets, with trailing ferns and laden with parti-colored foliage plants, swung in the arches between the vine-draped columns of the veranda. If one could imagine one's self afloat, or in some Venetian entourage, the diluvian scene might have seemed, instead of the dreariest expression of disaster, to have elements of picturesque amphibious interest. What though the Arkansas shore were withdrawn from view—there was not much of it visible in its best estate!—and instead was an expanse of rippling sunlit sea of indefinite bounds, of a richly tawny hue, and with enlivening and unique incidents,—a couple of gayly whisking dugouts in the foreground, a steamboat in the middle distance, puffing columns of curling smoke as in the centre of the channel she steadily climbed the current, and in the offing a white flash of sea-gulls, describing eccentric curves, brilliant as stars against the depressed horizon, blue and hazy and dimly discriminated. There was an absence of briny odors, which are not always acceptable, however, and instead a pungent fragrance of bark came from the inundated woods, and the honeysuckle twining about the balustrade and bravely blooming from out the floods sent forth a subtile and delicious perfume.

"'A life on the ocean wave,'" Mrs. Faurie exclaimed joyously, as he turned a corner and came suddenly upon her. She had been rifling a wire flower-stand that lifted its redundant growths against the wall of the house, and she held in her hand a cluster of pink and white carnations. As she stood in the blended sheen of the bland day and the refulgent reflection of the blazing waters, she looked not unlike the bloom itself. She had upon her head a wide hat of delicate pink organdy, the brim variously bent and shirred and frilled, and her morning dress was of sheer white lawn. He strove within himself to avoid its recognition as the simplest toilet, such as any country girl might wear, for she took no grace from it, but embellished its every suggestion. Her slim, lissome figure lent it such distinction; the exquisite fairness of her complexion was so emphasized by the unrelenting clarity of the tints of her costume; the shoaling lights and shadows of her beautiful gray eyes, her rich brown hair piled high amongst the carnation-like frills of the hat, her delicate dewy lips, her dainty hand and arm and throat, all were more assertive in their demand for homage in the simple not to say stereotyped attire. And she looked scarcely twenty years old, as her laughing, long-lashed eyes met his.

"Can you keep your sea-legs in the contemplation of that weltering main?"—she glanced at the waterscape. "Will you feel less as if in an indigestible dream and more like a landlubber if I give you a boutonnière?" She selected a very perfect carnation from the cluster, and as she advanced to place it in the buttonhole of his coat, he caught her hand with the flower in it.

"I want to say something very serious to you," he protested. "I want to speak as freely to you as if you were my daughter."

She glanced up, gayly laughing. "Your sister, you should say."

He perceived his error,—on the very point of age, which was to be the gravamen of his remonstrances! But he had unconsciously been allured by her aspect,—as she looked scarcely twenty.

"Well, hardly young enough to be my daughter, indeed," he said craftily, "though Desmond is really young enough to be my son. My dear madam, you will make yourself a laughing-stock if you contemplate this marriage. You ought to remember that you are ten years older than this boy."

"Should I mind that if he does not?" she queried, holding up the cluster of carnations no fresher than the flush in her cheeks.

"And now that, by the grace of God, you are to have Great Oaks unincumbered, you will put him into the position of making a mercenary marriage; he is sensitive on that score,—I can see that already,—though of course he is glad that your future comfort is assured, however meagrely in comparison with the old days."

"But ought we to consider the public,—if it will accord us so much distinction as to gossip about us as a nine days' wonder,—or only ourselves, and our own mutual happiness?" She slipped the carnation into his buttonhole and drew off, standing in her graceful slimness, her head aslant, to observe the effect.

"Ridicule deals a vicarious stab, which is peculiarly sharp. You should consider your children, dear Mrs. Faurie," he urged.

"And I will," she promised heartily. "Trust me for that! I will do nothing contrary to their wishes."

He made no secret of his intentions. He turned at once. She stood looking after him, smiling at his haste, as he went bustling down the veranda to find the boys. His method of busy progression was not unlike that of the puffing steamboat in the channel, bustling up the river. Though he had no fear of her interference or adverse influence, he was so impressed with the importance of his mission to enlist some potent opposition to the marriage that he made no effort to enliven the seriousness of the crisis with jocose preamble, in view of the juvenile character of his interlocutors, or to minimize its significance. In logical and definite fashion he set forth the fact and its aspect to the world at large, with its effect on their mother's future and their own, in very unvarnished phrase. They silently heard him out, seated before him in a row on the sofa in the front parlor, very attentive, and with more friendly faces than he had heretofore seen them wear.

"It rests with you three," he said in conclusion, seeking to impress them with a sense of their responsibility. "Your mother cares more for you than she ever did or ever will for any man. She is the most maternal woman I ever knew. You can prevent her from making a ridiculous marriage,—a foolish marriage,—a disastrous marriage, that will bring unhappiness upon everybody connected with it."

"Oh, no! Mr. Hartagous!" promptly responded the rosy and beaming Chub, taking the pas, perhaps instinctively on the principle that the youngest officer on a court-martial speaks first. "It is the very best thing that we can do. Ever since I have found out that Mr. Desmond was going to marry us, I have felt that we-all were so safe!" He gave himself an affectionate little hug to express his sense of security.

Horace administered a rude nudge with his elbow. "Nobody is going to marry *you*!" he admonished his junior, shamefaced for the ignorance he manifested.

"Oh, yes," protested Chub, wagging his round head, evidently having mastered the situation; "when a gentleman marries a widow lady, he marries the whole family!"

"You certainly have an interest to consider," said Mr. Hartagous, gravely. "Your affection for your mother, your respect for your father, ought to urge you to a course of discreet remonstrance,—nothing unfilial, or likely to estrange you, but to prevent an absurd and most unseemly marriage that must necessarily be, too, unhappy and unfortunate."

"I don't see it in that light, Mr. Hartagous," said Horace, slowly. His face had an intimation of precocious force, and there was even a mutinous spark in the glance of his eye. His was the complex and difficult disposition of the three brothers. His convictions were obviously strong, and his opposition likely to be of a strenuous order. Mr. Hartagous hearkened with an access of attention. "I don't see it that way. I think that Mr. Desmond cares more for her and for us than anybody else ever will. I think his proposal when he had reason to think her fairly bankrupt shows that he was willing to make every sacrifice for her. Then look at him! Why, you are obliged to see that he is head and shoulders above anybody—though he is not rich. But he is younger, just as you say, though he does not *seem* young. He is old in mind and disposition. And Lord! the heaps he knows about everything! As to your fear about what people will say,—well, *I* have seen a lot of the world, and it seems to me that if a certain kind of people don't laugh at you for one thing, they will for another. If you stay at home, they call you 'a swamper'; if you travel abroad, they call you a 'globe-trotter'; if you dress well, they ridicule you as 'a dude'; if you take it easy, they say you are 'tacky.' *My* idea is to go right ahead and do what you think is right and properest, and—let them laugh! I'd hate to deny myself anything good and valuable 'cause Mrs. Kentopp might giggle over it."

"She left us out of her house-party,—and we ain't dead yet!" said Chub, banging the heels of his shoes back and forth against the sofa.

Reginald took a deeper view. "I think, sir, that her happiness ought to be considered first. She is young, after all is said, and has many years yet to live, I hope. She ought to have her independence,—to be a free agent! When I was in India, there had been a recent case of suttee way off somewhere in some remote district,—I heard a great deal of talk about it. People had supposed the practice was suppressed. And without meaning any disrespect to my father's will,—for I can understand how the idea of a stranger in the family circle would influence a division of property,—I always thought an objection to second marriage was a sort of civilized suttee. As to Mr. Desmond, himself, I should prefer him as a stepfather to all the world."

And thus Desmond was welcomed without a dissentient voice.

At first Mrs. Kentopp, who might be taken as representing the gossips at large, was so rejoiced that Great Oaks Plantation would not come immediately on the market in competition with Dryad-Dene that it mitigated the acerbity of her views, and although she twinkled and dimpled much in commenting on the disparity in age and fortune and prospects of the couple, her talk had not the rancor which it developed later when Mr. Loring seemed indisposed to console himself with Dryad-Dene, and gradually drew off without making any offer.

A golden era of happiness had dawned on Great Oaks; the waters of the overflow gradually disappeared, and during the brief interval of the wedding journey Mrs. Kentopp drove over through the mud, bogging down once or twice in the alluvial sloughs, on a tour of discovery, and recounted with facetious distortions of effect afterward Chub's simple boastings in great pride as to the preparations that were making for the reception of the couple on their return. Mr. Stanlett had designed and supervised these, and was very important and happily busy. "I hope he furnished the money to pay for the changes, for otherwise I don't see where it was to come from, for Desmond must have put all his pedagogic savings in the expense of the bridal tour," she jovially speculated. Great Oaks was very judiciously embellished, and looked most genially hospitable on the day of her visit, for the old man had a pretty fancy and an accurate discrimination of the appropriate.

"I always said there was another will or codicil, or, to be accurate, 'paper-writing,'" he cheerily averred, as he handed Mrs. Kentopp into her carriage. "This is not of course the provision that was intended for Honoria, but it passes,—it passes fairly well, and Edward, my nephew, Mr. Desmond, you know, does not care for money."

And when Mrs. Kentopp repeated this, she was wont to point out gayly the incongruity of this statement with the fact that "Edward," Mr. Stanlett's "nephew," should have contrived to surround himself comfortably with that useful commodity in a wife so well endowed and three very rich stepsons, over whom he had now paramount influence. She found much joy, also, in Horace's simplicity in believing that the sentimental interests between the two had been settled before the discovery of the last codicil which had put a new aspect on the financial status, and she sought to convince people in Deepwater Bend and elsewhere that the comfortable estate, more than the phenomenal beauty of the lady, had served to obviate the disadvantage of the disparity of years.

Mrs. Kentopp said later that its vogue—an absolutely unreadable book, on all sorts of political conditions, for nobody had really read it—was because a notable English statesman, very meddlesome with pen and ink, had canvassed its positions in a London quarterly, duller, if possible, and less read than the book itself, and another English quarterly had published Desmond's reply, and for some time the counter-arguments of other political economists who found the work of vital interest caused the effusion of much printers' ink. And when the family went to London the next year, Colonel Desmond was lionized in distinguished circles, and was given an additional learned degree at a great English university where he had taken one in his earlier youth.

"Deepwater Bend is a literary centre now, and don't you forget it, and has its learned light," Mrs. Kentopp dimpled, "though none of us of course have read or ever will read the Great Book."

But even Mrs. Kentopp's flings were destined to disregard and discontinuance. A javelin, however skillfully aimed, must needs have a point to take effect. "I don't think there seems a disparity in age," a stranger in a social company had dubiously replied to her delighted mention of the ten years' difference. "Colonel Desmond does not look so much as ten years older."

And after the company's somewhat mischievous burst of laughter had shown their comprehension of her intention and hopelessly mystified the stranger, who could not imagine what had been said amiss, Colonel Kentopp had taken occasion to admonish his wife in private. "You do yourself no good, Annetta, by harping on that woman's age. People will only think you carping and jealous."

And, indeed, Desmond was fast growing older and graver. Other books had succeeded the first; and while they added distinction in differing degrees, they added, too, the marks of thought on brow and mien. Now the light always burned late from the library window on the water-side, and the river pilots counted its faint, far glow in their midnight bearings. Often they pointed it out with pride to some passenger admitted to the wheel-house, seeing it shining with a sort of stellular isolation amidst the darkling riparian forests of Great Oaks, and repeated the titles of his volumes, although perhaps, like Mrs. Kentopp, they had read none of the works.

But this was really not the illuminated hour of the library, the time of its signal triumph. Regularly every afternoon when the western sunlight, striking in long, slanting bars athwart it, turned from burnished gold to ethereal, hazy red, his wife appeared, and seated one on each side of the fire in true Darby-and-Joan fashion, as Kentopp's prophetic eye had long ago beheld them from the veranda, Desmond read aloud the result of his day's labor, while her beautiful, listening, reflective eyes dwelt on the coals and his voice filled the quiet spaces of the scholastic old room. She never criticised. She gave no word of applause. She offered no monition of advice. When he laid down the papers and their eyes met, her comment was always the same.

"What did I tell you long, long ago, the first afternoon that you and I ever sat here before the fire?"

"Why, that I ought to write for publication,—to write books."

"And what did you say?"

"Well," he always laughed as he replied,—"that I couldn't,—that I was not capable of it."

"Then," she was wont to solemnly rejoin, while her eyes danced with joy and mirth and pride, "do you never *dare* to contradict me again as long as you live."

www.ingramcontent.com/pod-product-compliance
Lightning Source LLC
Chambersburg PA
CBHW010805250626
47156CB00010B/3009